THE DARK PATH
TO THE RIVER

JOANNE LEEDOM-ACKERMAN

THE DARK PATH
TO THE RIVER

Saybrook

Publishing Company

Dallas San Francisco New York

6/1988
amitd.

The Dark Path to the River began and ended in imagination.
Any resemblance to real people or events is coincidental.

Second Printing

Library of Congress Cataloging-in-Publication Data

Leedom-Ackerman, Joanne, 1948—
   The dark path to the river.

   I. Title
PS3562.E3668D37 1988   813'.54   87-23418
ISBN 0-933071-16-7

Saybrook Publishing Company, Inc.
4223 Cole Avenue, Suite 4
Dallas, TX 75205

Printed in the United States of America

Distrtibuted by W.W. Norton & Company
500 Fifth Avenue
New York, NY 10110

For my husband Peter, whose love has long nourished me,
and for my sons Nate and Elliot, who kept me writing

Acknowledgments

The Dark Path to the River is a book of discovering faith in one another and in life. In its creation I am indebted to many who had faith in me. These include my husband Peter, who has understood the long road I've been on and the necessity of keeping on it; Jane Wilson, who read the first draft of this book and encouraged me; my publisher Pat Howell, who provided the editorial support of himself and Judy Karasik; their insight and questions kept me digging deeper and stroking harder. Also at Saybrook my thanks to Joan Howell and Nathan Mitchell. And to Julia Wheatley.

Friends who offered their specific knowledge include: Dr. Gene Sharp, director of the Program on Nonviolent Sanctions at Harvard University's Center for International Affairs and director of the Albert Einstein Institution; Dr. Edwin S. Munger, professor and director of the Munger Africana Library at the California Institute of Technology; poet Clayton Eshleman, editor Caryl Eshleman, and Dr. Carolyn Stremlau. I'd also like to thank the professors at the University of California at Los Angeles who allowed me to audit their courses on African politics, history and folklore.

I'm grateful to the staff of experts at the Los Angeles Natural History Museum, whom I called dozens of times during the writing of *The Dark Path to the River* to ask questions such as: why and when does a lizard break off its tail? how does a silkworm make silk? does a python hiss? They always answered with patience and professionalism.

And finally I want to thank my family, especially my mother, my father and my children, who have grown from infants into thoughtful, exuberant boys during the writing of this book.

THE DARK PATH TO THE RIVER

Part One

Chapter 1

Olivia Turner stood under the heaters on the marble steps of the Plaza Hotel waiting for the doorman to hail her a cab. She had no money, not even enough to tip the doorman, who came back soaking with her taxi. When the driver asked her destination, she asked him the time. "Twelve ten," he said.

"Eighty-ninth and Riverside," she answered. She looked out the window at the lights on Fifth Avenue. The stores were illumined even at this hour, bright empty windows along the dark streets. As the driver turned west on 57th Street, she leaned her head against the seat, drew her coat around her and fell asleep.

At Eighty-ninth Street the driver called through the bullet-proof shield between them, "Which corner, lady?" She peered into the rain and pointed to a greystone building across the street. As she got out of the cab, she explained that she didn't have any money but would borrow some upstairs and be right back.

"Christ, lady, you don't take a cab without money," he said.

"I'll be back," she insisted, and dragging her belongings with her, she darted into the rain. The driver opened his door and started to follow, but the downpour turned him back. At the doorway Olivia pushed the intercom, identified herself, and when the buzzer granted her entry, she felt a small release inside.

She started apologizing even before she stepped into the apartment. "I'm sorry. I'm sorry. I should have called, but I couldn't." She moved in quickly. She wore a wrinkled beige pants suit under her raincoat and was loaded down with bags and brief cases and too many appendages even for her broad shoulders. Her short black hair had grown nappy in the rain, and her make-up had long since worn off her smooth sepia skin.

"I didn't even have change for the phone . . ." She dropped her bags to the floor. ". . . and I have a cab downstairs waiting to be paid." She looked at her friends with their arms about each other, and she wrapped her arms about herself in a gesture both insecure and dogged.

In the shadows Jenny Reeder and Mark Rosen looked like one body. Jenny's cheeks were flushed from sleep, and her face showed the slight imprint of the cordoroy velvet sofa where she'd been stretched out. On the floor by the sofa were pages of manuscript and drawings. Jenny smiled and bent down for Olivia's bags. The act was friendly, and the anxiousness eased in Olivia's eyes. Mark reached for his wallet on the hall table and handed Olivia a $20 bill.

"I'll explain everything when I get back," she promised, then disappeared down the stairs.

When she returned, she entered in the same flurry. "At least you're awake. You have any coffee? I'd give all my money if I had any for a cup of coffee."

"What happened?" Jenny asked as the three of them moved into the kitchen. The wide planes of her face spread open even wider with her smile. She felt herself steadying to ground Olivia's scattered energy. She went to the stove and turned up the flame under a pot of coffee.

"When's the baby due?" Olivia asked.

Jenny looked around, brushing her light brown hair from her pale face. She was tall, slim except for the roundness of the child pushing at her belly, obscured for the moment under her husband's faded Harvard sweatshirt. "In May . . . so what happened?"

"I don't know where to begin." Olivia sat down at the table in the corner. She dumped spoonfuls of sugar into her cup as Jenny poured the coffee. Beside her on the floor two briefcases were crammed full of books and papers, and from her battered suitcase peeked the edge of something red. She leaned back in her chair, took a long breath, and when she started to speak again, she was calmer.

"I flew in this morning. I called Alan at *The New Centurion* last week to see if he wanted a piece on the National Liberation Association's appearance at the UN. This morning at seven I get a call telling me to catch a plane to New York; I at least got expenses guaranteed. I tried you earlier; you weren't home. I called Mark's office. You get my message?" Olivia glanced at Mark now, who stood leaning against the stove, a sturdy, dark-haired man she thought of mainly as Jenny's husband.

"We always expect you," he offered.

"Thank you." She reached into the yellow tiger cookie jar, her gift to them when their first child Erika was born just after she'd returned from four years in Africa. Leaning towards Jenny, she said, "You wouldn't have recognized them. There they were among the crystal chandeliers of the Plaza, sitting on gold-leafed chairs. I kept remembering them around those wooden tables sticky with that awful beer. Do you remember? That's when they first planned a separate state."

"I think I'd left by then," Jenny said, pushing out a chair for Mark to join them. "I only stayed with you a month, remember?" As Mark sat down, Jenny rested her stockinged foot on his knee.

"Oh . . . that's right. That was your mistake, trying to see everything. Instead you saw nothing."

Jenny exchanged a smile with her husband. Olivia had made this point before, in fact retreated to it as a place of security: that Jenny had mistaken geography for knowledge in her six months in Africa. At the tip of the point was always the suggestion that anyone who knew and studied less than Olivia risked superficialty. Yet because Jenny understood both the truth and the burden of Olivia's point of view, she didn't argue.

"They looked like bankers in pinstripe suits," Olivia complained. "They had a full court press: Peg from *Newsweek*, Guy Rhodes from *The New York Times*—Do you know him? We met years ago at the Ellsberg trial when I got trapped into introducing

Kay around, and he was lusting after her. Nyral told the press conference he feared a civil war if the U.N. didn't act. I think he's going to call for partition."

"Did he say that?" Jenny drew a pencil from behind her ear as if she would take notes.

"No. He was circumspect today, but that's my instinct. Anyway, after the press conference Jamin told me to come up to his room for an interview. No hello, how the hell are you after four years, just an order to come to his suite. When I got there, Jamin and Nyral and some men I didn't know were standing by the window looking down on the park. All of them except Nyral were laughing like school boys as if they'd just pulled off a great prank; but when they saw me, they got serious. Jamin came over and put out his hand. As I took it, I couldn't help but smile; then he smiled too." 'So what do you think, Olivia Turner?' he asked. 'Did I not tell you we would get here, and you did not believe me.'

"He introduced me to the other men: the Finance Minister and his aide, the Minister of the Interior, the Minister of Transport. 'Olivia is a friend from the camps. She will write nice things about us for the Americans,' he told them. And the men all smiled patronizing smiles as though I were Jamin's lady friend they were to amuse. Then Nyral came over. He's the one real statesman among them, but before I could talk to him, the Transport Minister said he had something to give me . . ." Olivia smiled. "You won't believe this; I've got to show you . . ." She started rummaging through her case, extracting papers and books until she produced a little plastic box which she handed to Jenny.

Jenny opened it. "What is it?"

Mark leaned over. "It looks like an amoeba."

"That's it. I've been trying to figure what it looked like. He was so serious when he handed it to me, but I didn't know what to make of it." She took back the box, and from pink cardboard velvet she lifted up a black enameled shape on a cheap silver chain. "What it's supposed to be . . ." she said, "is their new country. A pendant in the shape of their new country."

"It's a piece of dimestore jewelry," Jenny said.

"Exactly. He opened his briefcase to show me it was full of these enameled . . . amoebas. My god, I thought, surely he's not going to go around giving them out. But he had pendants for women

4

and cuff links for men. I looked over at Jamin to see what he thought, but he was busy making himself a drink. Nyral just looked on as though these souvenirs didn't concern him.

"I told the man—he was strange, short and squat—I told him that in America if he went around showing off his goods out of a suitcase, he'd be called a traveling salesman. But he just smiled this obsequious smile, and said, 'Yes. That is what I am, a salesman of the revolution.'"

Mark, who'd been leaning back in his chair, rocked forward now and laughed. "My god, who are these people? Why are we taking them so seriously?"

Olivia turned and looked at him. "Because they are serious," she answered. She wished suddenly she hadn't made Mark laugh. She took off her glasses and rubbed the bridge of her nose. Her dark brown skin was freckled. She had a thick nose, a gentle, elaborate mouth, features which some might call plain except the intelligence in her eyes lighted her whole face. "Only something's wrong," she said. She slipped the trinket back into her bag; then she reached up to the stove and poured herself another cup of coffee.

"They're acting the way they think they're supposed to: sipping scotch at the Plaza, giving out cheap jewelry as though if enough people wear it, they'll be recognized, hoping the world at this level of sophistication will believe them. But believe them or not, they are serious."

Olivia cupped her hands around the coffee mug, and a sadness passed through her dark eyes. She looked away from Mark. She wasn't sure of her relationship with him. She was suspicious of bankers and wealth and power. Though she didn't understand all that Mark did, she knew he worked on Wall Street, raising money and buying companies. He and Jenny lived modestly, yet she dwelt with the possibility that at any moment they might slide to the other side and join those protected by money and its privilege. This fact made her feel tangential to Jenny's life.

"The distance is enormous, isn't it?" Jenny said.

Olivia glanced at her. She nodded at this bit of mind reading. "Amen."

Mark reached to the center of the table and plucked a pear from a wooden bowl. "So what happened next?" he asked.

5

Olivia put back on her glasses. She frowned. Then shifting her weight at the table, she continued: "The Transport Minister made an excuse to leave, and the other ministers followed. One minute I was speaking to Nyral, then even he was leaving. I thought I must have offended them when I turned and saw Jamin smiling. I realized he'd orchestrated the whole thing. He was standing by the bed with a drink in his hand watching me. He's changed, Jenny. He looks much older—his hair's half grey; he's thinner. He still towers, even over me, but . . ." she hesitated, "he seemed somehow tenuous.

"He moved over to me and looked out the window on the park. 'Ah, America, how easy life is here,' he said. He put his hand on my shoulder, then stared at me for almost a minute as if trying to remember who I was. Finally I asked if I could have a drink. At first he didn't move, just kept his hand on my shoulder, holding me within reach. I couldn't tell what he was thinking, but I felt sure he knew what I was, including the fact that I was still attracted to him. He laughed as if this is what he wanted to see. He let go then and went over to make the drink. As I watched him, it occurred to me that he'd invited me up there precisely for that purpose: to prove to himself and his colleagues that he was still in control, even in America.

"I started trying to interview him. He answered two or three questions but glanced at his watch and said he had to get ready for the reception. That's when I knew I'd been used."

"Are you sure that's why he invited you up?" Jenny asked.

"The more I think about it, I'm convinced. He needed a boost before facing all those people tonight, and he brought me— member of the American press—up there to give it to him. It was all very subtle, very understated, but I know Jamin. And as he told me goodbye at the door, we both knew what had happened, and there was nothing I could do about it."

Olivia cast a sidelong glance at Mark, drawing up her shoulders as if ready to deflect his judgment, but he didn't speak. His mouth opened slightly as though he might, and she remembered when she'd first met him here at the kitchen table playing his harmonica, his head leaning against the wall, his hands flapping wha-wha-wha-wha while Jenny cooked supper. That night

6

she'd understood why Jenny had married him. She studied his eyes now—spirited, direct, shifting regularly to his wife—and in them she saw no judgment of herself. Silently she thanked him for that.

"You know we have mines over there," he said instead.

"What? We who?"

"Afco. An investment group, in partnership with the government, there and in other countries. We reopened several of the mines that had closed down."

"Shit." Olivia reached into the bowl of fruit and took out an apple. "You picked a hell of a partner. I hope you haven't invested much."

"More than we could afford to lose, but I don't think they'll hurt the mines. That's their lifeline."

Olivia laughed abruptly. "Who is 'they'? They don't think that way, Mark. A mine is a hole in the ground."

"The government's assured us we'll be protected should events get out of hand."

"You're aligned with Bulagwi?" Olivia bit into the apple.

"I'm not aligned with anyone. I simply don't want our investors to get hurt."

"You should have thought of that before you invested," she said dryly. "You know, there are a few other issues at stake here."

"I'm aware of that."

"Like the rights of half a million people."

"I'm not involved in the politics," Mark repeated. "I just raised money for a company."

"Ah-h . . . And did you invest yourself?"

Mark glanced at Jenny, who had stayed out of the conversation. Jenny took her foot off his knee. She picked up her blue and white mug and went to the sink. She wondered that Mark didn't know better than to debate Olivia on his investments in Africa. "Jenny was against it so we passed," he said.

"But your investors are in with Bulagwi? How much is Bulagwi getting?"

"I can't tell you that." He started to peel the pear. "I don't know how much worse the other side might be. Personally, I think the only hope for some of these countries is to get businesses going,

7

partnerships with the developed world. If the partners aren't perfect, well, they never are."

"Shit," Olivia said.

But Mark turned towards the door now for a cry stirred somewhere in the back of the apartment. Jenny also looked up. Small, quick feet padded down the hall, then in the doorway the sleepy face of their daughter blinked into the light. As Jenny stepped forward, the child ran across the blue tiled floor into her mother's arms.

"What's the matter?" Mark asked, rising and going to his daughter whose tiny bare feet hung out from under a ruffled pink gown.

The child reached out to him and held both parents around their necks with her arms. "Snakes," she whispered. Yet already her dream was fading, and she was beginning to look around, interested to find herself here, with her parents and this other person in this lighted room, at this unexpected hour of night.

"There are no snakes," Mark offered.

The little girl peered at her father with dark, serious eyes. "Yes. There are," she affirmed. "In the corners."

Jenny shifted her daughter onto her hip. "Come, I'll take you back to bed. We'll turn on a light, and it will eat the snakes."

As they moved out of the kitchen towards the dim corridor of bedrooms, Mark reached out for his daughter and kissed her on the cheek. "There," he said, "that will keep the snakes away." The child smiled now, pleased with the magic bestowed and with the conversion of her father.

When Jenny returned, Mark and Olivia were arguing over railroads. "That's why Afco paid a fee to the government, to protect the rail lines during the trouble and keep extra trains running to ship the ore."

"Bulagwi's pocketed that fee, I guarantee. He doesn't even have control over some of those lines, Mark. The NLA does."

"I agree it's a risk being there," Mark conceded. "But your alternative is for us to stay out of the country entirely."

"Now that's an idea," Olivia said.

Jenny poured herself another cup of coffee and sat back at the table. "So, did you go to the reception?" she asked.

Olivia glanced at her. She hesitated, but finally she yielded to Jenny's direction. She heaved her shoulders forward in a sigh. "Whoever's imagination created that had no idea of these people. There was more food than a village eats in a month. Shrimp. Lobster. Prosciutto. There were baskets of flowers. And a player piano tripping out show tunes. The whole thing was so jarring, I expected the earth to crack right down the middle of the White and Gold room and swallow us all up. I don't know who was paying the bill. Not the U.N. And the NLA doesn't have those kinds of funds. When I asked a UN official, he just stared at me as though I'd inquired about the color of his underwear.

"I never did find out because the delegation arrived. They were as out of place in that room as slugs on the silver trays. The Minister of Transport strutted in, fitted out in a military uniform with medals weighing him down like ballast, and he was carrying his briefcase. I almost wish I'd stayed till the end to see how many people left wearing amoeba cuff links and pendants, but I lost sight of him and didn't see him again. Next came Jamin and Nyral. They were whisked away to meet some dignitary. Several junior members of the delegation found their way to me. They were feeling lost and were glad to see a familiar face.

"We were standing around gossiping when Guy came over. Well, when Guy found out I actually knew these people, he latched onto me for the rest of the evening. There I was telling Guy about Jamin and the others as though they were old school buddies. I had to keep reminding myself that to many people these men were terrorists. Not Nyral. And Jamin takes pains to distinguish between a guerrilla and a terrorist, but to most people, the distinction's lost."

Mark leaned forward on the table, the small pen knife in his hand peeling an unbroken chain of brown skin from the soft, white pear. "They *were* the ones responsible for the bombings in the Capitol, weren't they?" Jenny cast him a warning look.

But Olivia answered matter-of-factly. "Yes. In spite of Nyral's nonviolence and Jamin's definitions. That's what's frightening." She set down her coffee mug and frowned, her thick penciled eyebrows meeting in a V over her nose. "It's so easy, or at least convenient, to abstract the violence, politicize it and forget it's part of these people I know. Yet I don't forget. Tonight I saw a man at the reception I remember from Angola, a mercenary. What was he doing there? When I tried to go over to talk to him, he disappeared. At least I couldn't find him. I don't know if he recognized me, but I remember he had a bad left eye. I'm sure he was the same mercenary I'd interviewed once in Angola.

"Jamin stepped over to me then. I asked him about the man, but he shrugged off the question. Then Guy came trotting over. Before Guy could introduce himself, Jamin put his arm around my shoulder and told me I'd left my purse in his room. He spoke with a familiarity . . . no, an intimacy Guy picked up right away. I knew Jamin was still using me to bolster himself, but Guy didn't know that; and by the look on his face, I saw he assumed what my relationship was with Jamin. I saw too what that meant to him. I wanted to shake off Jamin's hand and make my role clear. Then I thought the hell with Guy. And then I thought the hell with Jamin. Because as soon as Jamin found out Guy was from *The New York Times*, I might as well not have been there.

"I left them to each other. I went to try to find the man; I looked in the hallway, but he was gone. I tried to get one of the younger delegates to take me up to get my purse, but no one was allowed into Jamin's room. The reception went on and on. I would have had to wait until Jamin went back himself, and I refused to be put in the position of following him to his room at one in the morning. All my money, my credentials, everything is in that purse. So you see why I'm here . . . and broke . . . and in a state."

She leaned back in the chair and threw open her hands as if depositing the story with Jenny and Mark to do with as they pleased. She kicked off her heavy leather flats and began rubbing her toes. "I've been on my feet all day . . ." she exhaled. And putting her feet on the extra chair beside her, she leaned her head against the wall and finished her coffee.

Chapter 2

Olivia awoke to the phone ringing. She was lying on the couch in the living room under a tangle of hanging plants, the sunlight skewing through the leaves. She was between sleep and waking in the bush in Africa on the soft hard earth, the sirens, the guns, the phone was ringing. She rolled over and opened her eyes. Her large naked feet poked from the velvet comforter, then landed on the wooden floor as she sat up. She drew her robe around her. Sunlight poured through the French windows, shined off the parquet floor, the brass coffee table, the glass doors of the bookcase. She blinked into the light. Across the room in a wing chair a large silver cat sat watching her. There were two blue velvet wing chairs with matching foot stools, a floor lamp with a fringed Victorian shade, a baby grand piano, a mahogony dining table and plants, dozens of plants, hanging and standing.

She stretched her long limbs and rose from the sofa. She padded over to the chair where the cat was curled and lifted it onto her lap, then sat down and stared at the room from this angle. In the corner under the gauze curtains a bucket of red and yellow blocks spilled out, a doll in pink tights sprawled half naked, and a puzzle lay undone. Olivia carried a version of this room—sun-filled and filled with a child—in her head. She had carried it in her head before she ever saw this room: in Africa, in the dirt-floor hut of her friend Mushambe, with Mushambe's child and all the children Olivia carried in her head. She had no children herself though she wanted children. She woke up this morning remembering that in three weeks she would turn forty. She also awoke thinking of Mushambe teaching the village children in the afternoons when the African sun was high and hot on the hills and their mothers and fathers were working in the fields between the hills or in the veneer factory. Mushambe taught them while the flies buzzed the loudest and the sun pressed sleep upon them. She taught them letters and the shapes of words and the meanings of words and their magic. Olivia often came and sat in on Mushambe's class with her guitar and sang to the children songs of another time and place: "We shall overcome . . ." "I'm gonna sit at the welcome table . . ." "This land is your land; this land is my land . . ." And the children would join in: "From New York City to the gulfstream water" with a fervor born of the innocence and struggle that was their own, under the acacia trees in the dusty, open-aired classroom, in the pause between day and evening before their parents returned.

In the kitchen Olivia heard Mark laughing with his daughter. In the hallway Jenny had answered the phone. Olivia rose, and taking up her canvas suitcase, withdrew into the bathroom to dress.

Jenny had just returned from jogging along the river, and the flush was still high on her cheeks when she entered the kitchen. Her hair was pulled back off her forehead with a pink sweatband accentuating the squareness of her face. At the refrigerator she gulped down orange juice from a plastic bottle, then went over to kiss Mark and picked up her daughter from the counter, hugging her chubby body against her own angular figure, clad in grey sweat togs. She kissed her, then set her back down on the butcher block counter.

Mark glanced around from the stove where he was cooking pancakes. "Who was on the phone?" he asked.

Jenny took a banana from the bowl on the table. "You want one?" she asked Erika.

"Who was on the phone?" Mark repeated.

She began slicing the overripe banana into a bowl. "Kay's in town," she answered. She sliced another banana—slip, slip, slip—into another bowl. She took a spoon from the drawer. Mark watched the muscles tighten at the back of her neck. "She said she hasn't seen us in ages and asked if she could come over. She wanted to know if Olivia was here. Do you mind?"

"Why should I mind?"

Jenny handed the bowl to Erika.

"I made another picture," Erika announced. "*Another* bee kissing a butterfly."

"Do *you* mind?" Mark asked his wife.

"Can I see it?" Jenny answered her daughter. Then: "Why should I mind?"

"You can have it," Erika answered, presenting her mother with a damp piece of paper from the counter.

"I don't know," Mark said.

"I like this one even better." Jenny examined the paper scrambled with green and pink lines. Then to Mark: "I hope Olivia doesn't mind."

"Mind what?" Olivia stepped into the doorway. She wore the same wrinkled pants suit of the night before, but she had changed into a fresh white turtleneck. She'd put a brown shadow and pencil to her eyes and some lipstick on her lips; her hair was more or less combed, and she looked revived. "My god, Erika, you're a giant!" she exclaimed. The child on the counter smiled. "You remember your Aunt Olivia? I was the only one who'd take you to the zoo in the rain last summer." Erika nodded and Olivia reached out and gave her a hug. "I still say you look more like me than your mother," she observed of the olive-skinned child with the dark curly hair. "Are you sure you're not my little girl?"

"I couldn't be your little girl," the child said. "You're never here."

Olivia laughed. "I see I'm going to have to take my duties as an aunt more seriously or you'll take away my title."

"I won't take it if you want it," Erika answered earnestly.

As Mark explained to Erika what a title was, Olivia asked again, "What will I mind?"

"Kay's coming over for breakfast."

"Kay? What's she doing here?" Jenny poured orange juice into plastic tumblers. "You're kidding, right?" Olivia asked. "You're not kidding. Don't tell me. She's covering the NLA. I don't know why I didn't expect it. Goddamn, how do you think she swung that assignment?"

"She does cover State Department," Jenny said.

"It's been over two years since I've seen her. Did you tell her I was here."

"She asked right off if you were."

"How did she know?" Olivia reached over to the stove and poured herself a cup of coffee.

"She ran into Guy Rhodes when she got in last night."

"Oh shit. And what else did Guy tell her?"

"I don't know, but she's coming to see you." Jenny stacked knives and forks on a tray.

"Why do you think she wants to see me?"

Jenny gave Erika a handful of napkins and asked her to take them to the table. "Maybe she's just trying to be friendly."

"Friendship is not among Kay's motives," Olivia observed.

"What do you think her motive is?" Mark asked.

"Let's just say Kay is more self-serving."

"Aren't you?"

Olivia looked over at him. He didn't appear hostile, but she didn't understand his point. "I'm jealous of her if that's what you mean. I'm the first to admit that. If I were writing half as much as she, I'd be happy. Besides she's five years younger, good-looking and white. My feelings towards her are none too pristine." She began rummaging through the drawer for a spoon. She dumped sugar into her coffee. "But Kay knows I know this story in a way she doesn't. She knows I could introduce her around. I'll probably end up introducing her just to prove I'm not jealous, but allow me to find it curious that she's coming over here at 7:30 in the morning to see me after almost two years when all I heard from her was a clipping in the mail with her byline on it."

Olivia drank her coffee. Mark turned back to the stove. Jenny began counting out plates. She and Olivia and Kay and another friend, Elise, had all been reporters together a decade ago at *The Boston Record*. Of the four, Kay was at the moment preeminent though each had had her moment of success. Elise was now dead, and Jenny and Olivia had been out of the mainstream for several years.

"I already know what will happen," Olivia went on. "She'll suggest we share a cab to the opening meeting. She'll even pay for it on her expense account, and then there I'll be once again ushering *The Washington Tribune*'s star beauty into my territory like I did at the Ellsberg trial. But at least give me credit for knowing my own insecurities."

"What does beauty have to do with anything?" Mark asked.

Olivia passed her hand through her hair which curled on her head like an untrimmed plant. She stood beside Mark at the stove, and at 5'10" she was almost as tall as he.

"You're better than Kay," he said, "only you don't take your talent seriously enough."

Olivia's hands flew up like birds startled to flight. "But I do," she protested at the same time she wondered if Mark really thought her better than Kay; she was surprised that he had given the attention to come to any judgment. "That's the problem. I take myself much too seriously." She glanced at Jenny for support, but Jenny stood with her back to them. She stacked cups and spoons on the tray, and without turning around, she took the tray into the dining table as the telephone rang.

Mark reached for the phone on the wall. Olivia took her cup and followed Jenny. From a drawer Mark took out a pencil. "Yes, I saw that," he said into the phone. He pulled Erika's picture to him and began making notes on the back. "I marked the same question. The Afco meeting's at four. Why don't you come?"

As he talked, he paced, and the coiled telephone cord slapped back and forth against the photographs on the wall. He stopped and scribbled another number then stood listening, looking at the picture of Erika burying him in the sand in Nantucket last summer.

"I'm concerned too, Reynolds, as concerned as you are." Reynolds, his partner, ten years his senior, was sometimes so cautious and skeptical that Mark had trouble keeping his patience. They'd left the same investment bank two years ago and had formed a small merchant bank, acting as advisors and arranging financing for companies.

"Look, come to the meeting. We simply don't have all the facts. Okay?" This "okay" was part question, part summation. He hung up the phone. He stood for a moment looking at the other pictures: Jenny and him under a waterfall in Mexico on their honeymoon, Jenny and Erika and him the morning Erika was born, a red, wrinkled, large-eyed child cradled in Jenny's arms.

When he came into the living room, Jenny and Olivia were talking quietly at the end of the table and Erika was standing on her chair watching a parakeet in a cage by the window, her small round face solemn and inquisitive as the bird pecked at its mirror.

The intercom buzzed. Jenny exchanged glances with Olivia, then rose and went into the hall. The buzzer sounded again. Jenny pressed the button and waited. In a moment a small, energetic woman with blue-tinted glasses on top of her head strode off the elevator on the third floor and through the doorway. She was carrying a briefcase in one hand and a handful of flowers in the other.

"I couldn't resist daisies in January," she announced. She handed the flowers to Jenny, whom she kissed on the cheek. "You look wonderful," she said.

Jenny stood in her sweatsuit, her hair uncombed, hanging straight to her shoulders, her face dry, without make-up. But before she could respond, Kay had moved past her and into the living room. She walked with a flat-footed, awkward gait Jenny had always found incongruous to her good looks. "Olivia!" she cried. "My god, it's been years. How are you?"

Olivia looked up from her plate. "Hello, Kay."

"When Jenny told me you were here, I couldn't believe it. I haven't seen you . . .well, not since I got back from Europe. Did you know I was in Europe myself for a year? Did Jenny tell you?" Kay glanced quickly around the room.

"You sent me your clippings, remember?"

"That's right. I thought you might be interested since I was in some of the places you'd been."

16

"Is that why you sent them?"

Jenny stepped between the two women. "How are you, Kay?"

"Ah . . ." Kay heaved her shoulders. "Frantic, if you want to know the truth." She turned back to Olivia. "I'm in for the NLA meeting . . . . I guess Jenny told you. That's why you're here, right? But I think I'm a little out of my depth." She sat down at the table across from Olivia and next to Mark, whom she glanced at from the corner of her eye.

"Kay," Mark acknowledged.

"Hello, Mark." She leaned towards him, offering her cheek to be kissed.

"I see you're writing all the time now," he offered.

"It's been unbelievable. If you want to know the truth, I'm floundering a bit though don't dare say that to anyone."

"Not you," Mark said.

"I fought to get this assignment for instance, but now that I'm here, I realize how poorly contacted I am. I have good U.N. sources, but this is a different game. No one *knows* these people." She pulled off her sweater. She was wearing a sky blue cardigan, a silk blouse, a blue tweed skirt and brown leather boots. Pushing her hair out of her face, she held it back in a pony tail for a moment and looked like a young girl confessing some transgression.

"Then why did you fight for it?" Olivia asked.

She shrugged and let go of her hair. "Habit, I guess. This *is* the biggest news around this week. I wanted to be here." She reached out and poured herself a cup of coffee. She could hear herself talking too quickly, saying too much. She sipped the coffee to slow herself down. She was trying to win over these friends who weren't really friends because they didn't like her. At least Olivia didn't. She wasn't sure about Jenny. In some unexplored corner of her feelings, she felt hurt by Olivia, who had been her mentor of sorts when she was starting out. Essentially though Olivia didn't count anymore as a journalist, except that she was the expert on this country which had jumped into the headlines the past few months, this tiny, obscure country which for some incomprehensible reason Olivia had made her specialty.

Kay lifted a pancake onto her plate. "I don't mean I'm *totally* ignorant," she retreated. "I probably know as much as half the

17

people covering the story, but that's not enough. Do you know what I mean?" She turned to Olivia, who was cutting Erika's pancakes.

Olivia met Kay's smile with a steady gaze. "Sure, Kay," she said.

Kay reached for the butter. Then as if noticing Erika for the first time, she exclaimed, "That's not . . ." she hesitated, forgetting Erika's name. "The last I saw her she was crawling. Oh dear, I'm afraid she won't like the present I got her." She opened her briefcase and produced a yellow rattle with a mirror on one side and three bells on the other. "It was all I could find at the hotel this morning. I'm sorry if she doesn't like it."

"It was nice of you to think of her," Mark said.

Kay handed the rattle to Erika as though she were handing her a microphone and expected an appropriate comment. Erika simply said thank you and put the rattle beside her plate. "It's so hard to tell with children," Kay apologized. She wanted to say she never knew what to give her own son either—he was 11, in boarding school in Massachusetts—but only Mark, whom she had dated years ago, knew she had a son.

Kay turned now to see how Jenny was surviving motherhood. She hadn't known Jenny was pregnant again. Why would she do that to herself, she wondered. And yet Jenny looked more robust than ever. Her square face gave her the illusion of carrying more weight than she did though Kay noted the bones at her neck still protruded. Jenny too had faded from the ranks of those who mattered in the press, ever since she'd had a child and left the paper. Jenny had actually met Mark through her years ago. She'd invited Jenny to be the date of one of Mark's business school friends, only she'd made the mistake of going off with the friend and leaving Jenny to Mark. The rest was . . . well, history. She'd always found it puzzling though that Mark had chosen Jenny over her when in anyone's estimation Jenny was the plainer of the two.

"So, Jen, how's your book coming?" she asked.

Jenny looked up from her plate. She too had been making comparisons and wishing she had at least combed her hair and put on make-up. Kay's thick blonde hair swept stylishly off her face; her face was flush in olive and rose tones, and Jenny saw Kay's pale green eyes taking in all the details of herself and her home.

"Which one?" she asked.

"You're writing more than one?"

"I've been writing children's books."

"Oh, yes . . . I heard something about that." Kay laughed. "No, I meant your grown-up book. Weren't you writing one about women and Africa . . . or something like that."

"Something like that," Jenny said.

"I'd love to read it sometime. Are you letting people read it yet? Have you read it, Mark?" Kay reached out and touched Mark's arm on the table. "You must have."

Mark looked up. "What? Oh yes, it's good." He'd been skimming the newspaper and had paused at a small article on a threatened boarder closing where Afco had one of its largest mines.

"I would think so. It must be perfect by now. It's been what . . . four years?

"Jenny's children's book went through three printings," Olivia announced, "and she has a contract for another one."

"Oh?" Kay's eyebrows raised. "Well, that's wonderful, isn't it? I guess we'll just have to wait for your grown-up book." Jenny didn't answer. "Did you know I've been asked to write a book?" Kay went on. "I always thought if I could get some time off, but six months . . . that's my limit."

Jenny rose from the table; she wouldn't spar with Kay; she wondered why Olivia allowed herself to. "Would anyone like more pancakes?" she asked.

Kay took a bite of the one pancake she'd set on her plate, a pancake she'd topped with a small pat of butter and no syrup. "Oh not for me. I don't think I can even finish this one."

Jenny turned towards the kitchen. As she left, she noted Kay's hand again on Mark's arm. "Didn't you help finance one of the mines there?" Kay asked, nodding to the story Mark was reading.

Mark looked up, surprised that she knew.

Kay smiled. "See, I've been following your career through the business pages. You think you're going to have trouble?"

Mark set the paper down. "It's possible."

"The people already have trouble," Olivia inserted.

Kay and Mark both looked over at her, a similar query on their faces. But Jenny returned then, and Kay rose. "I'd really better be going," she said. "I just wanted to drop by to say hello. Could I make a call first?"

Jenny pointed to the phone in the hall. "Or if you want privacy, there's one in the back."

As Kay left the room, Olivia muttered, "Shit."

"Sh-h-h," Jenny answered.

Olivia began gathering her papers and books and loading them in her briefcase. "Goddamn it, she just gets to me."

"Let her be," Jenny said. "Why do you argue with her?"

As Olivia bent down to pick up her case, the cat rubbed under her arm. "Cassie's getting fat, Jenny," she said.

"He's getting old," Jenny answered. "He keeps getting fatter and fatter."

"I know how he feels." Olivia sat up with her briefcase on the table and rearranged her body in the chair. "Was I terrible?" she asked.

"You were less than friendly," Mark observed. He looked over at Olivia, not with censure, yet with an expression that suggested he expected more from her, though why he should have any expectations puzzled her.

When Kay reentered, Olivia stood. She glanced at Mark, then said to Kay, "I guess we might as well share a cab."

Kay smiled. "That's a good idea." Taking her sweater from the back of the chair, she leaned over and kissed Jenny on the cheek, then she kissed Mark. Turning to Olivia, she asked, "Who are you writing for anyway?"

"The New Centurion," Olivia answered.

On the landing Olivia stowed her clothes in the hall closet; then she looked back at Jenny and Mark and shrugged.

As she and Kay left the apartment, Kay said, "I understand you know Jamin Nyo . . . personally, I mean."

Chapter 3

Olivia folded herself into the backseat of the taxi and let Kay direct the driver to the U.N. The rain had stopped from the night before; the gutters of upper Broadway were filled with trash that yesterday had been covered by snow. Olivia stared out the window at the passing store fronts and fruit stands opening for business. Kay glanced over at her; then she reached into her purse and pulled out a cigarette. The smoke spun a thin spiral into the center of the cab as the two women rode in silence.

It was Olivia who finally spoke. "Could I borrow $20, Kay?" Her voice was resigned and matter-of-fact.

Kay turned to look at her. "You need money?"

"I'll pay you back this afternoon." She had meant to borrow money from Jenny but had forgotten when Kay arrived. Until she retrieved her purse, she was without money or identification, and she was beginning to worry that she wouldn't be able to get into the meeting without press credentials. "Well, if you need it . . ." Kay opened her purse and handed over a $20 bill.

"Thanks." Olivia took the money without explanation.

"I guess it's hard making ends meet as a free lancer," Kay offered.

Olivia didn't answer. The cab had cut through the park and was now turning onto Fifth Avenue. She was considering asking the driver to drop her off at the Plaza; but she was afraid Kay might follow. She didn't want to have to explain anything. She decided to go to the U.N., then catch a quick cab back.

"You should try to get a job at the *Tribune*," Kay suggested. "Everyone there is very professional, not like the *Record*." Kay blew more smoke into the cold air of the cab. At the *Record* Kay had been Olivia's assistant.

Olivia took off her glasses; she cleaned the lenses with the edge of her jacket. She was sure Kay knew she'd applied at the *Tribune* when she'd returned from Africa. She'd been asked back for three sets of interviews, but in the end, they hadn't offered her the job. "I don't know . . ." she answered vaguely as the Plaza rushed by her window, "maybe I will."

Kay lit another cigarette. Olivia's problem was that she acted so damn superior. At least that's what she'd told the national editor when he'd asked her opinion on hiring Olivia. Though to look at her, sitting petulant in her wrinkled suit, Kay didn't understand why Olivia should think herself superior; and she didn't understand why so many of their colleagues thought her so too, but she knew they did. Olivia hadn't written an article of note in almost three years, though supposedly she was writing a book. Kay opened the window and flicked out her ashes. "I'm sure you'll do just as you please," she said.

"What do you mean?"

"I don't know why you don't like me."

Olivia roused slightly. She didn't want this confrontation, not now. "I've been in a bit of a slump; that's all," she offered.

"That's what I told Guy."

"What do you mean you told Guy?"

"He said you acted odd last night. I said you must be tense because this is an important assignment for you."

Olivia frowned. "I don't need you interpreting me to our friends," she said. She remembered again the man she'd left Guy in order to pursue. She jotted a note to find out who he was.

Kay put out her cigarette. This time she stiffened at the rebuke. "In case you're interested, I came over this morning because I thought I might be able to help you. I know you haven't been publishing. I know it must be hard on you. I thought maybe I could be a friend, but as always you don't want help."

Kay's voice was shaking for one of the few times Olivia could remember; she wondered at the cause of the emotion. Kay reached into her purse for another cigarette. She lit it with a silver lighter, then she turned calmly back to Olivia. "So what did Mark tell you?" she asked.

"About what?"

"The mines. Is he involved in any of this? I assume that's why you're there."

Olivia expelled air in a surprised laugh. "I'm not staying with Jenny to use her husband as a source."

"Oh?" Kay's eyebrows arched.

Olivia shook her head. "You never change, do you, Kay?"

Kay opened the window and flicked out more ashes. "Neither do you."

When the taxi drew up at the U.N., Kay got out first. She paid the driver; then over her shoulder she said in a level voice, "I'll see you." And she strode off towards a small group of protesters chained to the front fence.

Olivia sat for a moment. She had been certain Kay had come to borrow her sources; she still thought that was her motive although she wasn't as sure. Perhaps she'd come to pump Mark. Olivia hadn't realized he was involved with the mines. She wondered why Jenny hadn't told her, but then she hadn't seen Jenny in six months. When they talked on the phone every month or so, Mark's business was not a topic between them. They talked of the books they each were writing, of Erika, of Olivia's love life or lack of it. Yet Olivia couldn't help but wonder if Jenny had been keeping Mark's involvement from her, knowing what her reaction would be. However, the mines were not, she thought, a focus in this drama. There were no mines in the North, and the NLA, she felt certain, would announce the secession of the North today.

As Kay moved to the fence, Olivia noted with passing interest that she'd singled out the best-looking man to interview. Gathering her briefcase, Olivia made her way out of the taxi. The morning was chill, and her coat was still damp from the night before. Heading across the street, she was about to hail a cab back to the Plaza when a fleet of limousines drove up with tiny red and black flags flapping on their hoods. Jamin and the delegation had arrived. Her purse was lost for the day.

As the limousines filed into the grounds, she felt jealous of their easy access. She stared up at the rows of multi-colored flags agitating above the expanse of concrete and granite and glass that was the United Nations. She didn't know how she would get into the meeting now. She saw reporters she recognized from yesterday start to move through the gates. Down the block a taxi stopped, and Peg got out. She thought of asking Peg if she could get credentials through *Newsweek*, but Peg was a friend who respected her; she didn't want to risk that respect. She thought of calling *The New Centurion*, but she'd only confirm Alan's worst expectations of her. She'd rather get in by her own wits. She was adept at hiding in the shadows and slipping past, but the thought of masquerading one more time so depressed her that she didn't move. She was 39 years old and still living by improvisation and sleight of hand. She wasn't sure where her next money was coming from. She managed to pull it from odd corners of her life, dashing off quick articles for newspapers or lecturing to classes at a university or winning grants. She was very good at winning grants. Foundations gave her money because her credentials were impressive—BA magna cum laude from Barnard; MA, Brown University; MS, London School of Economics—and they became more impressive with each grant. She talked, cajoled, and won her way in and out of places, had just enough luck to keep ahead of herself. She called it luck at least, for now and then when she surveyed the decline of her career from its promise a dozen years ago, she was at a loss to explain what had happened. Though she still had faith in her abilities, she no longer believed she could make things happen. Yet because she felt something important was waiting for her, she kept on, holding to the person she sensed she could be. Because Jenny was one of the few people who also believed in that person, she relied more than she liked on Jenny as a friend.

Picking up her briefcase now, Olivia started back across the street. She didn't know when she could retrieve her purse. She resented the fact that she was even thinking about it.

Most of the press corps had already gone inside, but Kay was still at the fence talking to the protester. Kay was her only hope now. She began digging into her briefcase for anything that resembled a press pass. From one of her books she pulled out a library card. She walked towards Kay as if to speak to another demonstrator. When Kay turned around, she waved. "You going in?" she asked, smiling as if nothing had passed between them. She couldn't bring herself to tell Kay she needed help. Instead she began reconsidering her feelings towards her former colleague. Kay worked as long and hard as anyone she knew. She herself should be so disciplined and fearless; Kay would go anywhere for a story. What she lacked in sensitivity and imagination, loyalty and friendship, she made up for in guts. When Kay joined her, Olivia asked in as friendly a tone as possible, "How did you do?"

"That man was the husband of one of the teachers killed in a bombing last year," Kay said. "He flew all the way over to protest this meeting." She sounded impressed with the man's story. Glancing at the white, ruddy-faced man in a suede jacket, Olivia wanted to say he must be rich and to ask what his wife was doing in a railroad yard, for those had been the targets of the bombings. But instead she said, "We'd better hurry."

She let Kay walk slightly ahead of her and on the inside, and she kept her in conversation. As they passed through the entrance to the press gallery, the guard checked Kay's pass first. Meanwhile Olivia asked questions about the *Tribune*, making it clear she and Kay were colleagues. When the guard asked for her pass, she held up her library card and at the same moment asked him the time. As he checked his watch, she put her card back in her briefcase and told him to have a nice day.

Kay glanced over at her. She didn't say anything, but from her disapproving look, Olivia knew that Kay knew she had just been used. Olivia kept on walking. Okay, so now she owed Kay one, she told herself.

As they descended to their seats, she said, "If you'd like, maybe I can introduce you to Jamin."

Kay moved into the row. She nodded to Guy at the end of the aisle and pulled out her notebook. Flipping to a clean page, she said, "I'll get my chance." Then she picked up the earphones and plugged in for the invocation.

Chapter 4

The dishes from breakfast still sat in the sunlight on the dining table, and last night's dishes lay unwashed in the sink when Jenny came in after walking Erika to school and Mark to the subway. She went straight to her study, for the quiet of a morning apartment, of domestic objects at rest, threatened the momentum of her whole day unless she bore past them with the conviction that the world awaited the energy she was prepared to give it.

On the window ledge the clock glowed 9:10. She was late starting today. Usually Mark took Erika to school, but today she had wanted to be with him and so had accompanied them and lingered with Mark afterwards. As they scanned the headlines by the subway station, their heavy coats arm in arm, she asked, "What did Kay want?" Mark glanced over at her. "I heard her ask you about the mines."

"She saw the article on the border closing; she asked if we had mines there." Mark bought *The Wall Street Journal* and tucked it under the arm still linked with hers.

"How did she know?"

"She did her homework I guess."

"Be careful," Jenny warned.

"What do you mean?"

"Remember, she's the press."

He smiled. "So are you . . . so are half your friends."

"But Kay's never off duty."

"So, what's she going to write? I'm not doing anything newsworthy . . . or wrong," he added in a slightly defensive tone.

Jenny didn't answer. She'd worried before that this investment was a gun waiting to go off, and Kay, she knew, had an instinct for setting off artillery.

Mark picked up his briefcase from the sidewalk. "We have that dinner tonight, remember? I'll meet you at the restaurant." He placed his gloved hand around her shoulders and kissed her. "I asked Mrs. Rousseau to come up at seven."

As Jenny sat at her desk now, she stared out at the alley and at the pots of brown geraniums on the fire escape. She opened her bottom drawer. Instead of pulling out *Nagundi Heath in the Tunnel of Mirrors*, her children's book, she drew forth a set of manila folders labeled: *African Women: The Ultimate Colony or Revolution in the Making?* She hadn't looked at this book for months, her "grown-up" book as Kay had called it, Kay who always inserted enough truth under the skin to act as an irritant, her "grown-up" book she kept setting aside.

She turned to Chapter 11—"Patronage and Violence." She'd left off her revisions here in the fourth or was it the fifth draft, about the time she'd found out she was having another child though she had not linked the two occurrences. She spread the manuscript before her now and began reading the story of a market women's riot in Nigeria in 1929 in protest over British taxation of women. The phone rang.

"You think Erika would like a doll house?"

"Mother . . ."

"I'm sorry. Am I bothering you? I just saw one on sale on the way to work this morning. I wondered if Erika were old enough."

"I'm in the middle of work . . ." Jenny answered.

"I know. So am I." Her mother was managing editor of a magazine in Houston. "But I thought I'd buy it on the way home and send it, along with a little something I got for the baby."

"I'm sure she'd like it . . ." "By the way, don't forget it's your father's birthday tomorrow."

Jenny laughed.

"What?"

"You've been divorced ten years. Why are you still remembering his birthday?"

Dorothy Reeder sighed. "Habit. I'm sorry. I'll let you go. So I'll buy the doll house?"

"Fine." Jenny hung up the phone. She switched on the answering machine, then rolled her screen to the next page, shifted a paragraph, and read the page. Kay was right; she'd been working on this book forever. She'd written her first children's book as a diversion from finishing this one, when Erika was toddling and she had neither time nor ability to stretch an idea beyond naptime, when the ideas themselves raised questions she couldn't answer. She wished suddenly she had gone to the U.N. meeting with Olivia and Kay. They were out on the story, and she wasn't. Was that what was bothering her? Something was burrowing under her peace of mind. But she hadn't been on a story for years. She'd left the rush of news to raise a child and write a book, only the child and the book required a patience she sometimes wondered if she had, unremitting patience before which no empires fell and no echo was heard. Was that it? She heard no echo of herself anymore. Kay's visit this morning had borne down this silence upon her. The whole time Kay had been in the apartment she'd felt a heightened sense of her own boundaries. She'd felt too a vibration, as animals are said to feel, in the presence of danger. She sat now listening to that vibration in her inner ear.

The key clicked in the front door. She heard Aida's immediate attentions, picking up papers, gathering dishes, cleaning what they should keep clean themselves but seemed unable to do. She picked up her pencil. It was already eleven; she had only an hour and a half left. If she didn't finish her work, she would be on edge all afternoon. There had been a time in her life when she had been much more relentless, not for a few hours a day but for days and weeks on end. The six months she'd spent in Africa, she'd kept moving and writing all the time. Her newsletters back to the

Foundation which sponsored her outweighed those of any other Fellow. Yet the whole time she was in Africa, she'd sensed she was missing what she'd come to find, for she'd been too busy tracking down stories. She had never settled down, never let the slow, relentlessly slow, pace of life there work its change upon her. It was only since Erika was born that she had finally begun slowing down, for without words or argument her child was bending her to another rhythm.

The clock glowed 12:45. She punched keys in a rapid series of codes to save her day's work, then filed her papers and went into the hall where she grabbed her coat. Pushing open the kitchen door, she saw Aida feeding the cat scraps from the breakfast dishes. In her early twenties, she was pretty with bright black eyes, though in her eyes was a loneliness Jenny saw but rarely had time to attend.

She paused now and asked, "Is everything okay for you?"

Aida watched her. Seeing her rush, she nodded, "Okay," relieving Jenny of responsibility for what she saw.

"You'll make him fat," Jenny said of the cat; then letting go of the door, she hurried out of the apartment into the cold afternoon.

As she waved down a taxi, the sadness in Aida's eyes flashed again in her mind. She tried to guess at the cause. Because the possibility always existed that money was the problem, she decided to give Aida another raise —it would be the third raise in seven months—and on Monday she would make sure to take time to talk with her. Then as the taxi turned down the block for Erika's school, she felt a quiet excitement rise as she went to meet her child.

Chapter 5

In the beige and green auditorium the world's representatives shifted on vinyl chairs as they waited for the gavel to drop. Olivia put on her horn-rimmed glasses and peered over the railing. Jamin and Nyral sat stiffly behind the podium with their eyes shut in the moment of silence before the committee session began. The auditorium was about half-filled; this hearing on human rights was one of several meetings requiring delegates' attention today.

"International statesman . . . theologian . . . author . . ." the Under-Secretary General droned as he introduced Nyral. "Threatened by a civil war . . . Fire feeding in our neighbor's brush can leap into our own if the winds pick up . . . Robert Nyral."

Nyral rose from his chair. Half a dozen African representatives clapped, but the official chairs of Nyral's countrymen were empty in protest at Nyral being given this forum. He moved slowly to the podium. From the window on his left sunlight was diffused through a gauze curtain. He squinted at the light; his face was strained. His hand passed over his grey hair. Above his lip a thin moustache struggled. He shut his eyes and bowed his head. He stood without speaking for a long moment. Kay glanced at Olivia for an explanation, but Olivia was watching Nyral. Peg touched Olivia's shoulder.

"He's praying," Olivia explained.

Finally opening his eyes, Nyral took hold of the podium. When he spoke now, his voice was strong. He spoke without notes. "I am sad to be standing before you," he began. His small eyes peered into the assembly searching for his audience. His broad mouth and nose, the planes of his face were softer, less demanding than his eyes. "I am sad for my country; I am sad for Africa; I am sad for myself." He wiped his forehead. His face already glistened under the spotlights.

"As you know, my country claimed its independence fifteen years ago. Like most of our African brothers, our colonial days left us with disparate formations of geography and peoples which we were told were our nation, peoples split across national borders, speaking different languages, following different customs. In the first years after independence we struggled to maintain our union. However, in pursuing our freedom, we allowed ourselves to believe the only oppressor was from the outside; and we allowed to remain in our land the false gods of wealth and power.

"Fifteen years ago the man now our Prime Minister lived in a house that had but three chairs, a bed, and a table. Today our Prime Minister owns apartment houses whose monthly rentals are more than most of our people earn in a year. He owns three palaces within our country and two houses abroad. He owns theatres and hotels. He and his family have become the new imperial power in our land, and his people rule all other people.

"For seven years I served in the government of Amundo Bulagwi because I believed a platform for opposition was better than no platform at all. But then in 1976 my colleague and close friend Joseph Untoro was murdered in his bed. Untoro was Minister of Finance. He too had challenged the extravagances of the government. He was slain the night before he was to deliver a plan for reform to the Parliament. The next morning those in his office were arrested and imprisoned. His wife and children fled across the border. A state of emergency was declared.

"The people were told Untoro had been plotting to overthrow the government. I know for fact his plot was only a plot of ideas. Along with others who saw the blood on the wall, I went into hiding. The death of Untoro was the beginning of the National Liberation Association.

"Soon political opposition was banned in our country. The Cabinet was dismembered. The Prime Minister named himself President for Life and passed laws which took all power from the northern region and gave it to his people in the south. My own people and all those of the north are now exiled to the hills where the river bed is dry much of the year and only the simplest crops grow. The farms—the coffee plantations—are in the South. The platinum mines are in the South, and we live by what little the land yields to us." Nyral mopped his forehead with a white handkerchief he drew from his pocket. He took a sip of water.

"We have been living in these hills for the past eight years. We have lived now for most of a decade in exile. The sons of Untoro have returned to us as men. Our young people have grown up, and these men and women have an energy that will not wait. Their energy can be used to build a new nation, or, I fear, to tear one down."

He stared out at the representatives with sad, insistent eyes. In the audience a number of delegates were working on other papers at their seats; several were whispering among themselves. Such was typical of committee sessions, Olivia noted, for while this hearing was vital to the NLA, it was of moderate importance to these representatives, accustomed to the speeches and pleas of nations.

Nyral continued: "There is a contingent ready at this moment to declare war on the South. Others outside our land have come in for their own purposes to encourage this war; they offer weapons for our aid; they move as shadows in our land. They covet the riches from our mines; they want paths into our country; they want our allegiance against their own enemies.

"From my earliest days my father, a chief among our people, warned against tribe turning against tribe, region against region. He knew it was the white man's way to divide us so we would fight each other and not him. It was the very early allegiances of the southern people with the Europeans which marked the beginning of the conflict we see today. The Europeans gave away our land to them in the generation of my grandfather.

"Yet my father warned us to give up the bad blood between us lest it turn to poison in our veins. Though my father was not a man of books, he knew the history of many nations of Africa. He knew of the Hereros and the Namas, how the Hereros made league with the Germans to destroy the Namas and how this destruction once wrought was turned on them. The chief of the Namas warned his enemy, 'This giving of yourself into the hands of whites will become to you a burden as if you were carrying the sun on your back.'

"I fear the sun now weighs upon the backs of us all. I fear I no longer see how to reconcile with my neighbor who is no longer my neighbor but tries to be my master, and so I choose to part from him. Out of the poorest of land, out of the strife of a once greater nation, out of the largest of spirit, I call for a new nation to be born. Let us go in peace."

Scattered applause broke from the floor. Nyral acknowledged the applause with a simple nod and then returned to his chair. His face was troubled. There was a wariness in his eyes as though he heard some other, high-decibel sound.

In the press gallery Olivia scribbled the end of the speech, shaking her head. Other reporters seemed to be recording Nyral's words routinely, but she thought the speech had been shattering. She was relieved when Peg leaned over from behind and asked, "Am I wrong or did he just accuse Bulagwi of being a murderer and thief in front of the world body of nations?"

Olivia turned, glad to see Peg's surprise matched her own. "I think that's what happened."

"Will he get away with it?"

Olivia glanced at the representatives, many of whom had stood up now and were talking with each other. "It looks as if he has for the moment."

"I thought that was against the rules here."

Kay glanced at Olivia. She hadn't heard the interchange with Peg. Olivia guessed she wanted to know what she'd missed, but she said nothing.

Rising, the Under-Secretary thanked Nyral. "We are grateful

to the representative of the National Liberation Association," he said, "and we are grateful to have his colleague, Jamin Nyo, with us . . ." The passion of Nyral's plea was reformed now by this man's monotone which accommodated passion within the boundaries of diplomatic amenity.

Jamin rose. He moved to the podium. Delegates continued to talk with each other. Jamin stood in silence as the auditorium gradually grew quiet. Unlike Nyral, Jamin neither bowed his head nor shut his eyes. He towered above the gathering dressed in a three-piece navy suit, pale blue shirt, maroon tie, gold tie stud and dark glasses, the same glasses he wore when he toured the camps of his country, glasses used to shield his eyes from the sun and sand and dirt as his jeep clambered over the hills. But here at the United Nations, his dark face took on an aggressive, almost sinister, look behind the glasses. Olivia guessed this was as he intended for Jamin did not leave his appearance to chance. She felt heightened attention in the room.

Jamin allowed the silence to continue to the point of unease. Then he spoke. His voice was not the impassioned voice of Nyral. It was a stage voice, practiced and pitched in the monotones of power. "You will forgive me if I begin today with a story," he said. "I was not trained as many of you in politics. I was schooled in my own country and then here in the United States and in Britain as a student of literature. I have a different view to offer of Africa and my country. I see them as mother and child, as woman nourishing her child without a husband and as a jealous wife without a child.

"I go to a tale of the Bakongo people, our neighbors. It is the tale of a man who leaves his two wives while he goes to trade in the bush. He instructs them to take care of his children; each wife has one child. Now the older wife is jealous of the younger's child, who is more intelligent and handsome than her own. When the younger wife goes off to fish for her husband's return, the older wife sharpens her razor, and in the night she murders the babe. The next morning she goes to hide the dead body and finds she has killed her own child.

"On the husband's return, he asks for his elder wife and child, and when he is told what has happened, he will not believe that a mother would kill her child. He asks his friends to help him find his wife. The first day they find nothing, but on the second day one friend reports seeing a woman hidden in the forest nursing a babe, shaking it and singing, 'Why do you sleep like this? Awake! See! Your mother nurses you.' The husband follows his friend and through the trees he sees his wife still shaking the dead body of their child and singing her sorrowful song.

"I see our fine, strong country as that child, slain by its own jealous mother. I see our government, handed to us by our colonial rulers, as that jealous mother. But I also see a new country in the bright, honest child who is spared. I see it in the young mother who nurtures and protects her brighter child and in the father who must now watch over them both. The tale of the Bakongo does not go further, but I would see the husband unite with his second wife and protect her and his remaining child, see them attend to the grave of their dead brother and learn the cruel lesson of the jealous wife. Let not the elder wife come back and demand the younger child for herself.

"Centuries ago, perhaps in the same time as the legend of the Bakongo, another child's life was tested before the wisdom of King Solomon, who granted the living babe to the mother who would nourish it and not divide it as a spoil. A true mother looks to nurture and sustain her babe, not to take from it its life.

"I was called back to my nation by Robert Nyral eight years ago from my studies at Oxford. I returned to my country because I had known Robert Nyral since I was a boy. He had been my teacher in school; later he had sponsored me for my scholarships. I knew him as a great man. I joined him in the hills of our country to begin to plan our new nation. I put away my books, and I began to learn how to farm maize on a hillside, how to build a hut from grass and mud, how to live on the land with my people whom I had forgotten. The strength of our land is in our people. Had Robert Nyral not asked me to return into the hills, I might have forgotten this truth.

"I have been called by some a poet revolutionary as though by being a man of literature, I am less of a revolutionary. Should we be surprised that our revolutions are now being fought by our poets and artists whose charge it is to watch over their people and shape a vision, to live by that vision though it run in the face of accepted ways, whose charge it is to reach for a higher way and in the reaching carve a road to that way? Our surprise should be that not more of us become poets and artists in the living of our lives."

Jamin paused and sipped the water beside him. Olivia reached into her bag for another pad. Jamin's words as always were eloquent, yet in the rhetoric Olivia heard a dissonance, a sound so faint she wasn't sure if she were hearing it or remembering it, and she wondered if Jamin himself were aware of its presence. On seeing him in dark glasses and now hearing his display of education, Olivia heard and felt the restiveness and hopelessness of Jamin.

Jamin spoke for half an hour. He declared that the colonial tie in his country hadn't been severed but only spliced with new cords. He challenged imperialism and colonialism and then indirectly he called to question the policy of the Organization of African Unity which prohibited a member from challenging the sovereignty of another, no matter how that sovereignty had been abused. He called upon the history of his people before colonization, the history of Europe during the Roman empire and finally upon the political theory of half a dozen thinkers of the past two centuries to establish the inevitability of a new nation being formed in Africa.

The speech was impressive in its scholarship, and yet it was inappropriate, Olivia thought. Jamin's considerable intellect had been kept dormant too long and now given a field in which to perform, he was running a marathon rather than the 100-yard dash that was required of him. That his 500,000 people and 8,000 square miles of earth were ordained by history to a separate statehood was at the least an inflation of history, she thought. That his hills offered alternative routes for shipping ore from the interior to the coast and shipping arms from the coast into other countries was more to the point. That the superpowers of this earth were now interested for their own strategic reasons in his same African hills carried more historic analogues. Certainly wars in the past had been fought over less land and fewer resources though Olivia could not name many.

Olivia and Kay entered the delegates' lounge together, but Kay quickly moved off to a group of other reporters. Olivia wished Kay would simply get angry at her, show some emotion, but Kay behaved like a gentleman. She wondered if Kay had grasped the significance of the speeches. That Jamin and Nyral had been provided this forum and attacked Bulagwi here signified to her that some larger powers were at work and that some shifting of allegiances was underway. The question was who were those powers and why were they acting now?

She was looking about for someone who might give her the answers when an aide to Jamin stepped over to her. He told her that she could pick up her purse in Jamin's room after the afternoon session. She glanced at Jamin in the corner speaking with the ministers from other African delegations. She was surprised that he would think of her today, but she told the aide she would come. She would ask Jamin her questions. The aide bowed, then returned to Jamin with the message.

At the time Kay had been talking to Guy, but she hadn't missed the transaction. Now she made her way over to Olivia. "I guess you know him rather well," she said.

Olivia turned. "Who?"

"Jamin Nyo."

"Oh . . . Yes. I guess I do."

"Maybe I will take you up on that introduction," she said.

Suddenly Olivia was sorry she had capitulated to Kay, but she couldn't back out. She made a date to meet Kay at the Plaza bar at 6:30. That would give her enough time, she reasoned, to go to Jamin's room, retrieve her purse, conduct an interview with him, then persuade him to meet an attractive young reporter from *The Washington Tribune*. The latter she felt sure would prove no difficulty.

Chapter 6

It had been four years since Olivia had written the cover story on Jamin and Nyral and the National Liberation Association for *The New York Times Magazine*, a story which had caused a minor stir in Washington. Until that time few people had paid attention to this small underdeveloped nation. Those concerned with African affairs were focused on the independence struggles in southern Africa or the power struggles on the Horn. That a pro-Western government was systematically persecuting its minority, that Western corporations routinely paid bribes to government officials to keep their operations open, that periodic disappearances of government opponents took place were accepted as givens, no cause for alarm.

What Olivia had pointed out in her story, however, and what finally roused concern was the strategic possibilities of the country and the interest of outsiders in the dissident tribes of the NLA. The old colonial railroad through the northern hills remained an alternate shipping route both for ore and arms. Olivia had discovered Cuban and Lybian consultants in the hills. She pursued the thesis that the NLA, naturally sympathetic to the West, was being courted by others and if ignored by the West, might well turn elsewhere. It was an old thesis, she granted. Yet when the Bulagwi regime toppled, as it inevitably would from its own excess she argued, the West might again find itself on the wrong side.

Her article had succeeded in gaining some sympathy for the NLA and at least covert support from several nations, including the U.S. The country itself was of marginal economic consequence, a producer of coffee and sisal, a few manufactured goods like wood veneer from a factory in the North. It had been a small exporter of platinum and chrome during its colonial days, but many of the mines had closed. Last year, however, production in a number of mines had resumed; production was still modest though the potential was large. It was the country's strategic relation to its neighbors which had made it important to Washington lately for through it the ore and arms of many countries could pass, especially now that one of its neighbors was embroiled in a civil war.

For her part Olivia had initially visited and then stayed in the country for professional and personal reasons. She'd been freelancing throughout Africa, stringing for *The Record, The Washington Tribune, The London Times, The Economist,* covering independence battles and post-independence governments in Mozambique, Angola, Zimbabwe, and she was tired of moving around. The fact that no big news was here, no swarm of journalists, attracted her. She'd won a Guggenheim, a year's grant which, spent in Africa, she might stretch to two or even three years. She was ready finally to write a book. She wasn't sure of the focus: the influence of independence movements on post-independence governments or a consideration of civil war, a constant threat in half the nations of Africa. Or perhaps a study of the NLA's nonviolent struggle with the regime of Amundo Bulagwi. Rather than organize a guerrilla army as other countries' opposition forces had done, Robert Nyral had established a parallel government in the hills with the aim of ultimately displacing the Bulagwi government. He appointed ministers of education, transportation, employment, housing. Those in the villages in that area recognized these men and women as their leaders, obeying them rather than government officials in much the same way that their ancestors had obeyed tribal chiefs rather than the chiefs appointed by the Europeans. For reasons of his own, Bulagwi had rarely challenged the NLA in the hills, perhaps because the region was isolated and of little economic importance to him or because Robert Nyral in his fashion and by the force of his character threatened Bulagwi, who was a superstitious man. Olivia, attracted to Nyral's vision, had stayed two years recording the story of his people. Somewhere along the way she had also fallen in love with Jamin Nyo though he was a story she had not pursued, at least not personally.

Jamin was sitting alone by the window sipping a drink when Olivia arrived in his Plaza suite. The sun had set; shadows were draining the last pools of light from the room. Jamin motioned for her to join him. She had determined that if she didn't interview him now, she might never get the chance so as she settled in the chair opposite him, she began rummaging through her carry-all for her notepad. When she straightened up, Jamin nodded as though affirming some statement she had made.

"I have few friends in this country, Olivia Turner," he said, "but perhaps you are one of them." His voice was quiet. He turned and watched the street lights begin to flicker on outside. "You know, when I lived here, I used to watch the lights turn themselves on every night. You do not like to live with darkness in America, and you do not have to. It is no wonder your people do not understand mine."

Olivia glanced out at the high intensity beam which illumined the street in a yellow haze. In the hills the night had been absolute, had had the power to seal itself from day and send the people to rest.

Jamin reached behind him and switched on a lamp. "I prefer to sit in the dark, but you cannot write in the dark though I wish, Olivia Turner, you would put your notebook away."

"I have a list of questions I'd like to ask you," she said instead.

He nodded. "Let me hear them all."

Olivia opened her pad. "Who arranged the meeting for you today? Whom are you negotiating with? Do you see this hearing as a beginning of a larger power play in your country? If so, who are the players? How and why have you altered your nonviolent strategy?"

Jamin lifted his glass from the table. "Would you like a drink?" he asked. She shook her head. "Do you know I never drink except when I am with rich people. When I was at Oxford, I drank every night." He stood and went to the dresser to fill his glass. He was in his stocking feet. His tie and vest were draped over a chair; his blue shirt was unbuttoned at the collar.

"I thought you'd be in high spirits after your success today," Olivia offered.

"What success?"

"You were eloquent, Jamin. Half the audience was standing in applause . . ." He stirred the drink. "You know as well as I, applause is the world's cheapest commodity." He moved back to the window and sat down. "Those people who called themselves friends today will be our enemies tomorrow." He continued agitating the drink with a red plastic stick. The light from the street lamp glistened off his dark skin which stretched tightly across high cheekbones and a broad forehead and at his eyes fanned out in small lines as if here energy found a release.

He reached to the table and picked up the extra pen Olivia had taken from her purse. "In my view . . ." he began, "we are here because our neighbors are at war, and we may soon be at war; then those who mine the riches from the belly of Africa will have no way to get their riches out without great expense. I do not know all those who arranged the hearing today. I assume, as you have assumed, that we were finally granted the hearing we have sought for years because it was in the interest of powers larger than ourselves. Bulagwi has begun to offend even his friends, I believe. That is the folly of a man who thinks himself to have power; he does not understand that power is always on loan. As for our nonviolent strategy, we never had a strategy, I'm afraid, only an ideal. That is perhaps *our* weakness, for ideals, as you know, are costly, sometimes too costly for a poor nation."

He studied the pen as though it were an object of unusual interest. "Now . . ." he said, setting the pen down. "I have my own question . . ." Olivia gestured for him to go on. "What became of the book you were writing about us?"

Olivia looked up. "I'm still working on it."

"Ahh . . . ? You have grown grey working on it, Olivia Turner." He smiled. "But I too have grown grey so, you see, we are still keeping pace with each other."

Olivia smiled too. Jamin and she were the same age, in fact shared the same birthday, a coincidence neither attached significance to, yet which made them feel some small bond.

"Did I ever tell you I started a book once?" he asked. "Of poetry. But I too did not finish. So we have something else in common." Olivia watched him and wondered what point he was moving towards. She watched his long, almost feminine, fingers holding the cocktail glass and tried to imagine those same fingers holding a gun or making a bomb, for she had been told that Jamin had consented to the bombings of the railroads which had killed forty people. "We must both sacrifice the personal, only I accept the sacrifice and you do not."

"What do you know about me?" she asked. She had come to interview Jamin, but he was turning the focus from himself. She'd often watched him manipulate reporters, contradict himself just to throw a reporter off too easy an evaluation. She'd heard him disparage his training at Oxford, for instance, when she knew he prided himself on it.

"I do not know all about you, it is true, but I've always been able to tell much from little. You see, our people must take from what they have if they are to survive; but you, you accumulate much and use very little." He met her eyes, his own eyes yellow-white around the dark center. He smiled, knowing he had caught her in her own truth. "When we last met in my country, you had more notebooks and words than my people are worth. You know us as well as any Westerner will, but you don't trust yourself to say what you know because you have too much pride in yourself."

"I have very little pride," Olivia answered. She was surprised she'd say that to Jamin, but he didn't seem surprised.

"Ah, but you do. Otherwise you would have returned to my room last night for your purse. I knew you needed it. I told the guards to let you through, but you didn't come because you wouldn't go to a man's room and ask for what you need. That is why I say to you life is still personal. And why I think, Olivia Turner, you are not made for your business."

Olivia blinked behind her glasses. She rubbed the bridge of her nose. She stood up. She wanted suddenly to set distance between them. She went over to the desk on the other side of the room where she saw her purse on the floor. Picking it up, she said, "It's the only business I have."

"Why did you leave your purse in my room?" he asked.

"I didn't leave it on purpose."

"I think you did."

"Why?"

"Because I think you are a very bright woman who has not met a man who thinks as quickly as you do, and you are afraid of who you become with a lesser man. I think you left your purse in my room because you wanted to go to bed with me." He nodded affirming his analysis; then he smiled, an ironic, but not unsympathetic, smile bridging the time that had passed between them. "Circumstances, however, have changed between yesterday and today. I am afraid we will not learn what we might have taught each other."

Olivia laughed. "You are very sure of yourself."

"No." Jamin pulled out a gold tie stud from his pocket and began rolling it in his long fingers. "I am not so sure. I think you know that too. Only I act on what I see. That is a difference perhaps between a man and a woman. A man will act even if he knows there is more to see, but a woman will wait and try to see all, and since she can never do that, she waits and waits. You, Olivia Turner, see like a man but act like a woman."

Olivia sat on the edge of the bed. "I happen to be a woman," she said.

"I have noticed."

"But you don't think much of women."

"On the contrary." He moved again to fill his glass. He spoke now with his back to her. "A woman is the deepest, most hidden part of a man. A bond to a woman is far more difficult than any bond to a country." He turned and sipped his drink. "But that bond is personal, and for a long time I've had no room for the personal in my life."

"What would you have done if I'd come back to your room last night?" she asked.

"I would have given you your purse."

"Personally?"

"Well . . . at least not impersonally." He drank the chilled scotch and watched her, her large body balanced on the edge of the blue bedspread like a bird too big to fly. Yet in her eyes was the will towards flight. "But perhaps you were right not to come. You need more I think."

Olivia leaned back on one elbow. She felt her caution towards this man giving way to his view of her. "Not necessarily."

He laughed, but there was an edge to his laughter; his wide nostrils flared. He sat down on the bed beside her. "None of us knows what we need, only what we want. I want a country for myself and my people; you want a book with your name on it and a man perhaps with your name on him. Very likely neither of us will achieve our ends."

"Why not?"

"Ah . . ." He raised his hand as if to draw down an answer. His eyes, which only moments before had bid her to him, now held her at a distance, judging her. "Because, like your country, Olivia Turner, you are bound by your image of yourself." He finished his drink.

Olivia heard the scorn beneath his words. This scorn sprang up between them at times like nettle. Because of its spike, she never entirely trusted him. He changed too quickly, wearing different roles for different people—scholar, revolutionary, diplomat, poet, lover—shifting his point of reference as soon as anyone got too close. "Aren't you bound by your avoidance of any image?" she asked.

He put his hand on top of hers. "You would not be an easy woman for a man," he said.

Olivia looked down at their hands—the black and brown skin upon the powder blue satin bedspread. For a moment she wanted to yield to both the logic and the improbability of this proposition. She leaned towards the pressure of Jamin's arm. She didn't know how firm it would hold or if she should trust it, but she leaned into the weight of this man because she wanted, at least for the moment, to surrender the weight of herself. Neither she nor Jamin spoke. Her head touched his arm; she could smell the fading starch of his shirt and the slightly sour odor of his body. She felt the taut muscles in his chest; his whole body was hard and rigorous. She wondered how her own soft toneless flesh might fit with his.

But before she could allow the question, he said, "I am leaving tonight."

"What?"

"Our whole delegation is going back. No one is to know."

She turned and looked at him. "But why?"

"As we are talking, our arrangements are being made." He peered into the darkening room as if at some vision moving at the periphery of light. "There is a group among us opposed to what we are doing here, opposed to us breaking off into a separate state. They have been led to believe by those outside our country that they could win a war against the South and take control of the whole country. They have been financed by these interests and have taken up arms. While we are here, they have struck the Capitol. When the honorable men and women we were speaking to today learn what has happened, they will not much believe our speeches of peace."

"Can't you stop them?"

"The attack has begun, and I am here. I tell you because I would like to think we have a friend in America. By tomorrow it will no longer make you popular to be our friend."

Olivia lifted her hand from the bed. She wondered suddenly what kind of friend Jamin wanted. Did he want simply a friendly journalist? Was that what this meeting was about? He knew how important her article in *The New York Times* had been though he had no way of knowing how little she had written since then or how her own doubts had intruded the last few years. She asked now who these outside interests were. Were they the Soviets? Cubans? U.S.? Were they business interests? But Jamin wouldn't clarify. He said instead that they wore many masks and all claimed noble goals. She tried to remember the dissidents in the NLA, but she had been away four years; and they too wore masks.

Other, more personal, doubts crowded in. Why was Jamin really holding her? Was it only for what he thought she could do for him? She watched the way light moved on the surface of his eyes yet failed to penetrate the interior. She wondered if he were waiting for her to reassure him, to tell him that all was not lost, that his purpose for the last decade hadn't been foolishly spent

46

by those who had no comprehension of history or power. She tried to find within herself that assurance, but instead her mind prowled through the facts and players and arrived at a question: "Who do you think set you up?"

All at once Jamin laughed, a hard, condescending laugh. " It is we who will set them up in the end."

Olivia frowned. This mutability, this refusal to see or to be seen alarmed her. In the mirror above the dresser she watched him touching her hair now. He was tense and preoccupied as if this stroking were not giving him pleasure or comfort but were an interval before some battle. "Who financed this attack?" she asked.

"I can't say."

Olivia sat upright. "What is it you want from me, Jamin?" The question came out more abruptly than she intended, but she let it stand between them.

"Why do you ask that?"

"I would like to believe we are friends having a farewell talk, even a farewell affair, on the evening you flee my country, but there is a voice inside me that doesn't believe."

He watched her, his arm linking their bodies, the possibilities between them still open. "Is it not the voice of the woman who keeps a pencil and paper between her and life?" he asked.

"Perhaps. But am I not talking to a man who has placed a gun between him and life?"

Jamin lowered his arm. "Is that what you see?"

"That's not all I see . . ." she mitigated.

"But you cannot see beyond it." He released her. She wondered if she were making a mistake to set distance back between them, but she told herself the chance was too great that he was using her. For what purpose she wasn't sure, but she couldn't take the risk. She couldn't surrender that much of herself; she didn't have that much esteem left. Besides, he would be returning to his country to kill his opponents or be killed. She couldn't even trust that he would stay alive. "So you're leaving tonight," she said.

"Yes." He stood up from the bed. "I don't know when I shall see you again."

Olivia stood too. She couldn't help but feel she was acting against her own will and yet acting according to an instinct of self-

47

preservation. She went over and picked up her notepad. "Tell me at least what you think you've accomplished in the time you were here?"

"We have accomplished nothing except to learn how ephemeral power is. Now, there will be no more interview." Jamin started towards the door. Before he opened it, he stopped by the desk and wrote something down on a piece of paper and handed it to her. "If you ever want to contact me . . ." he said.

Olivia took the paper.

"You asked what I wanted from you?" he went on. Olivia nodded. "I'd like you to tell your friends of the press who expect to see us tonight that we are suffering from food poisoning, and that is why we are not there."

"What?"

"We will send the same message through our spokesmen, but if you say you have seen us and confirm the story, we may be believed a while longer. It is important that we return to our country unexpected."

"That puts me in an awkward position . . ."

"No one will remember what you said. If they do, you can say you too were deceived."

So this was why he had called her to his room after all, she thought, to use her again. But when she looked at him, his expression said, so this is what you want to believe. "I don't know . . ." she answered.

He nodded. He stood at the door without opening it for a moment; then he leaned down and kissed her. "I am sorry, Olivia Turner," he said. And he opened the door.

As Olivia walked down the gold carpeted hallway, she wondered exactly what Jamin was sorry about and why she felt suddenly so sorry herself. But she didn't have a chance to form an answer for when the elevator door opened at the lobby, Kay was waiting.

"You've been in his room all this time?" she asked. "You must have gotten quite a story. When do I get to meet him?"

"He's not seeing anybody tonight."

"He saw you. Did you ask him about me?"

"He told me there would be no interviews."

Kay stiffened her shoulders and pulled her sweater around them. "You mean he would only give you an interview? Come on, Olivia, that doesn't make any sense. Why would he give you the only interview?"

"It was personal, Kay," she said. "And he didn't give me an interview."

"You mean you've been up there all this time, and you didn't even interview him? What happened? Did you sleep with him for nothing?"

Olivia stared at Kay then turned and walked away without answering. She wished suddenly she *had* slept with Jamin. Kay could go to hell.

"I'm sorry." Kay caught up with her. "I'm a little desperate. What's he like anyway? He's quite good looking. How did you meet him?"

"I lived in his country for two years," Olivia said dryly.

"Can I meet him tomorrow?"

"His schedule is uncertain."

Olivia slid into a booth in the Plaza bar. She wanted more than anything to be alone right now, but Kay sat down next to her. "I'm not trying to compete with you for this story if that's what you're afraid of. Your story won't even be out for another month. I'm filing daily so why not share your sources? You never used to be this way."

Olivia ordered a tomato juice then stared at the other reporters talking at the bar. She remembered when she used to sit among them at the end of the day after the stories were filed. They would compare notes and bits of information; they'd feed each other pieces of the story they'd gathered, and from each other's parts try to put together a whole, though each knew he was withholding the one part he considered vital.

"You used to be much more open," Kay was going on. "But you've changed. You didn't even ask him about me, did you?"

"He had other things on his mind."

"I don't know what you have against me." Kay sat forward at the table. "I don't recall ever hurting you, but I am getting a little tired of apologizing for you to other people."

"What other people?" In spite of herself Olivia found Kay drawing her into conversation.

"Guy . . . Peg . . . a lot of reporters who think you're hanging on by what you've done in the past. They think it's sad you're not writing and getting assignments. So do I. I tell them, I'm sure you'll make a comeback, but really I'm not so sure. If you want the truth, I don't think you'll ever write that book either. I'm sorry to say that, but it's time someone told you."

"Exactly what are you telling me?" Olivia asked.

Kay took her sweater off and folded it beside her. She pushed back her hair and frowned. "That people don't respect you any more. If you don't have respect in this business, what do you have? Our reputations are everything."

"I see." Olivia looked up and asked the waitress for vodka with her tomato juice. "What would you have said if I'd gotten you the interview?" she asked.

Kay fell slient. She sipped her glass of white wine, then answered quietly, "You may not realize it, but working for the *Tribune*, I can interview just about anyone I want. I'll arrange the interview myself."

"Fine," Olivia answered.

"The truth is I've thought of talking to you for some time. I know you don't consider me a friend. I'm a different sort of friend than Jenny. Jenny would never tell you what I will. Everybody likes Jenny because she tells them what they want to hear. Personally, I want a friend who will tell me the truth and let me know when I'm in trouble." Kay leaned back in the booth and pulled out a cigarette. "For instance someone should have done the same for Elise, you know. I've always thought that," she said, referring to Olivia's best friend and Jenny's mentor on *The Record*, who had been killed ten years before on a story when she had walked into an alley and never come out.

"You leave Elise out of this," Olivia warned.

"I'm only using her as an example. She had all these friends— you, Jenny—but no one had the courage to tell her she was losing perspective on that story. I could see it; you must have. I tried to tell her. She at least listened to me—she always gave that courtesy to people—but she went right on. I'm not saying what happened was your fault. I'm just saying sometimes you have to tell people what they don't want to hear, and I think you should think about what I've said."

She set her notebook on the table and began flipping through its pages. "You see, whether you help me or not, I'll get this story." She started checking off names in the back of the notepad. Her thin, polished mouth had tensed and her fingers tightened around the pencil. In her unquestioning will Olivia both envied and felt sorry for Kay.

After a moment Kay looked up. "You know, as long as we're clearing the air, there is one other question I've always wanted to ask you." Olivia waited. "Was there more than just friendship between you and Elise?"

"What do you mean?"

"You know you took her death *so* hard, quitting the paper, going off to Europe and then Africa. I've always wondered—it's nothing to be ashamed of—I've just wondered if there weren't something else between you."

Olivia's eyes narrowed. She held her glass very still in her hand. Suddenly her head felt light. She wanted to slap Kay. Instead she asked, "You want a tip, Kay, is that it?" Her voice was flat. "All right, I'll give you a tip. Jamin won't see you; no one will because the whole delegation is sick. The doctors think it's food poisoning. A spokesman will announce the news before the dinner tonight."

"You're kidding?" Kay picked up her pencil. "Do they think someone did it?"

"I don't know any more than that."

"Are they very sick?"

Olivia glanced at the bar at the other reporters. "You'll have to find that out on your own. You have a few hours on everybody else."

Kay hesitated a moment. "Look . . ." she said slowly, focusing now with intensity that surprised Olivia, "I didn't mean anything by that about you and Elise. It's your business; I don't judge. I just wondered." She gathered her notebook and sweater. "I won't forget this," she added. And then she hurried out of the bar.

Olivia leaned back in the cool leather booth alone now. Who else had wondered, she thought. Then out loud she said, "They can all go to hell." She felt pleased that she'd sent Kay off chasing the wild goose. The other reporters would be writing the same story in a few hours anyway. This way Kay could be the first with the misinformation. Kay wouldn't mind as long as everybody else made the same mistake; it would still be her scoop. In the end, when and if the truth came out, she could feel all the more aggrieved with Olivia. For all Olivia knew, she never would know the truth for when she discovered the delegation had flown home, she could attribute the retreat to food poisoning.

Olivia watched several reporters at the bar get up and follow Kay, who had left a little too purposefully. She decided she might as well go back to Jenny and Mark's. There was no more story tonight. She gathered her notepad and belongings and withdrew to the steps of the hotel, where she asked the doorman to get her a cab. It was the same doorman who had helped her last night. She tipped him a dollar.

A grey-haired woman in purple knickers and a purple and blue sweater greeted Olivia at the door. She introduced herself as Madeline Rousseau, the baby sitter. Right off she began answering questions Olivia hadn't asked: Erika was fine; she went right to bed like an angel, such a sweet child. Mr. and Mrs. Rosen would be home at eleven. They'd asked her to stay until Olivia got there, but if Olivia didn't mind, she'd just like to watch the end of the movie; her television was broken downstairs. She peered at Olivia from small, luminous eyes. Her features were frail and powdered and her hair was a puff of grey curls slightly askew on her head. Under the purple knickers she wore sheer white tights and on her feet matching purple pumps with tassles. Her figure was slim and pert.

"Madeline!" a voice insisted from the couch. In the living room Olivia saw a silver-haired man watching television. "Here is where you lost it, right here," he said sternly. Madeline Rousseau scurried over to the couch and sat at her husband's elbow. As she peered at the screen, her penciled eyebrows and thin mouth contracted; her face became that of an old woman. She nodded, "Yes . . . yes, Arthur, that is where it was all lost."

Olivia stood in the hallway watching the couple, wondering what was lost and when they would leave. She hadn't counted on this annoyance. She had wanted to see Jenny and talk with her or even better be alone. On TV the movie's theme song began to play.

The couple sat in front of the screen until the last credit; then Madeline Rousseau stood.

"My husband helped make that movie, you know," she said, stepping into the hallway. Arthur Rousseau rose without speaking. His face was florid and puffy, but he was a handsome man. He stood erect, almost a foot taller than his wife. He simply nodded to Olivia as he walked to the door. "Well, we'll be going now," Madeline Rousseau said. "So nice to meet you, dear." She took Olivia's hand. "Oh . . . there were several calls for Mr. Rosen. I left them by the phone. Tell Mr. Rosen he can pay me in the morning."

Olivia moved into the kitchen. She opened the refrigerator and peered at the lighted shelves. She took out a wedge of cheese and a salami. From the cabinet above the stove, she took down a box of crackers. She carried her rations over to the couch where she dropped in front of the TV. The movement of the light and the droning of voices relaxed her. She didn't know what she was watching. She reviewed the questions she had yet to answer: who had arranged the UN meeting? Was the NLA being set up? Or was Bulagwi? She began cutting little pieces of salami and cheese and matching them to crackers. She felt the events of the day slowly recede in her mind: her lost purse, her maneuver into the U.N. meeting, Kay's accusations . . . Elise . . . who else had distorted their friendship? But she didn't want to be thinking about these, especially she didn't want to be thinking about Kay. She wanted to be thinking about . . .what was it? She lay back on the couch. Oh yes, Jamin. She stretched out her legs. She wanted to be thinking of Jamin and what he was sorry about.

Chapter 7

The TV glowed in the darkened living room where Olivia had fallen asleep on the couch. As the hall light flashed on, she sat upright blinking. "What . . . ? What time is it?"

"Almost midnight." Mark stepped into the room. He and Jenny had met clients for dinner to celebrate a financing he'd just closed for a pipeline company. The deal he'd structured had been so well received that the financing had been oversubscribed. "Anyone call?" Mark asked, his voice full of the energy and goodwill of the evening.

Olivia peered at him in the glare of the chandelier and tried to orient herself.

Jenny disappeared into the back of the apartment to check on Erika. She was feeling subdued after an evening of self-congratulatory toasts and conversation about divestitures and oil prices.

"There are some messages by the phone," Olivia said.

Mark moved to the hall table. "Did you hear?" he asked, scanning the list of half a dozen people who wanted to talk with him tonight. He picked up the phone. "The NLA is going back. We heard it on the radio in the cab."

"What?" Olivia came suddenly awake.

Mark began dialing. "Check the news."

Olivia stood and went over to the TV where she began turning the channels. On the cable news station a commentator was explaining ". . . to regain control from opposition forces within their ranks, according to Katherine Bernstein Walsh in tomorrow's *Washington Tribune*. Taking off from Kennedy Airport an hour ago, the 747 is expected to set down around noon tomorrow . . ."

"How did Kay find out?" Olivia declared.

"Did you know?" Jenny stepped into the room.

"Yes. But how did Kay find out?"

Mark hung up the phone. "She's good," he answered matter-of-factly, stuffing the list of names into his pocket. "What does it mean?"

"It means they may all get killed or captured if Bulagwi finds out when and where they're returning."

"What does it mean for the country?" Mark clarified. "Will there be civil war?"

"I don't know. I'm not there." Olivia's voice had an edge. She felt censured for some reason by Mark's assessment of Kay and irritated at what she assumed was his myopia. "Your mines may shut down if that's what you're worried about."

Jenny stepped over to her. "How long have you been here?" she intervened.

"Hours. I had a drink with Kay then left. I didn't see any sense staying since I knew the delegation wouldn't be available."

"Did you tell Kay?" Jenny asked.

"I lied to Kay; that's what I did." She began to pace as she told Jenny and Mark what had happened. "I should have kept my mouth shut. I lied to her out of spite and gave her time to find out the real story." Olivia's large bare feet tracked a path across the pastel flowers on the oriental rug. Finally she stopped at the edge of the room and turned. "Jamin was right," she said. "To me it's still personal."

At five in the morning Olivia heard the newspaper drop outside the apartment door. The sky was dark. She heard a dog barking down the hall. She had been writing all night, sitting on

55

the floor in the living room with her back to the couch, her notes spread around her, Jenny's typewriter installed on the coffee table. Her story wasn't due for ten days, but suddenly she felt impelled to finish a draft. While she'd been sleeping, Kay had been out getting the story. She couldn't allow herself to sleep through this one, for at last had come her chance to reestablish herself. She'd written six pages so far, around half the article. She was trying to explain who the men of the NLA were, to fill in the history of Nyral's nonviolent movement, to assess its chances given recent outbreaks of violence, to analyze the prospects of a separate state.

She got up to get the newspaper and make herself a cup of coffee. She wasn't writing as quickly as she wanted, but at least she was writing. She went into the kitchen, plugged in the coffee maker, then retrieved the paper. Standing above the stove, she waited for the coffee to brew as she skimmed Guy's article. Guy had reported the food poisoning story with a last minute insert about the delegation hurrying home. His story left the impression that they had returned because they were sick. She was even more impressed that Kay had gotten the facts right.

Outside the faint light of morning was opening the sky. She returned to the typewriter and sat back on the floor. She picked up the pages she'd written so far and began to read. But as she read, she rebelled at what was on the page. The story sounded like a piece Kay or Guy might write, a flat, factual analysis, an explanation that missed the point. She could hear Jamin telling her she was missing the point, that she was avoiding what she saw, yet she couldn't quite distinguish what it was she did see because she wanted so desperately to finish the article, to establish momentum in her life. Instead she began page seven.

Olivia wrote without stopping until she heard Jenny and Mark in the bedroom. She heard them whispering to each other and then laughing and then whispering, "sh-h-h." She tried not to listen and wrote another sentence, but then she heard the bed start to move beneath them and their whispers lower into moans. She looked down at her story. Didn't they know she was out here? She blocked her ears with her hands and tried to think of the next sentence, but then she let go of her ears and heard Jenny let out a quiet cry. Goddamn it, didn't Jenny know she could hear? She picked up a piece of cheese and a cracker and ate it. She scratched out the paragraph she'd just written.

"Goddamn it!" she said out loud. Cassie, who had been sleeping at the other end of the couch, stood now and rubbed against her. Olivia stroked his back. She began packing her papers. She stuffed her rough draft and file folder into her briefcase and started packing her shopping bag and purse.

As she opened her purse, she checked for the slip of paper Jamin had given her. Maybe she could at least write to Jamin. He had come and gone, and she had taken no risks. She opened the paper, but instead of Jamin's address was the address of a woman in the Bronx, a name she'd never heard before. Quickly she folded the paper and stuffed it back in her wallet. She was standing to leave when the bedroom door opened.

"Olivia, you still working?" Jenny whispered.

She gathered her bags and moved quickly into the hallway.

"How about breakfast out . . .our treat?"

She took her raincoat from the coat rack. She wedged it under her arm and was about to open the door when Jenny stepped into the hall. "Olivia . . . where are you going?"

She turned and faced Jenny. "I've got to go," she said.

"Is anything wrong?"

She stared. Jenny stood barefooted in a yellow flannel robe tied at the waist, her belly small and round under the tie. Her hair was tossed about her face; her lips and cheeks were flushed. Olivia was ashamed of the anger she felt suddenly towards her friend. She couldn't explain the anger to herself, except that Jenny was lost to her here, connected to this man who walked in a world so different from her own. Or was her anger at the fact that she was not connected to anyone, that she had backed away last night from the person she had once longed to be connected to? She couldn't answer. She said simply, "I've got to go."

"Are you mad?"

"I've got to go, okay?" Then she added, "I've got to check out a lead."

"Oh . . ." Jenny watched her. She noted the sheets of manuscript left on the table. "You need those?"

Olivia glanced at them. "No . . ." She started to turn to pick them up.

"Don't worry, I'll clean up." Jenny searched Olivia's face.

The patient, inquiring look in her eyes made Olivia even angrier. "I'll call," Olivia said. Then in concession, she added, "Tell Mark I said goodbye."

Chapter 8

From Jenny's apartment Olivia had headed towards the subway, but not until she was standing inside the turnstile, forced to choose between the uptown and downtown ramp, did she decide to go meet Mrs. Hansa Patel. The address Jamin had given her was on Jerome Avenue, a seedy, littered street under the El in the Bronx. Since she didn't know where the apartment was, she got off at the first Jerome Avenue stop. The street was almost deserted. Shops lined both sides—used furniture, secondhand clothing, mom and pop grocery stores—half of them were boarded up or burned out; the rest were sealed off with iron gates. She wondered whom Jamin knew living here. The street numbers had long since been worn away. She hurried along the side of the buildings trying to shield herself from the wind as she searched for an address. When she finally located two consecutive numbers, she was somewhat relieved to find she had a ways to go. She looked about for a cab, but there were no cabs here. There were bus stops, but she hadn't yet seen a bus, and the wind was too persistent and the neighborhood too unsafe to wait so she lifted her bags and brief-case and kept walking.

She wondered who she would find at the address. She hoped she would find a lead to Jamin's whereabouts or at least to his connections in the U.S. She allowed the thought that Jamin had given her this name to help her with her story. She considered, but would not allow herself to believe, that he had given it to her for more personal reasons.

It was after nine when she finally arrived at a small tailoring shop. The street number was stenciled in chipped white paint above the door. In the window stood a giant pair of grey cardboard scissors and a bald mannequin draped in turquoise cloth. The neighborhood had improved slightly. People scurried along the street; the wind was still frenzied, but the sun shone, blocked only by the giant shadow of the El.

Olivia went into the shop. The proprietor, a dark-skinned Asian man with grey hair, appeared from the rear. She asked him if she were at the right address. "You have clothes in want of repair?" he answered.

"I'm looking for a Mrs. Patel."

The man tilted his head, and he looked at Olivia out of the corner of his eyes. "Everybody is looking for somebody."

"Do you know Mrs. Hansa Patel?"

"Who told you to look here?" he asked.

"A friend of mine." Olivia glanced around the store. Two full length mirrors reflected her on either side. Next to one was a crudely constructed booth with a torn white curtain hanging down. The counter was littered with tape measures and thread and scis-sors, but behind the counter the workspace was idle. The sewing machines sat covered, and on the clothes racks were only a few faded dresses and a pair of men's slacks. At the back of the shop, she could see a television flickering and hear the high, mimicking voices of a Saturday morning cartoon show.

"Perhaps you want a new dress?" he asked.

"I'm looking for Mrs. Patel," Olivia repeated. "Are there apartments upstairs?"

"You still have not told me who sent you."

"A friend . . ." Olivia wasn't sure if she should give Jamin's name, but she didn't know how else to get by this man. "A friend of mine . . . a man named Jamin Nyo."

"And how do you know this man?"

"Does Mrs. Patel live here or not?" She was getting irritated, but the proprietor didn't seem to care. Finally reaching into her purse, she presented him the slip of paper Jamin had given her.

The man studied Jamin's thin scrawl for a moment then he nodded. Moving over to the front door, he turned around a paper clock in the window and set it to say he'd return in ten minutes; then he locked the door. "Follow me."

He led Olivia through the back of the store, past the television, to a wooden staircase. He led her up two flights to a dark, narrow hallway and a single door. He knocked. When the door opened, he spoke to the person on the other side rapidly in what Olivia guessed was Gujarati. She heard that person speaking to a third person. A debate ensued between them for almost a minute; then finally the proprietor stepped away and presented Olivia to a girl of about seventeen or eighteen whom he introduced as Rhekka. He said a few more cautionary words; she nodded; then he nodded and turned away.

Olivia found herself in a small room with oriental rugs at each end, a couch, a table, a few chairs, and a television. Sunlight streamed in a back window. Sitting in the light was a small woman swaying back and forth in a rocking chair. She was wrapped in a sari and a shawl. In her lap she held a copy of *House Beautiful*.

"Mother, this lady is from Jamin," the girl said.

The woman looked up; her face brightened. She put out her hands, stood slightly and bowed. "You know my son?"

"Your son?" Olivia looked at the girl for an interpretation, but the girl's face accepted her mother's words.

The old woman said something to her daughter, and the girl nodded. "My mother would like to know if you want some tea?"

"Yes, that would be fine."

The old woman motioned for Olivia to come sit beside her. She started speaking to Olivia in her own language.

"Mother, she doesn't understand that," the girl said from the kitchen alcove. "My mother knows some English, but she doesn't like to speak it. She thought because you knew Jamin, you would know Gujarati."

"I didn't know Jamin spoke Gujarati," Olivia answered.

The girl turned around and looked at her. She was small with frail bones and clear brown skin and a black braid which hung to her waist. Unlike her mother she was dressed in western clothes, slacks and a print shirt. "Jamin speaks six languages," she observed.

"You know my son?" the woman asked again.

"I saw him yesterday," Olivia answered. She stared at this woman and tried to understand who she was. "I didn't know his family lived here."

The old woman nodded and smiled. "He is an important man. He was on the television."

The daughter returned to the room with the tea. "My mother watched television two days and nights to see him."

"Didn't he come to visit?" Olivia asked.

The woman smiled. "He is an important man."

The girl poured the tea and handed her mother the first cup. "He was afraid for anyone to know we are here," she answered. "If he came, someone might find out. I am surprised he told you to come."

"He didn't actually tell me to come . . ." Olivia said.

The girl frowned. She watched Olivia. The mother, seeing the daughter troubled, watched the daughter. "Then why did you come?"

Olivia sipped her tea. It was made with milk and sugar the way the British drank it—tepid and sweet—and she wished she could spit it out. "He gave me your address in case I needed to contact him."

"But you said you have just seen him."

"He's gone now."

The mother said something to the daughter. The girl turned to her and spoke quickly, translating the conversation. Then the mother turned to Olivia. "Why do you want to see my son?"

"I want to write to him. There was a misunderstanding between us."

The daughter translated the word "misunderstanding." The old woman nodded, keeping her eyes on Olivia. Olivia couldn't tell this woman that she wanted to find out if Jamin were still alive. Instead Olivia straightened in her chair and tried to think of something reassuring to say. She picked up her cup of tea. "Is your father here too?" she asked.

"That was my father who brought you up," the girl said.

"That's Jamin's father?"

"You do not know my brother very well, I see."

Olivia hesitated. "I'm not sure anyone does."

"That is true," the girl agreed. "He doesn't allow many people."

"But how could that be his father . . .?" Olivia was afraid she was overstepping her bounds, but she wanted to know.

"You mean because we are Asians? My parents raised Jamin since he was four. To them he is a son. His father was killed in an uprising; his mother died of a fever the next year. His father worked with my father. Though it was not common in our country, they were friends. It was not as difficult then as now for it was the Europeans who were the enemy; now we also are the enemy. Jamin moved us over here when he saw the trouble growing for us. He knew we would soon not be tolerated by the government. He said he could not lead his struggle if we were still there."

"Why here and not Britain?" Olivia asked.

"No one would find us here," he said. "People can get lost in America, he said, because no one holds you to who you are."

"Have you seen him since?" The girl didn't answer. "Didn't the government cancel his passport? He can only get into the U.S. with a special visa, I thought, " Olivia offered.

The girl picked up a magazine and began looking at the pictures. "It has been a long time since Jamin has lived with us," she answered.

The mother smacked her jaws together and sat forward. "You ask many questions about my son."

Olivia looked over at her. "I am his friend."

"Why do you say you are his friend?"

"I care about your son," Olivia answered.

The daughter translated for the mother, though Olivia was beginning to suspect she understood more than she let on. She rocked back and forth nodding and fingering her shawl. Her fingernails were painted bright red, and at the edges of her mouth she hid a smile that was not unlike Jamin's.

"Have you seen Jamin since you left your country?" Olivia persisted.

The girl continued to turn the pages of the magazine. Olivia thought for a moment she was going to ignore the question, but the mother, frowning and shaking her head, chattered something to her; and finally the daughter answered, "No, we have not seen him." But she didn't look at Olivia. The halting way she spoke and the determined way she avoided Olivia's eyes made Olivia sure she was lying. Suddenly the possibility that Jamin had come into the United States before, illegally, and visited his family interested her. She watched the girl, and the girl watched her out of the corner of her eyes.

"He has been here, hasn't he?"

"I cannot say."

"I'm not going to tell anyone," she insisted.

The daughter's deep brown eyes met Olivia's own, and the two women measured each other by their loyalty to the same man. Finally the daughter nodded. The mother, who had been listening, turned now and scolded her in a high, quick Gujarati. As they argued, Olivia tried to imagine Jamin in his jeans and combat boots mingling on the streets of the Bronx. She tried to imagine him standing beside Mr. Patel behind the counter of the store taking in other people's clothes for mending, or leaning back in the stick chairs at the dining table talking to his mother and sister as they cooked his supper. She was surprised how easily she could imagine Jamin in these domestic, personal scenes he'd disavowed. Perhaps with his adopted family he dropped the burden of who he was supposed to be and for a few days became only a mother's son, a sister's brother. She stared at the small Asian woman with red fingernails and *House Beautiful* in her lap. She would never have connected this woman as Jamin's mother, yet to the woman, Jamin was clearly a son. It occurred to her now that what she had been lacking all this time was the imagination to see past her own image of Jamin, and she wondered if he had been offering her this view by allowing her to meet his family.

"My son is a great man in our country," the woman said. "He brings freedom to all people."

Olivia didn't answer.

"He sends us money every month though he does not have much money himself. Do you not think he is great?"

Olivia didn't know if Jamin were great or not, but she nodded.

"He is an important man," the woman repeated, then she went back to rocking in her chair. She stared out the window at the light and closed her eyes. In less than a minute she was asleep.

Olivia glanced at the daughter, who nodded. "She is getting old. She does that more and more. She may not see Jamin again." In the girl's eyes Olivia saw the burden she bore for her family. "My brother must trust you," she said. "You are the first person he has sent to us."

"Do you know where I can write to him?"

The girl shook her head. "He has no address. We cannot write him for our letters would be read, and we would be found out. He writes only to us."

Olivia hesitated. But Jamin had told her if she ever wanted to contact him to come here. She looked at the girl, then over at the old woman. Was it through these women he meant for her to know him? She stood up. "Thank you for having me in your home," she said.

The girl rose from the couch. "I am glad you came. I don't get to meet many people." She stood in the doorway, a small, frail figure, and yet in her watchful eyes and her proud posture, Olivia could recognize Jamin.

"Perhaps we could see each other again," Olivia offered, "next time I come to New York."

The girl smiled, a shy smile, and nodded. "I would like that."

Chapter 9

On the desk in his forty-eighth floor office with the sweeping plate glass view of Manhattan, Mark kept a hard black squash ball which he banged against the window whenever he grew agitated. Sitting at his desk this grey January evening, he was whipping his squash racket forehand/backhand/forehand/ backhand, slamming the ball . . . bam . . . bam . . . bam against the glass without ever moving from his chair. In this manner he improved both the accuracy of his squash game and the precision of his temper. By the time Reynolds responded to his message and entered his office that evening, both Mark's temper and his stroke had narrowed to a six-inch radius on the glass, a shadowy smudge about the size of a hand grenade.

"Someday you're going to break the window," Reynolds said, settling onto the blue ultrasuede sofa in the corner of the room. Reynolds was a trim, neat man in his mid-forties with a thinning spot of light brown hair at the back of his head.

"I have faith . . . in the reliability . . . of the Puralex Glass Company," Mark answered, pausing as he spoke between slams. Bam . . . bam . . . bam. "They guarantee the glass . . . up to 100 pounds . . . of spot pressure . . . applied over . . . and over . . . again." He glanced at Reynolds then caught the ball as it returned to him. He set the ball in a brass cup which Jenny had given him for that purpose last year on his thirty-fourth birthday. "I had Louise check with the company. You see, Reynolds, I always measure my risks."

Reynolds picked up the latest copy of *Institutional Investor* and began leafing through it as though he were in no hurry and had little idea of what Mark wanted. Recently divorced, he had no one at home waiting for him, though Mark, glancing at the clock, saw he was already late.

"Could you tell me . . ." Mark began slowly, ". . . why I hear from Charlton that we passed on the pipeline stock? I told Charlton he must be mistaken, but he said, no, you'd asked for the fee instead."

Reynolds' pale, precise face twitched in an expression that could have been a smile or a grimace but resisted settling as though any emotion might betray him. "The fee is two and a half million dollars, Mark," he answered. "Though you may not agree, we need the cash right now."

"For what?"

"Expenses."

"What expenses? Our expenses were covered twice over by the Afco fee." Mark had argued for the past year that they should be taking more equity positions in their deals. In W&S Pipe Reynolds had finally agreed to take the new stock issue in the equivalent amount of the fee.

"There'll be other deals," Reynolds said without looking up. "Besides I don't think the return is as good as you project."

"What do you mean? You've seen the figures. It's gold."

"Comstock may be backing away from buying the oil services."

"Since when?"

"I talked to McMillan this afternoon; he was less than confirmed."

"I had breakfast this morning with Dave Robertson, and he's

buying. Goddamn it, McMillian's the treasurer! He doesn't have the authority to back away."

"It's the decision I made." Reynolds looked up. "Charlton was happy to take our shares."

"I bet he was."

"It's my call, if you remember. That was our agreement after we went ahead with the Afco financing." Reynolds had opposed Afco, their first major international project. But finally they had proceeded, raising $250 million to fund the reopening of mines in a number of African countries. The second round of financing of equal size was due in two months. In order to get Reynolds to agree to the project, Mark had yielded him discretion on W&S and two other domestic deals. "Charlton had to have the decision today," he added.

"Bullshit!" Mark exploded. "Bull . . . shit." He separated the words. "I'm busting my balls to get us business like this. W&S Pipe is going to be be worth four, five times as much in two years, and we're pocketing the change!" Mark took the squash ball and threw it against the plateglass. "You were never going to take equity, were you? You were leading me on . . .Yes, Mark . . . sure, Mark. Goddamn it, Reynolds, we have a problem. You and I have a *big* problem."

Reynolds continued flipping through the magazine, but his face was frozen. Finally he looked up at Mark as if he would endure this outburst but not participate in it. The furrow in his narrow forehead and the squint in his eyes gave him a wincing look as though he felt the lash of Mark's words, yet he was unable to respond or defend himself.

Mark didn't see this wince for he was facing the window. Bam . . . bam . . . bam . . . slamming the hard, black ball against the glass and catching it with his hand. Yet instinctively he backed off as though he knew he would soon draw blood, and he was not a blood-letter. He had to face the facts: Reynolds would not take risks. At least not anymore. Perhaps it had been the breakup of his family, his wife leaving him; whatever it was, Reynolds had retreated into the safety nets of their business, and Mark could not pull him out. Instead he felt himself trapped inside with him. He let the squashball fall to the floor, and he sank into his chair.

"And I'm uncomfortable with what I'm seeing in Afco too . . ." Reynolds offered as if here were his excuse. "The cash flow is inadequate."

"Then you should have come to the meeting," Mark said dryly. He began packing his briefcase. Reynolds turned the page in the magazine. Mark stood. As he opened the door to the outer office, he said, "Fifteen million dollars . . . that's what we're leaving on the table in W&S."

Reynolds didn't respond. Instead he turned the page and continued reading the article in *Institutional Investor*.

At the corner of Eighty-ninth Street Mark hurried towards his apartment as if by this last burst of speed, he might redeem time. But the quiet which greeted him when he entered suggested that he was already beyond its acceptable bounds. He glanced at the clock in the hall, a clock set into the face of a mirror: 9:15. As he took off his coat and hung it on the hook by the door, he began preparing his excuse.

He found Jenny, whom he'd neglected to call, in his office emptying his desk. At the specific moment he walked in, she was transfering his files from his bottom drawer into a box. Beside her on the floor were lucite cubes listing the billions of dollars he'd helped to raise over the years, dumped now into a Del Monte fruit cocktail carton. On the bookshelves dozens more trophies were yet to be extracted.

"What are you doing? he asked, setting one of two briefcases on the floor.

Jenny turned and smiled. "I'm taking over your office." She dumped out the middle drawer of his rolltop desk into a shoe box. He took a step forward but hesitated, uncertain for a moment how to advance. "It'll be simpler to switch contents than to move desks." She handed him the shoebox full of pencils and rulers and rubberbands. "I've already emptied mine." She pushed her hair aside with the back of her hand, then placed her hands on her hips for a minute to support her back.

"Are you doing this because I'm late?" he asked.

"Oh . . . are you late?"

"I couldn't get to a phone. I'm sorry. I was in a meeting."

She dumped his right hand drawer into another shoebox which she handed him so that he stood juggling two shoeboxes hugged against his chest.

He set down his other briefcase. "Look, Jenny, I've still got a lot of work to do tonight. Can't this wait?"

"I don't think so. Actually I've been waiting for four years." She looked up at him. This time she wasn't smiling though he couldn't read her face. It was true they'd agreed they should change offices but had never done so. His was a large mahogony study with a fireplace, built-in bookshelves, a bay window to Riverside Drive; hers, a former maid's room. When they'd first moved to this apartment, she'd offered to take the smaller office because she worked out of the news bureau and he was running an investment fund from home and playing in a jazz quartet three nights a week. They'd simply never made the switch when he moved to Wall Street or later when she moved home with a new baby.

"You could have asked me first if tonight was convenient," he said. "This is not the most convenient night."

She glanced at her watch. "Oh . . . well, I'm sorry. I called three times but couldn't reach you. Actually, it's not very convenient for me either. I just got Erika to bed fifteen minutes ago, and I was counting on working tonight. I needed to work tonight. You said you'd be home early so I could work." Her tone ran on an edge, neither indictment nor whine, in a zone Mark couldn't fix.

"I'm sorry. Reynolds backed out of the deal," he announced. "I can't believe it. He took the fee without even telling me." He hoped this news might excuse him, but by the silence which greeted it, he saw it held little recompense for him right now. "I was meeting with Charlton till almost eight, then I went back to the office to see Reynolds."

"Ummm." Jenny lifted computer printouts from the bottom drawer of the desk and stacked them in a box. "My desk is relatively clear," she said. "Shove anything you want to the floor. I've moved out most of my things. Your dinner's in the oven. We can finish packing the books later."

She lifted the carton full of computer sheets, a bond calculator, a racketball, a harmonica, and she started through the door.

Mark stepped in front of her. "Stop it, Jenny. Damn it, you shouldn't even be lifting that."

"I'm all right."

"I'm a few hours late. I've had people screaming at me all day. Why are you doing this?"

She met his gaze, only now her clear blue eyes blurred and her own gaze grew scattered, not cool and centered as she'd rehearsed, as she'd managed so far. "Because if I don't *do something*, I'm going to scream at you too." She moved past him. "Erika may still be awake if you want to see her," she said. Then she left the room.

Mark stood for a moment; he set the boxes down. He couldn't face this argument right now. He knew his infractions; he knew he'd been home late for the past three nights. But he still had figures to run and lawyers to call. He had to see if there weren't some way to get back part of W&S. But first he went in to his daughter.

Jenny returned to Mark's office carrying her computer which she set on his rolltop desk, but the desk had a bank of drawers and cubbyholes, and the terminal wouldn't fit. She and Mark would have to switch desks after all. She looked for her folder of work on the desk, then in the drawers, but she couldn't find it. The office was a mess, neither hers nor Mark's now. She leaned back in the chair and shut her eyes. She was too tired to work anyway. She would get up early in the morning instead.

Pushing away from the desk, she took a shoebox full of bills she needed to pay and went in and sat on the couch in the living room by the fireplace where gas jets burned a clear blue flame. She was sitting there paying bills when Erika came running in with Mark, grinning as though she'd been granted special dispensation. The two of them climbed up on the piano bench for their nightly ritual. As Mark began playing, they sang together: "Doe, a deer, a female deer; Ray, a drop of golden sun . . ." Mark's rich tenor overwhelmed Erika's toneless voice, which ignored the rise in scale and sang on the same two or three notes.

As they sang, Jenny paid the bills. When she finished the bills, she wrote a check for $500 to Oxfam, the world hunger organization. Five hundred dollars was her estimation of the dinner bill last night. She wrote the check as routinely as she'd paid the

mortgage and the phone bill. Mark called such checks her payments to the gods, her attempt to balance an imbalanced world she
couldn't account for. And yet he understood her need to give as a
way of ordering and rooting them in the world. When they went
on vacations, she came home and wrote checks to camp scholarship funds. When they bought new clothes, she contributed to
Goodwill. When she paid Erika's school tuition, she matched her
check with a donation to the school's scholarship fund. She also
gave money away to unweight them, to redeem more value from
the time Mark spent away from the family making money. She
wrote this week's checks: $1000 to CARE, $1000 to UNICEF, $500
to Southern Poverty Law Center.

Erika and Mark were tapping out "My Favorite Things" when
the phone rang. Jenny stacked the envelopes on the coffee table
and went into the kitchen to answer. She returned a moment later.

"It's for you."

As Mark rose from the piano bench, Erika protested. "I'll be
right back," he assured.

Jenny sat down beside her. "Here, I'll play with you." She
searched the top of the piano for the simplest sheet of music, and
with two fingers she began sounding out the melody. Reluctantly
Erika joined her, singing a dissonant and half-hearted rendition
of "Twinkle, Twinkle, Little Star," but midway through, Erika
shut the music on her mother.

"I want to go to bed," she said. Without waiting for Jenny, she
slid off the bench and padded to her bedroom alone. Jenny would
have followed, but the phone call had disturbed her too. She
remained on the bench staring past the music into the dark outside
the window.

When Mark returned fifteen minutes later, he asked, "Where's
Erika?"

"She went to bed. She's mad at you."

Mark turned and went into her bedroom. A moment later he
came back. "She's asleep." His voice was disappointed. "Why is
she mad at me?"

"It happens almost every night, Mark. The phone rings, and
you leave her."

Mark sat down on the piano stool. "What can I do?" He reached
up for Jenny to sit beside him, but she remained standing.

"You could have told Kay you couldn't talk," she said. "As far as I can see, you can tell everyone you can't talk until Erika's in bed." It was a point she had won before, but tonight it was not really the point.

Mark didn't answer. He didn't want to hear any more grievances against him. He wanted to hear the order and the rising of the music. He set his hands on the keys and began to play.

"What did Kay want anyway?" Jenny tried to sound casual; she thought she succeeded.

"Nothing."

"For fifteen minutes?" This question was less successful.

But Mark was building to the first crescendo in a composition he'd written years ago, and he didn't answer. Jenny rose. She wanted to caution Mark again if Kay were tracking him for information; she wanted Mark to warn her if Kay were tracking for other purposes though she knew for Kay the two objectives did not exclude each other.

Chapter 10

With a push of her hip Olivia knocked her scarred brown case through the turnstile at the subway entrance under Pennsylvania Station. She'd returned to New York after a week in which she'd finally finished her article, having found the voice she'd been seeking to tell the story. She wanted to deliver the article personally to the editor at *The New Centurion* in the hope she might also get an advance for other sections of her book. She'd called Rhekka from Boston and arranged to take her to lunch. She'd typed up her final draft until midnight then boarded the two a.m. train into New York.

At a kiosk in Pennsylvania Station she bought a roll of wintergreen Lifesavers for breakfast. After a night on the train, her mouth tasted thick and dry. She wanted to brush her teeth and wash her face and talk to someone about the story she'd just finished, so with several hours before her appointments, she headed uptown to Jenny's.

When she arrived, Mark was already gone. Jenny, still in her robe, looked pale and strained.

"I should have called," she offered.

"You never call."

She heard a rebuke in Jenny's voice but let it pass and moved inside. From her case she took out a manila folder and handed it to Jenny. "It may even be good," she said.

"Your article?" Jenny took the folder and went over to the couch. She seemed preoccupied, but as she curled her feet under her, she smiled for her pleasure was genuine that Olivia had finished her story.

"It's not like what I've written before. I decided not to play it safe . . ." Olivia began explaining.

"Please . . ." Jenny stood and went into the kitchen, shutting the door behind her.

In the bathroom Olivia brushed her teeth, washed her face, put on lipstick; then she returned to the living room where she began wandering about. She stepped over to the doorway of Mark's office. She had never been inside this room. She'd peered into it but had never gone in, sat down, made herself at home. Instead Mark had always come out to her.

She stepped inside now. The room was somber with mahogany walls and maroon carpet. It looked unsettled: boxes of books sat on the floor; Jenny's desk, not Mark's, was shoved into the corner. On the bookshelves were still Mark's books and his small lucite cubes which caught the Southern exposure and were refracting light in rainbows on the wall. She picked up one of the cubes: "$50,000,000 RedaTek, Inc. Cumulative Exchangeable Redeemable Senior Preferred Stock and Common Stock. The undersigned acted as agent in the private placement of these securities . . ." She picked up another cube cautiously as if it were an object from an alien culture and might harm her. Many of the objects looked like toys. A few were shaped like toys: one was the shape of an automobile with a price tag of six hundred million dollars, the sum Mark and his colleagues had raised for the automaker, she assumed. How one comprehended six hundred million dollars or knew where to find six hundred million dollars she understood only theoretically, as one understood the speed of light.

The cubes were scattered among Mark's books—books on stocks and bonds, music books, theological and philosophical works, even a half shelf of modern poetry. From Jenny she'd heard of these sides of Mark though she had never seen them herself. When she saw him working over his sheets and printouts, punching figures into his calculator, he'd seemed to her some conjurer calling forth hidden forces.

"Damn it, Jenny, do you always read so slowly?" she called, stepping out of the office. Jenny didn't answer. Olivia pushed the door open to the kitchen where Jenny was bent over the table with her ears blocked. Olivia opened the refrigerator and brought out a half gallon of milk; she took down a bowl from the cabinet and a box of raisin bran from the shelf. She returned to the living room where she ate her bowl of cereal as she waited on the couch reading *The New York Times*.

"So what happened to Jamin?"

Olivia looked up. Jenny was standing in the doorway. "Christ, did you like the article or not?"

"I want to know what happened to Jamin."

"I don't know. No one does. There are rumors, but no one can confirm. I tried to call through to the capitol, but there's a blackout. I'll have to add that in a postscript." Her thick eyebrows furrowed. "Jamin may be dead, and I'm fitting his death in italics."

Jenny shrugged and handed the manuscript back to Olivia.

"You don't like it."

"It's hard to separate what you feel from what's true sometimes," Jenny said quietly. Olivia watched her and wondered if she were talking about the article. "It may be the best piece you've written," Jenny went on. "It's beautifully written but frankly, I'm not sure *The New Centurion* will share that view. They'll want to know facts: who's financing the NLA, if American and European interests are involved. The tale of the hunter and his son . . . of Nyral and Jamin . . . it's wonderful; the story is wonderful, but Olivia . . ." her voice pleaded. "I almost wish I could help, research some of the facts for you."

"I've got fifty notebooks of facts on this story," Olivia defended.

"I know. But I mean recent facts. Someone's working behind the scenes here. You know that. Who? Where's the money coming from? I'd like to find that out myself."

"Why?"

"I'm starting to crack on the sidelines."

Olivia hesitated. "You want to share the byline?"

"The byline's yours. But there are facts I want to know, especially about the mines and the business interests."

"Because of Mark?"

"He thinks I'm paranoid; I think he's naive. But I've never been comfortable with Afco, though I don't have any facts to back up my feelings."

"Tell me what you do know . . ."

Jenny hesitated. "I don't really know anything. Besides, he's my husband. I just want to protect him if I can." Jenny handed the article back to Olivia. "Think about it . . . I'm here if you need me." Olivia took the manuscript. As she returned it to its folder, she felt a small black hole opening before her. Out of it flew tiny demons like biting black flies. She raised her hand as though to ward them off.

Jenny lifted her own hand for a moment in a slow arc which had no clear destination, as if she too heard the buzz of the flies and saw the hole. "Kay's in town again," she said without transition. "She called this morning and asked Mark if she could see him."

"What for?"

Jenny took a spider plant from the window ledge and began plucking off its dead tendrils. In her eyes a clear stream of blue light bore down on the question as if by concentration she might crack open its center and spill out a hard nugget of truth. But when she finally answered, it was not from this clear blue place but from a more cluttered ground. "I don't know. She only said that she wanted to see Mark and hoped I wouldn't mind."

"And you let him go?"

"He's a grown man. He can go where he wants."

"And he wanted to?"

"He was out of here in ten minutes. He took Erika to school half an hour early."

"Everything's all right between you two, isn't it?" Even as she asked the question, Olivia knew she didn't want the answer for she had come here to be reassured herself.

"He's under a lot of pressure at work. Sometimes it affects us."

"Is that all?"

Jenny pushed her fingers into the soil of the spider plant and took out a weed that had sprouted. "I'm relying on him more than I like right now," she said. "I've lost the edge, Olivia. I used to live on the edge of things."

Olivia leaned back into the sofa. "I fell off that edge so long ago, I've concluded the earth is round."

"Don't you miss it?"

Olivia shrugged. "You made your name already, won your honors."

Jenny dismissed the comment with a shake of her head though she had, when their friend Elise died, written the series Elise had meant to write and won a major national award. "Seeing Kay ..." Jenny went on, "... at least she's out there."

"Running the edge is a trap, Jenny. Besides, you can't run the edge and ask questions at the same time or you fall off. That's a point on Kay's side. She doesn't let herself get slowed down by doubts."

"Maybe that's why Mark's attracted to her."

"Jenny," Olivia protested.

Jenny wrapped up the dead leaves in the newspaper. She shrugged. "They'll probably just have breakfast, take a walk; but he'll come back tonight a little distant in his good humor, and I'll get depressed, and we'll have a fight over some insignificant thing."

Olivia frowned. She hadn't imagined this possibility for Jenny; she didn't want to imagine it.

"Actually if Kay had other motives, I don't think she'd tell me she wanted to see Mark," Jenny said.

Olivia stood. Outside a siren whined down as it approached the corner. "I think that's exactly what she'd do. You've always been more charitable towards her than I." She began gathering her manuscript. "I better be going."

Jenny stood.

"Wish me luck."

"The article's quality." Jenny made her offering.

"Are you serious about helping?"

"If you need it. To a point at least."

Olivia nodded. "I'll call you and let you know. At least I've found my voice for the book," she said. "Remind me of that if *The New Centurion* says no. And remind me that *The New Centurion* doesn't really matter, and *Atlantic* doesn't matter, and even *The New York Times* doesn't really matter."

"The story does matter," Jenny said. "And Jamin matters."

Olivia buttoned her coat. "Yes. Jamin." She wished she could offer Jenny some comfort. She reached out to her. Then as she opened the door, she turned. "Jamin once told me two essentials for success in guerrilla war: don't underestimate your foe and don't wait too long to fight."

The news was unconfirmed, but it was the first from anyone about what had happened to the National Liberation Association when it returned home the week before. A *Los Angeles Times* reporter had managed to get into one of the camps and out again. He was broadcasting from Nairobi when Jenny turned on the midday news in the kitchen. To the best of the reporter's information, the delegation had all been taken captive by government forces and shot. Those executed included Robert Nyral and Jamin Nyo, according to the report.

It was twelve o'clock when Jenny heard the news. She had phoned Mark's office twice already, but he hadn't come in that morning, his secretary said; and she didn't know when to expect him. As Jenny listened to the accounts of the executions of people she had once known and who were friends of Olivia's, she wanted to talk to Mark. The fact that he was out in the city with another woman suddenly made her so uneasy that she couldn't eat the lunch she'd prepared, couldn't sit at her desk and work, couldn't bear the thought of waiting in the apartment alone. She turned off the radio and left the can of tuna opened on the counter, the bread unwrapped; then she took her coat from the coat hook, and she plunged into the chill January sun and down to the river.

Olivia heard the news at *The New Centurion's* office. She arrived less confident than she'd intended after her talk with

Jenny, and she was fighting off a vague apprehension as she walked into the office on Park Ave. She kept reminding herself that she was turning in a major article days before its deadline and was presenting a solid book proposal with the hope of selling other chapters to *The New Centurion* as well as with the hope that the editor might open some doors at publishing houses for her. Yet as she passed into the reception room, her image in the mirror fixed her dread. Her hair was unruly—why hadn't she remembered to comb it in the elevator? Her dress, a navy shirtwaist she'd traveled in all over the world, was worn with small moons of perspiration circling under her arms. Suddenly the fact that she was even concerning herself with how she looked annoyed her, and the fact that she always looked the same depressed her.

Alan Michaels, the associate editor, didn't notice, however; or rather he saw what he expected as he rose to greet her. "I suppose you've heard," he said.

"Heard what?" She dropped on to the couch opposite him in the maroon and grey office. She'd known Alan for years, before he'd become an editor here, when they were both graduate students at Brown University and then when he was editing at a far less prestigious magazine. She'd even given him articles cheap and on his last-minute notice when she was reporting from Vietnam and he was in a bind. But now that he was embosomed at one of the country's leading magazines, she felt less than comfortable, not so much with him as with the power he represented.

"The NLA delegation were all captured and shot. It came over the wires this morning. You knew them, of course . . ." He went on to tell her the report as he'd heard it, how the government had crushed the rebel forces and were now striking at the camps and villages, burning many to the ground, how Jamin Nyo and Robert Nyral were both dead. He spoke in a slightly excited voice of one who stood outside events yet felt their happening animate his own life.

As he spoke, Olivia's throat went dry. Her stomach lifted somewhere near her heart. She thought she was going to be sick.

When he finished, he peered over the desk at the folder in her hand. "Is that it?" he asked.

She stared down at the manila folder and handed it to him.

"You'll have to make changes of course, especially now that

the main players are dead, but if the article's good . . . well, it may even make the cover."

"Yes," Olivia answered vaguely. She stood. "I have to go," she announced. "I have to have lunch."

Alan stared at her, but then he nodded, accepting her eccentricity. "All right. Why don't you stop by after lunch, and we can discuss the article and where we stand."

Olivia picked up her case and started out of the office. In the doorway she turned. "I have to meet someone," she added as if this were an explanation.

Plunging into the midday rush of people, Olivia made her way to Madison Avenue where thousands of bodies were pushing uptown, downtown, slipping under the scaffoldings of the new skyscrapers going up on all sides. Cars bumper to bumper honked while people spilled from around the barricades immobilizing traffic. The noise was deafening—CL-A-A-N-GGG RAT-TA-TAT-TAT—drills and jack hammers hammering: POW! POW! POW!

She had to get to Rhekka. She wondered if Rhekka had heard. Breaking out of the crowd, she walked in the middle of the street ignoring the cars grazing past her. Who was building all these buildings, she wondered as she walked. POW-POW- POW-ER! Who had this much power? Who had the power that had killed Jamin? The possibility seemed likely that the United Nations meeting had been a ruse to get Jamin and Nyral out of the country and effect this suicidal coup. But who had that power? The West, tied to Bulagwi and the mining interests? Or the Soviets, acting as spoilers of Western overtures to the NLA? Jenny's questions this morning echoed her own. Where *had* the money come from that had financed this visit and to whom was it paid?

And the final question: was Jamin really dead? She couldn't believe he was dead. She walked faster as though she might outrun his loss. She searched the faces on the street for someone she knew. If she could tell another person, perhaps the death would become real to her, but she saw only strangers racing past. Suddenly the city seemed too big, too concerned with itself and its power.

As she hurried crosstown, she remembered the first time she'd met Jamin, in Mushambe's hut where they both came to visit

Mushambe's son Albert, a boy with wide, intelligent eyes. The hut was off a road in a clearing by a parched creek which rose only once a year and flowed for a month during the rainy season into the Izo River below. Mushambe lived on a small rise where she nurtured a vegetable garden in the dirt yard behind her hut and set out bleached gourds in front filled with water for the dogs who roamed the village. In the evenings sometimes when Olivia and Jamin had both come to Mushambe and Albert's, the four of them would sit outside in the moonlight where the gourds glistened like giant pearls upon the ground. Mushambe urged Jamin and Olivia to talk with Albert, to bring the outside world into the generous spaces of his thirteen-year-old mind, for Olivia and Jamin were among the few in the hills who had traveled the distance between Mushambe's hut and Manhattan's throng. On those evenings Olivia had always felt more than friendship lingering between Jamin and her, like shadows beyond the firelight, yet Jamin had held himself apart. But last week, finally, he had set forth the possibility between them. Now this risk not taken, this loss of possibility began to stir the grief within her as she reached the restaurant on Sixth Ave.

Standing in the red and gilt doorway of the Golden Pagoda West, Olivia searched among the faces inside. When the hostess asked if she could help, Olivia just stared as if she didn't hear the question. The hostess shrugged and seated the couple behind her. Olivia stood for several more minutes until her eyes finally focused on a back corner where she saw the face she had been looking for: the quiet, light brown face of Rhekka sitting among strangers.

Rhekka didn't see Olivia approach, and she started when Olivia sat down, then smiled shyly. "I came early," she explained, "to watch the people. Father doesn't allow me to go out alone, but since I was meeting a friend of Jamin's, he brought me today."

Olivia glanced around the restaurant. "Is he here?"

"He will meet me at the subway when we are finished."

"You should have invited him."

"He will wait in a shop until we are done." Rhekka sat upright at the table. She was dressed in an outdated navy suit with a straight skirt and short jacket. She wore stockings and navy pumps. She looked as Olivia might have twenty years ago dressing up for lunch in midtown as if she had come to a major event. Olivia thought of what she had to tell her about Jamin, and she felt sick. Picking up the menu, Olivia asked, "Have you ordered?"

"I don't know this food very well."

Olivia glanced around the room. She wished she had chosen another place. This restaurant was too bright, too impersonal for what she had to say.

Rhekka watched her. "Thank you for inviting me," she offered.

Olivia just nodded, then signaled for the waitress. Avoiding Rhekka's eyes, she ordered; then shutting the menu, she finally looked over at Rhekka. "I don't know how to tell you this except to tell you," she said. "It doesn't appear that you've heard. From what I've been told Jamin was killed when he returned to your country last week. The news came over the wires this morning." Her tone softened. "I'm sorry." She met Rhekka's gaze. In the girl's eyes, she searched for her own feelings. The full grief she wanted to feel still hung suspended. Rhekka took the news without emotion. "I'm so sorry . . ." Olivia said again. "I don't know what else to say."

Rhekka stared down at the table. She was quiet for a moment. Finally she looked up. "Jamin is alive," she said.

"What?"

"He is alive."

Olivia leaned forward. "How do you know?"

"We have heard. I don't know where he is, but he did not return to our country."

"Did he contact you?"

"We have heard," Rhekka repeated. "I can't say more. You must not let anyone know." Rhekka's voice lowered; she looked about her. Her thick braid hung over her shoulder. She held it with her fingertips as if it were a point of security. "I do not know everything, but I know he was not killed. I think that he would have wanted you to know too. But he is safer if people think he is dead for a time."

"Is there any way I could see him?" Olivia didn't know what she would do if she saw Jamin; she wasn't sure if she would interview him or embrace him.

Rhekka answered, "None of us will see him for a time I think.

But if you are his friend, you will see him again. Only he comes when you least expect him, and you may not recognize him at first for he changes the way he appears."

The weight Olivia had felt pressing on her suddenly lifted. In fact only by the lightness she felt did she realize how heavily the weight had set. Some larger sorrow also pulled at its moorings. When the waitress brought the fried rice and steamed dumplings, Olivia set into them with an appetite that made even this bland midtown food taste hearty. She looked up at Rhekka and smiled. "You must tell me about yourself now," she said.

As Rhekka began her tale of a settlement village seventeen years ago, Olivia did not think she was mistaken in spying the dark weathered face of Mr. Patel watching from the window outside.

At the *The New Centurion*'s offices Alan Michaels was sitting with Olivia's manuscript in front of him when Olivia entered unannounced. "Your secretary was out," she said.

Alan stood. He offered her a chair and forced a smile. "How was lunch?"

Olivia nodded. She motioned to the story on the desk. "Well?"

"Well, it certainly isn't what I expected."

She studied his thin-lipped smile and narrow face. His teeth were yellowed from twenty years of nicotine; his hair was thinning, making his face look even more gaunt. "You don't like it?" she asked.

"I wouldn't say that. Actually I kept reading to see what would happen next."

"But?"

"You must know it's not the sort of piece we publish. It's too . . . well, it is very personal. Not that that's necessarily bad, but all the characters—and I want to call them characters—well, they're dead now. I mean essentially your story is irrelevant."

"The forces at work are the same," Olivia defended. "I was showing the forces through the people. The drive for secession versus revolution, nonviolence versus violence . . . the forces still apply."

"In an abstract, perhaps philosophical, sense, but practically . . . for the country's future . . . you've tied your whole focus to the people. With the people gone, well, I'm afraid you have nothing."

"I can update the article," she offered. "It won't take as much work as it appears. There is time."

Alan rubbed his balding head. "I won't tell you no. If you want to give it a try, but frankly I can't encourage you. You see . . ." he looked embarassed now, " . . . I didn't want to mention this before; I wanted to read your article first, but we've received another piece, not as well written as yours but straightforward, objective. Frankly we don't need two articles. I hoped to take yours, but well, you know me . . ." he offered a familiar, apologetic smile, ". . . I like to play it safe."

He began gathering up Olivia's manuscript from his desk. "The other article was unsolicited, I want you to understand. It was offered on speculation, but the writer's well-respected and knows the subject."

"Who's the writer?"

"You may know him; he covered the meeting for the *Times*. Guy Rhodes."

Olivia didn't answer. She accepted her manuscript back and stuffed it in her briefcase. "And the book proposal?"

"Well, of course we always like to have first look."

"But an advance?"

"As you know money's been tight lately, and without a manuscript . . ."

"But you know my work, Alan. I need money to finish." Olivia felt herself beginning to beg. She suddenly grew silent. She rebuked herself for letting Alan see how important this project was to her, how vulnerable she was right now. Instead she needed him to see her as independent and confident. She knew well that the spoils went only to the victors and the assignments to the already successful.

"We wish you the best of course," Alan was saying, "but frankly who knows if the public will even be interested in the subject by the time you finish another section . . ." He stood and handed the proposal back to her. "Remember, don't make it so personal next time." He stepped out from behind his desk. "When you do finish though, I hope you'll give us first look." And then gently, ever so gently, he ushered her out the door.

Olivia didn't return to Jenny's. She went directly to Penn Station where she caught the next train to Boston. Before she left, she phoned to tell Jenny that she could use her help, but Jenny wasn't home so she left a message on the machine.

She arrived at her Back Bay apartment around nine in the evening. Inside, she dumped her papers and clothes on the couch that doubled as her bed, then went over and pulled down the window shades. Her apartment was one large room at the back of a nineteenth century brownstone with high beamed ceilings and walnut moldings. She had lived here, at least technically, for the last thirteen years. When she was abroad, she'd managed to sublet to some student or other who would then sublet to a friend.

When she'd left for Europe after Elise's death, she had sold all her furniture to raise money for the fare, but by the time she returned four years later, the apartment was completely refurnished with the discarded pieces of those who had passed through its doors. Included was a convertible brown tweed couch, burned in several places by cigarettes and frayed at the arms, but to Olivia a prize for it accommodated her incommodious frame. She'd spent nights and days lying on the couch staring up at the beams of the ceiling telling herself she was thinking, sorting, preparing to write until finally she would fall asleep.

But this night she didn't even pause at the couch. Instead she pulled out the folder with her article and went over to the door balanced on two filing cabinets which served as her desk and sat down. From one of the cabinets she brought forth half a dozen spiral pads and arranged them around her. She swept the rough draft pages of the *The New Centurion* story into a box on the floor then pulled out clean paper from another box on the desk. The desk was cluttered with other papers and books and cups of cold coffee. It took her several minutes to clear a working space.

Finally she turned on her desk lamp. From the window ledge she picked up a red plastic pencil sharpener, the kind found in a child's pencil box, and she began to sharpen her pencils. To an observer she looked like a disciplined writer settling down for an evening's work, but at the moment she was angry, partly scared, but mostly angry, and she was taking up her work as a revenge to be wrought. She was angry at Alan and Guy and at Kay, at the whole world who passed judgment upon her.

She spread out the completed *New Centurion* manuscript and read it one more time; then she rolled the first page into the typewriter. At the top she typed "Chapter One." She began to write, continuing the manuscript on page 13. She wrote on the typewriter without stopping, without even picking up the neatly sharpened pencils until light spread under the window shades. Only then did she pause on page 28. She made herself a pot of coffee and picked out a stale donut from a paper bag she'd left on the counter; then bringing in the morning paper, she lay down on the couch.

She was awakened in the early afternoon by a phone call from a former student of hers she'd become friendly with. The girl was calling to tell her when the new exercise class was scheduled at the Y. After the call, Olivia got up, made herself a peanut butter sandwich and a glass of milk, sat down at her desk and started again to write. She moved from notebook to notebook checking facts and dates. She knew what was in all the notebooks, knew them almost by heart. On the pretext of organizing these, organizing, reorganizing and reorganizing again, she had postponed her writing for years. Now she knew exactly what she wanted and where it was to be found. By eight that evening she had written another eight pages, filed six of the notebooks away and brought out another set. She wrote into the early morning this time before falling asleep at her desk. When light roused her around seven, she moved over to the couch and slept there.

Olivia worked in this fashion for nine days. She rarely left her room except to go to the store at the corner to buy food or to take a walk around the block. She worked as she had only heard of writers, working with an intensity and single-mindedness which might have frightened her in the past lest she lose herself to it or perhaps discover herself in it. For reasons she couldn't even claim to understand, she was afraid of being who she could be. For the moment, however, she was able to hold these fears in abeyance. By the end of nine days she had produced 200 fairly intelligible pages. They were in need of editing, but the book was more than half drafted.

In these days Olivia lived in another sort of time, one defined by the events in her mind. She wouldn't allow herself to read the newspaper lest she get distracted by what was happening in the world. The fear of being made to break her concentration became the greatest distraction of all. She guarded against it by taking her phone off the hook and posting a Do Not Disturb sign on her door even though few people ever climbed the four flights of stairs to disturb her.

She hadn't worked with such intensity in over a decade, not since the days she was reporting from Vietnam. Back then she had worked in the same sort of time warp where the world outside didn't exist, and her work carried its own momentum and life. But at least then the stimulation had come from events outside herself. She'd never had to wonder if there would be a story the next day for the life around her was a story. But now the story was all inside her head and in memory and in the notebooks which were records of those memories. She was only beginning to trust the workings of the remembered past, but she was so well-schooled in the facts of that past that she could write quickly. After all these years it seemed now was the coming forth.

At times she wondered what had made the writing flow. The anger which had impelled her the first night had gradually dimmed as she caught the light of her own story. She still didn't understand why Guy would deliberately turn in a piece to *The New Centurion* when he knew she was writing for them, but she quit asking the question. She assumed he counted on her failing to produce, and she was tired of fulfilling other people's negative expectations. She could of course try the article at the *Atlantic* or turn the tables on Guy and try it at *The New York Times Magazine*, but she was afraid that Alan's hesitations would be theirs, and so instead she tried to forget about Alan and Guy and all the others and listen only to the heart of her story and let it guide her. She wrote from what was inside herself. In so doing she knew she broke the cardinal rule of a journalist to be objective. She knew too that in order to break the rule and get away with it, she would have to be very good. But even that demand she couldn't think about. It was the most insidious of all for it implied that she could also fail. She could not allow herself even to consider that possibility right now, for her work had to be an act of faith, one which forestalled doubts and faults of character and everything that mitigated against the full rush of life coming upon her. It had to be the kind of act that would allow Jamin to return from the dead. So she wrote, and as she wrote, she moved her way slowly towards that faith.

Part Two

Chapter 11

The phone was ringing when Jenny entered the apartment early on the same evening that Olivia had returned to Boston. She stopped in the dark hallway just long enough to listen to the silence between the rings, to note the empty coat hook behind the door, and to know by feeling, even more than by these signs, that her husband had not been home. Jenny had been out walking for the last five hours: on the arcade by the river, down to 72nd St., among the crowds and shops to Central Park, through the park and the snow to the East side, then up to the Metropolitan Museum where she passed through the vast high-ceilinged rooms and stared at the art of antiquity. She wandered almost two hours in the museum, sat in the coffee shop another half hour. She could not have described anything she'd seen or exactly where she had been.

Finally as the museum was closing and the sun was sinking somewhere in the Hudson River, she stepped outside into the dusk and caught the crosstown bus home. All the while she argued against what her intuition was telling her.

The phone rang again. She dropped her coat on the hall table and hurried for the phone. She was not one to brood on premonitions, but Olivia's visit earlier that day had unsettled her. And the news of the deaths of Olivia's friends had stirred her so that all afternoon she'd been moving in a state of anxiety, fighting off the proposition that the center could fall away. For her that center was her husband.

"Jen?" The voice on the other end of the phone was assured and familiar. "I've been trying to get you for hours. Mark asked me to call and tell you he won't be home for dinner. He'll go straight to his meeting. I'm afraid I kept him rather longer than either of us intended."

"I see."

"Where have you been anyway? I've missed a plane trying to get you."

"You missed a plane to phone me?" Jenny's voice was dry.

"I told Mark I would. He had to go to a meeting. He didn't want you to worry. It was the least I could do."

"Yes," Jenny said.

"I'm afraid I set him way behind his schedule." Jenny didn't answer. Kay was confessing accomplishment, not guilt.

"Well, I'd hate for you to miss another plane," Jenny said finally.

"There's always one the next hour. Listen, thank you for loaning me Mark; I needed him today."

The lilt in Kay's voice made Jenny want to cry out, but instead she asked, "What was I loaning him to you for?"

Kay paused for what seemed to Jenny an unnecessary amount of time; then she answered in a voice that strained to sound confidential. "I needed to talk, and you know Mark . . . he's such a good listener; he has a clear head where I'm much more emotional."

"You're emotional?"

"I may not show it, but Mark understands. You're very lucky, Jenny; you better watch out or someone may steal him from you."

"Are you trying?"

Kay laughed. "That's what I've always admired about you. You're so . . . well, so secure and normal, not like the rest of us."

The operator broke in then and asked for more money. Over the loud speaker Jenny heard the call for boarding of Eastern's shuttle to Washington. "Listen, I have to run," Kay said, "but thanks again." And she hung up.

Jenny was left standing in the early evening shadows holding the phone. She didn't know what to believe. She trusted Mark, yet she felt empty and bereft of judgment right now. The innuendo and the triumph in Kay's voice sank into her like a weapon with sharp points twisting inside her. She didn't think anything had happened between Mark and Kay. Yet why had he gone with Kay and for so long and why hadn't he phoned himself? Why had he let Kay deliver his message and come between them even in this small, yet personal routine of calling her at the end of the day? Because Kay had come between them, she wouldn't see him now when she needed to see him and talk about Olivia and the death of her friends and about herself. Thursday was their night to have dinner alone without Erika, for on Thursdays Mark's mother picked Erika up at school and had her over for dinner.

Jenny hung up the phone, then out of habit went to the back of the apartment to her study, only to remember it was now Mark's study. She stared into the darkened room, at the desk stacked with papers he hadn't gotten to. The room was crammed with boxes of files and books yet to be unpacked, probably never to be unpacked unless she did it for him. He was working longer and longer hours and complained that he had no time for himself. Yet today he'd spent hours with Kay, whose troubles she suspected were no greater than which congressman to sleep with next. Even as she thought this, she could see Mark frowning at her pettiness so she tried to grant Kay the possibility of grief. But the more she thought about the time Mark had given her, the more distraught she grew.

She went to Mark's desk and stood staring at the computer printouts, the bond calculator, just staring as though to claim this territory too as her own, not by rights of property but by years of shared living. Finally she moved to the front of the apartment to her office where she began sorting through the papers on her desk. She used the light from the street lamp to see. She pulled out a folder marked Chapter 12, picked up several other folders then quickly went back into the hallway. She didn't turn on a single light. With Mark not home, she wanted to come in and go out again without making any concessions to the darkness.

Jenny pulled open the door of Leo's Coffee Shop on the corner and hurried inside. The wind followed her with a gust of cold air, slamming the door behind her. She went over to the booth by the far window and slid onto the orange vinyl. The coffee shop was almost empty with only half a dozen patrons, each sitting alone. Jenny nodded to the owner, who was wiping the counter with a dirty white rag. "A bitch out tonight," he said. Jenny nodded again then began spreading her papers on the white formica table. She didn't look at the menu; she knew it by heart. The food here was mediocre at best, but there was always a space for her. She sometimes came here in the mornings to write when Erika was in school, when she didn't want to work alone in the apartment, or in the evenings after Erika was in bed and Mark was closed up in his study. She'd gather her folders and head out to Leo's for the coffee and the bright lights, for here at least, she felt some connection to the world.

"You're early," Leo said as he came over to the table. Leo Stein was a pot-bellied man with a broken nose and fuzzy grey tufts of hair. His hair grew in patches on his scarred head and looked as though it had once been seared off then grown in again. He had run this coffee shop deli for over two decades, arriving each morning at 6:30 from Queens with his wife Anna, who kept the books and ran the cash register.

"You eating alone tonight?" Leo sat down on the other side of the booth. Jenny nodded. She didn't want to talk. But Leo continued, "I had an editor in today," he said; his small brown eyes shined. "I told her about you. She said you should send her your book when you're finished." Leo pulled out his wallet and drew forth a business card. "Here. Jona P. Howe. Remind her she heard about you at Leo's Coffee Shop . . . she'll remember."

Jenny took the card. Leo liked to match up people, to fit pieces of the world together which he thought belonged together and to repair those which had fallen apart. She didn't know how he knew an editor when he saw one, but he managed to ferret them out and extract their business cards and then pass the cards on to her. She had half a dozen such cards in her desk drawer. "Thanks," she said.

Leo nodded. He got up then and returned to the counter. Jenny pulled out her pad of notes for revisions on Chapter 12: Migration to the City: the Search for Freedom. She read the opening, an account of the village woman's path after she's married. She moves away from what is hers to her husband's clan where she must accept the place assigned to her in the male-dominated family, a place subordinate to her mother-in-law, sisters-in-law and to her husband's other wives should she not be his first. To escape this destiny, some women were moving to the cities, Jenny noted, where they could have a measure of independence and freedom.

Jenny got up; she couldn't concentrate. She went to the pay phone in the back of the restaurant and dialed her apartment. What meeting was it Mark was going to? She didn't remember his mentioning a meeting. She listened to the phone ring . . . ring . . . ring. No one was home. She hung up. She dropped a quarter back in. This time she called Helene, Mark's mother. Jenny wanted to pick up Erika early tonight.

She wanted to be with Erika right now, but the phone rang there too without an answer.

She returned to the table where a turkey sandwich and coffee were waiting. She took a small bite of the sandwich then set it back on the plate. Why did Kay know where Mark was, and she didn't? All at once, across the street in a huddle of coats at the light she saw Mark. She thought it was Mark. She watched his shape moving towards her. Quickly she bent over her work. She waited for him to reach her. Out of habit he would look in to see if she were there. She waited for a knock on the glass or for the door to open, but she looked up just in time to see the heavy tweed overcoat moving on down the block. He couldn't have missed seeing her; she was sitting in the light of the window. She wondered if he had forgotten to look, and she wondered which was worse. She started to go after him, but she stopped. No. He should go home and find the apartment dark and empty as she had; he should have time to consider the consequence of what had happened . . . whatever had happened. The breach was probably in her imagination, she told herself. When she got home, Mark would hold her and kiss her and dismiss her fears. Yet tonight she couldn't make that image of Mark hold.

She looked at the clock on the wall. She would give Mark twenty minutes in the apartment before she returned. But she would have to walk to pass that time. She couldn't sit any longer and so she paid for her uneaten sandwich and went back outside.

At 8:30 Jenny put her key in the door. From Leo's she had walked down Broadway, past the lighted supermarkets, the fruit stand, the iron-gated stores, past the two prostitutes in mini skirts on the corner, past the police car parked on the opposite corner.

She had stopped in at a bookstore, a tiny cubicle with magazines from all over the world crowded on shelves downstairs and a loft full of paperbacks upstairs. She paused on the steps between, staring at notices on the bulletin board: tenants looking for apartments, apartments looking for tenants, tutors looking for students, kittens for homes, men and women advertising for each other . . . fragments all searching for some whole. She climbed the winding steps to the top, stood for a moment staring at a cat calendar, then abruptly asked if she could use the phone. The night manager, who knew her, let her make a call in the back. She phoned Helene's apartment one more time, but still there was no answer. Suddenly her anxiety focused on Erika. Where was her daughter? Hurrying out of the bookstore, she jogged the whole way home.

As she opened the door of the apartment, she half expected to find Mark at his desk brooding by one small lamp waiting for her to return. Instead all the lights were on; the television was going, and Mark was in the kitchen talking to someone. She stepped into the doorway. At the counter Mark was making himself a sandwich from the tuna she'd left out earlier in the day. Beside him Erika sat eating a chocolate donut, and perched on a high stool was Helene. "So here she is!" announced her mother-in-law.

"Where have you been?" Mark asked.

"Where have *you* been?" Jenny countered. She went over to Erika and picked her up.

"I had a meeting over at Afco with DeVries. You knew that."

"No, I did not know that," Jenny said. She stood in her navy pea jacket with her plaid muffler tossed about her collar, her brown hair spilling out from under a cap. Her face was flushed from the heat and cold.

Mark glanced up from his sandwich. "Kay called you, didn't she? She told me she did."

"Why didn't you call?" Jenny glanced at Helene, who was sitting with her legs crossed on the stool, interested in this exchange.

A tall, elegantly-set woman, she looked stylish even in the simple brown sweater and slacks she was wearing.

"I tried to call you, but you weren't here, and the machine wasn't on," Mark said.

Jenny shifted Erika on her hip. She wanted to ask how he knew Kay had reached her, but she hesitated in front of Helene. She got on well enough with her mother-in-law though had they not been bound to the same man, they might have found little in common. She knew she was not the daughter-in-law Helene had hoped for her third and favorite son. She wasn't Jewish; she hadn't attended a prestigious Eastern college as her other daughters-in-law had. She certainly wasn't stylish like Helene nor much interested in style and the society which occupied Helene. Yet she'd heard Helene express more than once that she knew how much Jenny loved her son and that was what counted. Jenny felt she had worked hard on coming to this sentiment and now practiced it on others. Because she wanted her mother-in-law's sympathy, Jenny asked, "So you had Kay call instead?"

"She offered to when I couldn't get you. She knew how pressed I was. Then she phoned me back to let me know she'd talked to you."

"She phoned you back?" Jenny sat Erika on the counter as though she needed suddenly to be unencumbered.

At this point Helene slipped off the stool. "I'd better be getting home myself or Grampa will wonder where I am."

Jenny turned. She restrained from asking Mark why he hadn't bothered to phone then himself once Kay told him she was home. Instead she said, "Tell Irwin hello." Helene nodded.

While Helene's affection for her was practiced and achieved, her father-in-law's was genuine. He liked her spirit, he'd told her once and had been pleasantly surprised when Mark, whom he'd always known less well than his older brothers, had brought home such a partner.

"Come on, I'll walk you down," Mark offered his mother, then he cast a stern sideways glance at Jenny.

Jenny took Erika into her bedroom and lingered with her daughter, holding her on her lap. As Erika narrated her day, how she and Granma had gone shopping and then to have ice cream in a *tea* room, Jenny felt an order returning. Erika spoke the phrase "tea room" with an air of importance as though she were now privy to special information.

Jenny was wiping the chocolate off Erika's face when Erika demanded, "But where were *you* tonight?" The intonation was Helene's.

"I was working."

"We were very worried."

"Why were you worried?"

Erika thought for a moment trying to remember the reason. "We didn't know where you were, and you should have been home."

"Who said I should be home?"

"Granma. She said you shouldn't be out at night with no one knowing where you are."

"Daddy knew where I was."

Erika hesitated. Jenny could see in her small round face that she was sorting through this information trying to fit it to some order of her own. But then abandoning the task, she looked up and smiled, "You want to see my tea bags?"

"What?"

"Granma let me have them." She wiggled out of her mother's lap and ran into the living room returning with a beaded evening purse turned yellow with age and missing several strands of beads. "She let me have this too." Erika held up the purse. Opening it, she produced two Earl Grey tea bags. Jenny laughed. "Don't laugh at me." Erika's dark eyes grew serious. She was dressed in a pink flannel nightgown, the evening bag clutched in her hand. How earnestly she took life already, Jenny thought.

"I'm not laughing at you, sweetheart. I'm laughing at the tea bags. What do you do with them?"

Erika stared at her mother as though she'd asked a stupid question. "You make tea," she said.

"Of course. Well, tomorrow let's make tea together."

Erika grinned. "That's what I was thinking." Then she rolled over, and as Jenny kissed her good night, she fell asleep, clutching the evening purse full of tea bags.

While she was putting Erika to bed, Jenny had heard Mark return. She resisted going into the living room now and facing the argument she knew they would have so she lingered instead in the security of Erika's room. Erika slept in a canopy bed, enclosed in red and white gingham. On the walls pictures of ducks and rabbits and clowns smiled down upon her. In one corner was a rocking horse, in another a slide.

Jenny sat down in the chair by the window on a cushion which matched the gingham bedspread. Helene had helped decorate this room. Mark had pursuaded Jenny to let Helene help, pointing out that Jenny was writing a book and didn't care about decorating, and it would save them both time. Helene had run from store to store matching fabrics and comparing beds, and Jenny and Mark approved only the final choices. Erika's room now looked like the room Jenny had always wished she'd had, a magazine version of childhood. Her own room in Texas had doubled as a den and guest-room so that every night she'd had to take all the pillows off the couch, which the newspaper staff or neighbors had sat upon during the day, then fold it out for her bed. Because she shared the room with adults, there was little in it which was a child's, no posters of ducks or giraffes, no clown light switches, only plain maple furniture suited for a den in the flat, treeless housing development outside of Dallas where she'd grown up.

Jenny heard an increasing clatter in the kitchen and knew Mark was growing impatient for her to come in, yet still she lingered. A plate dropped. Rising from the chair, Jenny kissed Erika one more time.

In the living room she settled on the couch and picked up her book from the coffee table. In a few moments Mark stepped into the doorway. He was still dressed in his navy pinstripe suit, his pale pink shirt opened at the collar, his tie loose about his neck, his black hair disheveled. When Jenny glanced up at him, she felt a momentary pang at how handsome he looked.

"Could you tell me what the hell that was all about tonight?" he asked. His face was strained; he looked in no temper for a discussion.

"What?" she asked innocently.

"That innuendo about Kay?" He stepped into the room carrying half a sandwich and a bottle of seltzer in his hand. He dropped into the blue velvet armchair. "Mother asked me who Kay is and why you're so upset about her. What's the matter with you?"

Jenny didn't answer. She wondered if this were Mark's protest of innocence or simply a quibble over timing.

"What were you thinking of?" he repeated.

"What were you thinking of?" Jenny answered. It was a feeble counter, but she resisted plunging in with her real question. She hoped by circling it, she might get to it without exposing herself.

"I don't know what you're talking about."

She wondered if he really didn't know. He should have known. She counted on his knowing her vulnerabilities and not making her lay them bare. She knew his, knew the men who made him uncomfortable around her. She knew that around Paul Cronin, whom she had once cared for, Mark was not at ease so she had stepped back from her friendship with Paul. She knew other vulnerabilities, knew his father's favoritism of his older brothers still undermined him. She knew his exposed spaces, and he knew hers. Or should have known. If he had to see Kay, he should have known enough to call her himself and offer reassurance. He should have known . . . he should have known, she repeated to herself.

"So why *did* Kay want to see you?" she asked.

"She had a problem; she wanted advice."

"A problem with a story?" Jenny felt the muscles in her face tense; she tried to show no expression.

"No, personal."

"And you were the only one who could help her?"

"Perhaps I was the only one who would listen." Mark took a bite of his sandwich.

Jenny smiled a disbelieving smile. "Yes. That's what she said." Mark didn't answer. "She came all the way to New York just to use your shoulder?"

"I never asked her why she was here. You should have asked."

"She was too busy telling me how wonderful you were."

Mark regarded his wife coolly. This tone of hers, her display in front of his mother angered him. It was a glimpse of Jenny he rarely saw and didn't like. It was a small-minded, jealous woman whom he had specifically not married. He had specifically not married Kay or a woman like his mother. Both were overly concerned with what other people were doing and saying. While he'd been raised to know what was socially acceptable, Jenny didn't know society from taxi drivers or doormen; she treated everyone the same. He wanted her to maintain his ideal of her, to be unimpressed with the money and success he'd achieved while he himself was impressed, wanted her to pursue the artistic vision he had not. He wanted her to be what he might also be, all the while binding herself to him for who he was. It was not after all an unreasonable expectation of a marriage partner, and it was not very different from what Jenny was demanding of him. At the moment, however, as they faced each other across the living room, they each felt the other had failed.

"What was Kay's trouble anyway?" Jenny asked.

"She asked me not to talk about it."

"That hardly seems fair, does it?"

"What?"

"To have Kay's secrets between us." The sarcasm left Jenny's voice. Her blue-grey eyes leveled on her husband in a gaze without innuendo or pettiness, her vulnerability exposed but in check.

"Kay's secrets aren't between us," he said quietly.

"Why didn't you call me?"

"I did call you three or four times; you weren't here. Kay caught me as I was running uptown and said she'd been trying to get you and would keep trying and pass on my message."

Jenny watched her husband. He'd been out since early this morning; she knew how tired he must be. "Weren't you with her all morning?"

"We had coffee; I spent maybe half an hour."

"But I called your office at noon. Louise said you hadn't been in, and she didn't know where you were. Kay told me she'd put you way behind your schedule."

Mark shook his head almost without interest. "I don't know what Kay's talking about. Louise, if she'd bothered to check my calendar, would have known I had a nine o'clock meeting with DeVries." He leaned his head now against the wing of the chair.

"I met with him all morning and tonight. I don't see how the company can make its interest payment, and I don't know how I'm going to face my clients or Reynolds if they default. Reynolds was dead set against the financing."

Jenny rose from the couch. She went over and sat on the arm of Mark's chair. He leaned into her. "God, Jen, I don't want to face this."

"Are you sure?" she asked.

"And the Hastings acquisition . . . that's gotten tangled in a web of regulations over insurance companies." He looked up and gave her a tired smile.

She stroked his hair. "Look, I'm sorry about tonight with your mother." Mark nodded. "You should have stopped at Leo's; we could have talked."

"I didn't know you were there. I took a cab home with Mother and Erika."

Jenny fell silent. But she'd seen Mark out the window. At least the coat, the stride, the shape of the man had all looked like Mark. Yet it had not been Mark. Suddenly she felt wrung out by the emotion she'd expended all day. In a flat voice she said, "Jamin, Nyral . . . everyone was killed when they returned last week. It came over the news this afternoon."

Mark looked up at her. He took her hand. "I'm sorry. I hadn't heard."

"I guess the cat's been walking for me today," she said.

Mark squeezed her hand. They both knew this cat. They'd named the feeling after Cassie, who prowled the apartment in the middle of the night. They would hear his claws clicking on the hardwood floors. In the worst cases the clicking came faster and faster until Cassie was racing around the apartment, and one of them would have to get up and go into the living room and catch him and hold him and stroke him into a calm. They sat for a moment holding hands, then Mark asked, "Would you mind if I played the piano for a while?"

"I'd like that."

As he went to the piano, Jenny rose and went into the kitchen where she made herself a cup of tea. She put away the bread and the lettuce on the counter. Cassie followed her limping slightly. She examined the bottom of his paw and saw it was cut, saw a spot of blood on the counter, and realized Cassie had tried to pry open the can of tuna. She washed the paw then scooped out the rest of the tuna and a can of cat food into his bowl. Returning to the living room, she sat back on the couch with her book and listened to the music.

Mark and Jenny went to bed together late that night. They made love before they went to sleep. In the middle of the night they awakened and made love again. In their deep sleep after the second love-making, they didn't hear Cassie darting across the hardwood floors, over the couch and the blue velvet chairs, strung tight in his own animal disquiet.

 *Chapter 12*

Mark set *The Washington Tribune* on the hall table the following evening, then went into the kitchen where Jenny was standing at the stove. He put his arms around her waist and kissed her on the back of the neck. In the hall wooden wheels clacked across the wooden floor towards them.

"She's been waiting for you all day."

Mark kissed Jenny again before he let go. "Then I guess I better go to her."

Jenny followed him into the hall where she saw the newspaper. She roused when she saw Mark had bought the *Washington Tribune* rather than the *New York Times* or the *New York Post*. She took the paper back into the kitchen and opened it on the counter. As she waited for the spaghetti to boil, she read Kay's front page account of massacres halfway around the world.

UN Weighs Massacre Evidence,
Considers Emergency Meeting

by Katherine Bernstein Walsh
Tribune Staff Writer

NEW YORK—The reported massacre of over 6000 members of the National Liberation Association (NLA) by government forces of Joseph Amundo Bulagwi has touched off charges and countercharges at the United Nations and a call for an emergency session of the Security Council.

According to first reports from journalists out of the country, President Bulagwi's armed forces gunned down hundreds of countrymen in a bloodbath which started Friday and continued through the weekend. Included in the toll was the entire National Liberation Association delegation returning from the United Nations.

Soviet and Cuban officials have laid responsibility for the killings on the United States and their Western allies. "Through their continued economic and political support of the barbarous Bulagwi regime, they have encouraged this action," said a Soviet spokesman.

President Bulagwi, breaking a week-long news blackout, insisted in a press conference yesterday that the killings were only of NLA guerrillas found entrenched outside the Capitol. The rebels were armed with Soviet weapons and assisted by Libyan and Cuban advisors, said Bulagwi from his palace residence. "The rebels planned to overthrow the government; the army took appropriate action," he said. "My enemies used the great body of the United Nations to distract the world from their true aims, but I was not fooled. I am always awake. I see my enemies before they see me." President Bulagwi admitted to having arrested the NLA delegation when it returned, but he claimed the members were now in prison awaiting trial.

Los Angeles Times reporter Sage Davis, however, reported two eye-witness accounts of the machine gunning of the whole delegation as it got off the plane. In addition, Mr. Davis reported personally witnessing a raid into one of the camps by government troops who shot at "anything which moved, including children."

The course the United Nations will take has not been determined at this writing. "We are still gathering the facts," said the Secretary-General in an interview. "But I am appalled by reports of wholesale killing, and I will use every means within the power of the United Nations to press for a peaceful solution."

The United Nations charter prohibits the body from interfering in a country's internal affairs unless invited by the recognized government. President-for-Life Bulagwi has made it clear he would regard U.N. interference as hostile and would respond accordingly.

State Department analysts in Washington, who have watched President Bulagwi over the years, suggest that these killings may be Bulagwi's response to the recent U.N. hearing. One analyst did not rule out the possibility of Bulagwi's instigating the attack on himself so that he could retaliate. As to what the incident means to U.S. relations with the Bulagwi government, Washington's official response has been cautious and noncommittal. "We are following the situation with gravest concern," said a senior State Department spokesman.

Jenny looked up from the paper. The water in the pot churned on itself. She heard laughter in the back of the apartment. She hadn't known of the massacres; she hadn't known the extent of the killings. She felt suddenly uneasy. She set the dinner plates on the counter and drained spaghetti onto them. She set salad into bowls, poured juice into glasses. Kay of course would return to cover the story. She took the dinner in to the table and called Mark and Erika.

She was quiet during dinner; Mark himself was tired, but Erika chattered enough for both of them. After dinner she told Mark to play with Erika; she would clear. She took the plates back into the kitchen and dropped them in the sink. She dropped the *Tribune* into the trash.

Erika and Mark were at the piano when she returned, but instead of joining them, she went to her study and dialed Olivia's number. Olivia had said she wanted help. Jenny needed to know what kind of help. Olivia must have heard about the massacre by now. She wanted to talk to her, to be there for Olivia if she needed to talk. She wanted Olivia to be there for her though Jenny did not want to talk. But Olivia's line was busy. She hung up the phone.

At ten o'clock she tried Olivia again, but the phone was still busy. She read for half an hour, tried one more time then went into the living room. The lights and the television were on, and Mark and Erika were asleep in each other's arms. She didn't wake them but went over and turned to the news channel.

On the floor she spread out the week's bills and appeals and began writing checks: the electric bill, the heating bill, Master Charge. She sorted through requests for donations: CARE this week showed Afghan rebels huddled in tents across the Pakistan boarder; Save the Children appealed for children in the Sahel. Amnesty International sent a calendar with its envelope, each month dedicated to an individual imprisoned for political opposition, along with instructions of who to write in protest.

She wrote her checks: $1000 to Save the Children this week, $1000 to CARE, $800 to Amnesty International. Then she wrote to the President of the Republic of Indonesia to protest the disappearance of 17-year-old Maria Gorete Joaquim, abducted after her opposition to Indonesia's invasion of East Timor, wherever in the world East Timor was. She felt cut off from this world she was giving to, her own existence unfathomably separate. As she sat in front of the flickering TV stuffing checks into envelopes, casting her and Mark's money out on the world, she felt a kind of terror overtake her as if she were glimpsing some demon stronger than herself, some force that pulled the world apart and shattered unities. She feared the demon was not just in the world, but in herself, its shape and origin as subtle as the shadow in her own heart.

She rose now and carried Erika to bed. Returning to her office, she took out a pad of paper and began to list questions she might help Olivia answer. Next to the questions she noted possible sources of information:

—Who financed NLA UN visit?
               —Airline records
               —Travel agent
               —Hotel records
               —Airport log book/charter flight?
               —Af. UN delegates?

—Source Bulagwi funds: personal/political?
                          —Bank record
                          —Library file
                          —UN reps
                          —Embassy
                          —Afco—ck Mark?

   She could help Olivia to a point. Olivia had helped her time
and again, reading her work, offering her clear-sighted judgment.
She would phone Olivia again tomorrow. Setting the questions
aside, she pulled out her own manuscript, Chapter13: Beasts of
Burden or Women of Power?

Chapter 13

In the year and a half Mark had been doing business with Benjamin DeVries, he had never introduced him to Jenny. Usually she met his major clients, but he was protective of DeVries, she thought. She had heard of Benjamin DeVries even before Mark knew him, primarily because of the controversy which hung to his name. In the early 1960s he and his Belgian bank were rumored to have helped finance the coup and possibly assassinations in the Congo at the time of independence. The charges were never proven, and DeVries' role in the upheaval in central Africa remained to this day merely a shadow which followed him. He had since run a major European mining company whose size he'd almost doubled in his decade there. After he retired from Generale de Metaux six years ago, he had set up his own merchant bank which had been investing in mineral companies in Europe, had garnered mining concessions in a number of African countries and was expanding its investment base into U.S. markets.

Jenny finally met Benjamin DeVries with Mark on Friday evening for dinner. They met in the entryway of Windows on the

World among dozens of yellow chrysanthemums blooming in brass pots. Though Jenny had seen photographs of DeVries in news magazines, she was still surprised when Mark put out his hand and put on his warmest, most respectful smile to a slight, white-haired man in a black suit and bow tie who looked more like a waiter than a renowned international financier.

"Mrs. Rosen." DeVries bowed and offered his hand. "I've been after Mark to have us meet." His eyes blinked behind pale lashes. His lashes and eye brows were white and his skin pink and translucent. DeVries was an albino. "My wife, Rosa." He presented a woman Jenny's age in silver lamé pants with thick curling black hair about her face. The woman smiled carefully.

"Mark talks of you a great deal," DeVries said, taking Jenny's arm and leading her up the steps. "It is a good thing when a man loves his wife." He escorted her into the main dining room which was arranged on three levels, separated by brass railings and gold pillars rising to the ceiling. On the main level a brass and chrome structure displayed cakes and tarts and fresh fruit. DeVries led Jenny past these to a separate room behind a glass and gold door. On the far wall enormous purple irises were painted on a gold canvas. DeVries pulled out a chair for Jenny at a table by the window and positioned himself beside her. He left the maitre d' and Mark to look after Rosa. No one else was in the room. As they sat down, a helicopter flew by the window, its lights blinking red and yellow against the Manhattan skyline.

"Must be nice working up here among the gods," DeVries bantered to the maitre d', whose flushed, portly face brightened, and smiled.

"Yes, sir. Nice to have you back with us, Mr. DeVries.

Waiters in white military style jackets appeared; one with pink decorations poured water; one with gold epaulets took orders for drinks. Jenny picked up her menu, but she hadn't had time to note more than the appetizers when DeVries took it from her. "If you don't object, I've ordered a special dinner for us tonight. Do you trust my taste, Mrs. Rosen?"

Jenny nodded, but already she resisted this man's easy charm.

Speaking quietly to the waiter, DeVries set out the sequence of the foods he'd ordered; then he turned towards Mark. "So tell me . . . " he said.

Mark smiled and shut his menu. He leaned forward on the table. He began explaining the new idea he had to postpone interest payments on Afco. When Mark had raised the money for Afco a year ago, DeVries had projected that with the financing and the cash flow from the mines, Afco would double its asset base in two years. However, ore prices had plunged; a coup had taken over in one country and closed the border; civil war threatened rail lines in another. Instead of the large projected profits, Afco was precariously close to default.

As Mark spoke, his dark, serious face animated. DeVries began nodding. "Yes . . . yes . . . " he said, "yes, that might be a possibility."

"It came to me in the shower," Mark explained. "It's a long shot. It will depend on the insurance companies rolling over. And the banks."

"I think I can handle the banks," DeVries said. "Yes. God damn, you think like I do!" The two men smiled at each other. Jenny had tried to follow the conversation, unlike Rosa DeVries who sat staring out the window. Jenny had listened to Mark for enough years to understand that he was talking about turning 15 percent bonds into zero coupon bonds so that rather than getting paid every six months, the bondholders would be paid more money in a lump sum at the expiration of the bonds. She understood that the change would give breathing room to the company's cash position. The subtler implications of the transaction, however, she did not understand; and so when DeVries paid Mark his compliment, she was not sure of all that it meant, and she felt a vague uneasiness. Afco, it seemed to her, treaded close to simply offering a plan for new colonialism with bribes to officials like Bulagwi. She and Reynolds had both pointed out that the operation took their firm into an area it knew little about. But in the end the reputation and expertise of Benjamin DeVries and the promise of large returns for investors and a sizable fee for the firm had won Mark and finally Reynolds over.

As Jenny listened and watched Mark now, it occurred to her that perhaps he'd been keeping DeVries from her as some vulnerable and changing part of himself.

The gold-shouldered waiter pushed open the door and rolled in a buffet table full of food. He spread out half a dozen appetizers. With quick professional strokes he divided them on four serving plates: croustade with chicken livers and artichokes, prosciutto with papaya, galantine of duckling and foie gras, coquille of scallops and shrimp, cold asparagus and finally ravioli stuffed with truffles. This last, DeVries noted, was a delicacy served only in selected restaurants in the world, one he'd had to order specially for tonight.

As the procession of food began, DeVries turned his attention to Jenny. "You have a little girl, I understand," he said, "and another child on the way. You are very lucky. I never had children." His voice was slightly high-pitched, not in keeping with the man Jenny had imagined. "My first wife and I didn't want to take the chance. Twenty-five percent possibility, we were told, that my difficult genes would pass on, though I was taking worse odds than that in business at the time." He smiled. Mark had told her he'd been married to the same woman for forty years until she had died six years ago.

"But now Rosa here has about convinced me to take that chance," he went on. "I didn't turn out so bad, she says. Wouldn't that be something . . . me a father at 73!" DeVries turned to Mark; his eyes blinked.

"You should," Mark declared. "An incredible experience . . . like closing A&L."

DeVries laughed. "Is your husband always so incorrigible, Mrs. Rosen? I bet he was checking the market while you were having the baby."

Jenny looked over at Mark and also wondered at his glibness. "No," she said quietly. "In fact he took the week off."

"I don't believe it. He works as hard as I do, and I don't say that of many people." Rosa DeVries looked at Jenny; her dark, flat eyes registered sympathy.

"You really should have a child," Mark insisted as the waiter set down a rack of lamb on the side table and began apportioning it. Around the lamb he fanned a rainbow of vegetables—zucchini, carrots, broccoli, squash.

Jenny wondered why Mark was pressing DeVries to have a baby. He sounded as though he were selling him a stock, and it made her uncomfortable; he didn't sound like himself. DeVries, however, seemed pleased by Mark's enthusiasm.

"Don't you agree, Jenny?" Mark said as the waiter set a plate in front of him. He began telling DeVries about an episode Jenny had told him when Erika smeared rouge all over her face and body. He told the story as though he had been there, only he was inventing and exaggerating what had happened. Jenny wondered if he had persuaded himself that he had been there. DeVries laughed as Mark described Erika admiring her rouge-smeared body in the mirror and announcing that now she was a lady. Jenny strained to recognize her husband. He sounded like so many men who knew their children's lives through the secondhand stories of their wives at the end of the day. Yet Mark knew Erika better than that. Why was he going on this way?

On the side table the gold-decorated waiter was slicing up a duck as his assistant opened a new bottle of wine. Jenny had counted nine separate foods and four wines so far. She looked at DeVries. He seemed to take this spread as a matter of course. The only evidence of such eating on his spindly frame was his paunch which fell slightly over his waistband like a child's baby fat. As the waiter set the new plates on the table, he turned to her. "Your husband tells me you like Peking duck so I take it you need no introduction on how to eat it." He smeared thick sauce over a pancake. "It is one of my favorites too." He picked up a slice of duck, a piece of crisp skin and a scallion and rolled it in the pancake. Then with manicured fingers, he picked it up and stuffed it in his mouth, eating it with a relish Jenny couldn't muster, mopping sauce from his chin with the edge of the tablecloth which he mistook for his napkin.

Across the table Rosa DeVries half-heartedly dabbed plum sauce onto her pancake. She had yet to speak. Instead she stared at the three of them with bored, tolerant eyes even as they had discussed her hypothetical child. Jenny looked down at her own plate and wondered where she would stow this food; the new baby's weight was pressing upon her full stomach; she was beginning to feel light-headed.

DeVries was asking her about her writing and the award she had won when the waiter set before them a giant fish with mottled scales and dead eyes. Jenny's face blanched; she felt blood rush to her head; her throat suddenly filled. Covering her mouth, she stood. "Excuse me," she mumbled, then as quickly as she could, she fled into the mirrored, pink-walled bathroom where she stumbled into one of the stalls and threw up all over the toilet. Kneeling in her crepe skirt on the pink and white marble, she retched the foie gras and chicken livers and lamb. She kept her eyes closed. She could hear the clink of quarters in the maid's dish outside. As she knelt, she breathed in the strong clean odor of disinfectant.

"Oh god," she moaned waiting for the nausea to pass. She opened her eyes and stared at the smoked glass bulb above the toilet. Finally raising herself from the floor, she stood shakily. She tried to wipe up the mess she had made; then she flushed the toilet and pushed open the door. The attendant at the sink was waiting for her with a damp towel. "Thank you," she muttered.

The woman's dark face remained expressionless as though she were used to cleaning up after rich white ladies. Jenny's own face peered back at her from the mirror wraithlike, brown streaks under her eyes where her mascara had run. Her hair had tumbled down. She had left her purse at the table so she had neither powder nor lipstick to make repairs. She tried splashing water on her face. She wished she could brush her teeth. She was leaning on the sink swabbing her blouse with a wet paper towel when a slightly Southern voice spoke from behind.

"I know how you feel, honey." Rosa DeVries handed her her purse. "I thought you might need this."

Jenny turned. "Oh . . . thank you."

"You got to forgive Benny. Sometimes he goes overboard on food. I'm afraid he's showing off tonight."

Jenny stared at this woman with the broad, bright mouth and sleepy eyes. She wondered where she'd come from and where she had met Benjamin DeVries, but she didn't ask. Instead she began trying to reconstruct her hair.

"Here, let me help." Rosa led Jenny into the dressing room where half a dozen vanity tables were set up with mirrors and tiny light bulbs, with brushes and hair spray and kleenex and perfume. Jenny sat on one of the brown leather stools, and Rosa De Vries with a professional hand began coiling Jenny's hair on top of her head. At the other end of the room a bride stood fussing in front of the mirror in an ivory satin 1920s gown with a satin scarf tied about her head. Her bridesmaids in purple were primping, laughing about the wedding which had just taken place. At the other vanity tables other women were complaining about themselves, trying to recreate themselves under these lights, in these mirrors. Mirrors on the walls and the ceilings reflected the women, the perfume, the silk and satin, the rustling dresses as well as the dark, silent figure of the attendant in the corner with the porcelain dish.

"Why is your husband showing off for *us*?" Jenny asked.

"He's trying to snag your husband, don't you know?"

"No," Jenny said. "What do you mean?"

Rosa DeVries stared at her in the mirror. "You mean you don't know what this dinner is about?"

Jenny's expression grew alert; the color returned to her cheeks. "Mark's been talking about my meeting your husband for a long time."

"Oh shit," Rosa said flatly. She pushed the last hairpin into Jenny's scalp. "You better get out there to listen to what comes next."

As Rosa DeVries opened the door, Jenny reached into her purse. She dropped a crumpled $5 bill into the dish. The attendant stared at her without expression.

When Jenny and Rosa reappeared, the two men stood. "Are you all right, Mrs. Rosen?" DeVries asked. Jenny glanced at Mark, who reached for her hand. In the gesture was both comfort and a question. She looked at him with her own question. On the side table the half-eaten fish stared up at her. She sat down without answering. DeVries motioned for the waiter to remove the fish. Then as if on cue, he leaned towards Jenny.

"You have a remarkable husband, Mrs. Rosen," he said. "One of the comers on Wall Street today. You must know that. He reminds me a lot of myself at that age. Frankly I still think of myself at that age most of the time. I think as quickly as I ever did, but a man at 73 can't keep the physical pace as a man 35. So you know what I've been telling myself?" Jenny didn't answer. "I've been telling myself it's time to get a young partner, someone who can think as fast as I can but move faster, someone who can make those trans-Atlantic crossings and be awake on the other end. I've been thinking about this ever since I left Generale de Metaux and set up my own shop. And you know who I've been thinking of lately?" Jenny watched the way light failed to penetrate this man's eyes. His eyes were the same mottled color as the fish.

"Your husband. He has an outstanding record as you know and a fine future ahead of him. I also happen to know you are the backbone to that future, which is as it should be, so I've asked Mark to let me personally place my proposal before you." He blinked and opened his hands on the table displaying thin, ringed fingers. He wore a gold band with a fleur-de-lis on one finger, a university graduation ring on another and a gold and diamond wedding band. Jenny glanced at Mark, who was watching her. His smile faded when he saw the expression on her face.

"Mark has probably told you for the past few years I've been investing my own and investors' money in a number of mineral corporations we now control. In the near future these companies will be used to leverage much larger purchases. Mark has strong knowledge and experience in U.S. markets and a reputation for integrity. I want Mark to come in with me as a partner. We could merge our two organizations. Mark is young and just moving into my side of the business. I have considerably more experience, but frankly I could use Mark's U.S. clientele. We'll make investment decisions together, and Mark will have an opportunity to travel all over the world."

DeVries looked at Jenny expectantly, but the tight line of her mouth and the fixed stare of her eyes were not what he expected. Thinking she was unhappy about Mark's traveling, he quickly added, "And of course you may accompany him whenever you choose."

But Jenny still did not respond. She picked up the silver spoon beside the parfait glass which had just been set before her. She took a bite of the raspberry sorbet. She glanced again at Mark. As she watched her husband, she tried to understand how he could have led her here without a hint of what this dinner was about. She wondered how long he had been keeping this proposal a secret from her and more importantly, how Benjamin DeVries had persuaded him to do so. As she watched him, she thought he looked ready to leap at the offer with or without her.

"Don't think me conceited," DeVries was persisting, "but I'm offering your husband a chance which may not come again in his lifetime."

Jenny sipped her coffee. "Why are you offering him this chance of a lifetime?" she asked. Her voice was steady. "Your business is considerably larger than his. You don't have a reputation of giving anything away for free." She avoided Mark's gaze though had she looked, she would have seen him smile; he took pride that his wife would stand up to Benjamin DeVries.

Her question caught DeVries off guard. "Well . . . Mrs. Rosen . . . Jenny, you ask that like a good businessman. And you are right; no one gets something for nothing. Even considering your husband's considerable talents, I would be asking Mark to make an investment of his own; that is only fair, you will agree."

"How much of an investment?"

"Oh . . . " DeVries blinked. "The assets of his company and perhaps an additional seven or eight million."

Jenny did not blink. "I see."

"Or we may strike a deal so that over time, if the company grows according to certain figures, I'll sell Mark my stock at its current value until we own equal shares. You see, the most important part of Mark's investment will be his time, his reputation, and his energy. He will run the business day to day so I'm willing to trade money for time."

Jenny wanted to ask if he were also trading money for reputation, but she remained silent.

DeVries leaned forward on the table now and took Jenny's hand, which was cold to the touch. "Unless I am mistaken . . . and I have a long career of not being mistaken . . . this is the ideal time to move into the marketplace in a big way. Businesses everywhere are undervalued and fighting for cash; stockholders are worried, just waiting for someone to come in and take their worry off their hands. For an investment of a few million ourselves, along with investors' money and bank financing, we can leverage a deal and buy control of a company that will be worth a hundred million in a few years. And then we can use that company to buy another. American business is still the strongest in the world. There are investors all over the world looking for a place to put their money.

117

But one has to act in the face of other people's fears to be a success. That is what I can do and what I think Mark is capable of doing." DeVries face flushed slightly; his eyes narrowed. "There is fear built up everywhere, Jenny. Often people aren't even sure what they are afraid of. And fear tends to fulfill itself unless someone acts in the face of it."

"So you and Mark will buy companies cheap to save people from their fears?" Jenny asked the question in an even tone straining out the irony, but Mark shot her a warning glance.

DeVries, however, rocked back in his chair and laughed. "I like your wife, Mark. Yes, I do. Perhaps she and I should go into business." But Jenny's eyes remained steady on DeVries. The banker waved to the waiter and ordered more coffee. He leaned back onto the table then. Seeing he had not yet won this pregnant, modestly attractive, yet skeptical wife, his own face grew more stern. In the harder light of his eyes Jenny saw what she had been looking for: the encompassing will of the man.

He answered in the same uncompromising voice as she. "No, my dear. I expect we shall earn ten times our money in three years. I expect the man who is my partner will be on his road to the heights of American enterprise. In the process, it so happens we shall be strengthening the businesses we buy, paying stockholders more than they can get in the marketplace, freeing their money for other investments and at the same time pumping new capital into the companies, increasing their value. We will also be employing many of those fearful people."

He wiped his eyes with a napkin and turned aside for a moment. In his palm he blinked out two grey contact lenses, and for the first time Jenny saw his glazed, colorless eyes. Rosa quickly wrested from her silver evening bag a pair of thick-lensed glasses which he put on. When he turned back to Jenny, he looked different, more remote and imperious. All at once Jenny wondered if she had the will to oppose this man or if he should even be opposed.

"But of course you and Mark need time to talk," he said. He signaled the maitre d', who had been hovering near the doorway, for the check.

As the four of them proceeded through the narrow, mirrored gallery to the lobby, no one spoke. On the walls were enlarged photographs of man's achievements around the world—the

Sphinx, the Eiffel Tower, the Tower of London—and between these panels stood enormous semiprecious stones on brass pedestals: a three-foot amethyst, a four-foot rose quartz. The hallway emerged into a lobby with gold carpet and gold walls. They waited for their coats here then rode the speeding elevator down the 107 floors to the main floor with its royal purple carpet and cathedral windows. The whole time Jenny held tightly to Mark's arm.

"I should have told you," Mark said as soon as they entered the taxi. DeVries had offered them a ride uptown in his limousine, but feeling the pressure on his arm increase, Mark had declined
.Jenny didn't answer.

"You have to admit it is a very generous offer," he said. He tried to keep his tone noncommittal. He wasn't sure what his wife was feeling. "You know I've talked to you about making a change. Reynolds and I simply do not see the business the same way. In fact he told me yesterday he's thinking of retiring, that I could buy him out. I need another partner. Well, out of the blue a while ago DeVries came up with this idea." He put his arm around Jenny, but in the stiffness of her body, he felt her anger or hurt or disappointment; he wasn't sure which; but his instincts told him not to press the offer right now. He said instead, "DeVries certainly liked you."

"DeVries does't know me," she answered quietly. "Whether he likes me or not is beside the point." The words came slowly, but Mark felt their momentum building. In his mind he searched for a place to dodge the impact. But Jenny didn't go on. She turned and stared out the window. The night was pitch; it looked as if it might snow.

Mark glanced out the other window. His gloved hand rested on Jenny's, but she didn't respond. He leaned his head against the back of the cab. His face was pained; his deep-set brown eyes closed, his jaw, set. "It would mean an opportunity for you too," he suggested. "You can travel and write from all over the world."

"And what about Erika?" she asked.

"She'll come with us."

"And the baby?"

"We'll bring him too."

119

"Him?"

"Her, him . . . we'll bring the baby."

"Who will take care of Erika and the baby if we're both working?"

Mark hesitated. He hadn't thought about the details, but he was sure they could be worked out. "We'll hire someone."

Jenny stared back out the window. As she thought: he hadn't even considered what the job would mean to his family. It was her first consideration. What it would mean was less time for Erika and no time for the second child for the reality was that Mark would go away, and she and Erika and the baby would stay at home waiting for his return. DeVries wasn't fool enough nor was Mark to add four superfluous bodies—a wife, two children, a nanny—on business trips. Besides she didn't want a nanny. Mark's complaint about his own childhood was that he had known the governess better than his mother and father; now he was suggesting the same fate for his children. She didn't say any of this, however, for at the moment she didn't trust her own feelings. She thought she should be soaring over this possibility for Mark; yet instead she felt earthbound and threatened and hurt at not being told. "How long have you known?" she asked.

Mark looked over at her. "A month . . . a couple of months."

"A couple of months!"

Mark stirred. He didn't understand what was bothering his wife. Suddenly he felt agitated himself. Why did she always have to be the skeptic? Why couldn't she allow him just once to feel the way he thought he should feel, the way he thought she should feel? "Damn it, Jenny, what's wrong?"

She drew her hand from under his and pulled her coat around her. "I feel manipulated," she said. "I feel taken for granted and manipulated by two men who are going to get what they want anyway." She avoided his eyes. Her lips were drawn tight; her voice poised on words she didn't want to speak.

"Oh shit!" Mark said. "How can you say that?" He removed his own hand from her lap. "How am I manipulating you? I thought you'd at least be a little excited. I even thought tonight might be fun. DeVries went to a lot of trouble to treat us to a special dinner, and he did it mostly for you. You don't know that part, do you? He called me twice this week just to ask what foods you liked. He had the restaurant make the Peking duck specially for you."

"I threw up the Peking duck," she reminded.

"Well, that was your problem, wasn't it?"

"Who does DeVries think I am that he can buy me with a duck?" Her tone was tough, but Mark thought he heard a slight humor in the word 'duck'"

"He wasn't trying to buy you. He was making what he thought was a nice gesture. Actually, he was excited about the whole thing . . . as if he were giving you a surprise party."

"I don't like surprise parties," Jenny said. And whatever else was disturbing her—the opulent world she feared would lure her husband away, the demands on his time that would take him from her and his family—whatever the objections that were yet to be discussed or argued between them, this for the moment was central: "You should have told me."

"I already said that. Didn't you hear me? That was the first thing I said when we got in the cab. I got caught up in the idea with DeVries. I'm sorry. I realized as soon as I saw your face . . . we should have talked first. Really, Jen." Mark's eyebrows rose in a protest of innocence. "I wasn't trying to manipulate you. There's plenty of time. Nothing's settled. I told DeVries I wouldn't make a commitment without you. I mean that."

Jenny fell silent. She resisted the idea. She felt apprehensive over DeVries though she couldn't have explained why. She wondered exactly what his relationship was with Bulagwi. For the moment, however, she asked only, "Where do you propose to get seven million dollars?"

"That is the least of my worries," Mark said. "You are my main worry." He started to kiss her, but seeing her still tense, he refrained. Instead he reached out for her hand.

They both knew to let the question rest for the time being. They rode home in silence. In his thoughts Mark returned to the options still available to Afco, and Jenny returned to the smiling, sightless face of Benjamin DeVries.

121

Chapter 14

Olivia was holed up in her room on the ninth night of her writing siege. She had written two hundred pages so far. All over the blue-patterned carpet were scattered papers and notecards. On the desk more papers and notebooks were stacked, leaving only a small clearing in the middle for her typewriter. It was 5:30 in the afternoon, and she was wearing a red plaid robe which she'd been wearing since she'd come back from the corner grocery where she bought a quart of milk, a box of shredded wheat and a loaf of bread. She'd made herself cereal and toast at around four, then in the waning light she'd changed into her robe, thick woolen socks and a black cardigan sweater. She turned on the electric heater for though it took its toll on her electric bill, the room was too cold without it after the sun went down.

She was nursing a cup of over-brewed coffee and staring at the same set of notebooks she had been studying for the past two hours. In these was a record of her last interview with Jamin before she left Africa. Next to the notebooks was the past week's *New York Times* which were delivered each morning but which she had allowed herself to read only a few hours ago. Until then she had heard nothing of the general massacre, nothing of the Security Council meeting set for Tuesday or of Bulagwi's impending trip to New York. She had been living in time defined by the light outside her window and by the needs of her body to eat and sleep. She had hidden her clock lest she distract herself by counting minutes and hours and days and pages. She knew how many days had passed by the number of unread *New York Times*.

Instead in her mind she had been walking the hillsides with Jamin and eating yams with Mushambe and visiting the school where children sat on narrow benches in front of wooden slats used as desks, in a clearing used as a school room. She had been dwelling at a different point of history, on the upward curve of a cycle before it arced and dipped in another direction. The momentum of the decline she had just been reading about in Guy's flat and factual stories on the front page. After all the speculation, all the opinions and facts, there remained for her one question: Where was Jamin? This question had led her to her notebooks.

Her last interview with Jamin had taken place at the veneer factory on the other side of the hills. Jamin had insisted on meeting there for he claimed this would be the seat of his nation's future. The corrugated steel building sat on the flat grassland. Telephone and electric wires threaded into it out of nowhere as if to tie the building to the brown earth lest it rise and disappear into the shimmering heat. The only American company in the hills, Flatbush Veneer was the largest employer of villagers in the North and the chief source of the area's income. Veneer was stripped from logs here and sold to Europe and America.

Bulagwi allowed the factory to remain, the elders said, because he was afraid of the "elephant man," the American who had started the company. No one knew who this man was, but in the tattered green-carpeted entry of the factory hung a blurred black and white photograph of a fat white man leaning on a chieftan's cane. Bulagwi demanded heavy taxes from the factory which the factory never paid and Bulagwi never came to collect. His soldiers had set fire to other businesses which did not pay their taxes. But to the Flatbush Veneer Company he only sent letters every few months demanding hundreds of thousands of chalas, letters typed on gold-embossed stationary, letters which no one answered.

Olivia had met Jamin outside the factory her last morning as the sun was rising over the hills. She had spent most of the night before in her hut with Mushambe, packing and drinking wine. While Albert slept on the dirt floor in the corner on her air mattress, she and Mushambe divided up her pots and spoons and curtains and furniture for different friends in the village. Mushambe would distribute them after she'd gone. To Mushambe she gave her bicycle and her frying pans. To Albert she gave her army surplus air mattress she'd bought at a shop in Brazzaville. To Jamin she planned to give a box of books that she'd decided to leave behind. The books were in the back of her Landrover in the parking lot where she was waiting as the workers pulled up in yellow buses.They would work from six till noon, then they would take off in the heat of the day to eat and rest.

Jamin pulled up in his jeep. He was dressed in his usual army camouflage pants and a khaki shirt. With quick, impatient strides he made his way across the lot to her car. Under his arm he carried a satchel and a large roll of paper. He was about to say something to her when she presented him with the box of books. "A goodbye present, you might say." For a brief moment she had been afraid she might cry, but Jamin's expression undercut any sentiment.

He'd opened the box as though annoyed, rifled through the titles then returned it to her. "I have them already," he asserted. "Come inside." He strode ahead of her towards the factory.

Inside, the noise of the machines made it impossible to hear so they didn't speak until they reached a glassed-in office. The ruddy-faced foreman whose office had been donated for Jamin's use was pacing by the drinking fountain. The office was a small, improvised space set a few feet off the ground to give a view of the one enormous room filled with stripping machines and workers. Jamin took no note of the man by the fountain, but entered the foreman's office, shut the door and closed the blinds.

Jamin unrolled his papers on the metal desk. Along with the desk there were two chairs, a private water cooler and a small bookcase sparsely filled with Reader's Digest volumes and European girlie magazines. With the blinds closed, the only light in the room came from a small bulb on the ceiling. Jamin swept his hand above the desk. "Here it is," he announced. "My plan."

Olivia moved over and stared down at the papers. From the pocket of her skirt she pulled out her horn-rimmed glasses.

"Three parts," he went on. "A cost analysis, plant expansion design, and auxiliary road development plan." He lifted the large roll of paper and spread it on top. It was an architectural drawing of the Flatbush Veneer Company extended to approximately twice its size. Next to it he lay a plan for a road system which would lead to the factory from the four major villages in the hills. And finally he presented a proposal by which Flatbush Veneer would double its exports in three year's time with a payout to the workers from the profits and an increase in local ownership of the factory. He began explaining each document. He spoke in a matter-of-fact, almost pedantic tone answering questions before Olivia could ask them.

To the best of her remembrance this plan was new among Jamin's plans. He conceded he had worked it out late at night over the past month. Now he was convinced it held the key to the nation's future. In the two years Olivia had lived in the hills, she had heard and witnessed half a dozen of Jamin's development plans. The projects were always set out in careful detail at the start, meticulous constructs of the future which Jamin would then set into motion by gathering the laborers, setting up work schedules, time tables, due dates. But when reality impinged, as it always did, in the form of the weather or lack of funds or materials or skills, the projects would falter. Rather than face failure, it seemed to Olivia that Jamin would lose interest, never admitting that his singular will was not enough to transform the land. Only the reconstruction of the old railroad through the mountains, which Nyral supervised, had moved slowly but steadily towards completion. Jamin's large projects dwindled out or were abandoned. So it had been with the water project to irrigate the lands near the Izo River. So it had been with the bread factory in the eastern settlement.

As he came to the end of his explanation of this plan, Jamin sat down in the chair at the desk. "So you see, this is where we shall be in a year's time. Should you stay, you may witness this project."

He looked up at Olivia. The tension had eased in his face. He smiled the slightly superior smile she knew well. The proposition that she should stay, however, took her by surprise. She was going that afternoon, driving over the border and catching a flight the following morning to London. She had made her plans to leave a month ago. Until today he had never once suggested that she do otherwise. She had gathered all she needed for her book; she had enough grant money to get home and to support herself for a few months while she looked for a job. She needed, she longed for a personal life which she had not found here.

"And of course this is just the beginning of what we are to accomplish," he added. "There will be another factory in the second year. I will arrange this with the Americans when they visit."

She didn't ask which Americans. She supposed it was the investors who had started the factory a decade ago, investors she had never met but who, rumor had it, were sponsored by the CIA. Why the CIA had spent American tax dollars in these hills was still a matter of speculation. But at this point she didn't care. Her bags were packed. She had given away her things, said her goodbyes. She had been away from home almost four years. Ever since she had made her decision to return, she had felt herself filling with a long-denied nostalgia. This meeting with Jamin was to say goodbye.

But Jamin was pacing now in the small, hot office slapping a wooden letter opener on his palm. "I am arranging all this, you see. I hadn't told you before because I wanted to make certain of our plans, but I believe . . . I am told the Americans will come at the end of this month. You will of course meet them, and you may sit in on our negotiations."

Jamin was talking rapidly. His face beaded with sweat. There was no ventilation in the room with the door and windows closed. The room was so small that after Jamin had taken only two strides, he was at its border and had to turn and step the other way. Olivia didn't move lest she interfere with his path. She felt warm herself, felt her underarms growing damp on her white sleeveless blouse. She picked up the architectural plan for an expanded corrugated steel factory, all neatly drawn in blue and red pencil. "Who drew this?" she asked.

Jamin smiled, a boyish smile. "You didn't know I studied architecture too, did you, Olivia Turner?" He was flirting with her now. She recognized this appeal to her as a woman, recognized his confidence as a man.

126

She picked up the economic projections, also carefully worked out and typed on Jamin's dim-ribboned typewriter. "And these?"

"They are rough but accurate, I believe."

As she studied the projections, a small clock on the desk chimed. There was a knock at the door. Jamin turned. His expression grew suddenly angry as if the knock had reminded him of where he was. "We are busy!" he snapped. "Can't you see?" He turned back to Olivia. The footsteps fell away.

"I am impressed," she conceded.

"So you will stay. You can watch us build."

"Jamin . . ." She paused. "I can't stay." She didn't understand why he was asking her. Why now? She would listen to his plans, suspend disbelief, grant him all possibilities. But she was going home.

He stared at her across the desk. She stood with her slightly fat arms folded around her waist, her armpits sweating now, her glasses low on her nose. She was not attractive, and in her eyes he saw her sympathy, even sorrow for him. This both touched him and made him want to strike out. He flung the letter opener at the desk, its point thrust downward cutting into the wood. "So go then like all the rest," he said, gathering his papers.

"Jamin, I've been here *two years*," she protested.

"Yes," he said dryly. "Two years."

Only as she read back through the notes of that meeting did she understand the panic her going must have stirred in him, for she was his contact to the world outside the hills, his only chance for his action to have an echo in that larger world. The master plan he had worked out, pinning the future of his unrealized nation to the Flatbush Veneer Company, had within it the fusion of fantasy and reality she had witnessed so many times in Africa. She felt suddenly pained to think of it overtaking one as talented, yet isolated as Jamin. Perhaps Jamin had also felt the pull of himself and his people over that arc of history, and the plan, all the plans, were his attempt to keep some control of his destiny.

Whatever he felt, she had left him to his corner of the earth with his fate tied to Flatbush Veneer. She had forgotten even to ask him about the factory and his plan when she saw him last week. For all she knew, he had accomplished his goal though it did not much matter now for she had just read in the third to the last paragraph of today's *New York Times* that a veneer factory in the North had been blown up by government forces, and several hundred workers, reportedly sympathetic to the NLA, had been killed. As Olivia read the *Times* story, she felt again her ambivalence towards Jamin, but she also had a clue of where she might find him. It was a long shot, but one she could pursue, and so she continued searching through her notebooks this Friday evening, for tomorrow she would return to New York.

Chapter 15

The phone rang early Saturday morning. Jenny grabbed for it out of instinct, afraid the ringing would rouse Erika.

"Hello, Jen, is that you? I'm sorry, am I waking you? Is Mark there?"

"Who is it?" Mark asked as Jenny handed him the phone, then rolled over and put a pillow on her head. Mark took the receiver. He listened for a moment. "Yes," he said finally. "I see. All right . . . I understand." He hung up.

He moved to Jenny and put his arm around her. "Good morning," he said softly. She didn't answer. He stroked her shoulder then kissed her on the cheek. "You think the phone woke Erika?" She didn't respond. She held her body motionless and pretended to be sleeping. He lay next to her for a while longer, but finally when he got no encouragement, he rolled away.

A moment later he slipped out of bed, and she heard the blast of the shower. She continued to lay there with the pillow over her head. Why was Kay calling him again . . . at seven in the morning? Why hadn't he told her what Kay wanted? He shouldn't make her ask. She heard him come back into the room;

she could feel him looking at her, gauging if she were asleep. She didn't move. She heard him quietly open the drawers to his dresser, saw him out of the corner of her eye as he started to dress. She noted his underwear discarded on the floor in a pile which she would have to pick up, and this thoughtlessness suddenly exploded something in her. She leapt out of bed, snatched the underwear off the floor and marched into the bathroom.

"I was just about to pick it up," he called after her as she shut the bathroom door. She threw the underwear in the hamper then sat on the toilet. She heard Mark dressing. She took her time washing her face and brushing her teeth. When she finally emerged, she found the bed made, the clothes all hung and Mark gone from the room. The sight of the neat room did not appease her, however; it suggested instead Mark's guilt, though over what she wasn't sure. Over their dinner last night with DeVries, over Kay. Of what did she think he was guilty?

She sat down and began brushing her hair at the dressing table, a French provincial table with a three-paneled mirror, a hand-me-down from Helene. The whole room was furnished with pieces Helene and Irwin had cast off about the time she and Mark had married eight years ago: a fourposter bed, a blue velvet chaise. The room looked like the boudoir of some aging French nobility. She'd been uncomfortable with the furniture at first, but now that she and Mark could afford to buy what they wanted, she felt no inclination to go furniture shopping.

She finished brushing her hair. On Saturday mornings Mark took Erika out so the apartment would be quiet for her to write. Usually she went straight to work, slipped on jeans, a sweatshirt, but this morning she paused to dress. She touched a shiny peach color to her cheeks and lips, went over to the closet and put on blue corduroy slacks, a blue and yellow sweater. By the time she went in to see her daughter and husband, her anger had dissipated.

"What do you two have up for this morning?" she asked.

"Mommy!" Erika ran up and gave her a hug. Mark looked over at her from the dresser where he was taking out Erika's clothes. His glance took in and approved of her appearance. "We're going to a Plaza and the zoo," Erika announced.

"The Plaza?" Jenny asked. "That's rather fancy."

Mark pulled out Erika's corduroy velvet jumper and a blouse and slipped it over her head. "That's why I have to wear a dress," Erika mumbled from inside her clothes.

Jenny watched Mark to see if she had missed anything. Mark was concentrating a little too hard on buttoning Erika's dress, she thought. She waited to see if he would offer an explanation, but he sat Erika on his lap and began pulling on her tights and buckling her shoes.

"I'm sorry I'll miss the outing," she tested.

Mark glanced up. She saw the distance in his look. "We're having breakfast with Kay," he said matter-of-factly. "She's staying at the Plaza."

"Oh?" Jenny heard her voice as if it were separate from her. "With Erika?"

"Of course with Erika," he rejoined as though she were implying he would leave Erika behind.

Jenny didn't say anything. She began making Erika's bed. She swept her hand across the sheets, pulled up the bedspread, folded it over the pillow. "Was that why she called you this morning?"

"She has some questions she thinks I can help her with."

"She couldn't ask them over the phone?"

Mark stood Erika up. "It's personal, she said." He went to the closet to get Erika's sweater and coat.

"What kind of questions?"

"I don't know, Jenny."

Jenny hesitated. She didn't want to expose herself, but in a minute they would be gone. She started putting blocks in a bucket. "Well, before Erika goes, she has to pick up her toys," she declared.

"You can do it, Mommy."

"I'm not your servant," Jenny said in a voice harsher than she intended. Mark got on his knees and began gathering the red and yellow blocks. "Erika should do it," Jenny said.

"If it wasn't important, I wouldn't go," he answered quietly. His eyes met hers, searched hers, then looked sad as though she were failing him. He stood. From the floor he picked up two stuffed bears and a dog and tossed them on Erika's bed.

Jenny held out her arms to her daughter, buttoned her coat then hugged her. She felt Mark still looking at her, but she didn't return his gaze now nor did she answer when he told her to write well. She was still on her knees in Erika's room when the front door clicked shut.

"Damn," she said out loud. Why did Mark make her feel guilty when he was the one going to have breakfast with Kay? She hadn't even said anything. She hadn't pressed why. Yet he knew she was jealous, and he was disappointed with her for being jealous; and even more annoying, she felt ashamed herself. It wasn't only Kay; his whole world seemed to her to be pushing between them right now, trying to dislodge her from him and take him away.

She rose and went into her study. She began putting away the bills she had tossed on her desk. The injustice of her position stirred her as she stuffed the heating bill, the electric bill, the phone bill back in their envelopes. At the Master Charge bill her glance snagged on one of the charges. Her eyes stopped on a store she had never heard of before: Chez Couche Lingerie. She didn't remember buying lingerie. The charge was dated Dec. 15. Had she bought anyone lingerie for Christmas? Had Mark given her lingerie? No, he'd never given her lingerie. Why then did she think he might buy it for someone else? The thought caught her off guard. Was that really what she was thinking? No. Rather the thought hovered like the possibility of something she might think if she chose to.

She pulled the phone book from under her desk and began looking up the store in hopes she might remind herself where it was and when she had visited it. But Chez Couche Lingerie wasn't listed. She called information and asked for further listings in Manhattan, then in Brooklyn, in Queens. Finally in the Bronx on a street she had never heard of, there was a Chez Couche Lingerie. She hadn't been in the Bronx in a year. What would Mark be doing in the Bronx? An image of him and Kay hiding away in some remote room flashed into her mind. She didn't choose the thought; she didn't even want to be thinking it, but there it was. She dialed the phone number of the store, but there was no answer. She glanced at the clock on her ledge: 8:52.

She pushed up from her desk and went into the living room where she paced in front of the bay window, then into the kitchen where she put on water for coffee. She dropped an English muffin into the toaster and picked up the paper, glanced at Guy Rhodes' account of further evidence of a massacre, of the debate set for the Security Council. She paced back to the living room and sat on the piano stool. The apartment was quiet, too quiet. On the keyboard she sounded an F-sharp which rang a dissonant tone into the silent, sun-filled room. She got up and returned to the kitchen where she made her coffee. She left the English muffin in the toaster.

In her room she dialed Olivia. She needed to talk. She wanted to hear Olivia's account of the NLA; she wanted to lose hereslf in Olivia's point of view. But Olivia's line was busy. She stared out the window at a naked elm tree. Downstairs the Rousseaus were arguing. "Shut up," she said out loud. She glanced again at the clock: 9:21. She dialed Chez Couche, and someone answered.

Calmly she explained her problem: their shop had appeared on her bill; she didn't know the store; she wondered if they had any way of tracing who had made the purchase on Dec. 15 for $85. The woman asked where Jenny lived; she told her.

"Ah then . . . you must have purchased from our store at 88th St. Chez Boudoir. We are the main store so the billing is done through us."

Jenny fell silent. Almost immediately she remembered she had gone into a new boutique on 88th St. She had bought Helene a bed jacket for the holidays. Chez Boudoir. Yes. She thanked the woman and hung up. She might have felt ashamed of her suspicions had she not felt so relieved. She had not really believed that Mark would betray her, she insisted. It was only the possibility, her own fear fixating her so that she had lost sight momentarily of what she knew.

Suddenly hungry, she wanted to go somewhere. She began packing her folders into her briefcase. She flipped on the answering machine. Then without considering exactly where she was going, or rather without admitting where she was going, she hurried outside and flagged a cab. She told it to take her to 59th Street and Sixth Ave. The Plaza was on 59th and Fifth. She wasn't going to the Plaza, however. She wouldn't spy on Mark. He had told her the meeting with Kay was important or he wouldn't have gone. She believed him. But she was no fool, and Mark could sometimes be naive. She simply wanted to be in the same neighborhood with her husband and child as if some animal sense would alert her should danger stir.

Jenny turned into the Park Lane Hotel, an elegant, European-styled hotel with an enormous second-floor dining room which looked out on the park. She had come here before to write. The dining room was rarely filled so she could sit for hours and work as long as she could pay the inflated price of a meal. She unpacked her papers at a table by the window. Outside, snow capped the bushes and trees in the park. The sky was clear blue; the streets, dry. From her table she could just glimpse the path to the zoo, but she turned away. She had not come to watch for Mark. She ordered coffee and orange juice, opened her folder, pulled the pencil from behind her ear and started to work.

She was reading Chapter 14 today: The Colonial Syndrome: Woman as Second Class Citizen? As she read, she jotted notes to herself. She bent over the papers, her head between her hands, her thumbs blocking her ears; her fingers forming a shade over her eyes so that all she saw was the manuscript before her; all she heard were its words in her ears. She didn't see the other patrons in the dining room, nor did she notice the two new arrivals who had sat down near her and were watching her work.

When she finally finished the chapter, she paused. It was better than she remembered. She took a sip of orange juice.

"Tell me, Benjamin, what do you say about a young woman who works that hard and on a Saturday?" Irwin Rosen asked.

"Anyone who works that hard I'd like working for me," Benjamin DeVries answered. Jenny glanced up. The expression on her face made her father-in-law laugh.

"How long have you been there?" she asked.

"Long enough to report to Mark that your powers of concentration are awesome," Irwin answered. Irwin Rosen at 71 resembled an aging college athlete, his grey hair thinning but still generous and his shoulders broad, if slightly stooped. He was not a large man; Helene in stockinged feet stood even with him, but he radiated energy. Until he had retired five years ago, he had been an executive vice president at one of Wall Street's middle-sized investment banks.

Jenny wondered what Irwin was doing with Benjamin DeVries. Mark had never mentioned that they knew each other.

"Benjamin tells me he met you at dinner last night," Irwin said, "and that you gave him a hard time."

Jenny glanced at the small, white-haired man, dressed as he had been the night before in a black suit and bow tie. "I wasn't aware that I gave you a hard time," she said.

"I told him that was my daughter-in-law."

DeVries nodded to Jenny. "I said only that you seemed to me a woman of definite opinions." His tone was cool. With a delicate sawing motion, he was cutting his steak.

Jenny wondered how he could eat anything after last night. "I wouldn't say that . . . " Jenny demurred.

"Of course you are," Irwin declared a little too robustly. "And we agreed Mark's got his hands full." What he meant as a compliment, however, stung. Jenny glanced down at her papers.

"Are we bothering you?" DeVries asked. "Or would you like to join us?"

Jenny heard his reserve; she didn't want the disadvantage of his dislike. "Perhaps for a moment," she answered. She took her coffee and orange juice to their table.

"Benjamin tells me you have reservations on the proposal he made Mark," Irwin opened.

Jenny glanced from Irwin to DeVries. Was it possible that Mark had spoken to his father and not to her? She wished she knew the relationship between the men and how much Irwin knew of the proposal. "I would like to know more," she said simply. "Mark and I haven't had a chance to talk."

"It's quite straight forward," DeVries declared. "I need a partner, and I am impressed with your husband." He ate a mouthful of steak, holding the fork poised between his left fingers and thumb, European style. He spoke with a more pronounced French accent than Jenny remembered from last night, and it added authority and condescension to his words.

"I'm afraid I don't understand why you're willing to bring Mark in as an equal partner." Jenny sipped her coffee. She tried to keep her tone friendly though in fact she was questioning DeVries' motives.

"I have explained that," he answered with a slight impatience.

"It seems to me you are selling the partnership cheap."

DeVries made a movement with his mouth that resembled a smile, exposing an even row of stained teeth. "Well, when you are my age, my dear, money is no longer everything."

The patronizing tone and the implication that money to her was everything stirred Jenny, but she didn't answer.

"It's a damn generous offer," Irwin interposed. "Damn, wouldn't I have loved an offer like that when I was Mark's age and from a man like Benjamin DeVries."

Irwin's deference to DeVries cast him in a light Jenny hadn't seen before. "How do you two know each other?" she asked.

"We have done some business in the past," DeVries answered. "Only I wasn't aware that Irwin Rosen of Davis and Wilkes was Mark's father until . . . well, until a colleague did some research and informed me of the connection."

"You've investigated us then?" Jenny asked.

DeVries' mouth again agitated in a smile. "We are talking of a good deal of money, Mrs. Rosen. I investigate everyone I am associated with."

The edge in his voice let Jenny know she was pressing the limits of his geniality.

"As always Mark's been tight-lipped," Irwin declared. "He hadn't told me a thing. Benjamin called me late last night to see if we could talk. I had no idea."

"I have been telling Irwin that should a partnership occur, we would become a considerably larger organization and would need someone with his breadth of knowledge to bridge the two firms." DeVries began sopping up the blood on his plate with a piece of bread.

Irwin cast a sideways glance at Jenny as if to gauge from her what his son might say. But Jenny frowned. Without consulting Mark, without considering the complications of feelings between father and son, DeVries was proposing a bond which would require at the very least a revision of family history.

"I told Benjamin, of course, I would have to speak with Mark," Irwin interjected. "It is after all Mark's company."

"I am hoping you will help persuade him in my favor," De Vries said. "And Mrs. Rosen," he turned back to Jenny, "I hope you will see how important this step can be for your husband's career.

Mark and I would be missing a major opportunity if we continued separately. Tax advantages this year alone justify the merger."

The tax advantages, Jenny suspected, were DeVries' losses on the mining operation set against Mark's gains, but she said only, "I'm afraid that it's Mark you must convince, not Irwin and myself."

DeVries smiled appreciatively at this pose. "I happen to know decisions are not so simple," he said. "I've been told by more than one source that you are the backbone of Mark's future."

"I assure you, Mark's backbone is intact without me," Jenny answered.

Irwin laughed. "You see what I mean."

Jenny glanced at her father-in-law and for the first time she saw his insecurity. She saw too that for Benjamin DeVries he was only a second-string player who might be useful. She wondered at Irwin for letting this man manipulate him by holding out a job as enticement to persuade his son. She felt suddenly uncomfortable. "I'm afraid I have to get back to work now," she said, standing.

The two men stood with her. She glanced one last time at Irwin. From the ardent light in his eyes, she knew he had already been convinced, but she saw too that it was not the job which had convinced him but the prestige of having his son in partnership with a legend. The eyes of Benjamin DeVries she still could not penetrate.

When Irwin Rosen and Benjamin DeVries left the restaurant, the latter stopped to speak a few words to the maitre d'. The maitre d' had treated Jenny with condescension when she'd come in, but now he came to her table and poured her coffee himself.

She was sipping the coffee and glancing out the window at the park when suddenly she saw Mark. She was certain it was Mark this time because next to him in her pink and blue parka, with her navy tights dangling, was Erika. They were sitting in a carriage across the street. The black chassis was decked with flowers and sported lanterns on either side. A dapple grey mare was hitched to its front. On the other seat, with a boy of eleven or twelve, Kay sat wrapped in a white fox coat. She was laughing; Mark was smiling, and Erika was telling something to the boy, who listened attentively.

As Jenny absorbed the scene, she sucked in air as if her brain and heart all at once needed an infusion. She'd known Mark was with Kay, but actually seeing them . . . and in a carriage . . . what were they doing in a carriage? She and Mark had planned to take Erika on her first carriage ride together. Jenny didn't know who the boy was; she didn't care. She saw only a picture she was left out of: a happy couple, her happy husband and child with another woman. And the other woman was glamorous, a woman who would not be condescended to by a maitre d', a woman who was what she was not, what she chose not to be, yet what she feared her husband wanted. A flood of self-righteousness suddenly rushed over her, and she felt paralyzed by the sheer pressure of her own emotions. She stared out the window as if she had no power over what she saw.

What she saw next was Irwin Rosen and Benjamin DeVries crossing the street. She watched as one watches two trains moving towards each other. She watched Mark give a start when his father and Benjamin DeVries approached. He half stood, then sat, then stood again, relieved of his uncertainty only by Erika, who reached out her arms to her grandfather. Irwin hoisted Erika out of the carriage with a hug. He introduced her to DeVries, who looked pleased by the little girl. Erika was the only one oblivious to the awkwardness of the situation. Everyone focused their attention on her.

Finally Mark gestured to Kay, who stretched out her hand. DeVries exchanged several words with her; then Irwin spoke to Mark, and Mark turned and looked towards the hotel. Irwin replaced Erika in the carriage, and the two men moved on.

Jenny waited for Mark to climb down from the carriage now and come over to her in the dining room. But he didn't come. Mark had been caught off guard seeing his father with Benjamin DeVries, and he had manned his defenses instead. He looked like a guilty school boy, though his guilt rose not from being with another woman but from the fact that he was making a major business decision independent of his father; and now here was his father obviously knowing of it, perhaps even instigating it.

When Irwin announced that Jenny was across the street, Irwin's disapproving tone only roused Mark to prove he was doing nothing wrong. Mark signaled to the driver now that they were ready. The driver, dressed in a gold braided coat, mounted his seat; the horse stretched out his neck, and the carriage and four passengers trotted off into the park.

Only then did Jenny rally. She didn't know what to do, but she knew she had to do something. When she signaled for her bill, the maitre d' informed her that Mr. DeVries had already taken care of it. This gratuity annoyed her, but she let it pass. Quickly gathering her folders, her briefcase, her jacket, she hurried from the red and gold velvet room to the street outside.

The cold air braced her. She stood for a moment staring into the sun at the park entrance where the carriage had disappeared. She thought of climbing into a taxi and following it, but the carriage could trot along jogging paths and bike lanes into the heart of Central Park where cars were banned. She darted across the street holding up her hand to the traffic which blared horns as she crossed.

On the other side a lone carriage with a faded yellow ribbon woven through its meshings stood empty. A stocky horse was feeding from a pouch tied round its neck. Against the monument a few steps away, the driver, wearing baggy pants and a wool great coat decorated with medals, stared disinterestedly at the horse.

"A quiet drive through the park, m'am?" he queried as Jenny stepped over to the carriage.

"I have to catch someone," she declared, climbing into the chassis. The seat was torn, and the driver tossed a coarse blanket over it, then handed her another blanket for her knees.

Slowly he began disengaging the horse's feed bucket. "I'm in a hurry," she pressed.

"A hurry, is it?" He continued the disengagement with no particular change in speed. "Well, you got the right horse and driver: Ranklin and Jones." He folded the feed pouch and stored it under his seat. With effort he mounted his platform; then he turned round, and winking, he asked, "Which way?"

No sooner had Jenny pointed than the horse pulled forward jolting her against the seat. Jones called back to her as they turned into the park on Sixth Ave., "What'd you say the carriage looked like we're chasing?" Jenny described the carriage and driver. "Ah, that's Murphy's coach. I know his route." And he took an abrupt right.

Jenny peered around the carriage to see if she could spot Murphy and his passengers, but all she saw were a few hardy bikers and joggers in the quiet snow-capped expanse of Central Park. The driver tapped the horse again; the coach began to pitch from side to side so that Jenny had trouble sitting still. She felt as if she were riding on top of the wheel which might fly off at any moment. "Is this safe?" she called.

"What's that?"

"I said, is it safe to be going this fast? We don't have to go so fast."

"Well, that depends on who you're after I guess." Jones turned around, his face flushed, enlivened by the chase. Jenny too was feeling invigorated by the cold and the speed and by the fact that she was doing *something*. She hadn't focused on what she would do when she caught up with Mark, how she would explain chasing him through the park. She wondered if he would be angry. She didn't care. She would explain nothing. She'd simply say hello, tell him she was finished with her work and would take Erika home. He could spend the rest of the afternoon with Kay if he wanted, unencumbered, but she wanted to be with Erika. She would not act angry or jealous. On no account would she show weakness. "I'll just take Erika off your hands," she'd say. "Hi, Kay." And smiling she would trot off with her daughter. But her point would be made. And the point was that she was there. That she could act. That she would not yield so easily nor flee from what she feared, but would fight. Yet as the wind flew through her hair, and she pushed the strands from her eyes, she wondered exactly what it was she was fighting.

All at once Jones cried out, "There they are!" Far up ahead, around the corner was Murphy's carriage. "Hold on!" And the horse pulled away.

When Jenny saw the carriage, she felt a rush inside. She opened her purse, pulled out lipstick and a brush, but then abruptly she stopped. What was she doing? She was missing the point. Why did Kay make her feel so inadequate? Was that the point? When had she lost her confidence? She didn't know what the point was right now. She felt only hurt, and for the first time, she feared the hold this hurt had on her.

She brushed her hair quickly and put on lipstick. She again practiced what she would say. "I just came to take Erika . . . Hi, Kay." She would be friendly. Yes, she would simply smile and take Erika. Yet nonviolent as her stand might be, she would take a stand. If only the panic inside her would subside.

As they closed the distance on the coach ahead, Murphy spotted them in his mirror. Suddenly he cracked his whip. "Son of a Tory!" Jones exclaimed. "He's going to give us a chase." He snapped his own whip, and the stocky brown horse lunged forward.

There were few people in this section of the park so the coaches had an open road for their run. Jenny's driver was grinning and talking to himself. "Goddamn Tory red-coat putting on airs, are you? We'll see whose nag can run." And the horse broke into a canter. The carriage rushed into the wind. The trees flew by. Suddenly Jenny wondered if the horse had taken over. His hooves crashed against the concrete; the coach rocked precariously from side to side. "It's too fast," Jenny called. "We're going too fast!" But the driver didn't hear.

Jenny held to the side of the carriage. She worried suddenly for the safety of the child she was carrying. She saw the coach in front of them fly round the corner at 86th St. In that coach were her daughter and husband, and they were definitely going too fast. "No!" she shouted above the wind. "No, it's too fast."

Jones glanced back at her, his sunburned face inquiring. "Never had an accident yet," he assured.

But Jenny felt a deepening panic. She had not liked the way Murphy's carriage had taken the last corner. "No! They're going too fast. Please . . . I'm sorry . . . Stop!"

Jones shrugged and reined in his horse with effort. The wind at once died down. "We won't catch them now, you know," he said disappointed. Jenny didn't answer. The chase had lasted less than a minute, but in that burst of speed at the edge of control, she had felt what chaos lay on the other side. As the familiar world returned to her, she looked disturbed. What was propelling her to that edge? She wondered how long it would take Murphy to see they were no longer in pursuit and to slow down.

"Well, we had some fun, didn't we?" offered Jones.

But Jenny was peering ahead, anxious for her carriage to turn the corner so that she might catch sight of the other coach and see that all was well. The horse trotted along slowly breathing great puffs of air. The click of his hoofs, the rattle of the coach wheels, the vague hum of traffic outside the park were all Jenny could hear. But as they approached the corner, she heard, or thought she heard, a dissonant sound, a stirring ahead. The carriage took the turn at a gentle trot.

Down the road a short ways off, a crowd had gathered. Jones stood up on his perch to see what had happened. "Jesus Christ!" he exclaimed after a minute. "Murphy's pitched over." He picked up speed.

Jenny saw the crowd. As they drew nearer, she saw toppled to the ground Murphy's carriage. And then she saw the car. A silver-grey Mercedes. It had not heeded the signs and the barricades banning automobiles from this part of the park but had thought to take a short cut. It had not been going fast, but fast enough so that the driver was unable to brake in time to miss the speeding carriage which had turned into his lane. The driver and the Mercedes were pulled up at the side of the road unharmed, but the horse and carriage were smashed. The dapple grey mare lay in the snow exhaling draughts of steam into the air, his legs splayed out at unnatural angles. In red and gold livery Murphy stood above the horse half-stunned, calling out, "Does anybody have a gun? Doesn't anybody have a gun?"

Jenny jumped from her carriage before it even stopped, and she hit the ground running. She was heading towards the coach searching the crowd for Mark and Erika when she turned suddenly as if a voice had spoken inside. There under a tree she spied the tiny, hooded figure of her daughter. Erika was standing near the crowd, her dark eyes opened wide, her bottom lip quivering. When she saw her mother hurrying towards her, she broke down into the tears she had been holding back. "Mommy! Mommy! Mommy!"

Jenny swept her up in her arms and hugged her. She buried Erika's head in her own. Then she looked at her, checked to make certain she wasn't hurt. "What happened? Oh, thank God. Where's Daddy?" She hugged her daughter again. Erika was sobbing too hard to answer questions. "It's okay," Jenny assured. "It's okay." She began moving into the crowd looking for Mark. The crowd seemed to have grown out of nowhere. The road had been almost deserted when she was riding in the carriage, but now joggers in sweatsuits, bikers, passersby from Fifth Ave., elderly men and women who had come to the park to sit in the sun, all stood around staring, slightly excited by the fact that something had happened. A police car moved slowly towards the gathering.

Jenny looked but could not find Mark. "Where's Daddy?" she insisted. Her tone startled Erika. For a moment she stopped crying.

"I don't know." Her small lip quivered as if she were at fault for not knowing.

"It's okay. It's okay." Erika's expression touched a chord so deep within Jenny, that her own eyes glassed over. She held her daughter tightly, remembering herself the feeling of inadequacy to explain the adult world and the assumption of blame for what she could not account for, including the disappearance of her own father. "It's all right. Mommy will find him."

"He told me to stand by the tree and not to look," Erika said.

"What? He told you that? You mean he's okay? All right. We're going to be all right." Hugging Erika to her, Jenny moved with new vigor into the crowd.

When she finally broke through the front line of spectators, she didn't comprehend what she saw. There sitting in the snow, her white fox coat stained with blood, her hair wild about her face, was Kay. In her lap she held a boy who looked unconscious, the boy Jenny had seen in the carriage but paid no attention to.

His face was buried in her skirt and on Kay's face was a look of surprise. Kneeling beside her was Mark. On the other side a policeman was trying to persuade her of something she didn't want to do for she kept shaking her head as she held tightly to the boy.

Jenny hurried towards them. Her relief at seeing Mark and holding Erika was jarred by the look on Kay's face. She dropped to her knees. She reached out to Mark.

143

"Jenny," Mark said as though stating a fact. Jenny looked over at Kay. Though she didn't know what had happened, she reached out and touched her hand. Kay stared up blankly.

"Take Erika away," Mark said. "Take her home."

"Can I help?" Jenny asked. "Who . . . " she stared at the boy.

"Please," he declared. "Just take her home. I'll come home as soon as I can."

In the distance a siren broke the cold still air. The whine grew louder and louder as it neared. Suddenly a shot rang out. The crowd gasped. Erika clutched her mother. Her dark eyes looked to Jenny for an explanation, but Jenny drew her up, enfolded her in her arms. "Yes," she said. "Yes, I'll take Erika home." She touched Mark's hand again and kissed him. He hadn't looked surprised to see her; rather he'd looked impatient as if he had expected her, and she was late. She wanted to ask him why he had left Erika alone, afraid under a tree, to ask him who this boy was. But right now she had to get Erika away.

"Call me," she said to Mark. He nodded. With one last look at Kay, Jenny hurried Erika to her waiting coach.

Erika balked at getting in, but Jenny insisted that they go in a carriage. She told the driver to take them very slowly home. She held Erika to her and spoke softly and told her a story about a magical giraffe who lived in the jungle. The horse clomped at a walk through the park across to 86th Street.

When they got into their apartment, Jenny suggested, "Let's make tea. You go get grandma's tea bags, and I'll put on the water."

Erika's eyes brightened at the suggestion. She hurried to her room for her evening purse. When she returned, she began telling Jenny how grandma had told her you had to make sure to let the tea "sleep" for five minutes so it would taste right. She said the word "sleep" with authority as though this much of the adult world she had comprehended.

Jenny made the tea, and she and Erika made cookies. They took the tea and cookies into Erika's red and white room. There they had a tea party, and for Erika at least the world began to reassemble itself.

Chapter 16

Jenny spent the afternoon coloring with Erika, making paperdolls, reading books, trying to set Erika's world aright all the while holding off the collapse she felt in her own. She fed Erika dinner in the late afternoon darkness in the kitchen while they watched a children's movie on television. She didn't know the name of the film, but she blessed the TV for the distraction.

She then went to bathe Erika, but without thinking she poured the bubbles into the tub rather than letting Erika, and her child dissolved into tears. "I wanted to do it."

"Here, you pour the rest."

"No! I wanted to do the whole thing." Without transition or reason Erika threw herself naked on the cold tiles.

"Get up," Jenny said quietly. "You can pour the rest."

"No! It's too late! It's ruined!" And Erika, who had taken no nap and was exhausted, pitched over an edge and would not let her mother put her right. "You stupid mother!" she cried.

"Erika, get up!" Jenny lifted her from the floor and put her into the tub, but this exertion of will sent her daughter into a rage from which Jenny could not recover her. Though she knew Erika was tired, though she knew the trauma of the day, this fit touched her own irrational stirrings. Where was Mark? Why hadn't he called? They needed him right now. She felt she had little more reserve than her daughter. She lifted Erika from the tub and marched her into her room. "You will go to bed now," she declared. "And I don't want to ever hear you talk to me that way again. Ever! They're only bubbles. Goddamn bubbles!

"Stupid mom! Stupid mom!"

Erika was screaming, and she was shouting, and the whole ending of the day was the very opposite of what she had intended. She watched herself and her daughter in a rage at each other. She smacked the naked backside of Erika with her palm. Then she pulled a nightgown over her head and dropped her onto the bed. Her fury frightened her. Where was it coming from? "God, no," she exhaled. "No." Suddenly she drew Erika up into her arms. "No. No. It's all right. Mommy loves you. I'm sorry. It's all right." She began to sway with Erika back and forth on the bed, rocking her into quiet, rocking herself. "It's all right." Erika's cries faded into whimpers. She buried her head in her mother's bosom. "I love you. I love you," Jenny intoned. "I'm sorry." She began singing softly:

> *I went to the animal fair.*
> *The birds and the beasts were there.*
> *By the light of the moon*
> *The old baboon was combing his auburn hair.*
> *The monkey, he got drunk;*
> *He fell on the elephant's trunk.*
> *The elephant sneezed and fell to his knees,*
> *And that was the end of the monk, the monk, the monk.*

Erika fell asleep to this familiar refrain. As Jenny looked down on her child's face, quiet now, her lips in a soft line, she began to weep. Her tears fell in such a rush that they dropped onto Erika's clear olive skin and dark lashes. She wiped them away with her hand, but she couldn't stop weeping over this child in her arms, over the child in herself. She felt as if something were breaking up deep inside or was it breaking down? Finally she reached out and turned down the bed she had made precipitously that morning. She placed Erika on the clean flowered sheets and tucked the covers around her. She kneeled beside the bed. "God . . ." she implored out loud. Where was this anger coming from? She listened to her child's regular breathing, then finally she stood and turned out the lights. Let her sleep, she thought. Erika would wake in the morning with little or no memory of the rage of the night before. That was the way with children. But she would stir for hours.

Jenny went into her study and took out her folders. She had not finished her work for the day, yet as she brought out her pages, she couldn't work. Why hadn't Mark called? She picked up the phone and began to dial hospitals in the area. However, she didn't know the name of the patient. She described the boy and his attending adults, but without a name, no one could help her. She thought of calling the morgue, and this thought sent a chill through her. She stood up. She was standing, staring out the window when the phone rang. She grabbed for it, but Olivia, not Mark, greeted her.

"I'm at Penn Station," she explained. "Did you get my message?" Jenny looked over at the blinking red light on the answering machine. "Could I stay over?"

Jenny had been trying to reach Olivia for days, but now she didn't want to see her. She was strung too tight. She didn't want to tell Olivia what had happened. She was afraid Olivia would draw the obvious conclusion about Mark and Kay. Yet she told Olivia she could come. Then she went again to Erika's room where she stood in the doorway and stared at her sleeping child at peace with the world. Erika was tuned so finely to her sometimes that Erika felt what she felt without even knowing why. For Erika alone she must find and keep the peace.

As Olivia sped uptown on the subway, she half dreaded seeing Jenny. She had returned to New York reluctantly. For almost two weeks she had kept the world out, and she was afraid now lest she be drawn in and lose the momentum of her writing as suddenly as she had found it. She worried that Jenny's long pause on the phone, the tremor in her voice might threaten this momentum. Yet Olivia had a clue of where to find Jamin so she was taking the risk. Jamin, she was convinced, was the key to the questions she needed answered. She also wanted to go to the UN meeting to hear Bulagwi. Had she the money, she would have stayed at a hotel, but according to her last bank statement, there was only $825 between her and charity.

The two friends greeted each other with reserve. "I've tried to call you several times," Jenny said.

"I had the phone off the hook. I'm finally writing." Olivia offered this information matter-of-factly.

Jenny nodded. "Good." She took Olivia's canvas bag. She felt a passing anxiousness when she saw Olivia had also brought a portable typewriter. She wondered how long she planned to stay. She stationed the bags in the hall closet, then she and Olivia went into the kitchen. The room was warm from the stove where she had cooked dinner earlier in the evening in anticipation of Mark's coming home. On the stove still sat two plates of chicken and rice and broccoli.

"You want dinner?" Jenny set her own plate on the small table in the corner. It was 8:30. If Mark came home now, he could make his own dinner. She was tired of waiting.

"Where's Mark?"

Jenny shrugged. She set the other plate in front of Olivia. For a moment the two women ate in silence. Jenny stuffed bits of chicken into her mouth without pausing between bites in order to fight off the nausea she felt rising.

Olivia watched the quick, perfunctory movement of Jenny's knife and fork. She didn't want to get involved, but she was touched by Jenny's evident pain. Finally she asked, "Will Mark be home soon?"

Jenny put down her fork. She had been holding back tears, and now her eyes filled, and her throat closed.

"Jenny . . . ?"

Hearing the apprehension in Olivia's voice, Jenny hesitated, but she needed to talk; and so finally she began telling Olivia what had happened. She told her about Kay's calls, about Mark meeting her this morning, about seeing them in the park and panicking and chasing them, about the accident and her fear that she had set off events whose end she couldn't foresee and over which she had no power. She didn't tell her about Benjamin De Vries and his offering Mark a partnership; she didn't tell her about the overwhelming pull of the world she felt taking Mark away.

While she talked, Jenny stared at her food rather than at Olivia. The few times she did glance up for encouragement, Olivia's face looked pained, as though she were being asked more than she knew how to give. When Jenny finally finished with an apologetic shrug, Olivia was silent. "Can I have some coffee?" she asked.

Jenny stared at her. She had just poured out her heart, and Olivia wanted coffee. But Jenny got up and went to the stove.

As she made the coffee, Olivia strained for a vision to offer her friend. "I think you're watching the water rather than the glass," she said finally as Jenny set the cups on the table.

It was not the response Jenny expected. "What?"

"That's what my grandmother used to tell me. When I'd come in upset after somebody'd treated me bad . . . 'You watching the water again,' she'd say. 'Watch the glass, girl. Keep your eye on the glass, water take care of itself.'" Olivia looked up from her coffee and saw that Jenny was waiting for an interpretation.

"My grandmother used to give me a glass full of water and tell me to walk across the living room without spilling it. She used to make me walk back and forth, back and forth till I could do it. She told me to concentrate on the rim of the glass, keep it high and proud. The water would follow the rim. She used to carry water a hundred times a day at the restaurant where she worked. Got so good carrying water, after only nine years, they promoted her to waitress, first black waitress in Hudson Landing. God, she used to tell me that story over and over, even when I graduated from Barnard, she said if things got bad, at least I knew how to carry the water."

Jenny wasn't sure what the story had to do with her and Mark, but its effect was calming, and she smiled.

"Why did you marry Mark anyway?" Olivia asked.

"I loved him."

"And that's changed?"

"No."

"So why are you letting somebody come in and make you act as if it has?"

"You think what happened today was my fault?"

"I don't think fault has anything to do with anything. If you're right, Mark's a fool. But the fact is, he married *you*, not Kay." Jenny didn't answer. Olivia got up and brought the cookie jar to the table. "You know, my grandma also once marched into the local bar where my grandfather'd taken to hanging out rather than coming home, and she dumped his dinner in his lap in front of all his friends and girlfriends; then she marched out and locked him out of the house for a week." Jenny laughed.

"Grandma never had patience for a man didn't know who kept his bed warm."

"What do you think she'd have done today?" Jenny asked.

"Probably the same as you."

Jenny pushed her plate aside. She smiled, then her face again grew serious. "So where does that leave me?"

Olivia stared into her coffee. Finally she looked up, her brown eyes unsentimental. She answered quietly, "With a man who loves you."

Jenny didn't miss the poignancy of her words. She only wished they could restore the peace for her. But Mark still was not home, and she needed him. Lately she'd needed him more than usual, and he'd been distracted. She didn't know why she needed him so right now, maybe because she was about to have another child, or because she was coming to the end of four years of work on her book and was overcome by her own limitations. Or because she had been apart from the world too long and when the baby came, she would have to retreat from her work even further. Or because Kay had appeared. Or simply because the need existed within her and was now rising and asserting itself. Whatever the cause, Mark did not see it, and she could not abridge it, and she felt their balance faltering. The only person who did see the trouble was Kay. She discerned not from insight, Jenny thought, but from practiced self-interest; and she did not underestimate the potential of what she saw.

"Maybe you should ask why Mark married me," Jenny offered.

"Goddamn it!" Olivia declared. "You know that makes me mad."

"What?"

"That you even ask that question." She stood up. "What's happening to you?" She moved over to the coffee pot and refilled her cup. "Mark was smart enough to know the difference between you and Kay and make a choice. I've always given him credit for that."

Jenny didn't answer. Olivia drank the coffee, then moved into the hallway where she began hanging up her clothes. She wedged her dress and a pair of slacks between Jenny's and Mark's coats. "You have an iron?" she asked. From the closet Jenny pulled out an iron and an ironing board. Spreading her shirtwaist on the board, Olivia concentrated on smoothing the pleats, but she was agitated. Finally she turned. "Damn it, Jenny. You have a man who loves you, a child, a book, and you're . . . you're so . . . " she sought for the right word, "so blind or ungrateful, I don't know which."

"Why are you mad?" Jenny'd expected Olivia to comfort her, to be an ally.

Olivia didn't answer. She dropped the iron on the first pleat and instead pressed in the wrinkles. She had her own troubles. If Jenny wasn't happy, who could be? Jenny's questions had taken her back to her own doubts and betrayals. Why had Guy turned in an article he knew she was writing? But she couldn't allow the questions right now. She wanted simply to find Jamin, write her story and get her own life underway. "You have everything, Jenny," she said as her defense.

The two women stared at each other. They had been friends for over ten years; yet still there were barriers between them.

"I need, Olivia," Jenny rallied. "I don't know why right now. Mark won't see it. You won't . . . "

Olivia watched her; she struggled to see from her point of view. "You scared?" she asked.

Jenny moved over to the windows and closed the curtains to the dark. She nodded. "Look, I know in the scheme of the world, what I'm feeling isn't very high on the scale of suffering, but I thought . . . " She hesitated; then she waved her hand, abandoning the thought. She sat over on the couch. She said instead, "I tried to call you when I heard about Jamin. It makes one feel helpless, doesn't it?"

Olivia folded up the ironing board and hung up her dress. Jenny was yielding to her point of view. She felt both annoyed and relieved at her retreat.

"At least you're writing," Jenny went on. "At least it got you writing."

"Yes," Olivia said vaguely.

"I drew up some questions I may be able to help you with," Jenny added, pushing her own life further away from them. "But you'll have to tell me the specifics of what you need."

Olivia hesitated, wondering if she should bring Jenny back, but instead she answered, "I need to know who's financing both sides. Is Mark or Afco involved?"

Jenny reached over to the end table for a pad of paper. "I don't think so. You should ask him that. Kay's already asked."

Olivia frowned. "Doesn't it bother you that he might be? How do you allow that?"

"Allow?" Jenny roused. "Olivia, he's a grown man. I can't allow or not allow him, anymore than he can tell me what to do."

"But if he's financing Bulagwi's government!"

"He's not financing Bulagwi's government," Jenny defended. "He thinks he's offering some value. Look, he and I've argued around and around about Afco. It's not easy for me to talk with him about it anymore."

Olivia watched her, trying to understand her. She stepped down into the living room. Suddenly she stopped.

"What's wrong?" Jenny followed her eyes to the floor by the dining table. There, under a chair, lay the half-eaten body of the parakeet. "Oh no! Oh damn!" Jenny exclaimed. She leapt up. "Cassie! Cassie!" she shouted. "Goddamn it, Cassie!"

The cat, who had been curled in the blue velvet chair, suddenly bolted to the back of the apartment.

Olivia moved over, between Jenny and the bird. "Sit down. I'll clean it up," she said. "Sit down."

"Damn. Oh, why, Cassie? What am I going to tell Erika . . . ?"

Olivia was on her knees with a dustpan, and Jenny was on the couch staring at her when Mark opened the front door. Beside him, with hollow, startled eyes, stood Kay. "I've invited Kay to stay with us for a while," he announced.

Part Three

Part Three

Chapter 17

Mark supported Kay into the apartment, holding her under his arm and leading her to the couch where Jenny was sitting. When he tried to sit her down and move away, she grabbed for his hand. Her frosted hair flared about her pale face, and her large eyes glittered. Her mouth opened to him. "Please don't leave me, Mark." She took his hand into her lap over the blood stains on her coat and held it there. "You mustn't leave me." She appeared not even to notice Jenny or Olivia. She held to Mark's hand as if it were a lifeline she would not let go. That Mark was Jenny's husband and Jenny was watching her appeared as irrelevant to her as the cat watching from under the hall table.

"God . . ." she intoned, dropping her head onto Mark's shoulder. Mark awkwardly touched her hair with the flat of his hand, but he was clearly uncomfortable. He glanced at his wife, but she offered no expression. He glanced at Olivia, who was still kneeling on the floor. His own expression grew defensive.

Olivia rose with the dustpan and walked into the kitchen where she dumped the dead bird into an empty cereal box and stuffed it in the trash. When she returned, she addressed Mark, "Cassie killed your bird," she said. "Jenny's a little upset."

Mark looked again at his wife. "What happened?" His voice strained for sympathy.

"Someone left the door open, I guess. He got hungry." Her voice was flat. "Or maybe it's his nature." The answer was matter-of-fact, yet there was a plaintiveness in her tone which touched Mark.

He tried again to rise. "I'll make everyone a drink," he offered. "I don't want a drink," Jenny said.

Kay held to his hand. "Neither do I." Her eyes insisted. "It's only a bird, Mark," she declared. "A goddamn bird."

"It was Erika's bird," Jenny said.

Kay turned and for the first time acknowledged Jenny. Jenny was sitting in the corner of the couch with her knees tucked under her, her face washed and plain. Kay's face was drained of color except for the dark circles where her mascara had smeared; her eyes looked hollow, and her gaze was cold. "You are so *protected*," she said in a low voice. She didn't bother to hide her contempt. "So protected. My child may not walk again so you will forgive me if I don't cry over a bird."

Jenny picked up a pillow, and Kay saw that she had hit her mark. She continued, "Can you tell me why? Why should that happen?" Her voice dropped into an inquisitional tone. "It was you chasing us, wasn't it? You couldn't allow Mark and me a few hours together? Why can't you allow us to be friends?"

Jenny faltered but started to answer when she saw Mark watching her, his eyes asking the same question. She didn't answer.

"What child?" Olivia interjected. "You don't have a child, Kay."

"Oh?" Kay's voice arched. Then she laughed. "You always know everything, don't you, Olivia. Yes, I have a child, and he may be paralyzed." She sucked in air. "Goddamn! Goddamn you!" The words spit out barely audible, and it wasn't clear if they were addressed to Olivia or Jenny.

"Kay, it was an accident," Mark interceded. "Jenny didn't intend to hurt David." He looked carefully at his wife, trying to grant her the benefit of the doubt. "Were you chasing us?" he asked. But Jenny's gaze had hardened, and her body curled into a tight fist on the couch.

"How old is your child?" Olivia asked. That Kay had a child astounded her. That the child might be Mark's occurred to her. Mark answered that David was eleven. She exhaled, "Oh." Kay hadn't known Mark that long. She looked at Jenny expecting to see the same relief, but Jenny wasn't even listening. "Why didn't you ever tell anyone?" Olivia asked.

"It's nobody's business." Kay drew her coat around her. She took Mark's other hand. "I am very tired," she said. "I need to go to bed."

"Of course." Mark stood. "There's a trundle bed in Erika's room. You can sleep there."

"That will be fine."

"No!" Jenny roused. Mark and Kay looked over at her. "I'll sleep in Erika's room. Kay can have my bed . . . . You and Kay can sleep together for all I care, but I will sleep with Erika."

"Jenny," Mark protested. "What are you talking about?"

"I don't want Kay sleeping with Erika."

"Why?"

"It's all right, Mark," Kay answered. "What's wrong with you?" Mark stared at his wife as if she were suddenly a stranger.

"You really don't know, do you? Goddamn it, you don't even know." Jenny rose. Without answering, she went in to her daughter.

Mark stood for a moment in silence. Olivia and Kay avoided each other's eyes. Finally Mark said, "All right, you take our bed, Kay. I'll sleep in the study."

"Look, I can go somewhere else," Olivia offered.

"No." Mark turned. "Please . . . stay." Olivia heard the entreaty in his voice. "Please." She nodded.

As Kay followed Mark into the back bedroom, Olivia went over to the closet and took out the pillow and blanket and sheets. She didn't want to stay; she didn't want to be part of this confrontation, but she would stay for Jenny. She tucked the blue-striped sheets onto the couch; she unfolded the blanket. In the front bathroom she changed into her plaid robe. She had never seen Jenny so vulnerable before. She wanted to shake her. Jenny was the person she counted on for stability, Jenny who wrote every day, who didn't consider the possibility of writer's block or failing love affairs or faithless friends, who mothered her and everyone, perhaps, it occurred to Olivia for the first time, as her own defense against the world. Why was Jenny letting Kay unhinge her?

As a reporter, Jenny had had courage and imagination. In Africa when Jenny had visited after Bulagwi had taken total control, it was Jenny who urged that they too go into the hills. Untoro had been killed; Robert Nyral had fled to the North; Jamin Nyo had returned. Together she and Jenny had packed up her Landrover, and two hours before curfew one steamy November evening, they had headed towards the mountains, uncertain who or what they would find.

They took backroads and sometimes no roads, but finally they'd had to resign to the single-lane highway that ran to the foot of Mt. Ako. There in the flat grasslands they were exposed to whomever might see them. When the soldiers suddenly appeared over the rise at a roadblock with red lights flashing against the pitch-black of the African night, Jenny had nudged her awake. "They're here," she whispered, "looking for ghosts. We better convince them we're flesh and blood."

Jenny had understood the drama of this land. The government was indeed chasing ghosts, chasing the spectre of an enemy which was, Olivia had once written, the shadow of itself. And while Olivia had felt her own heart stop at the approach of the soldiers in the middle of the night, their teeth luminous in the glow of the headlights, cast a leer at two women alone on the road, Jenny had held out her press card and announced with authority, "We've been cleared through."

The guard took her card, studied it, then finally handed it back to her. "Pass!" he called out and waved them on.

As they left the roadblock behind, its red light a small monotonous blinking in the dust, Olivia exhaled. "Luck must be riding on our bumper."

"That and the 2000 chalas I gave him," Jenny said, her eyes fixed on the road as the car cut clean through the night, racing to its destination before dawn's exposure.

Olivia wondered now what had happened to this friend who could look a soldier in the eye and take his measure. She had been serious when she told Jenny that she could use her help; she could use the help of the clear-sighted friend she'd known. But Jenny too, it seemed to her, was parrying with ghosts.

Olivia slid under the sheets, stretching out the full length of the couch. Her feet were cold on the clean cotton, and she rubbed them together for a warm space. She turned off the light. She was lying, staring up at the plants by the glow of the street lamp when Mark came back into the living room. He sat down in the chair across from her and leaned back his head. He didn't speak at first. She continued staring at the tangle of unpruned plants wondering if she would ever find Jamin when Mark asked, "Can you help me?"

She looked over at him.

He hesitated. Then in a flat, exhausted voice, he said, "Kay was telling the truth. The doctors think her son's neck may be broken." Olivia waited. Mark leaned forward on his elbows. He pushed his fingers through his hair. "I feel so bad for him. No one cares shit for him, Olivia." He looked up at her. "I include his mother. He's just run away from his third boarding school. I used to know him when he was a child, and Kay asked if I'd try to talk to him, but now . . . ." He stared across the room then looked back at Olivia. "What's wrong with Jenny? What the hell was that all about tonight?"

"You don't know?"

"No. I brought Kay here because I thought Jenny might help her. I thought she might be able to offer her some comfort, might even be able to help Kay understand what a mother's supposed to do and feel . . . ."

"Mark!" Olivia exhaled. Mark stared at her. "You're not that naive, are you?" She sat up on her elbow. "Kay is making a play for you, and you expect your wife to school Kay in motherhood?"

"That's not fair," he said stiffly. "You think I'm having an affair with her?"

"No. As a matter of fact I don't. I told Jenny that, though I'm not sure you're being honest about how you feel. But whatever you feel, Jenny's your wife, and you're out playing Galahad to a woman who wants to take you from her." Olivia dropped her large bare feet onto the floor. From her bag she pulled out a pair of yellow warm-up socks and slipped them on, then she sat back up.

"I don't know what's wrong with Jenny right now," she went on, "but as far as I see, if your wife isn't perfect enough or . . . or . . . Christian enough to love her enemy, then I say you goddamn better be Jew enough to stand with her against the enemy."

"What enemy?" Mark rallied. "What are you talking about? Kay's not an enemy." He stood and began to pace in front of the couch. "She used to be a friend of both of yours. Only she's succeeded in a way neither of you has, and frankly I think you're both a little jealous."

Olivia wrapped her arms around herself. "Is that what you really think?" she asked.

"Yes, I think that's a part of it. Not all, but part. I'm sorry, I do. Jenny hasn't published in four years, and Kay's publishing all over the place."

"Jenny is raising *your* child, Mark. She chose to quit and raise a family and *be* a mother."

"You don't have to tell me what she's doing. I know. And I know it's not easy for her, but she's also writing a book which she can't finish because she's got some fear of being a success. I know Jenny, even better than you, and I know what I'm talking about. She won't try for what she can be, and she's jealous of Kay who does."

Olivia didn't answer. Her shoulders had begun to twitch as they did when she grew angry. She stared at the empty cage by the window.

"What ever you may believe, I don't want Kay," Mark went on. "But I do care about her son right now. I don't want to abandon him like every other adult in his life just because Jenny's jealous. I'm sorry. Jenny used to be more generous than that."

"Well, Mark, we're not all as generous as you, I guess." Olivia knew her retort was petty and defensive; she also sensed this might have been a chance to grow closer to Mark, but she felt the sting of his words herself and so instead she took sides.

Mark moved to the window. Without speaking, he lifted the empty bird cage from its stand and set it on the floor out of sight behind the curtain. He turned then and without rancor, but with a weary voice, he said, "Good night, Olivia." And he went into what used to be his study and shut the door.

Chapter 18

Olivia left Jenny's apartment before anyone else was awake. The street lights were fading into the dawn which crept along the rows of buildings from the East River to the Hudson in a cold grey light and then suddenly exploded with the appearance of the sun.

Olivia squinted as she caught sight of the glare between the buildings on Broadway. She turned and headed uptown. She had not slept well. She had tossed on the couch and only knew she slept at all because of the succession of dreams which drew her on towards morning—dreams of a child wandering alone on an empty road. Dreams of marabous hovering over a river—was it the Charles, the Hudson, the Izo? hovering over a barge of . . . of what . . . she couldn't see. She woke up half a dozen times during the night with these dreams, or more likely because she was waking, she had the dreams. Every time she woke, she saw Mark's light on in the study. Mark and she seemed unable to close the distance between them. Mark came from a world that left her out, his world of power and money, only he didn't see that she was left out, and so he never entirely saw her, she thought. For her part, she couldn't see him except through the prism of this world and so she never really saw him either. They ended up arguing when left alone though neither wanted to argue. For this reason they avoided discussing their lives with each other even now when they appeared to have a stake in the same obscure patch of earth. She resisted his point of view as he resisted hers. And though she didn't understand Mark, she had seen his pain last night over Jenny, but she had even less idea of how to approach this territory with him.

When she finally awoke the last time, Mark's light was off. She got up quietly. She folded her blanket and sheets at the end of the couch. On tiptoe she gathered her coat, her papers, her purse, and she crept out the door. She didn't want to be there when everyone woke up. The circumstances at Jenny's had grown too threatening.

She walked towards the subway now. A cold wind kicked up papers around her ankles. It was ten minutes to seven. It occurred to her that she couldn't arrive where she was going for at least two more hours, and so she stopped at a coffee shop and peered in to see if it were open.

Leo Stein had just arrived and was raising the blinds when he saw Olivia at his window. "We ain't open yet," he said, opening the door, "but you can have coffee if you want." She thanked him and came inside. "Anna, a girl wants coffee," Leo called.

Anna Stein emerged from the back in a black shapeless dress with a coffee pot in her hand. "We got a few donuts left," she offered.

"A donut would be fine," Olivia answered. She then went to the back of the restaurant to the small tiled bathroom where she drew out her toothbrush and toothpaste from her purse and began brushing her teeth. With the remnant of Camay on the sink, she washed her face. She combed her hair and emerged slightly refreshed. At her table a stale jelly donut and coffee waited.

When the griddle's hot, I'll make you some eggs if you like," Leo offered, opening the blinds by her table.

"Oh . . . " Olivia hesitated. She'd brought only $100 with her to New York, and she'd already calculated she'd have to move to the Y if Kay remained at Jenny's. "No . . . thanks. This is fine."

Leo watched her, then he nodded as if recognizing the quick calculation of a purse. He moved behind the counter where he turned on the griddle.

Pulling a yellow pad from her shoulder bag, Olivia leaned forward on the table. She took a bite of the jelly donut, a sip of the coffee, and then she began to list what she didn't know:

1) Whereabouts Jamin?
2) Whereabouts Nyral?
3) Money source: Plaza reception?
               delegates' clothes?
               room bill?

4) Kay's source on NLA departure?
5) Bulagwi plan at U.N.?
6) U.S. position v.v. Bulagwi?
               NLA?
               Jamin/Nyral?

7) Soviet position on same?
8) Rebel uprising: how start?
               who start?
               spontaneous?
               orchestrated? (by whom?)
               suicidal? homicidal?

9) Mercenaries involved? Name of merc. at Plaza reception?
10) Mushambe/Albert fate?

After she listed her questions, she listed sources for answers. Then on a separate page she asked a single question: Is there a Flatbush Veneer Company? She got up and returned to the back of the restaurant to the phone where she asked Brooklyn information the same question and was given an answer, at least a telephone number and an address. The intuition had been growing within her that *Flat bush* had nothing to do with the African landscape as she had always assumed but was instead the name of a street in Brooklyn. That the mythical American responsible for Flatbush Veneer should turn out to be a Brooklyn businessman seemed to her now plausible. That the Brooklyn business was sponsored by the CIA seemed more likely.

Her real hope was to find Jamin, if not through his sister, then through Flatbush Veneer. She had phoned Rhekka yesterday, but Rhekka had refused to give her any clues of where Jamin might be. Olivia didn't think he had gone far, however. She suspected he was not only still in the country, but in New York City. He knew New York. He had gone to school here before he went to Oxford. He had driven a cab all over the city to finance his studies. He would know how to get lost here. He had told Rhekka that one could get lost in America. If that maxim fit anywhere, it fit in New York. Jamin was a master of disguise. Olivia remembered in the villages he would sit on the edge of gatherings in the glow of the fireside, and he would appear as one of the elders. He wore their simple maroon-colored cloth, smoked their pipes, and only on coming near him would she recognize him. Or in the factory she had come upon Jamin once seated in a row of workers; he was dressed in the same grey pants and loose print shirt chatting in their dialect. She hadn't noticed him until he spoke to her. When she'd remarked on his constantly changing according to his environment, he'd challenged her: didn't her observation say more about her inability to distinguish her environment? "A chameleon is hidden only to the outside, never among his own," he'd said. "Perhaps it is you who cannot see me rather than me who masquerades from you." Yet Olivia knew this argument itself was a masquerade. As an amateur of improvisation and protean ways, she recognized a master. As a journalist who assumed the dress and manner of her surroundings in order to get a story, as a woman who was expected yet unable to blend and yield to her environment, she too knew the ways of Proteus and the dangers.

Finishing her donut, Olivia began matching her questions to her sources and setting out an agenda for the day. She pulled off her coat and left it in a heap beside her. The steam was pumping through the pipe near her booth now and warming the room. She felt a stirring of excitement inside. She was ready to pursue this puzzle. Her method was partly Socratic, partly gumshoe: question and answer, question and answer, intuition, logic and footwork. She must first find all the parts of the puzzle and then fit them together. She knew the real story lay in the more complex terrain of emotions and history and unseen powers, some personal quest of her own; yet after last night at Jenny's, she was ready to flatten out reality to the simple pursuit of who, what, when, why, where and how. She wanted to shake off introspection like a cloak which impeded her movements. There were times, Jamin had told her, to quit asking why and act. She had come to such a time.

Leo set down a plate of fried eggs, hashbrowns and toast in front of her. "Oh . . . I didn't order . . ." she protested.

"On the house," he said. "Good luck for the first customer on Sunday. It is a custom."

Olivia arrived at the tailoring shop on Jerome Avenue at 8:45. A CLOSED sign hung in the window, but inside a small Asian man with greying hair and slackened gums stood at the counter talking excitedly to Mr. Patel. Olivia knocked on the glass. The door was ajar so she pushed it open. When the bell jingled, Mr. Patel glanced up. "We are closed," he said. The man at the counter turned. He had no nose, only a slash across his face. Quickly he began gathering papers spread out on the counter.

"Is Rhekka here?" Olivia asked.

Mr. Patel hooked wire spectacles around his ears. "Ah . . . it is you," he said.

"I'm sorry it's so early, but I need to see Rhekka if she's awake."

"Yes . . . " Mr. Patel moved from behind the counter. "Well . . . I don't know."

"I need to see her," Olivia persisted.

"Ah, well . . . " He said something in Gujarati to the other man then nodded to Olivia. "I will go and see." He disappeared up the back stairs.

Olivia sat on a high stool beside a full-length mirror which reflected the man and the back room of the shop. The man was holding his papers to his chest as though he feared Olivia might try to snatch them. He glanced at her furtively. Even sitting, she towered over him. She sat with her dark arms folded across her red wool coat as though she were passing judgment. He began talking to himself in rapid, indistinguishable words. Olivia glanced away and instead stared at the postcards tacked up on the walls: faded black and white pictures of the capitol where the Patels had lived before Bulagwi started building office towers and hotels on the market roads. There were color postcards of London, vintage 1960—Trafalgar Square, Picadilly, Buckingham Palace— postcards of the Washington Monument and the Statue of Liberty.

The cards were pinned up in no particular order with thumbtacks which had rusted around the edges.

Mr. Patel reappeared in the doorway. "Our mother is still sleeping," he said, "but Rhekka is waiting for you. You may go up." He nodded to the man, who reluctantly set his papers back on the counter.

As Olivia passed him, she let her eyes rest for a moment on his face. There was a large swollen scar with an airhole where a nose had once been. His other features were fine, possibly even handsome when he was younger. Seeing Olivia stare, he spat on the ground. She moved quickly past him and up the narrow stairs.

Rhekka stood at the top with the door open. She wore a loose dress of Indian print. She nodded to Olivia, and the two women stepped inside. Olivia glanced about the room looking for some sign that Jamin had been here, some change from her memory of the place, but the room looked the same. By the window was the stick table and chairs with three white linen placemats and a single cup of tea. On the opposite wall the faded orange couch sagged next to the formica table which held a plaster lamp and half a dozen magazines. The rocking chair sat near an electric heater in the middle of the room today, across from the old wooden box of a television. If Jamin had been here, the evidence had been cleared away. Nothing was out of place, no clothes lying about, no stray cigarette butts or unaccounted dishes on the table, only spareness and tidiness and loneliness in this room.

Olivia sat down with Rhekka at the table in a patch of sunlight. "Who was the man downstairs?" she asked.

"You mean my uncle?"

"I don't know. He seemed very nervous when I came in."

"That is Uncle. He is over here every day now after what has happened in our country. He is planning his return. He says the massacres will bring the fall of Bulagwi. He has been gathering his papers and money to go back. He is trying to persuade my father to do the same. I do not understand why. My uncle was almost killed before he left."

"What happened to his face?"

Rhekka averted her eyes. "Bulagwi's men cut off his nose. He owned many businesses; he also published a newspaper. They said he had his nose in too many places so they sliced it off."

Olivia took in air. Rhekka looked at her. "He nearly died. He lost much blood and infection set in. The soldiers dropped him on our doorstep. I still have nightmares seeing his face all covered with blood. It was then Jamin insisted we all must leave."

Rhekka glanced out the window. For a moment her eyes seemed to focus. Olivia followed her gaze but saw only a taxi edging out of the alley. "Have you heard from Jamin?"

"Would you like some tea?" Rhekka offered.

"I won't betray him."

Rhekka fingered her braid. She unfolded the rubber band at the end and began replaiting the hair.

"Please, won't you tell me?"

"I don't know where he is."

"I think you do. I need to talk with him. I've told no one he's alive." Rhekka watched Olivia carefully, yet still she didn't reply. Olivia tried another line of questions. "Then tell me, have you ever heard of the Flatbush Veneer Company?"

Rhekka held her braid before her as she retied the rubber band. She kept her eyes on her hair rather than on Olivia. "Was it not a business in our country?"

"Have you heard of it over here?"

She glanced up. "I do not understand . . . "

"There is a Flatbush Veneer Company in Brooklyn. Have you ever heard anyone speak of it?"

"There is nothing I can tell you." She stood and went into the kitchenette where she began busying herself with a tin of biscuits and a pot of tea.

"I think you're avoiding answers."

"You should not ask so many questions."

"Why?"

Rhekka hesitated. "I am afraid for my brother," she said finally. "My father, my uncle, they gossip all day about the news of the killings, about their businesses they left behind, the money they left behind. They buried their money before they went. They talk about that money as if it were still theirs. They have been away all these years, and still they live in the past. My uncle wants to return to dig up his money. He does not understand what has happened. And my father does not understand. He does not even see what is happening to his country and to his son . . . ." She stopped as if she had said too much. Her brown eyes cast their gaze to the ground; her mouth sealed itself around a biscuit.

"What *has* happened to Jamin?"

"I cannot say."

"But you have seen him?"

"Please do not ask me," Rhekka implored.

Olivia stared at her standing in the windowless kitchen in the Bronx before a chipped tile sink with roach cups set in the corners. She wore the faded red-print cloth of a sari she had stitched into a western-style mumu, brown woolen knee socks and loafers.

She was arranging High Kensington biscuits on a brown melmac plate. She seemed to Olivia alone at the edge of the world.

Downstairs her father plotted to dig up old gold to make new fortunes in a land he did not possibly understand. Upstairs her mother slept more and more, escaping this land and the present, cherishing a young African boy she had raised as her son, yet who had grown into a man she could not comprehend. Rhekka alone sensed the impossibilities and the dangers of this present grown from a divested past. Olivia was struck again by the similarities between Jamin and his unrelated sister. "All right, I won't ask. But if you do see Jamin, tell him I want to talk with him. Let him decide."

"If I see him, I will tell him."

Olivia reached into her purse and pulled out a pencil and scrap of paper. "If he agrees or if you need me, here is an address and a phone number . . . the woman there is a good friend. She will be able to get a message to me."

Rhekka took the paper. "I am afraid for my brother," she said again. "He is talking too fast these days."

And Olivia understood, for she too had heard Jamin at the edge of his control, talking too fast, planning schemes too grand.

Mounting the steps to the El at Jerome Avenue, Olivia hugged her coat about her and moved out on the platform to wait for the subway. The sun shone thinly through clouds which threatened snow later in the day. The platform was empty except for her, and she spent the time studying the map on the wall. The maze of colored subway lines weaved across the city to the far corners of Queens and Brooklyn and the Bronx. Tracing her route line by line, Olivia jotted down stops and changes of trains then took a seat on a wooden bench. She looked out at the network of power lines channeling into stores and apartment buildings along the avenue, lines crisscrossing without ever touching, funneling power from an unseen source.

The train shrieked around the track, the massive thrust of its engines hurling towards her. The brakes screeched; the doors clattered open; she got on; they clanged shut. The train roared on, carrying her along the El: past the zoo, Yankee Stadium, tenements, stores. Suddenly it plunged into the dark under the city and thundered into Manhattan. Olivia could remember feeling awed by the subway when she first returned from Africa, dwarfed by this power of civilization, she who had grown up outside New York and ridden the subway since she was four. The reaction had only been part of a larger paralysis she'd felt on returning to her own country. Sometimes she thought she'd lost the ability to synthesize, to act and assert herself into the world. This paralysis of will had nearly crushed her more than once. But today as she hurdled past Times Square, Penn Station, 23rd St., 14th St., past the explosion of graffiti on the walls of the stations, through the cold, dark channels of the city, she did not feel removed from the power or frightened by it, but rather directed, almost carried by it towards a destination.

The trip under the city took over an hour. Few people got on the train. One drunken man slept on a far seat. Two women dressed in Sunday suits and flowered hats got on with a little girl between them then got off again a few stops later. One or two students, a cook, a transit authority worker.

Finally at the last stop, Olivia emerged from the roar underground into the daylight and silence of Flatbush Aveue. She began walking south towards the address of the factory or warehouse. Along the blocks in this section were warehouses, hardware and parts stores. She had gone several blocks when, between an auto body shop and a reupholstery store, she spotted a squat brick building with bars over the windows and a faded black and white sign: Flatbush Veneer Company. The building, like the block, looked deserted. There was one car parked out front. Across the street a taxi was stopped with the driver asleep inside.

Olivia approached a large metal door and rang the bell. She waited. She rang again. She moved around to the side of the building and peered in one of the windows. The bars and the dirt on the glass obstructed her view. She walked to the back of the building where she found a paper towel on the ground. With it she reached between the bars and rubbed one of the windows. Through a hole in the soot she glimpsed a room with bare floors and bare walls. She returned to the side of the building and applied the same towel to another window. Again an empty room. She walked around the whole building window by window. At each was the same view. In two rooms she saw desks, but they appeared empty. In one larger room there was a machine of some sort, but no evidence of its use. Either Flatbush Veneer Company had gone out of business, or it was a facade.

Olivia moved back to the front steps. She rubbed the window by the door with her coat sleeve and saw more empty rooms opening into each other. In a middle room she saw a light. She cleared more of the glass. A light, a table, and a figure of a man. She rang the bell. The man was large, dressed in a black coat and leaning on a cane. Olivia pulled out her glasses and squinted into the window. He was sitting at the table and looked as if he were playing some game. She again rang the bell and knocked on the door. "Hello . . . " she called out. The man didn't move though for a moment he glanced up as if he sensed some agitation, but then he looked back down at the table. "Hello . . . Hello . . . " But the man continued playing.

A horn honked. Olivia turned. The taxi from across the street was stopped at the curb. "Na be anyone dere today," the driver called to her.

She walked down the steps. "Do you know if anyone works here during the week?"

"Na be work done dere long long time I think. You want taxi?"

She wished she could take a taxi. The promised snow was beginning to fall, and she was cold and suddenly discouraged. She had been sure she would find a clue here. Now she wasn't sure where to go next.

"Subway long way away. Na can get dere on Sunday," said the driver.

Olivia knew he was right for on Sunday the station she had come from was an exit only. The next entrance was many blocks away. Yet she couldn't afford a taxi. "No thanks, I'll walk."

"You na want ride? I take you one dollar. No am fare round here for me."

She hesitated. The comfort of the taxi was tempting. "If you could just drive me to the next subway entrance . . . for a dollar." She peered in at the driver. He was slouched in the seat with a cap over his eyes. He wore blue jeans and a dirty canvas jacket with the collar rolled up around his neck.

"I charge you one dollar only," he repeated.

"All right." She climbed in. "Just to the first subway stop." She shut the door and looked out the window as the cab eased into the snow falling fast now in thick white flakes. She didn't know where to go next. She couldn't go back to Jenny's. She couldn't face the dissolution; she didn't know how to help, and she couldn't bear just watching.

"I take you dere bery quick," the driver said.

"Fine . . . yes. Thank you." Olivia glanced in the front seat. "Where are you from?" she asked.

"Africa."

"Oh? I used to live in Africa."

"You know am my country maybe?"

"Which country is that?"

The driver straightened, his head rising towards the roof of the cab. His eyes stared at Olivia in the rearview mirror, dark black eyes with a frantic light in them. Olivia gazed into the mirror then suddenly she gasped. A kind of terror and excitement rushed through her. "Oh my God . . . oh God. You are alive."

Chapter 19

While Olivia slept fitfully the night before, Jenny had crept from Erika's room and entered her study where she found Mark asleep at her desk, his head turned to one side resting on his arm, the desk light burning into his eyes, sweat running down his face. A small flow of saliva wet his sleeve. He was asleep over the balance sheets of Afco Mining. The sight of the papers from DeVries' company stirred her. While she had been awake in Erika's room, tight with apprehension, repentant in her anger, her head spinning till she thought she'd fall out of consciousness and yet remained awake, Mark had been working. She had come here to see if they might talk through what had happened, yet now these papers reminded her of the other issue they had not yet settled between them.

She bent over the desk and turned off the light. With her fingertips she wiped the sweat from his brow. She kissed the back of his neck. He stirred. As if from sleep, he reached out and drew her onto his lap. She kissed his mouth, drew his head between her breasts, rested her own of top of his, smelled the musty campfire odor of his hair as her tears fell. She began stroking his hair. He kissed her neck. Her chest began to rise and fall in heaves. He looked up at her.

"What is it?" he whispered.

"Do you love me?"

"You know I love you." He stroked her hair. "Why don't you know that by now?" He reached up and touched her face, wiping away the tears.

"Sometimes I don't." He lifted her and took her over to the couch where he lay down beside her. He began kissing her lips, her breasts, her belly. He pulled up a blanket from behind the couch and covered them. "Then let me show you."

He made love to her gently in the silence of the dark, book-lined study which was neither his nor hers anymore, but a junction of their lives. Outside the study Olivia stirred. When she awoke, she saw that Mark's light was finally off. Mark was asleep by then. Jenny alone heard Olivia rising, heard her go into the bathroom then back to the living room, heard her take her case from the closet and go quietly away.

Mark woke up two hours later. He turned to Jenny with a contented smile she knew well. He started to speak, but she touched his mouth. He stroked her hair. "I love you, Jenny," he said. She nodded.

He sat up. He began drawing on his slacks and his yellow Oxford shirt and black sweater. As Jenny stood, he stepped over and held her naked body in his arms. "I brought Kay here because I thought she could use your help," he said. "That's the only reason. She needs a friend."

The mention of Kay here between them jarred her. She began picking up her clothes. "I'll do what I can," she said finally.

"I know you will."

Together Jenny and Mark went to Erika's room. They wanted to lie beside her and kiss her awake, but Erika's door was already open, and from their own room they heard the quiet, confidential chatter of voices.

Kay, dressed in one of Jenny's nightgowns, was sitting up in bed reading Erika a book. Kay's hair was brushed out full about her face, and her face was revived this morning. When Mark and

173

Jenny looked in, she smiled. "We've been up for hours," she said. "We were letting you sleep."

"Yes!" Erika declared. "I showed Aunt Kay how to hide from snakes and monsters." Suddenly Kay and Erika lifted the blankets and disappeared beneath in one of Erika's favorite morning games.

Kay emerged. "Erika thought I was you," she said to Jenny, "and crawled in next to me and began giving me wonderful kisses."

Mark stepped into the room. "Yes, Erika is a very good kisser." He turned to Kay. "You seem much better this morning."

"Oh, Mark, I am so relieved. I woke up early. I heard your front door shut. I thought maybe Jenny had gone out. I called the hospital, and David has been taken off the critical list. He'll have to stay in the hospital for a while. I guess I'll move up here, but my story's here anyway. The important thing is the neck isn't broken and no nerves were severed . . . " She smiled. "He'll be able to walk and move and . . . and everything."

Erika emerged from the covers. "And then this little one came wiggling into bed kissing me . . . " Kay looked up at Mark. "This has been one of my better mornings-after in a long while."

Mark turned to Jenny, who still stood in the doorway. "Isn't that wonderful?"

"Yes," Jenny said.

"Mommy, Aunt Kay's going to buy me a bird," Erika announced. Jenny's eyes darted to Kay's. "I'm afraid I had to tell her," Kay apologized. "She wanted to show me her parakeet. I hope you don't mind. We've talked all about it, and we've decided I'll get her a cockatoo."

"Because they can talk back to Cassie if he ever tries that again," Erika declared.

"I see," Jenny answered.

"That's very nice of you, Kay, but it's not necessary," Mark said.

"No, please, I want to. In fact if Erika would like to go with me . . . ."

"She has Sunday school," Jenny answered, "and then we're having dinner at her grandparents."

"Oh, Mommy!"

174

"No," Kay said to Erika. "You let me get it. That way it will be a surprise. I'll bring it to you tonight." Erika smiled. Kay too was smiling. Jenny, however, stood in the doorway without expression; and Mark, feeling his wife's tension, remained silent.

"I do have one favor," Kay addressed Jenny. "I'd like Mark to come with me to the hospital this morning. I'm not sure what to say to David." She looked at Mark. "You're so good with him. He must be very scared right now."

Mark watched Jenny, but her face was a mask. Her feelings had coiled inside again. She saw Mark's pain at being caught in between her and Kay; she felt her own pain at being unable to extend herself to Kay. "You do what you want," she said to Mark. "We're expected at your parents at noon." Mark nodded.

"Fine," said Kay, "just let me dress."

Erika stayed in the room with Kay. Jenny and Mark returned to the study where Mark began gathering his papers from Jenny's desk. As he loaded them in his briefcase, he observed, "Erika seems to have taken Persephone's death pretty well."

Jenny folded the blanket and set it on the shelf behind the couch.

"At least she didn't seem too upset," he added.

"I don't suppose I would be either if I were getting a cockatoo as a replacement."

"Erika doesn't know one bird from another."

"A cockatoo is a $300 bird," Jenny answered. "I'm not very happy having Kay buy Erika a $300 bird."

"Then you should have said something. You want me to tell her not to buy it?"

"If you agree with me."

"I agree she shouldn't spend so much money. I'll give her a check, and we can all buy the bird for Erika together. But I think it was nice of her to offer."

"Oh, Mark!" Jenny's voice rose. "That's our place. My place. We should have been the ones to talk with her. It was the first time anything she's known has died. I wanted us to talk with her together about death. Then if it made sense, we could go and get a new *parakeet*. Erika is not Kay's child."

Mark stared at his wife. He neither understood nor liked this possessive, preconceived order of their family. "Jenny, it's only a bird. Just because Kay talked with her doesn't mean you can't talk to Erika about death."

Jenny sat down on the couch. She sensed the restrictions of her logic. She wasn't even sure if what she said represented what she felt, but instinctively she felt something was wrong. She got up and closed the door to the study then returned to the couch. "When I saw Kay in my bed, in my nightgown, with my child, it hit something so deep inside me . . . I don't think you have any idea."

Mark watched his wife; he strained to understand what she was feeling. By the way he tucked in his upper lip, however, Jenny saw that his patience was straining.

"Look, I don't want to feel this way," she said trying to soften her tone. "I feel bad about Kay's child, but, Mark, I've seen Kay. I know her. With Olivia and others again and again, she's come in and taken over: sources, contacts, Olivia's information, used it as her own. With Sarah in Washington . . . suddenly Sarah's fiancé was going out with Kay. It's as though she can't make her own life and so she steps in and tries to take over the lives other people have made. She usurps, Mark." Jenny paused.

Mark closed his briefcase. "So what does that have to do with us? She's not going to usurp me."

"You can't ignore who somebody is and what they want. Kay wants you. I don't take much comfort from your complacence."

"I am not complacent," Mark roused.

"All right, your indifference. It's naive, and frankly I don't think it's much of a defense."

Mark stood. The lines of his face tensed. "Have you ever considered there may be another way to look at Kay?" he asked. Jenny didn't answer. "You want me to tell you what I see?" She opened her hand for him to go ahead.

"I see someone who doesn't have real friends, who's afraid to let anyone get too close. Her success is her defense. But now her son has suddenly appeared in her life. For the third time he's been thrown out of school and has nowhere to go except to a mother who doesn't even know him. He's the first person to challenge the tight controls she's put on herself. Beneath all that facade, Jenny, she's scared. Now usually . . . *usually* you are the one to see that sort of thing and to help."

Jenny didn't answer. Outside the door she heard Erika scolding Cassie for what he had done and then forgiving him and telling him next time there would be a bird who could talk back. She sensed that what Mark saw in Kay was true; yet she also knew what she saw was true. She shut her eyes. "Why did Kay want to see you yesterday?" she asked in a level voice.

Mark stood looking down at her. "She wanted me to talk with David. She thought he might listen to a man since he doesn't have a father."

"Why you?"

"I don't know. I'd known David before, when he was a child, before I knew you, Jenny. We always got on well."

"I see. And did she also ask you about Afco and the mines?"

"Yes. Why?"

But before Jenny could answer, there was a knock, and the door opened. Kay stood in the doorway. She was wearing a white wool dress with a gold belt around her slim waist, grey leather boots and her white fox coat on her arm. Her hair fell softly about her face. Jenny felt pained at how lovely she was. "I'm ready, Mark," she said quietly. Jenny wondered if Kay could have overheard their conversation; then she decided she didn't care.

"You want breakfast?" Mark asked.

"I don't think I could eat. I'm very anxious to see David."

"All right." Mark picked up his briefcase. He went over and kissed Jenny. "I'll see you at Mother's," he said. His eyes searched hers for a response, but she just nodded.

"I'll see you," Kay offered.

On the way out the door, Kay leaned down to Erika. "Did you tell the cat what I told you?" Erika nodded. "Then I don't think there should be any more trouble."

It was beginning to snow as Jenny mounted the granite steps of the church on Central Park West. She held Erika by the hand while Erika stretched out her small legs to climb the stairs.With her other hand Erika held onto the brass railing. She was dressed in a navy double-breasted coat and white tights and navy shoes. They were late. Jenny finally hoisted her up in her arms and scrambled to the doors at the top where she set Erika down and took her quickly to the Sunday school.

She slid into a back pew of the church as the first hymn was over. The services here were simple, without rituals: hymns and readings from the Bible, with an emphasis on the bonds of Judeo-Christian thought. This morning's readings began with passages from Genesis then moved to Exodus. As she listened, she tried to grasp some thought larger than her own.

And the Lord said unto him, What is that in thine hand? And he said, A rod.
And he said, Cast it on the ground. And he cast it on the ground, and it became a serpent; and Moses fled before it.
And the Lord said unto Moses, Put forth thine hand, and take it by the tail. And he put forth his hand, and caught it, and it became a rod in his hand."

But where did the serpent go? Jenny remembered asking that question in Sunday School in Richardson, Texas. She remembered walking up the white-washed steps to the church between her mother and father, holding their hands as if she herself could keep them together, remembered staring out the colored windows in the Sunday School at the hackberry trees outside, blue or red or yellow depending on which pane of glass she peered through. It was the year that her father left her mother for the first time. She had learned that year that things could change according to how she looked at them. But did Moses see a serpent or a rod when he put forth his hand, she had asked; but no one had known the answer.

The readings moved through the Bible now to Revelations where the serpent grew into a great dragon, and woman was called upon to slay it. But her concentration was lapsing. At least she had told Mark this morning how she felt about Kay. The issue was in the open between them. She had posted her signs. But Mark didn't understand, and her own fear was no respecter of signs.

The congregation stood for the final hymn. Jenny gathered her coat. The mahogany doors swung open. As she approached the Sunday School, Erika came running up to her holding out papers in her hands. "I learned to read," she announced. She thrust the slips of paper at Jenny. "See: God . . . Love . . . Life," she read. "See, I can read. Wait till I show Daddy."

Mark was arguing with Irwin when Jenny and Erika arrived at the apartment on Fifth Avenue. The two men sat across from each other at a game table in the living room. The living room opened to a view of Central Park and through the trees, a glimpse of the zoo.

"I'm afraid they are at it," Helene said, taking Jenny's coat. "Why don't you go in and see if you can stop them."

Helene took Erika off to the kitchen. Jenny stepped into the living room onto a laquered wood floor and oriental carpet. An oversized chandelier hung from the ceiling above French provincial furniture upholstered in peach and turquoise flowers. On mahogany end tables lamps of crystal and brass shone. The room was bright, fashionable, yet overdone, as though Helene couldn't restrain her need to show off.

"Jenny . . . " Irwin reached out his hand. "You were there. Will you tell Mark there was no conspiracy going on yesterday."

"I didn't say conspiracy, Dad," Mark declared. "I said that I didn't appreciate your meeting with DeVries behind my back."

"And I say it wasn't behind your back. If it had been behind your back, would I have had Jenny come sit with us? I was the one who saw you, right, Jenny?" Jenny nodded. "I could have as easily gone somewhere else if I were trying to hide anything. Goddamn it, Mark, you're as touchy as a thirteen-year-old."

Mark stood and kissed Jenny on the cheek. "Here . . . you sit down," he said. "I want to see Erika."

As Mark left, Irwin shook his head. "How old is Mark now? Thirty-four, thirty-five? I would have thought by now he'd have let me off the hook."

"Why were you meeting with DeVries?" Jenny asked.

"He told you. He wanted me to help persuade Mark to go into business with him."

"If Mark knew DeVries had offered you a position without consulting him, he'd be even more upset," Jenny said, lowering her voice.

"I had nothing to do with that." Irwin pulled out a cigar from a box on the table. "The offer surprised me too. Frankly, I'm not sure I'd take it even if Mark agreed."

"Why not?"

He lit the cigar. "I don't need it. Now if it were another son . . . Arnold or Sam . . . sure, I'd like to help my sons build something. But Mark's got a chip on his shoulder about me. I'm not sure it'd be any fun working with him. Frankly I'm too old and too rich to do it for any other reason."

Jenny sipped the orange juice Mark had left. "I'm sorry." "So am I. I don't know why we can't get over the past. Look, I raised two sons. By the time Mark came along, I was just very, very busy. Besides, for a time Mark was against everything I stood for. I admit I was tempted yesterday, but I'm no fool. I see how Mark feels." He puffed on the cigar. "But I tell you, Mark will be giving up a hell of a chance if he doesn't take DeVries' offer. Frankly, I don't understand why he hasn't jumped at it."

Jenny knew Mark was waiting for her. She knew too that her objections were not in her father-in-law's frame of reference so she didn't answer.

Mark came back into the room with Erika, who scurried to her grandfather's lap. Mark sat over on the couch. As Erika climbed into the chair beside Irwin, Jenny stood and joined Mark.

"Erika says you have a surprise for me," Mark said.

"Erika has the surprise; she'll show you on the way home."

"I won't be going home with you."

"Why?"

"I have a meeting with DeVries."

"What? Since when?"

"It's just for a few hours. I'll be home by dinner."

"Mark!"

"What's wrong?"

"Why didn't you tell me?"

"I didn't know until I called him when I got here. He needs to see me."

"So do we," Jenny insisted. "That gives us no time together this weekend."

"We're together now."

"And *I* wanted to work today too," she added.

Mark picked up a handful of pistachios from a brass dish. "I thought you said you wanted us to be together. If you work, then we will hardly be together."

She hesitated. She knew her argument made no sense, but if

she couldn't claim time for herself from Mark, she demanded time for her work. "So that means lunch is it?"

"We'll be together all evening. Or if you want to go out and work, I'll take care of Erika."

"Kay will be there tonight."

"So?"

"So even if I don't go out, we won't have time alone."

Mark thought for a moment. "Why don't you go work, and I'll make dinner for Erika and Kay; then when Erika goes to bed, I'll ask Kay to baby-sit, and you and I can have some time."

Jenny fell silent. Mark's appeasement oppressed her. He was missing the point; she wondered why he didn't know that. For his part Mark was wondering why she was making such an issue out of a few hours. Jenny looked over at the game table where Erika had set up the chessmen. "Kay will definitely be back then? How's her son?"

"He's better . . . "

But before Mark could go on, Helene announced, "Lunch everybody."

The family moved into the dining room. "It's simple," Helene apologized. "I meant to cook last night, but there's so much to do before the trip, I didn't have time."

Lunch was set out on a buffet table at the end of the room. The dining room was long and narrow with panels of mirrors on one wall enlarging its appearance. Mark filled his plate with herring and white fish and bread and slices of cheese then sat down beside his father. "When do you leave?" he asked.

"Next week. What . . . Wednesday, isn't it?"

"You know it's Tuesday," Helene said. "He tries to act as if this cruise is all my idea."

Irwin heaped herring and onions on a cracker then looked up at Mark. "I'm told we go Tuesday."

Mark smiled. Jenny saw he was trying to make up with his father. "You sure you're up to all that sunshine and sea breezes for two weeks?"

"Please, Mark," his mother protested. "We are going on Tuesday, and your father is going to have a wonderful time."

Mark laughed, and his father laughed. "Is anybody staying

here while you're gone?" Mark asked.

"No. Reneta will come a few hours each day just to check up on things."

Mark glanced at Jenny then asked, "Could a friend of ours use the apartment?"

"Who?" Jenny asked.

"Kay. I was thinking, it might be a perfect answer." Mark turned to his mother. "You see, her son's in the hospital nearby. They may be able to release him the end of next week if he can come in each day for treatment; but she doesn't have any place to go with him except a hotel room."

Mark began explaining to his parents what had happened. He was careful not to implicate Jenny, but as he told of the accident, Jenny grew more and more uncomfortable. Why was he telling his parents? Couldn't he see he was reviving the crash for Erika, whose expression now turned inwards; then Erika began adding her own details in a quiet voice, joining herself with the victims of Jenny's outburst. Helene looked horrified at the vision of the falling carriage and her granddaughter thrown to the ground. Irwin's face turned crimson.

"But how could that have happened!" he demanded. "It's outrageous that your driver should have been going so fast. Did you report him? His license should be taken away."

"I'm sure the police took care of everything," Mark said. He glanced at Jenny for the first time. He saw her lips closed tight and her hands trembling slightly on the table. "I only mention it . . . " he added quickly, "because I wanted you to understand how helpful it would be if Kay could use your apartment."

"Well, of course, she can," Helene said.

"Perhaps I could pay Reneta to stay during the day to help out with Kay's son while she works," Mark added.

"I'm sure she'd be glad to. I'll call her up after dinner. You know, I remember Kay now," Helene said. "I'd enjoy seeing her again. Bring her by before we go. I'll show her a few things about the apartment. Didn't we see her on television not long ago? She was guest host for . . . what was that show?"

"News in Review," Irwin said.

"Yes. She was quite good, I thought." Helene glanced at Jenny now; Helene too noticed Jenny's discomfort. She hesitated. "You know, Jenny," she said, "I meant to tell you when you came in how lovely you look today. Blue really is your color."

"Doesn't she look beautiful?" Mark confirmed.

Jenny stood. "Would you excuse me please." She could endure the whole conversation, but she could not endure being patronized by Mark and his mother. She hurried from the room.

Irwin looked sharply at Mark.

"What's the matter?" Helene asked.

"Excuse me," Mark said. He stood and went to find his wife.

Jenny was sitting on the chaise lounge in Helene and Irwin's bedroom. She was staring out the window. Through the bare trees she could see the bird cages of the zoo. Because it was winter, only a few birds were out, mostly hawks. The more exotic birds were in the warm houses until spring. She was thinking if she were a bird, she would chose to be a hawk so she could take care of herself. A purposeful, efficient hawk.

She didn't look up when Mark came in. She felt him watching her. She knew they could have a fight or embrace depending on her response. She wanted neither. She simply wanted to be left alone. She would grant Mark the benefit of the doubt, grant that he was simply trying to be kind to Kay, that he was too naive to see the implications of his offer in Kay's mind. He felt responsible for what had happened, a responsibility she herself refused to feel. He was paying reparations for her act by offering to pay for the care of Kay's son. Yet the harder he tried to do the right thing, the more he hurt her and denied what she felt. Yet she would not argue; she just wanted to be alone. To finish her book, have her baby, raise her children. She wanted not to care for Mark so deeply.

"Would you like me to cancel my meeting today?" he asked. There was an edge in his voice.

"You do what you have to," she said, her own voice controlled. Was it control, she wondered, or had she simply achieved the right pitch?

"What's the matter, Jenny?" She heard his defense now, straining to sound like solicitude.

"Nothing. When you do have time, I'd like to ask you some

questions about Afco," she said instead. "I'm going to be helping Olivia on some research she needs for her book."

"What are you talking about?" Mark stared at her, trying to understand the transition. "Jenny, what is the matter? You ran out of dinner in tears."

"I did not run out in tears." She turned, showing him her dry eyes. "Olivia is tracking down financing sources. I offered to help." She stood. "I'll go back to the table now."

"Are you upset because I asked if Kay could stay here?"

"You do what you have to." The hawk, she told herself, the hawk. She started towards the door.

"I thought it was a good idea," he argued. "It will give her somewhere to go so we can get her out of our apartment." He said this last with an assumed annoyance, she thought, playing to what he assumed she wanted to hear. "I thought that's what you would want."

She turned towards him. Quietly she said, "You have no idea what I want."

He stared at her. The coolness, the separation from him, he had seen this only a few times before. Of all sides of Jenny, this one unnerved him; he didn't understand its source and had no control over it. "Thanks," he said. "Thanks a lot. Goddamn you, Jenny, why do you say that?"

"Have a good meeting with DeVries," she answered and stepped into the doorway, but he grabbed her. He pressed his fingers tight into her arm. He was hurting her now. She stared at him, her gaze remote, yet with a flicker of recognition and an entreaty that they might yet know each other well enough to stop hurting each other.

"How can you say I don't know you?" he demanded. His face was tense as though he wanted to strike her, but he simply jerked her arm instead. She tried to pull away, but he held her arm bent towards him to make her bend, bending her to her knees. Yet he knew he could not bend her to his will, could not control her. He could not keep her from separating from him, and this separation threatened his very core, taking part of him with her.

Erika stepped into the room then. When she saw her father hurting her mother, she stepped backwards. She had come in because she had thought now might be a good time to tell her father she could read. Mark quickly let go of Jenny's arm. He dropped to his knees before his daughter. "Honey . . . Erika . . . Mommy and Daddy were just playing," he told her, forcing a smile. She knew he was lying; they all knew he was lying. Jenny stood. "What did you want, honey?" Mark asked.

Erika looked at her mother. Instinctively her loyalty went to her mother, yet she felt paralyzed at having to make such a choice. She handed her father the slips of paper from Sunday School. He unfolded them and tried to focus on the words. He wasn't sure what she expected of him. "Those are very nice words," he tried. "Thank you." He missed the point that she could read the words. Jenny, however, didn't help him get the point, and Erika, afraid to expose herself, also let the point pass him by.

Chapter 20

"I'll be home by six," Mark spoke calmly yet with distance as the three of them stepped onto Fifth Avenue. Jenny nodded, then started walking uptown holding Erika by the hand.

"Don't you want a cab?" Mark opened the door of the taxi he'd stopped.

"You take it," she answered, lifting Erika into her arms and turning east, not west, on 64th Street. Reluctantly Mark climbed into the cab. He didn't know what was happening with Jenny, but right now he couldn't focus on Jenny; he had to attend to DeVries, who could not be asked to wait. The taxi delivered him a dozen blocks away at a canopied apartment building on Park Avenue.

DeVries met Mark in his stocking feet at the elevator opening into his penthouse. Wearing slacks and a green satin lounging jacket, he took Mark's arm and led him into the marble-floored entry hall. In the center of the room stood a six-foot Henry Moore sculpture of a woman.

DeVries nodded to the security guard sitting on a velvet chair in the corner. Mounted in the rafters of the ceiling cameras scanned the room. Dozens of paintings adorned the walls.

Though Mark had known DeVries for over a year, he had never been to his apartment. And though he knew DeVries was a collector, he was unprepared for the collection before him: Rembrandt, Caravaggio, Bacon, Goya.

"Rosa!" DeVries called. "Mark's here." He turned to Mark. "Everyone has the day off today so Rosa's making us a little snack in the kitchen." DeVries led Mark down another hall. There too the walls were covered with paintings: Rousseau, Matisse, Miro, Gorky, Picasso. "I'm glad I finally got you up here to visit," he said, watching Mark try to focus on the paintings as they walked by. "So you like my art? One of the finest personal collections in New York City, I dare to boast."

He pushed open the door to a kitchen with emerald green walls and cabinets and brass fixtures. The green tiled counter was fitted with a brass rim. "Rosa!" DeVries called, but no one answered. Scattered about the counter were cracker boxes and an opened package of American cheese. DeVries began punching buttons on an intercom. "Rosa?" "Rosa?" "Rosa?"

"I'm in the living room, Benny," she answered.

DeVries smiled over at Mark. "We'll be right in."

Leading Mark back down the same hall, DeVries stopped and opened the door to his study, dominated by a high-polished Louis XIV desk, along with two green satin sofas, wall-to-ceiling book cases, an inlaid onyx and jade game table, and a miniature billiard table. On every shelf and table and corner of the room lay some object: a sword in a jeweled sheath, a pair of marble swans, a brass sculpture of men with penises erect in tribute around a satyr, a bird cage with a porcelain bird, guns, daggers.

"And here," DeVries stopped in front of a glass-enclosed bookcase, "is my collection of first editions." He fished a key out of the pocket of his jacket. Mark wondered what other keys he carried around. Opening the bookcase, he presented Mark with Charles Dickens' *David Copperfield*. Before Mark could examine it, he drew forth a first edition of Flaubert's *Madame Bovary*, and of Proust's *À la recherche du temps perdu*.

"And, Mark . . ." he said, "this is my prize." He pulled forth a massive, ragged edged book. "Leo Tolstoy's *War and Peace*." He smiled triumphantly as though by possessing it, he had somehow helped create it.

Mark opened the pages and studied the unfamiliar alphabet. "Do you read Russian?" he asked.

"*Cela n'a pas d'importance*," DeVries answered, as though Mark had missed the point of the possession. Then more tolerantly, "My first wife and I collected these treasures from all over the world. We were both *great* collectors." He took the book from Mark and began wrapping it back up in its protective covering. "Just as you and Jenny can be if you chose." He placed the book carefully back on the shelf along with the other books, then he took the key from his pocket and locked the case.

At the edge of the room he stopped at a shelf with a small black and white photograph in a simple silver frame. He handed to Mark the picture of a young woman who looked remarkably like Rosa DeVries. "That was Christina and I when we were about your age, in Vienna if I recall." Then he turned out the lights and shut the door to the room.

As they walked past the dining room with its table for twenty, its door flanked by porcelain Nubian slaves, he said, "Rosa is less interested in collecting so I give it only a little time now. But I confess I lost my zeal for it when Christina died."

He led Mark into the living room where Rosa was curled into the corner of one of three couches, reading. When DeVries entered, she looked up. "I made the hors d'oeuvres, Benny." She rose. She was wearing a shocking pink blouse, silk pants and gold slippers. She went to the bar where she lifted a silver platter of Ritz Crackers topped with little squares of American cheese. She offered the platter to Mark.

Mark took a cracker. "Thank you."

"You want a drink?" she asked.

"Not just now."

DeVries also took a cracker without comment as though he required no more than this from his wife. "Now to business . . ." he said, taking the platter himself and moving to a sofa by a coffee table spread with papers and computer printouts. Returning to her position at the far end of the room, Rosa picked up her novel.

"Here is why I called you today." He handed Mark a news clipping. "I don't know if you saw this yet, but the border was closed yesterday to the East for our largest mine. The neighboring country sealed it, protesting the mass of refugees fleeing across. Railroad lines to the South have been sabotaged, we think by the rebels. It appears that our mines in that country are cut off. We are in the process of negotiating an opening in the northern border at the old colonial rail line, and I think by the end of the week, we will be successful. I'm waiting for a phone call right now, but as you know our cash position is very tight."

"What about shipping to the West?" Mark asked.

DeVries dismissed the suggestion with a wave of his hand. "No roads. No rails. Not possible." DeVries hesitated then smiled. "I'm afraid too that the government is changing the rules on us."

Mark, who was studying one of the clippings, looked up. "What do you mean, changing the rules."

DeVries laughed lightly as though this occurrence was to be expected. "You know how it is doing business over there. The government's trying to renegotiate our tax agreement and labor contract."

"What do you mean renegotiate?"

"Nothing to worry about . . . it's just when things get bad, they start to look around to see who they can blame, who can pay the bills for them. We've seen this before. Now, if we could get our second financing early, I think we'd be fine," DeVries said.

Afco, which was financed in two stages, was due to receive $250 million in March, contingent on returns the company had not yet shown. Mark was responsible for raising the second round of financing.

"It's very common in this business and in this part of the world, Mark," DeVries added. Then he turned. "Rosa, get Mark a drink. What are you drinking today?"

"I don't want a drink," Mark repeated.

"Bring me a spritzer, would you?" DeVries asked.

Rising from the couch, Rosa padded across the living room to a bar behind a wall of mirrors. "Why didn't you tell me this before?" Mark demanded.

"Don't overreact. I know you're not used to doing business in places where the rules change, but take it from me, it's nothing to worry about. We're just facing a shortfall of cash to accommodate them. If there's a way to speed up the financing, we'll be fine."

But Mark was staring at another sheet of figures. "According to this projection, you're going to need $350 million, not $250 million."

DeVries glanced at the paper and took it from Mark's hand. "How did that . . . well, yes . . . it's not clear. I wanted to wait until I was sure before I brought that up."

Mark leaned back into the pillows of the couch. He felt suddenly staggered by the prospect that DeVries not only had understated his risk but that he might have understated the cost, thus locking investors in and squeezing them to cover the shortfall.

Rosa handed DeVries his drink. "Look, Mark," DeVries said, "this business is risky. I told you that at our first meeting. I also told your investors; they're all big boys; they went in with their eyes open. It's not like doing business with American companies. On the other hand, you'll never find these returns with General Motors. We've run into some problems I'm taking care of . . ."

The phone rang. DeVries reached over to a marble end table and lifted an ornate gold telephone. "Yes. Yes. In an hour . . . ? I'll be there. Yes, I'll call the others."

He looked back at Mark. "All right," he said. "That was the call I was waiting for. Look, let me go to this meeting, and I'll phone you. I think we have everything under control."

"Why don't I come with you?"

DeVries stood. "No, that wouldn't do right now, but I'll call you as soon as I have news. I wanted to alert you, that's all. Give you time to consider advancing the second financing date. Now go home and spend the rest of the day with your family. When this is all over, you may even want to name that new baby after me . . . if it's a boy."

Chapter 21

Jenny carried Erika dozing on her shoulder as she scanned the names of stores on Third Avenue. Finally stopping at a pizza stand, she borrowed a phone book. Erika sagged in her arms, and Jenny set her down.

"I want to go home," she whined.

"In a minute." Jenny searched the pages. She'd seen the store she was looking for months ago. She had stood outside for a long while staring into its window.

"I'm tired," Erika argued.

"In a minute," Jenny repeated. "We're almost there. Don't you want a present?"

"What kind of present?" Erika brightened.

"You'll see in a minute." She took her daughter's hand and strode up Third Avenue through the Sunday shoppers, past fruit stalls and cafés. Finally she stopped at an empty shop. Inside a cardboard sign was taped: SPACE FOR RENT/ Caldonia's Moved to 2153 Third Avenue.

Jenny waved for a cab. She set Erika and herself inside and asked the driver to take them to 2153 Third. Erika dozed on her lap as the taxi sped up the half-empty streets, through the seventies, the eighties, nineties, into Harlem. The stores along the way changed from cafés and galleries and gourmet food shops to boarded-up fronts, mom and pop groceries, garages. Finally at 118th Street, the driver stopped in front of a small shop with two cages in the window. Across the street was a discount furniture store, a discount clothing store and an abandoned hardware shop. Jenny lifted Erika and herself out of the cab. "Could you wait?" she asked the driver.

"Sorry, lady." And he locked the doors and drove off.

"I want to go home," Erika said.

Jenny drew her over to the window. "See."

Erika blinked in the sunlight. She stared at the cages, then looked up at her mother. "Snakes," she said.

Jenny also peered into the cage where an enormous brown and grey snake lay coiled in the sand. In a smaller cage next to it a nest of baby snakes wriggled on top of each other. According to the sign, the snake was a python. As Jenny and Erika stared at it, it suddenly flattened its head and hissed towards the rear of its cage. Erika started and reached for her mother. "I don't like snakes," she said.

"Neither do I." Jenny took her daughter's hand and entered the shop.

Cages lined the narrow room: brown wooden boxes filled with sand and rocks and bowls of water. Many of the cages looked empty though on closer inspection, Jenny saw snakes hidden beneath the rocks or in the sand with only their tails or sides protruding. The only other customers were two boys standing in front of the python's cage. When the proprietor wasn't looking, they struck the snake with a stick, and the snake hissed again.

"You stop that!" the owner called from the back where he was washing sand. He came forward shaking his fist. He was a small black man. "Get out!" he declared. "You kids, get out!" The boys stepped away from the cage but made no move towards the door. "You come here frighten my snakes. You get out!" They looked at him with indifference when suddenly he opened the cage and hauled out the tenfoot python whose head thrust towards them.

"All right. All right." They tripped over each other to the door. Erika grabbed Jenny, who quickly lifted her in her arms and shielded her with her own body. Jenny wondered suddenly if she had made a mistake coming here. She too started for the door, but the snake keeper began to laugh. "Rikki scares away the riff-raff," he said. "I didn't mean to scare your child. Here . . ." He held out the snake, but Jenny stepped back. He stroked the snake who coiled about his arm and shoulders. "He won't hurt you. He wouldn't hurt those boys, but they don't know that."

"Yes . . ." Jenny said, disbelieving.

The man smiled showing his front teeth missing. On this cold day he was dressed in only an undershirt which was ringed with sweat. The shop was warm. He again offered the snake to Jenny. "You want to hold him?"

"No," she gasped.

"Rikki, he is very friendly."

Jenny bumped into the cages behind her, then jumped forward for fear the snakes inside might strike. Suddenly she felt breathless. Why had she come here? "No . . . no . . . really. Actually I'm afraid of snakes."

The man frowned. "Why you come to my shop?"

She was having trouble remembering herself. "I don't know. I don't want my daughter to be afraid." She wasn't sure that reason made any sense. She was beginning to suspect that coming here was not a rational act for she was in fact terrified of snakes. As a child in Texas, she'd been warned of rattlesnakes in the vacant lots around her house. Then one day she'd turned over a rusted oil drum, and in the same moment she saw the coiled brown body, she felt the needles in her leg. She'd screamed. Her mother, alone in the house now, stepped onto the porch. She kept screaming. She was ten years old, and the possibilities overwhelmed her. Her mother ran across the field as the snake cut through the brown grass and disappeared. Even when her mother reached her, she could not quit screaming. Her mother picked her up and quickly carried her into the house where she applied ice, cut the bite and drew out the blood with her own mouth. The snake, it turned out, had not been poisonous, and the cut took longer to heal than the bite would have. The fear had never entirely healed.

But her childhood fear was not why she was here today

though it had occurred to her while she was watching the hawks that she would face down this symbol of her fear, symbol and object in one so that she might master fear itself. She would come home with a snake, meet Kay's brightly colored bird unafraid with her own boa constrictor or python.

"What kind of snake would you recommend for us?" she asked.

"Well . . ." the proprietor slipped the python back into its cage. "You should start smaller . . . a garter snake perhaps or small king snake."

He pulled out a green snake and extended it to Jenny, who tentatively touched its scales. "Will it bite?" she asked.

"Wanda? No. She's a good snake. Even if she do, she don't hurt." He bent down to show the snake to Erika, who was growing curious. She thrust out her hand to touch it.

"Slow . . ." the keeper said. "Around snakes you got to move slow." He reached into another cage and brought out a larger brown and grey-ringed snake he called Pete.

"How do you know their names?" Erika asked.

"I give them names," he said. "It makes them seem more friendly to people."

He rested the tail of Pete in Erika's chubby hand. She touched the slick, smooth skin. "Snakes won't hurt you," he assured Jenny, "except poison ones, and I don't sell them. But a snake is a snake. It's not a cat or a dog. Mother snake has her babies, leaves them, never looks back. Or sometimes she eats them." At this revelation Erika's eyes opened wide. "She's got no mother feelings like most animals."

He placed Pete back in the cage. "But the worst thing you can do is be afraid of a snake because he knows." He opened another cage. "Take a boa . . ." He pulled out a mottled brown snake. "He feels you get tense, your muscles flex, he's going to clamp down. That's his instinct. He'll squeeze you. The only way to get loose from a boa is to relax. Don't be afraid, then he'll just let go."

Jenny stared at the snake nosing its way around the proprietor's neck. "How do you know which snakes are poisonous?" she asked. "I mean if I came across one?"

"I don't guess you would. Unless it was a rattler, and you could hear it."

"Can you take the poison out?" she asked. The snake keeper frowned. "People gotten poisoned trying to do that."

"I used to think I'd burn them out," she said.

"How's that?" "Growing up, there were rattlesnakes where I lived. I decided I'd burn them out if I ever found them."

The snake keeper laughed. "You'd of burned down your own home more likely. Snake would have only crawled deeper in his hole and hidden from the fire. Probably wouldn't even have got hurt. You want to get rid of a snake, you got to block up his hole, cut off his air and food. But first you have to find the hole and then make sure he's in it."

Jenny watched the baby snakes in the front window and the giant mother in the next cage. She wondered if the mother really would eat her own babies. Erika was peering into a different cage on the floor. Jenny kneeled beside her. "Which one do you like?" she asked.

"This one," Erika answered. She pointed to a snake about two feet long, an inch wide with red and black rings around it. He appeared to be staring back at her.

The snake keeper stepped over. "Rosy," he said. "Well, Rosy wouldn't be a bad one for a beginner. She's a little fussy about eating sometimes, but usually she'll eat a mouse every few weeks." He lifted Rosy out of the cage and showed her to Erika. "Rosy's a king snake," he explained. "She's pretty gentle though she will eat other snakes, even rattlesnakes."

"We'll take it," Jenny said.

The man set Rosy back in her cage, and he and Jenny went to the rear of the store. Erika remained on her knees in front of the snake. Jenny paid for the snake, a cage, a water bowl, a light for warmth, a bag of sand, an arched tile where the snake could hide. The snake keeper said he'd give Jenny the snake in the sand bag, and she could assemble the cage at home; but Jenny insisted that he put the box together and install the snake himself.

Finally after half an hour, Rosy was set into her new quarters, and Jenny and Erika were standing out in the snow on 118th Street with their snake, looking for a cab home.

Chapter 22

Jamin drove slowly through the thickening snow. Olivia sat beside him in the front seat. She was smiling. From time to time the
smile would expand and break into a laugh which had no relation
to what he was telling her but welled up from some unexpected
resevoir of hope she felt inside her. Jamin was relating what had
happened to him since they last met. Though he was not smiling,
it seemed to her he too felt pleasure at being acknowledged alive.

"So, you see, I hid in the porter's closet when the delegation
left. Christophe wore my coat and hat. Anyone who observed the
delegation would think I was among them. Nyral also stayed. If
Bulagwi had set a trap, we did not want our whole leadership
caught." He glanced at Olivia, measuring her response, but she
offered none. "The delegation voted that we should stay," he
insisted. "We were to continue making our case at the United
Nations. The others were to land in the hills and tell the people
Nyral and I were returning with aid." Again he looked at Olivia,
his eyes nervous, watching for her judgment. "As you know, that is
not what happened."

He rubbed his chin, now coarse with two and a half week's growth of beard. A streak of tomato sauce stained the sleeve of his jacket; his collar was soiled, his blue jeans patched at the crotch and knees. Olivia wondered where he had found these clothes.

"Why did you let everyone think you had returned?" she asked.

"As long as it was thought we were on the plane, we would not be looked for. This gave us time. We did not understand what was happening in our country. We did not know a massacre was already underway." Jamin spoke in a guarded voice, yet as one who has longed for conversation. "Instead we made secret, polite visits to our friends; we sipped tea, spoke of 'stability in Africa,' 'mutual respect'; we acknowledged the dangers of 'division,' 'bifurcation,' 'civil war.' We listened to the fears of our friends and tried to soothe them. We bowed and wiped our lips with tea napkins and listened to advice. Our friends love to give us advice about how to bring stability and economic progress to our people. All the time we talked, we did not know that the blood was already flowing over our land . . ." Jamin's voice drifted for a moment.

Finally he resumed: "But Nyral grew restless. He saw that our friends would help us only with words. Their concern was to be on the winning side when the last bell sounded. They danced first on one foot then the other, like children in a game back and forth across the line listening for the bell. Yet we continued to move secretly in and out of their chambers. Then one night two weeks ago, Nyral had a dream. When he woke he said the heart of our people was in pain. I assured him we would soon hear from our delegation and our friends would help. We heard the next day on the radio. Christophe . . . all were killed: lined up, stripped of their clothes, shot, left naked in the sun for an example and for the carrion eaters."

Jamin peered out through the snow. As he spoke, the base of his nostrils flared, a slight vibrating of skin as though some wind inside him at the edge of control was seeking a way out. "You see, Olivia Turner, our imagination failed us." He spoke in a flat voice now. "We did not understand the totality of the evil."

Olivia wondered exactly what the evil was. Was it Bulagwi? Was it a person? She'd believed the goals of Nyral, of a new nation nonviolently born, but ghosts had risen for the NLA too, and lately many had abandoned Nyral's vision; their fears had unleashed violence. Jamin himself and members of the NLA had blown up railroad yards and trains to disrupt the Bulagwi government, and in the process killed people, even children. She asked: "What is the totality of evil?"

But Jamin simply grunted as if the abstraction were not the point. He pulled to a stop at a light. The snow fell faster. The windshield wipers, swatting full speed, could barely clear a space for vision. Jamin slipped back down into the seat as he turned onto the Belt Parkway.

"When we asked our friends for help," he went on instead, "they told us to wait. See what happens, they said. After all, they said, it was your people who attacked the legitimate government." Jamin glanced at her. She wondered why he hadn't expected the massacre. He knew the record of Bulagwi and the army; he had seen the brutality to his own family. He himself had told her that his friends would become enemies. There was a naiveté in what he was saying now, a rhetoric she would have accepted in a speech or in a pose before the press, but he appeared convinced that he had been surprised.

"And your government, Olivia Turner . . . it believes in its own righteousness while it acts only to accomplish its will." He began calling up grievances against the United States, then against the West in general. "And the Russians . . ." he went on, ". . . are the worst opportunists of all." Grievances against all who had power and the will and ability to exercise it. He began talking faster, speculating who had instigated the uprisings. He suspected everybody. One minute he told her they were spies for Bulagwi; then he said these spies worked for the United States, who was trying to overthrow the NLA even as it pretended to be a friend; in the same sentence he accused the Russians of using the massacres as a propaganda tool, even facilitating the killings as a punishment because he and Nyral had resisted their overtures. "All are parasites drinking our blood to make themselves strong while we slowly die."

And then suddenly he stopped talking. He looked over at her. His feverish eyes took on a searching look as though inquiring what she thought, not about what he was saying, but about him. "And there is the possibility," he added quietly, "that we acted out our own destiny, set in motion our own death. We are simple people. We do not see that we are manipulated and do not know how to defend ourselves. Instead we only react."

He reached across the cab and touched Olivia as if to confirm that she was there. His hand dropped onto her lap, resting on her wool coat like an invitation as he accelerated along the parkway through the snow. She glanced at his hand, black at its base and rosy in its upward palm: an exotic flower or an open wound. She covered the hand with her own. She felt a sensation of unreality. Outside snow whitened the windows and the world so that she could distinguish nothing. Inside the car she and Jamin were holding hands as old friends, friends perhaps on the way to becoming lovers. And halfway around the world in the glare of an ever-present sun, six thousand people had been killed, were still being killed in part because of the vision of this man who sat beside her, dressed as a Brooklyn cab driver.

Jamin turned off the parkway into an enormous empty parking lot at Canarsie beach. He left the motor running to keep the taxi warm. He leaned forward on the steering wheel and peered out across the empty lot to Jamaica Bay. The pressure of his hand on hers increased. Jamin continued to look ahead rather than at her, but his fingers were circling her knuckles, stroking and massaging her hand in a slow, insistent rhythm. She breathed more quickly. She saw her breath filling the inside of the car, clouding the windows to the outside. She let her own fingers respond, fitting between Jamin's as he spread his palm over hers. She glanced at him, her eyes cautious and questioning. She felt a tightening of flesh, a longing not simply to make love to this man but to break free of the bond which restrained her, always holding her within herself and preventing flight. Even now it held her grounded and rational for she was asking herself how she could make love in a taxi with a man she had not seen for four years, whom she would not see again after the news events passed. She did not want a casual coupling with Jamin; she wanted the whole. She should be interviewing him instead, this man who owed and would pay her no responsibility, who could afford no responsibility. When the world opened the doors of the taxi as it inevitably would, when it peered in the fogged glass to see what had blinded the windows, there she would be under him, her papers and pad strewn on the floor, her story and reputation abandoned for the passion of a man who had no place in the world. This is where her imagination took her . . . to the end of possiblities.

Jamin slipped his hand and her own beneath her coat and onto her thighs. He looked at her. He saw her readiness and her need, yet also her reserve. His own face was more difficult for Olivia to read. The dark eyes . . . manic then becalmed, looking out with more knowledge and passion than the world would allow him . . . and the half-contemptuous smile . . . she knew this expression. But there was a hardness she did not entirely recognize and a resolve. There was not passion in the face he turned towards her but the need to dominate and control. This she resisted. He had enough knowledge of her to bring her to the edge of her own need, but not enough to draw her over it.

All at once Jamin reached into the glove compartment and brought out a flask of whiskey. He took a deep swallow, then offered the bottle to her. She shook her head. He took another swallow. As he set the flask back under the maps of the city, Olivia reached into her purse and switched on her tape recorder. Jamin turned to her now, his body surrounding hers. She smelled the musty breath of the fresh liquor and the odor of oranges. She didn't know why he smelled of oranges, fresh morning citrus they had sometimes feasted upon in the hills. He drew off her glasses. The sockets around her eyes were paler from the protection of the lenses and this lightness of skin made her weak eyes appear even kinder. Until that moment she didn't know what she would do, but the hardness she saw in his face and the rough way he had taken her glasses from her, made her say, "I don't think we will work, Jamin . . ." She smiled, knowing he could still redefine the moment, but the kindness he saw in her eyes threatened a core of him he had closed away. It threatened to strike at his resistance.

He hesitated. Then suddenly he laughed. "I cannot trust anyone anymore, Olivia Turner," he declared, drawing his hand from beneath her coat. "I cannot even trust you." His manner changed so quickly Olivia wondered if his move towards her had only been a ruse she had chanced to see through. He rubbed the window with his palm and peered back out at the ocean.

"So . . ." he said abruptly, "our nation has failed just as you knew we would."

Olivia watched him trying to find the transition. "I never said you would fail."

"Ah-h-h, but you did." He turned to her, and his smile mocked her. "You left us."

"I had to go."

"Yes. You had to come home. How comfortable to have such a home to come to."

He was baiting her. Why? They had talked too many times about the plenty of her country and the poverty of his, the rights and responsibilities in such disparity. There had been a time when he had held their poverty over her as his moral superiority, but she had moved beyond this guilt, and he knew that. Why was he provoking her? "You trust Nyral, don't you?" she asked.

"I have destroyed Nyral." He stared out at the pier thrusting into the water towards the horizon.

"What do you mean?"

He didn't answer for a moment. He seemed preoccupied somewhere else in his thoughts.

". . . And Christophe. Eaten by vultures and hyenas. No one was allowed to bury the bodies. Did you know that? They were left to rot in the sun. Anyone who tried to bury them was shot."

"How do you know?"

"Because I know Bulagwi . . . and so I know that the rumor in the paper that this happened is true."

Olivia had not read this report. "It's not your fault," she offered.

"I didn't say it was my fault," he snapped. Again she saw the hardness and the decision in his face.

"How is Nyral?"

Jamin reached to the glove compartment and pulled out the flask and took another swallow. "When he heard of the massacres, he wept. I have never seen him cry. He has seen much. He knows the price we pay, but he wept like a child. We should have been there, he said. They should not have gone back alone."

"Then all of you would have been killed," Olivia said.

"I am the one who persuaded Robert to stay."

"You were right. You didn't know what would happen. My God, you're alive. You can at least do something."

"I knew." Jamin looked over at her.

"How could you?"

"I am an educated man. I know Bulagwi. He could not allow us to survive. He does not have the imagination. He understands only the force of will."

"But you didn't know for certain. Christophe, everyone knew the possiblity existed."

"I knew more, but I did not want to die for Bulagwi's pleasure." His gaze held Olivia's; he was dropping his pretense now and defying her with this revelation of himself. "It would be a waste for Nyral and for me to be killed."

"And the others?"

"It is all a waste. But I could not save them all. We knew someone had to go back and try to take control. But I persuaded Robert he would do the most good here."

Jamin's gaze bore down on Olivia. He was asking her for judgment. This, she saw, was what he required of her. He would make love to her, court her, but from her he wanted confirmation: American to African? Woman to man? The man in him seeking the woman to confirm, approve, make whole? She didn't know upon which standards he wanted her to judge, and she didn't know how to judge him. For all these years she had sought him out because of her own need to integrate herself with the world, but now she wondered if Jamin had ever achieved this integration, or if he had always, only improvised moment to moment. Was he just a quick-change artist assuming whatever shape was required of him? Or, if she could hold onto him through all the changes, would he yield her knowledge?

"When I was three," he said, "my father was killed by a drunken British soldier. When I was four, my mother died of small pox. Robert Nyral has been my father and mother."

"I thought the Patels . . ."

"They kept me; they sent me to school. I am grateful to them. But Robert Nyral has been my teacher since I was seven. He always had a vision beyond other men. He shaped us all with his vision. In the last years though he has begun to doubt. He looked to me for advice, but I have never had his faith in man and God. I advised as any modern student of politics would advise. I said we needed to arm ourselves for defense. But now our people have taken up those arms. They have gone out to attack Goliath, and

202

Goliath, fought on his own terms, with his own weapons, will win."

"Should you not have armed then?" Olivia asked.

Jamin shrugged. He seemed hardly interested in the question. "Who can say? You can only live at the moment you find yourself."

Olivia peered at him through her horn-rimmed glasses. She wanted to ask him to explain what he meant, but in her purse her tape recorder had begun to make a clicking sound, and she feared Jamin would hear it. She should have told him she was taping the conversation, but she hadn't wanted to lose the intimacy, an intimacy she had wanted for herself, yet didn't trust only for herself. Later she would ask him if she could use what he had told her, yet even as she considered this technicality of consent, she felt she was betraying him and herself. Reaching into her sagging black purse, she placed her palm over the spools of the recorder, holding them down rather than turning them off, as they vibrated round and round. "Where is Nyral?" she asked.

"Would you like to see him?"

She nodded.

Jamin opened the car door. "Then come."

She glanced around the snow-covered parking lot and the empty benches along the walkway. "Where?"

Jamin stepped out of the car. Olivia reached for her purse. "Leave it," he said. She hesitated. He stretched his tall frame up into the sky; his eyes scanned the horizon. Olivia watched him for a moment. Would there ever be only the two of them? She turned off the tape recorder; then dropping her purse onto the floor, she slid across the torn vinyl seat and joined Jamin.

Outside the snow was falling more gently as if its rage to cover the ground had abated once its will was accomplished. Now the silent flakes descending seemed almost to be offering an apology. Jamin turned his collar up around his neck, and aiming his shoulders into the wind, he set off towards the water. Olivia pulled a black wool scarf from her pocket, but the wind caught it and sent it flapping out behind her. Jamin reached over and set the scarf on her head. Together they trudged across the wet, snow-crusted ground. Olivia's eyes peered up and down the path trying to distinguish where they were going. Jamin drew her over towards the pier where she saw at the end, a man fishing.

"Is that Nyral?" she asked.

Jamin nodded.

"What's he doing?"

"Thinking . . . and with any luck catching our dinner."

The waves from the bay kicked up around the posts of the pier spraying foam into the air. The sky beyond sat like lead on the horizon. Olivia drew closer to Jamin as they entered the open bay. When they neared Nyral, he turned; and seeing Olivia, he nodded. He was bundled in layers of old clothes. His grey hair cockled up under a cap with ear flaps pulled down about his head. On his hands he wore several pairs of knit gloves, thin at the fingertips. He looked like an old tramp fisherman. The disguise was so convincing that Olivia wondered if it were a disguise or a new identity.

Jamin peered into the bucket at Nyral's side. A thin layer of ice had formed across the top, but in the water beneath two fish were flapping about. "Not much of a catch," Jamin noted.

"Sea's rough," Nyral said. He watched his line agitating on the waves, his fingers resting lightly on the nylon thread. The sea whipped it back and forth; then all at once the line tugged. Nyral leaned forward. He placed one foot on the base of his aluminum chair to keep it from blowing away as he stood up. He didn't appear in a hurry, but he responded with the unbroken motion of one who understands what he must do. He drew in the line with a steady pull, a confident answer to the fish, momentarily allowed it slack, then with a quick jerk of the pole, he hooked the fish.

When he was certain he had his catch, he began reeling it in, slowly. Olivia watched the taut line. In waters rough as these it could break at any moment if too much pressure were applied. As the fish fought back now, Nyral again loosened his line; he gave the fish slack before reeling it carefully up through the heaving waters.

"I think you have it," Jamin said, noting the shadow beneath the surface.

But Nyral didn't answer. His eyes were fixed on the line, not the fish; the line would tell him what he must do. The fish, he knew, would fight; its most violent battle was yet to come as it made the terrifying ascent from water into air. At that moment he

204

needed to reel quickly to keep the fish from flipping itself off the hook.

As Olivia watched Nyral, she remembered in the past when events weighed heavily on his mind, he had gone to the river to fish. Since he was a boy, he had fished for his food. When he was troubled, he would cast his line deep and wait, for one could not will or rush a fish, he had told her. He would wait and listen for God to provide the fish and the answer he needed. In his face now Olivia saw this quiet attentiveness. From Jamin's description of him, she had expected to see a beaten man, but she saw only that he was turned inwards, listening.

She peered over the edge of the dock now, where a silvery shape was flapping between water and land in the open sky. Nyral lifted the fish above the railing and dropped it onto the pier. With his mittened hands he held the fish, took the hook from its mouth then tossed it into the bucket. The ice cracked as the fish made its way to the bottom and joined the others.

"You ready to go back?" Jamin asked. "You're not likely to catch much more."

Nyral stared at the sky. "The storm's breaking," he said. Olivia looked out but saw only heavy, grey clouds.

"You want to stay then?" Jamin looked impatient as if he didn't know how to bear the responsibility for this old fisherman.

"There are chairs in the house," Nyral answered, gesturing to the empty concession stand down the pier.

Jamin drew his jacket up around his ears. "It's freezing out here, Robert. Where's an old African like you get blood to sit in the cold?"

Nyral was baiting his hook with a shrimp. "Bring Olivia a chair," he said. Then he turned to her. "You like to fish if I recall."

Jamin disappeared down the pier. Olivia hadn't held a fishing pole since she'd left the hills, but she used to go to the beginning thread of the Izo in the evening with Mushambe and Albert and fish for dinner. Once she had interviewed Nyral after he'd retreated to the water on an occasion not unlike this. Bulagwi's soldiers had raided one of the towns in the valley and burned the crops. The people had urged Nyral to retaliate. He had closed himself up in his hut the whole night. Early in the morning before the sun rose, he left his hut and headed through the trees, down the dark path, to the river. When he finally returned, he announced there would be no retaliation. Instead, everyone in the hills was to go to their homes, gather their children and a week's provision of food. They were to be driven down to the town where they would share the food with the first people they met, including Bulagwi's soldiers. The children were to do the same. Many argued at the time that the children would be killed, but Nyral held firm, and the people obeyed. Not one person was hurt, and the town was supplied. The event came to be known as "ashana," the feeding. When Olivia had asked Nyral how he could risk so many lives, he had answered that they were not his to risk. She asked how he had come up with the plan, and he said he had listened all night, then at the river he had been given a fish.

Olivia wondered now if those days of clarity seemed as far away to Nyral as they did to her. She wanted to ask what he planned to do about the massacres, but he spoke first: "The fish are deep today; you must be patient. The ocean would make you believe there are no fish."

"Most people would wait for a calmer sea," Olivia offered.

"If you are hungry, you cannot wait," he said, handing her a pole. "And you cannot will nature; you can only listen to it and yield to it."

Jamin had returned with the folding chair which he snapped open with a quick flick of his wrist and set beside Nyral. He began pacing along the pier.

"Yield what?" Olivia asked. "How far can you yield?"

"Sometimes you must yield everything," Nyral answered casting his line back into the ocean. "You must yield and yield until at last you are in harmony with nature, which will then sustain you. You yield only what stands in the way of this harmony."

"You mean your own life," Jamin declared. "Your life stands in the way of harmony if you're willing to fight for it." Jamin stopped at the railing. Olivia saw she was in the middle of an old argument.

"By itself your life can save no one, Jamin."

"Losing it saves no one either."

"This is so." Nyral conceded. "But if called upon, this final yielding can . . ."

"No," Jamin declared. "I shall still kill the man who tries to kill me. Your religious morality enslaves a man's will, Robert."

Nyral cast his eyes out over the ocean. On the horizon there was a thinning of clouds and a faint lighting of the sky. The snow had stopped. "You do not see as I," he said. "But perhaps you are the better leader for our people. They no longer see as I do either."

Jamin pulled his cap off his head and started hitting it on the railing as he resumed pacing. "Why do you say that?"

"It is so."

"Robert, would you rather have returned and had Bulagwi shoot you down as meat for the hyenas?"

"I do not believe he would have shot me down," Nyral answered.

"There!" Jamin slapped his cap. "That is it! You still think of him as in the days when you planned a nation together. You do not believe in the corrupt and evil man he has become."

Nyral's quiet face roused; his brow furrowed. "Son, it is you who *believes* in the evil, fears it and fights with it and allows it its power. Evil is only darkness. In the presence of light, it is undone."

"Robert!" Jamin declared. His face strained with emotion. "How can you say that? Look at history. Jesus Christ, the consummate good man, was crucified. Gandhi, your ideal, was assassinated. Martin Luther King, whom you knew and admired, killed by an assassin's bullet."

Nyral looked away. His eyes searched the distance and his expression grew remote.

"That is the way you *want* it to be," Jamin went on, "but that is not the way the world is." As Jamin spoke, his own face grew sorrowful, as if in refuting Nyral's vision he was left with his own lack of vision. Olivia had never seen him so stripped of disguise and opened to another.

"You must study more than history, Jamin," Nyral said. "Truth is not the same as history." He stood up. "But now . . . I think you must take Olivia home. She is beginning to shiver, and I see by her line that the ocean has taken her bait." He reached over and took Olivia's pole and began reeling in the empty line.

"Aren't you coming?" Jamin asked.

"I will stay a while longer."

"How will you get back?"

Nyral swung the empty hook onto the railing. "I will make my way."

As Olivia and Jamin headed towards the parking lot, Jamin stopped and made a phone call at the pay phone by the concession stand. He spoke quickly with his back to Olivia. When he hung up, he offered no explanations but took her elbow and hurried her to the cab.

The clouds had broken. The late afternoon light scattered across the windshield. Jamin drove in silence into the sun. Reaching up to the dashboard, he brought down his dark glasses and covered his eyes. He pulled his cap to the rim of his glasses; his turned-up collar covered his ears; his beard covered his face. The disguise, it occurred to Olivia, was complete now. He could approach Bulagwi himself undetected. This thought drew her up. She turned and searched Jamin for the same thought, but his face was a mask. His eyes scanned the road. She hesitated to speak of what had just happened, for she knew it struck at a place in Jamin he would protect.

She reached down and drew her purse onto her lap. The tape recorder bulged in her bag. "Where are you staying anyway?" she asked finally.

Jamin swung the taxi onto the parkway. At first he didn't answer. Then he glanced over at her. "As you say, under their noses."

"Where's that?"

He smiled. "You want to come with me?"

"All right," she answered the question, not the smile. Instead she slipped her hand into her purse and turned on the recorder. "Who's paying your bills?" she asked.

"What bills?"

"The Plaza reception, your rooms, your clothes? If I'm not mistaken, the suits you wore were not from Samaldas'." Samaldas was a tailor with a two-room shop in one of the villages. He was among the few Asians who had remained.

Jamin nodded at her familiarity with his world. "You are correct. Poor Samaldas . . . would he not have liked so much business, but I'm afraid he knows only one kind of suit."

"So . . . who was your tailor?"

Jamin laughed. "You are the same, Olivia Turner. No one else would ask us our tailor while our people are being massacred."

Olivia recognized the diversionary tactic. "I'm asking," she said. Jamin glanced at her. The tape recorder had begun its clicking sound again. She placed her hand over it.

"I can say only that we share tailors with Bulagwi. I am not sure that he knows this, but I suspect he might."

"Bulagwi shops for his clothes in Europe and West Africa, I believe."

"Yes, I've been told that . . . among other places."

"And sometimes in America?" Olivia watched him. A distracted look had entered his eyes, or rather the beginnings of distraction as when one first hears a fly buzzing about one's head. "So you were provided by the same sources?" she persisted.

"The world can be generous when it suits its interest. You will pardon the pun."

"Could you be more specific? The silk looked French to me. Is that correct?"

"Ah . . . primary source is difficult with silk. It all begins with the worm, doesn't it? And who is to say where the worm begins. Such a small, inconsequential creature, yet its cocoon so valuable. It is not the worm which interests man, however, nor the moth that comes forth. Man wants only the silken cocoon. And to get it, he must kill the creature inside who created it, for if the metamorphosis takes place, and the moth emerges, it will break the cocoon's long silken thread. The cocoon will be worthless, and man will be left only with an ugly moth . . ."

Jamin was enjoying his metaphor and his evasion of her question. As Olivia listened to him, she wondered if he evaded her more than other reporters, as a way of keeping her attached to him, always seeking after him and his Africa.

Olivia was moving out on her own thread of thought when suddenly Jamin reached over and seized her hand inside her purse. "Ah-ha!" he declared. "That is it! That is what I've been hearing. A tape recorder. I had forgotten, Olivia Turner . . . you and your tape recorder." Without warning, he seized her purse. "You take from me; you take and take. I do not allow this of a woman." And before Olivia could reach for her purse or understand what was happening, Jamin rolled down his window and flung the purse outside. Its contents flew in all directions: mirror, lipstick, toothbrush, wallet, comb, tape recorder cast into the air. "You will not take again!" He leaned over the steering wheel, and bearing down, he sped onto an exit ramp and off the parkway, leaving Olivia's purse and belongings strewn across the highway.

"Jamin!" Olivia protested. "Go back! You have to go back!" But instead Jamin slowed down at the toll booth into Manhattan, paid the attendent then plunged into the Battery Tunnel.

"One can never go back, Olivia Turner. You should know that by now." As he drove into the dead corridors of Wall Street, he began talking rapidly. "Now tomorrow we shall see Bulagwi. He will arrive. He will be greeted by the same diplomats who greeted us two weeks before. He will be fed and fattened and allowed to speak. And there will be applause for him as there was for us. And that is the way it will be."

"Jamin, I need my purse," Olivia insisted at the same instant she knew it was lost. She checked her briefcase and found the money she had stowed there.

"Nyral, as you saw, has given up," Jamin went on. He didn't even acknowledge that she had spoken. "I cannot get him to come back and face what we must do. He says he is thinking, waiting for the answer. But one can wait a lifetime and never get the answer. Nyral has become like a woman, I fear, and I do not know how to save him."

Olivia fell silent. She realized how irrelevant her point of view was to him right now and how powerless she was to effect it.

"The world thinks I am dead, Olivia Turner. But Bulagwi knows I am alive. I must assume he wants me dead and Nyral dead. So you see why I must act first."

"What do you mean act first?" She looked over at him. He was stopped at a light on Madison Avenue, his taxi wedged between two buses and a concrete mixer. He glanced at her. His sun glasses still hid his face. In the dark lenses Olivia saw her own shape reflected. In this double image of her huddled body and Jamin's eyes, she saw their shared powerlessness as if for a moment they merged: woman and African facing a world they did not control. She thought of Jamin in all his guises—poet, diplomat, revolutionary, scholar—and they seemed a child's masquerade in an

210

adult world of uncomprehended power. And yet who or what held the power? If she could find the face behind the Flatbush Veneer Company, would she have found the power? If she could find who sent this concrete mixer up Madison Avenue to build a skyscraper, would she find the power? After two decades as a journalist she had never uncovered where the power lay. Was it in the people with money and influence? The powers of government and business often set events in motion, and yet it seemed to her that another inarticulate, insistent force took over, a reaction to the original assertion of will. Power was more like lightning, she thought, which, when conducted, created electricity, but untapped, burned down forests. She thought of Nyral now on the pier fishing. She wondered if he would even ask the same questions about power; she was sure he would not give the same answer. Yet she began to understand Jamin seen suddenly through herself.

"What do you plan to do when Bulagwi arrives?" she asked.

Jamin didn't answer. The light had turned, and he was moving out behind the concrete mixer. "You will be interested, I think, to see where we are staying," he said instead. "You see, when we were here, we made friends. They open the empty rooms to us each day." He turned over to Fifth Avenue, down to 59th Street and to the Plaza Hotel. He parked behind the hotel on 58th Street. He opened the door for Olivia.

"Wait for a moment," he said. Pulling his collar up around his neck, he went over and pushed a button on the side of the building. He opened the trunk of the cab and lifted out several boxes marked Flatbush Veneer. "Carry this and keep your back to the camera." He indicated a security camera mounted on an awning and pointed to the iron-grated hole in the sidewalk out of which an elevator was now rising to the ringing of a bell. Jamin led Olivia to the delivery elevator and nodded for her to mount the platform. He followed her onto the platform, rang the bell again, and the elevator began to descend into the sidewalk. As they went down, Jamin pulled the iron doors closed over their heads.

Olivia blinked, adjusting her eyes to the light in this hole in the ground. The elevator landed in the basement. Without speaking, Jamin led Olivia through back halls which smelled of garbage and coffee grounds. The walls were stained and scuffed. Beside a service elevator Jamin stopped and set down his boxes;

Olivia did the same. They stood waiting in silence before a luster-less steel door unlike the shining brass and glass elevator doors in the lobby. They rode up the service elevator with a maid and a maintenance man who accepted their presence. At the tenth floor Jamin nodded for Olivia to get out. Only when they were alone at the end of the hall did he speak.

"Today, we've been given this room," he said, pulling a key from his pocket. Before he inserted the key in the door, he looked over at Olivia. He took off his dark glasses. She saw in his eyes anticipation though she didn't know what he was expecting. "So, Olivia Turner, you have no pad, no paper and no tape recorder," he said. She wondered for a moment if he were bringing her here to consummate what they had left unfinished in the taxi, but he went on, "And so you are ready, I think, to meet my friends."

He opened the door. The room was one of the Plaza's dingier rooms looking out on a stairwell and the backs of buildings. There was only one window, which couldn't catch the sun because of the shadows of the buildings around it. A double bed jutted out from the wall covered in a faded yellow and gold spread. Over in the corner stood a small table and chairs. At the table sat three men: an elderly albino wearing a bow tie, a dark-skinned man with a bad left eye, and an elephantine white man in a black cape leaning on a cane.

Chapter 23

Kay clicked a manicured fingernail against the bird cage. A white bird with yellow tail feathers cocked its head and blinked its lidless eyes. "He already says, 'Give him the business!' and 'What's cooking, sweetie?' Don't you think Erika will like that?" Kay smiled. She waited for Mark to smile.

Mark sat on the piano bench across from her peering at the bird on the coffee table, but he looked distracted.

Kay kneeled beside the cage nearer Mark. She took a cracker from a box and tried to feed it to the bird, but the bird wasn't interested. Casually she rested her elbow on the stool by Mark's knee. "What's the matter?" she asked.

Mark looked at his watch. "I was wondering where Jenny was." He'd hurried home after his meeting with DeVries to see her. He didn't understand what had upset her so at his parents, but he wanted to talk to her now about himself or rather about DeVries. He was concerned over the figures he'd seen and over the cool way DeVries had dismissed what he should be concerned about. For the first time he wondered if he were being told the whole truth.

He'd come to trust Jenny's intuition though he argued with her. Now he wanted to know what she thought about DeVries. But she wasn't there. Because she wasn't there and he didn't know where she was, he couldn't work when he sat down at his desk. Finally he'd come in to play the piano; but then Kay had arrived.

"She's probably out shopping," Kay offered.

"Jenny hates shopping. She wanted to write."

Kay leaned towards the bird, increasing the pressure of her hand on Mark's leg. He looked down, noticing the hand for the first time.

"Thank you again for going with me to see David," she said.

Mark watched the bird pecking at its own image in the mirror. "You should buy David a bird," he said. "Have you ever bought him a pet?"

Kay glanced at Mark; she couldn't tell if he were criticizing her. "I don't even know if he likes animals."

"You know Erika less well, and you bought her a bird."

"But I knew she loved the other bird. She told me all about it this morning." Kay watched Mark. Her blue eyes shined behind a thin glaze of emotion. "She's a much more open child than David, Mark. You must see that."

"She's only three and a half. I don't know what she'll be like at eleven."

"Probably very much like you," Kay answered quietly. She met Mark's eyes with an assertion which made him pause. He stood and let her hand fall.

"In fact, Erika is more like Jenny," he said.

"Oh?" Her tone stiffened slightly. "I don't see that. Erika seems . . . well, more lively, but then I guess I don't know either of them that well."

At the piano Mark began straightening loose sheets of music. Kay moved over to him. "You've helped me a lot with David. Buying Erika a present seemed a way to thank you." She laughed then. "Certainly the bird is better than that baby rattle I brought her. That's the story of my life with David. By the time I think I know what he likes, he's become someone else, grown up, and I'm forever giving him baby rattles."

"Then spend more time with him," Mark answered. "Don't be so afraid of him."

Kay laughed airily. "You've noticed that. You always could see inside me, Mark. Why did I ever let you go? I'm scared to death of him."

"He's just a boy who needs a mother. I don't know where his father is, but . . ."

"Neither do I."

"So, you're all he's got."

"That scares the breath out of me. I don't know if you can understand—you're so close to Erika—but here's this person, a stranger really, who's part of me, yet doesn't even like me very much. Yet I *am* all he's got, and that makes him dislike me more, I think, because he's so dependent." She took in air. Then in a quiet voice she added, ". . . And yet sometimes I think he might also be my salvation."

She looked up at Mark. The sincerity in her face touched him, but it lasted only a moment before she grew conscious of herself and what she had said and the effect it might have. Mark saw in her eyes this change and this fundamental flaw. Jenny was mistaken about Kay, he thought. It wasn't manipulation of people or self-interest that was the flaw; it was sincerity she lacked, sincerity which came so naturally to Jenny. And yet his sympathy was stirred because of the insecurity he saw in her, because of his own doubts right now and because Kay cared for him. He put his arm on her shoulders. "I hope David can be your salvation," he offered.

The door opened. Erika stepped into the hallway, followed by Jenny carrying a large wooden box. When Jenny saw Mark with his arm about Kay, she stopped. She stared for a moment, then she took Erika's hand and moved towards the back of the apartment. Kay separated from Mark with an exaggerated motion, offering him a guilty look he did not reciprocate.

"Where have you been?" he asked instead, his own defense, instinctively an offense.

"Shopping," she answered.

Erika broke away and ran into the living room. "Daddy, you'll never guess what we got? One clue: her name is Rosy."

Mark dropped to his knees in front of Erika. "Rosy?" he said. "A bird?"

"No!"

215

"A cat?"

"No!"

"A mous-se?" Mark drew out the question to make Erika laugh. Jenny had paused in the hallway. They both knew he was really playing to her.

"No!" Erika declared in triumph. "A snake!"

"A snake?" Mark looked up at Jenny.

"Her name is Rosy, and I'm going to keep her in my room."

Mark watched his wife. "I thought you were afraid of snakes."

"I'm not afraid," Erika answered. "The man said you got to know them for a while, and I already know Rosy." She took her father's hand and drew him over to the box. "See." Mark stared in at the sand and the tile. Only the tail of the snake was showing. "She's hiding," Erika explained.

Mark glanced up at Jenny. Her eyes were luminous; her expression was tight with suppressed emotion. He saw this purchase was not a random act, though he had no idea what it meant. "Why did you buy it?" he asked.

"I don't want Erika to be afraid of snakes," she said.

"I didn't know she was afraid."

"She will be if she doesn't ever see one."

Mark frowned. He was missing some point here. "What about you?"

"I'll be all right," she answered. She looked at the snake instead of Mark. The snake had poked its head out and was peering about with a cautious gaze. "It's a king snake," she added flatly. "It eats rattlesnakes."

"Oh. Well, that's quite useful in Manhattan." Mark's irony had an edge. Jenny didn't smile. "Jenny, there are no rattlesnakes in New York City."

"You assume that," she answered. The fact didn't mitigate Rosy's value to her. "We don't know where Erika will end up living," she added. She set the box on the floor. "She shouldn't be afraid." She opened the lid, and with evident effort, she reached in her hand, and she drew forth the snake. She held the snake behind its head.

"Oh my God!" Kay declared. The two-foot Rosy dangled from Jenny's arm flicking her tongue from side to side. "Jenny, it's going to bite you! Put it back."

"She won't hurt me," Jenny recited.

"What if it gets loose. Erika's just a child," Kay insisted. "She's Erika's snake. She won't hurt Erika."

Kay stared at Jenny as if she were an alien being. She had never understood Jenny; she wondered that Mark did. She saw in Mark's face his concern, and she saw that something else was wrong. "Jenny," she tried more patiently, "don't you think Erika is too young for a snake?" She moved to the coffee table by the bird, who had begun making low gutteral noises as if it sensed the threat.

"Why don't you ask Erika?" Erika was holding Rosy's tail and stroking her. She hadn't even noticed the bird on the table.

"I hardly think she'd know," Kay answered.

Jenny replaced the snake in the box and closed the lid. "Well . . . that's a difference between you and me." Without elaborating, she lifted the cage and proceeded with Erika to her room.

Kay glanced at Mark after she'd gone, searching his face for a shared reaction, but Mark's expression had turned inwards. He stood for a moment without speaking. Then he said, "Excuse me," and he started after Jenny. But before he got to the door, Jenny returned. She was carrying her briefcase.

"I'm going out to work now," she said. "Erika says she's hungry. She hasn't had much of a nap so she should go to bed early."

"Where are you going?" Mark moved towards her.

"Out."

"Where?" He took hold of her arm gently, but she met his eyes with a look which told him not to try to stop her.

"I'm going out to work," she repeated. Then glancing into the living room, she added, "If I were you, I'd hang that bird up before Cassie eats it."

In the living room Kay watched Mark. He stood without moving. Then running his hand through his hair, he turned from the door. He yanked his tie from around his neck and threw it on the hall table. Kay looked away. She lifted the bird cage and carried it over to the window where she strained to raise it to the hook on the pole. Mark stepped over to help her.

"I'm sorry," she said. "I guess Jenny's mad at us?"

Mark glanced at her. He started to say, "There is no *us*, Kay," but he didn't bother. He was furious at Jenny. He had come home needing to talk to her. As he'd left DeVries' apartment, he'd wanted only to be with his wife and listen to her set his world in order, to comfort her too and help ease her pain, whatever it was. But now she had walked out on him for reasons he didn't even understand. The fact that she misinterpreted what she saw with Kay angered him even more. In his mind he justified himself and censured her for not knowing him better. Yet lingering behind his arguments was the possibility that he was at fault, at least he wasn't entirely guiltless. His infidelity was not that he wanted to have an affair with Kay but that Kay fed some vanity of his, some perception of himself as . . . well, noble or good. That was it, wasn't it? And Jenny saw and knew this vanity and had turned her back on it. He didn't answer Kay's question. Instead he asked, "You want to have dinner with us?"

"Yes. I'd like that," she answered. She was arranging the newspaper in the bottom of the bird's cage and picking up stray bird seed and putting it back in the feeder. She didn't look at him.

Mark moved into the kitchen. Kay followed. "What shall we have?" she asked.

Mark opened the cupboard and took down a can of soup. "Whatever you like."

Kay opened the refrigerator. "Would you like grilled cheese sandwiches? I make an outstanding grilled cheese sandwich."

"Fine." Mark emptied soup into a pot as Kay explored the vegetable drawer pulling out tomatoes and mushrooms. She set a skillet on the stove and dropped in a slab of butter then began slicing mushrooms into the pan. She was still wearing the white wool dress from morning and the high-heeled grey leather boots. As the mushrooms sizzled, she sat at the table, lifted up her leg to the chair and unzipped her boots.

She returned to the stove in her stocking feet. "I don't cook much for myself," she said, "but I think you'll like this." Mark didn't answer. He was staring at the water running in the sink. "Actually I enjoy cooking for someone else." Already she was imagining herself as the woman in his house. Today had only confirmed what she'd sensed two weeks ago. With no other reference than her own, she assumed the discontent she saw between Jenny and Mark arose from their discontent with each other; and now quietly, benignly even, with a show of goodwill, she was considering what kind act she might extend to Jenny as compensation for her husband.

Because Mark didn't see the consequence of his own goodwill towards Kay, he did not imagine the hurt his next words caused. "After dinner could you babysit with Erika for a while?" he asked.

Kay glanced at him. She wiped her hair from her face with the back of her hand. "Where are you going?"

"I want to find Jenny. We need to talk."

"Oh . . ." She pushed the mushrooms about with a spatula. "Well . . . I've been out all day, Mark . . . what with David and buying that bird. I haven't done any work myself." She hesitated. She searched his face. Perhaps he needed to find Jenny to discuss the breach between them, but his face offered her no encouragement. She didn't know what she did see—discomfort, distraction, pain— but she saw no clear opening for herself. She answered, "I've got quite a lot to do before Bulagwi arrives tomorrow. Ordinarily I'd be glad to help, but . . ."

Mark just nodded. He poured the water into the saucepan.

Mark and Kay and Erika ate chicken noodle soup and cheese and mushroom and tomato sandwiches in silence at the kitchen table. Erika was so tired that she almost fell asleep twice with her head beside her plate. After dinner Mark revived her long enough for Kay to present the bird, but by then she was too sleepy to focus on it. Mark carried her into her room where he put her to bed in her clothes.

In the living room Kay had gathered up her briefcase and was waiting at the table for Mark. She'd put back on her boots and her white fox coat. "I imagine I'll be quite late," she said, standing when he entered. "You still keep your key over the door? I'll just take a couch . . . in your study or the livingroom, whatever's available."

Mark walked her to the door. "I'm sorry I can't help you out, Mark." She forced a smile. "Maybe Jenny will be home soon." She leaned over and kissed him on the cheek; then she walked away with the awkward, flat-footed gait of a child.

It was 6:30. The apartment was quiet. Outside the dark pushed against the windows. In the living room the new bird was clicking

219

its tongue against its beak as if trying to decide what words to offer in its new home. In Erika's room the snake was asleep, coiled in his cage on a shelf of Erika's toys.

Mark walked about the silent rooms. He was wide awake, unable to work. Downstairs the Rousseaus were arguing with each other. Mark stood in the middle of the living room listening, then he went to the phone and dialed their apartment. The argument ceased for a moment as Mrs. Rousseau answered: "Now? . . . Well, well, yes. All right. Fifteen minutes," she said.

Mark went to the bedroom where he took off the sweater and shirt he'd been wearing all day. In his undershirt he stood at the sink and washed his face. He lathered his cheeks and shaved off the day's shadow. Then he brushed his teeth and returned to the bedroom. He put on a fresh blue shirt and blue crewneck sweater. He went in and kissed Erika again and covered her up. He then went to his study and took a large manila folder from his briefcase. It was the Afco file. He carried it in and left it on Jenny's desk so she could find whatever it was she wanted to know. He needed her to trust him. He wanted her to know that he trusted her.

Returning to the kitchen, he then began to wash the dishes. Whenever Jenny was angry at him for reasons he didn't understand, he washed dishes. The ritual dated back to one of their earliest arguments about household chores, and the act had an unspoken meaning between them. It was an admission of his own helplessness in the face of a rage he didn't comprehend.

When Mrs. Rousseau arrived, he told her he didn't know how long he would be. Then he left to find Jenny.

Jenny was at her desk when Mark returned three hours later. She was working with a concentration that encouraged him as he watched her from the doorway of her study. His own anger had eased, and he took pleasure observing his wife undetected. She sat with one stocking foot curved under her seat and the other tucked around the base of the chair. Beside her on the floor her books sat in boxes; his own books were still on the shelves. He was thinking that he should move his to give her space when she turned.

Seeing him, she grew still. Neither of them spoke. Finally Jenny asked, "Where have you been?"

Before he heard her question, he was saying, "I'll move my books out this weekend." She glanced at the shelf. He answered, "I went to look for you. When I couldn't find you, I went to a movie."

"I was at Leo's."

He stepped into the study and sat on the couch. "I looked at Leo's. I looked at the American, the Library, the Front Porch . . . I finally gave up."

"What movie?"

"*Battle of Algiers.*"

"Again?"

He shrugged. He leaned towards her. Part of him wanted to take her hand, but she was holding back and so he held back. "How are you?" he asked.

"Okay."

"I'm sorry," he said.

"For what?"

"For making you so unhappy."

"You don't make me unhappy."

"Oh? You could have fooled me." There was an edge to his voice.

Jenny's face filled with sadness at this distance between them. "Thank you for leaving me the Afco file," she said.

He nodded. "I wanted you to see there's nothing nefarious in what I'm doing."

"I never said you were doing anything nefarious," she answered. "Can I share this with Olivia?"

"I left the file for you," he said.

"I have a few questions . . ."

Mark stood. He began to pace. "I don't feel like answering questions right now, Jenny," he declared. He turned. "You walked out on me tonight. Why? Is it Kay? You're going to have to trust me." He felt the unfairness of his position and wanted to justify himself, but he refrained.

Jenny wanted to ask him why he had his arm about Kay, why he couldn't understand what that meant to Kay, if not to him. Why must he put his arms around her, hold her, touch her, even in the name of friendship. Jenny didn't do that with other men. Why did he do that with another woman? But she said simply, "It's not only Kay."

"Then what?"

She breathed in deeply. Finally they were alone together. Mark wasn't somewhere else in his mind. He was looking at her and listening to her.

And then the phone rang. Jenny paused. It rang again. She picked it up. Mark watched her. She handed him the receiver.

"Who is it?" he whispered.

"DeVries."

"I'll just be a minute." He stood and took the phone. "I promise." He kept his eyes on her. But then they shifted. "What? . . . What do you mean? That's not acceptable!"

Jenny watched him. He held the phone in one hand, the re– ceiver in the other. She stood. He cast a pleading look at her. She offered him a smile; then she took the folder and turned to leave the room. She glanced back, but he wasn't watching her now. He was leaning over the desk writing something down.

She went into the bedroom, where she undressed. She washed her face, combed her hair. She put on a pink nightgown and slid into bed. She turned on the light at her nightstand and picked up the Afco folder and her pad. She studied the dry convoluted prose: "herewith offered in the amount of . . . in consideration for . . ." She tried to set aside her questions about Mark and Kay. But even the most generous interpretation of Mark's embrace of Kay stung her, and the possibility of betrayal uprooted her. She tried instead to lose herself in these facts and figures, in dollars and cents.

When Mark finally came in, she set her pencil down. "Exactly how did Afco finance the mines?" she asked. Mark stared at her; he tried to judge where the question was coming from. "The pro- spectus shows that at least with Bulagwi, DeVries may have traded bank debt for Afco's royalty," Jenny added.

Mark sat on the edge of the bed. "Benjamin knew the banks in that case. He bought the country's debt at a large discount and traded it for a royalty on mining revenues."

"What spread did he get?"

"What do you mean?"

"How much did he buy the debt for, how much did he trade it to Bulagwi for."

"I know what a spread is, Jenny," Mark rejoined. "He doesn't get a spread. He used money we raised for him to buy the country's bank debt at twenty cents on the dollar. He traded it back to the country at twenty cents on the dollar."

"Are you sure?"

Mark hesitated. "I trust my partner."

Jenny set the prospctus on the bed beside her. "Why would the banks sell so cheaply?"

"They were glad to get anything for the debt; they'd about written it off. The country was ecstatic to get out from under almost seven hundred million dollars of debt. The government then raised new money to open the mines." Mark watched Jenny, looking for an opening for himself, but for the moment she was holding him at a distance.

"Mines that DeVries now owns," she said.

"He owns a royalty."

"Of almost half," Jenny emphasized.

"So?"

"So DeVries owns the main revenue-producing channels of these countries."

"No. He owns a portion of the revenue."

"But how can the country develop if someone else owns almost half its main revenue stream?"

"They would never have been able to open the mines and generate the revenue in the first place if DeVries hadn't come in."

"But that means DeVries and you and all your investors essentially *own* these countries or part of them." Jenny's voice rose as she found herself in an old argument.

"We don't own them. We're partners in a business deal. Because of us the mines are open for the first time in over a decade; people are working; a prohibitive debt is paid off. Frankly, if this project works, it could have enormous implications."

"But that also gives DeVries enormous leverage over the country."

"So?"

"So!" Jenny sat forward. "Why should he have that? What if his leverage is less than benign? He does not have a reputation for benevolence."

223

"Jenny," Mark roused. "First of all, DeVries was willing to put his own money on the line. No one else has done that."

"And he'll make an enormous profit," Jenny said. "What about the people in the country? It's their country. Shouldn't they be making this profit?"

"The people of the country are WORKING!" Mark declared. "Some of them for the first time in years. And with the government's profits they're creating roads and schools and other jobs. If there weren't a profit, believe me, DeVries, our investors, no one would put a penny into it. The fact is, he may not make a profit. The whole Afco Mining Company may collapse if we can't get the ore out. The railroads have been closed in two countries because of civil wars. Afco has less than a month's worth of cash and no more lines of credit. We may lose everything and so will the government."

Mark stood from the bed. He tracked a path between the bed and the closet. "The government has no more money to put into the mines, and we can't raise any more unless we can sell ore. Our investors will lose $250 million. DeVries will lose his $50 million, and I guarantee you, it will be a long time before anyone else will be willing to take a risk in those countries."

Mark stopped pacing and turned. "Frankly, for all you or Olivia talk about the third world, you can write articles and send care packages till the birds come home, but you aren't touching the basic problem which is capital and investment."

Jenny didn't argue. She watched Mark. She hated this argument which they usually tried to avoid. Instead they tried to accommodate their different economic views of the world into their shared sympathies for the world. But right now she was doubting those sympathies. She asked quietly, "What's Bulagwi's kickback?"

"What kickback?"

"The prospectus says that Afco pays five percent of its proceeds back to the governments."

"That's not a kickback."

Jenny raised her eyebrows. "What do you call it?"

"It's payment for taxes and other liscensing fees."

"Mark . . ." Jenny protested, "you believe that?" She picked up the folder and set it on the nightstand. "You're ignoring who the people are you're dealing with."

"And who are you to know so much about the people I'm dealing with?"

Jenny hesitated. "I don't know entirely," she conceded, "but I know history—especially Bulagwi's history and to an extent DeVries'. And I have intuition. I trust both of those. I also know that however innovative or brilliant your plan may be, it's only as good as the people you play with."

Mark didn't answer. Jenny fell silent. Whatever Mark's arguments, she came back to this point: she didn't trust Bulagwi, and she wasn't sure she would trust DeVries. She remained uncomfortable with Afco, especially now that she saw its hold over these countries. And yet none of this was the primary source of her discomfort right now.

Mark turned towards the door. "Where are you going?" she asked.

"I've got to call Reynolds," he said, his voice suddenly tired.

 *Chapter 24*

"The Izo Valley stretches sixty miles in all directions. Flaxen grass bristles across the flat land to the rim of the mountains in the distance. Over the valley the sky spreads in a white light so warm and sun-filled that only its apex is blue. In the rainy season clouds roll in each afternoon, and for a few hours water assaults the earth. But when the clouds recede, the sun again breaks forth illuminating the cream-colored land through a haze on the tips of the wet grass. For miles nothing breaks the line of the horizon. Then a clutter of mud huts springs up from the earth itself, a harmony of land and home. Sheep and chickens and children mill about off the dusty path to the road. A tree rises against the horizon. It too is the flaxen color of the earth and appears ready to be blown away in the next wind like a giant tumbleweed. The land here is reminiscent of the American West—broad and open and unsettled. I have driven for an hour and a half and have only now come to a stop sign where another road crosses this one-lane highway.*

"A few miles on the other side of the sign emerges a town of half a dozen streets and stores. One of the roads is paved; the others are beaten down to hard earth by the traffic of feet and animals. In this valley the people are undisturbed by the politics of the capital 300 miles away over the mountains. In the town a mother with a child wrapped about her hip pauses to watch the sun sink red and orange into the hills. The light reflects off the glass and the tin roof of a wood frame store. Ablaze on the windowpane, the sun illumines the dark figures within, then slowly flattens into a glow and disappears. Only an orange rim is left like the memory of the day.

"I continue to drive towards the mountains. I cross a creek filled with pebbles. The water will not rise again here for several months. As the town falls away behind, only power lines stretched along the roadside suggest civilization. A car speeds past in the opposite direction reminding me there are other destinations in this land. As the sky darkens, I draw near the mountains I have been looking towards all day and find they are only round, black foothills; but as I drive into them, I see suddenly Mt. Ako in front of me. At its base an abandoned freight car and a railroad track lie bent and rusted from years of disuse. The car and track are at the heart of the story now disturbing this land.

"I begin my way up the narrow road into the mountain. I see a light in the first settlement and drive towards this light where I will rest for the night . . . ."

These two sheets of manuscript were tossed somewhere on the Belt Parkway, tucked inside Olivia's purse. She had put them there to work on while she rode the subway from the Bronx to Brooklyn. The rest of her papers had been in her briefcase, out of the range of Jamin's fury, but as she stepped into the Plaza room with Jamin, she found herself thinking about these pages and wondering where she'd filed the earlier draft so that she might retrieve a copy. In them she had set out what she saw as a symbol of the conflict: the old colonial railroad through the hills, which foreign-owned companies wanted to revive as an alternate route to the coast now that civil war threatened the current rail lines. But the railroad ran through NLA territory, and as long as guerrillas could sabotage it, the railroad could not be repaired and used. In these pages she had set out a symbol of the conflict; now she was about to meet the faces.

No names were exchanged. She immediately recognized Benjamin DeVries, the international banker. The other two men she didn't know by name, but she recognized their faces and later learned their names. One was Anton Moreau, founder of Flatbush Veneer Company and a likely front figure of the CIA; the other, Willie Williams, the mercenary she'd spotted the night of the reception.

Jamin introduced her as his translator. He gave her no explanation of what she was to do, and she wondered why he was manufacturing this pretense. Did he finally trust her enough to take her to the inside of the story? More likely he had brought her here to throw these men off balance. As they entered the room, Jamin put on his sunglasses. The room was dimly lit by a goose-necked lamp arched over the center of the table where light pooled then spread thinly to the corners. The winter sun had set, and the patch of sky in the well of buildings was darkening. The room smelled of tobacco and peppermint. On the table an ashtray was littered with cigar butts and little squares of cellophane.

Jamin stepped up to the table and sat down in the light; he gestured for Olivia to sit on the bed behind him. From his pocket he drew forth a map; from another pocket he pulled out a pen. He spread the map on the table and traced a line from North to South.

"This is the route of the railroad," he began without introduction or transition. "Two-thirds of the rails are already operable. The rest can be repaired or replaced. The track through the foothills is where most of the replacements are needed. We could, if financed adequately and supplied, complete the replacement in a month." He glanced up, his abruptness masking his discomfort.

The three men stared at the map. Moreau lit a cigarette. "If certain conditions are met and financial terms agreed upon, we could also guarantee the safety of any trains running through the foothills," Jamin went on. "If our conditions are not met, it is fair to say there is no guarantee of the trains, the cargo, or of any outside workers who might try to repair the rails."

He looked up again. This time the men met his gaze. Benjamin DeVries stared slightly over his head. His thin white fingers were folded in his lap; he sat sideways to the table with his legs crossed. He showed no sign of a response.

Anton Moreau, however, shifted his bulk forward and arranged his face in a genial smile. A rim of sweat beaded above his lip. "You know of course that you may soon lose control of those hills," he declared.

"Is that your intention?" Jamin asked.

Moreau's fat lips spread on his face. "If it were, we wouldn't be talking with you now. But you should be aware of what is happening."

"I am aware."

"The situation's not in our hands or your hands; you may not be able to guarantee us anything in a few weeks," Moreau said.

"That is why we are here," DeVries inserted coolly, "to assure control."

"Yes . . . yes . . . of course," Moreau went on, "but such assurances aren't always possible."

DeVries turned to Jamin. He stared at him dispassionately. From the pocket of his suit he pulled out a red and white peppermint and began unwrapping the paper. "And what do you think, Mr. Nyo? Can you provide us such assurance?"

"I have been in touch with our leadership still in the country. I am assured if we rid ourselves of certain obstacles, our chances are favorable," Jamin said.

Olivia stared at DeVries' pale, expressionless face across the table to see if he believed Jamin. She wondered who Jamin had been in touch with and how. If any of the leadership was even left, it was unlikely that he could contact them, she thought. But DeVries seemed to accept Jamin's assurance.

"What would it take to clear the way of such obstacles?" DeVries asked. He placed the peppermint on his tongue then snapped his tongue into his mouth like a snake.

Jamin paused for a moment. He leaned back in his chair clasping his hands behind his head. "Commitments from our friends that once the path is cleared, they will not come in on their own to take advantage." His tone was aggressive, yet Olivia heard in it a whine in a high-pitched register.

"And what do you consider an adequate commitment?" DeVries asked.

But before Jamin could answer, Moreau interrupted, "That's all well and good, well and good, but you must realize events have gone beyond our *ability* to make such commitments."

"*You* must realize," Jamin said tapping the back of his head impatiently with his thumbs, "that if we lose control, the railroad will be blown up. Explosives were planted months ago along the whole track, not simply in the north. Should events take another turn, there will be no railroad to discuss." He unclasped his hands. He stared at Moreau, whom he thought he could intimidate. "You need to understand too that the safety of the railroad is not unrelated to the safety of Robert Nyral and myself."

At this point DeVries shifted in his chair. Olivia wished she could see Jamin's face. She wondered if what he was saying were true or a gigantic improvisation. To the best of her knowledge there was no immediate way for the NLA to know what happened to Jamin and Nyral over here. There were no newspapers or televisions in the hills; she'd read that telephone lines in most areas had been destroyed. It was true there were radios, but news could take weeks to spread. Jamin was isolated over here, without support. His only power was to weave strategems, and in that he was out of his league, she thought. She wondered if he knew this. His only bargaining tool was his willingness to destroy what these men wanted; yet the destruction was of his own land, not theirs. He had no leverage other than this ready nihilism, and she feared suddenly that his belief in his own protean ego would trap him. She looked at Benjamin DeVries on the other side of the table. In the dim, pink eyes staring past her, she thought she saw a will steady enough to spring the trap.

"That would be foolish," DeVries answered quietly, as if Jamin had simply threatened to throw a temper tantrum.

"The business interests of many nations are at stake here," Moreau reacted. "Ore and products could pass through to the ocean if that railroad were open. It would mean revenue for your country, improved trade, communications; it could link nations . . ."

"You are overestimating the value of a few miles of track," Jamin answered.

"The value to us is one million U.S. dollars," DeVries said flatly. "No questions. No records. All expenses—materials, labor—we will finance in addition; and we will pay for the use of the track."

Jamin laughed suddenly, a derisive laugh meant to diminish what had just been offered. Yet Olivia heard the breathlessness at its center. DeVries had summed up what he thought of Jamin and his power in an easy purchase in dollars and cents. Jamin watched the older man through the smoky lens of his sunglasses. The contrast between the two men was striking. Jamin towered over DeVries even at the table. He was a foot taller, powerfully built, a dark ebony color. He wore the soiled clothes of a street corner man or factory worker. DeVries wore a black silk suit and bow tie. His translucent skin and thin white hair seemed to let the light pass through. Yet he met Jamin's gaze without flinching. He folded his ringed hands on the table. Only in their hands, soft, almost feminine, with long manicured fingers was there a coincidence between the two men.

It was Jamin who turned away first. He leaned back in his chair toward Olivia. She had not yet been called upon to translate anything. DeVries too glanced at her. She saw the assumptions he made about her presence with Jamin. She wondered if Jamin had brought her here precisely for those assumptions to be made. She also wondered if Willie Williams recognized her as the reporter who had interviewed him years ago in Angola. If he did, he showed no evidence. He sat unspeaking, a great hulk of a man stuffed into a blue suit.

Jamin chattered something to her which she only partly comprehended, but she knew it didn't matter if she understood or not, for he was using this moment to recover his own poise. She answered in the same dialect, "Be careful."

Jamin nodded. He set the front legs of his chair back on the floor. "My translator agrees that you are trying to steal from us. And that you think we are thieves who will steal from our own people."

Moreau smiled even wider, as if his face knew no other response. DeVries, however, did not smile. "What is it your people would require?" DeVries asked. "A similar sum for them to be disbursed as you see fit?" He was seeking only Jamin's price; that Jamin could be bought he took for granted.

"I like to know whom I am doing business with," Jamin said now.

"I have always been a man of my word," DeVries answered.

231

Jamin stood up. He moved to the desk, where he picked up a bottle of scotch. He poured a few ounces into a water glass. He looked over at Moreau then back at DeVries. "The two of you have worked together before if I am not mistaken," he said. "Your word in the past has preceded killings in our country and in our neighbors'." He sipped the warm liquor.

DeVries had been sitting at the table calmly, almost detached from the proceedings, but now his back arched over his shoulders, and his body drew up almost like an animal's ready to pounce. His hands curled in on themselves; his jaw jutted forward. "You make a mistake with such impudence," he said.

His look frightened Olivia, but Jamin didn't appear to notice. "Yours is not the only offer we have received," he replied. "I am telling you my terms. I do not do business if I don't know the other side."

Olivia wondered why Jamin was asking to know the other players. Did he hope to gain some advantage? Exactly what was the game being played?

"We have not asked you to name *who* will remove the obstacle. I do not see that we need to give names that you yourself are not prepared to give. We have come ready to make our first payment tonight; another payment will be made when the obstacle is cleared; a final one when our project is complete."

Olivia realized now that they were talking about more than a railroad. An obstacle. Who or what was the obstacle? She wanted to reach out and caution Jamin.

As if sensing this response, DeVries added, "I also would suggest that if you want candor in the future, you not bring your *fille de joie* with you." He acknowledged Olivia with a twitch of his mouth that she supposed was meant to be a smile.

Moreau quickly placed a fat hand on DeVries' arm; he streatched out his other hand towards Jamin, who stood by the window. "I'm sure this young woman wouldn't mind stepping into the other room if it would make this gentleman more comfortable." He too smiled at Olivia.

Jamin motioned for her to remain seated. "This is my translator," he said.

DeVries squinted at Olivia through the light. She shifted uncomfortably under his stare. She could, she thought, get her story

232

better in the other room anyway, listening at the door, where she could take notes while everyone spoke more candidly. Yet she also knew this was how she reacted to the assertion of power: she stepped aside and found an alternate space for herself, then later bristled at having lost her footing.

DeVries arched his lip. "I meant no offense to the young woman," he said.

"Of course not. Of course not," Moreau assured. His grey hair flared about his face. "We have larger purposes to settle tonight. And we don't have much time." He glanced at the leather watch-band pinching his wrist. "Realities are changing quickly; we must decide what part we want to take." He glanced again at Olivia. "It is always nice to have the company of a lady, but it might be difficult to speak as frankly as we must, you understand, when we do not all know each other. Perhaps if my colleague could accompany your translator to the bar for a drink just while we finish our business . . ."

Olivia didn't move; she held her position for Jamin. Willie Williams stood. His left eye quivered as if it might open, but it remained half closed. He still had not spoken. It occurred to Olivia that she could interview him, could perhaps find out what was going on from him. She began to cast about in her mind for the most advantageous place for herself when she felt a change in the room: a sudden quiet as if reality were about to shift. She looked at Jamin. He had poured himself another drink and stepped into the shadows by the curtains. He had been moving progressively away from the light and the people until now he was barely distinguishable from the heavy braided drapes. He sipped the drink. His mouth was set in a contemptuous line, his head cocked slightly to the side. She wished she could see his eyes behind the sunglasses. She noticed in his face the hardness had returned she had seen earlier in the day, the distance of a decision made. Then all at once, as if light shot into the room, she saw how the pieces connected. She understood what this meeting was about.

Jamin set his drink on the window ledge and stepped over to her. "Go on," he said abruptly. He took her arm and lifted her from the bed. "I'll find you if I need you." His back was straight; his attention focused, not on her, but on what was before him. She realized now that he had brought her here to give himself time to

233

find his footing with these men, but now his time was up. These men had come to take him across a line. They were preparing to pay him well so he would take the action they themselves would not, to change an order by sheer exertion of will. Bulagwi arrived tomorrow; tonight they were planning his assassination.

The door shut behind Olivia. Willie Williams escorted her to the lobby, where the patrons of the Palm Court sat eating and laughing at marble tables. Three violins filled the room with the music of Vivaldi. Panic rose within Olivia. All day Jamin had been preparing to cross this line. Why had it taken her so long to recognize the signs? Did he really think he could change the realities of his country by killing Bulagwi? Instead he would assume the one guise from which he might not return. As an assassin he left the company of men. All day he had been moving towards this point—his rationalization for letting others die, his tirade against the powers that be, his attempt at intimacy with her, his guilt over Nyral, his cajoling, his rage, his defense—he had been moving through the mine field of his emotions until tonight he had at last resigned to the calm, dead center from which he could act. She wondered if he sensed she might understand. Or was it possible that he wanted her to stop him?

Chapter 25

An hour later Olivia returned to Jamin's room. She had learned what she could from Willie Williams: that he'd met Moreau in Angola, that Moreau knew DeVries from his days in the Congo. Williams had been Moreau's aide and bodyguard for the past five years. Finally she had asked, "What are they planning exactly?"

But at that question Williams had grown suspicious. "Why you ask so many questions?" he'd demanded. He'd taken hold of her arm and began leading her to the rear of the hotel. But as an after-theatre crowd rounded the corner by the gift shop, Olivia had slipped away from Willie Williams. She darted into the ladies' room where she locked herself in one of the stalls. Surely he wouldn't follow her in here. She had listened. She waited and listened for almost half an hour. When she finally emerged, there was no sign of Williams.

She hurried back to Jamin's room, checking all the time for Williams. She knocked on the door, but she was greeted not by Jamin, but by a balding white man in a bathrobe. He held a toothbrush in his hand, and he looked as puzzled as she did when he saw her standing there. She glanced again at the room number, then explained that she'd been visiting with a friend in that room only a short time before.

"I don't know about your friend," the man replied. "No one was here when I checked in half an hour ago."

Olivia apologized, and the man shut the door. She stood for a moment trying to figure out where Jamin could have gone. She knocked on the doors on either side, then on the door across the hall, but she only managed to awaken an elderly woman and a young couple. There was no sign of Jamin.

She went to the lobby, where she used the house phone to ask for Jamin Nyo, but he wasn't registered. She asked for Robert Nyral then Benjamin DeVries, but none were registered. All the while she kept looking over her shoulder.

She remembered the taxi outside and hurried through the revolving brass doors. Ladies in fur coats and men in evening dress were arriving as she left, milling beneath the heaters under the canopy. She quickly made her way to the corner of 58th Street. There she caught her breath. Still parked in the yellow zone was the cab. She walked towards it, keeping her head turned from the security camera on the awning. As she passed, she saw a parking ticket on the windshield.

Glancing inside, she saw her briefcase on the floor and felt a small release as if order might still be restored. The taxi was locked, but the street-side window was cracked open. With her back to the camera and with the deftness of one who has broken in and out of situations half her life, Olivia worked her arm into the window and flipped the lock. She quickly retrieved her case. She checked the pocket. Ever since the incident with her purse in Jamin's room, she'd divided her cash between her purse and case, a lesson which now yielded her $50 and a measure of freedom.

She crossed the street to wait for Jamin. She could have waited in the cab, but she was afraid if Jamin saw her there, he might not return. She was afraid to hide inside and surprise him for she didn't know who else might be with him. She went over to the Paris Cinema opposite the Plaza, where she pretended to be reading the billboards while she watched the taxi. She was afraid if she went to look for Jamin elsewhere, she might miss him, and she thought at some point he would return to the cab.

It was 11:10. It was cold. She paced in front of the theatre then in front of the office building next door. At one point she thought she saw Jamin. A tall man in a khaki-colored jacket with a black cap passed and glanced into the cab; but as she hurried towards him, the man turned, and she saw his white face. She stepped away, back across the street into the shadows. She didn't know what she would say or do when she did confront Jamin. He had told her once that a revolution did not allow the personal, yet she wondered if what he was about to do was an act of revolution or the most personal act of all: an expiation of his own guilt over those he had sent back to die, over Nyral, over his own preserved and superior life.

She looked up. The snow was again falling. The flakes veered into the yellow light of the street lamp at odd angles then disappeared into the darkness. She remembered Jamin noting how the street lights turned themselves on in America, for Americans did not like to live with the darkness, he insisted, and they did not have to. Yet for years she had been peering obsessively down a dark hole into which she had yielded her confidence and her ability to act. But now she *must* act to find and stop Jamin, whose destiny she had once believed in and for whom she still cared.

As she paced under the marquee, she found herself thinking about Nyral and his fish. She imagined Jamin and Nyral eating the fish on the Plaza's gold-rimmed plates with lemons wrapped in yellow netting. She considered running up and down the halls of the Plaza looking for discarded room service trays with fishbones and lemons in hairnets in order to find Jamin. Or maybe she should go back to the elevator where she and Jamin had left the boxes of veneer and wait there, strips of veneer with which to cover the tables and televisions of the Plaza. Her thoughts were bouncing off each other and dissolving into their own darkness when across the street a policeman stopped beside the taxi. He walked slowly up to the car. Olivia stood still. Could he know about Jamin? She drew in a breath of cold air. How could he know? But he checked his watch, then pulled a pad from his pocket and began writing another ticket. When he went to place his on the windshield, he paused at seeing the first one, shrugged, then lifted the wiper and set his beside it.

Olivia resumed pacing. "Show's over." A voice spoke from

behind. Olivia started and turned. An usher had come out of the theatre and peered now into her face. "Aren't you freezing? I kept thinking you were coming inside." The lights under the marquee dimmed. A few patrons wandered out. Inside, behind the candy counter, the lights went off. Olivia didn't answer. The girl moved on.

Olivia turned to look back across the street, and there, from wherever he had come, was Jamin getting into the cab. Olivia darted off the curb in front of a car which slammed on its brakes. She raced towards the taxi. Jamin shut the door. He started the motor. She thrust her fingers into the opened window on the driver's side as he shifted into reverse. She held onto the glass as though she would hold the car by sheer physical force.

Seeing the hand propelled towards him, Jamin bolted around and slammed his fist against the fingers on the window. He hit with such force that the glass cracked. Olivia shrieked. She snatched back her hand. A sharp pain shot through her whole arm. Her eyes opened wide, filling with tears. She tried to speak, but the pain was so intense that she couldn't make a sound. Jamin stared at her. His own face looked wild for a moment, then recognizing her, froze as if in a question, then just as quickly grew distant. He rolled up the window, and without a word, grazing her coat with the taxi, he sped away.

Olivia clutched her bare hand against her body. The cold sharpened the pain. She was sure her fingers were broken. A car honked for her to get out of the street. She made her way to the curb. Across the street the last light went out at the theatre. She tried to bend her fingers, but the middle two on her right hand were rigid. She wanted to cry, not so much because of the pain but because she knew now she had been right about Jamin. She'd hoped she'd misinterpreted what she'd heard in the room, but now she knew with certainty that Jamin had made the crossing.

Olivia stood on the curb for a moment. She didn't know where to go next. She couldn't bear going back to Jenny's and facing Jenny and Mark and Kay. She was freezing so she trudged up the steps of the Plaza and through the revolving doors. The Palm Court was still open, but even if she had been able to afford to eat there, she didn't want to sit out under palm trees among the marble urns and crystal lamps listening to other people's chatter. She worried suddenly that Willie Williams might still be in the hotel and spot her. She went to the bar, but it had already closed. She dropped onto the steps in the back hall behind the bar. Her fingers throbbed in a dull pain. She leaned her head against the wall and shut her eyes. She longed for sleep but had no bed, wanted comfort but had no one to comfort her.

The man she had been pursuing . . . how long?—it seemed to her now her whole lifetime—had leaped off the edge of the world tonight. As she drifted towards sleep, old images returned: a naked child in the dust, a marabou stork, a barge on a river, images from a darkness over which she seemed to have no control.

Then suddenly a hand was shaking her shoulder. "I'm sorry, you can't sleep here." Opening her eyes, she saw the dusky face of a man in uniform. She had trouble for a moment remembering where she was. The security guard reached down to help her up. "I'm sorry, miss."

She straightened her bright red coat around her. Her face took on an apologetic look. "I got left by my group," she began to improvise. "My purse was stolen. I can phone in the morning; they'll wire me money, but I've no place to sleep tonight." Almost without thinking she invented, instinctively creating a place for herself in the world.

"What time will your group be home?" the guard asked.

"Seven. If I could just sleep here till seven."

"The Plaza don't allow transients . . . not that you're a transient, but I'd lose my job if I let you stay."

It was after midnight; she would have to wake up Jenny and Mark, use her money to get uptown. She was so tired. She picked up her briefcase.

"But wait a minute . . ." he amended, "there's a cot in the back stairway. You couldn't stay as late as seven, but I could let you sleep till my last round. Then you'd have to get right up and go, but at least it'd be light out. The streets would be safer."

She stared at this earnest-faced black man in his mid-fifties. She nodded to his terms. She remembered the man this morning at the coffee shop who'd given her breakfast. Suddenly she felt overcome by this unwarranted kindness.

"I'm sure your friends will get you home all right," the watchman said. "Come on now." He led her to the second floor stairwell where he rolled out a small cot. He handed her a blanket and pillow. "Now you get some sleep; you'll feel better. But you got to go soon as I wake you. And I can't let you do this again. The hotel's going to be tight as a drum tomorrow. Some important people coming in."

He left, but every hour or so, Olivia stirred in her sleep as the watchman passed on his rounds. Twice he covered her with the ends of the blanket she'd knocked to the floor.

At 6:30 the guard shook her awake. She rose obediently; together they folded the cot. Neither spoke, but as they stuffed the bed back into the closet, Olivia said simply, "Thank you."

He nodded and led her downstairs to the lobby where the newsstand was just opening. There she bought a *New York Times* and a *Washington Tribune*. As she paid for the papers she tried to bend her fingers, but the two middle ones were stiff. Jamin's blow had been so instinctive and so violent that she felt sure if she'd stuck her head into the car instead, he would have broken her neck. There had been nothing personal in the attack, only a reaction to what he feared. She wondered now who he thought she was. She realized how foolish she'd been to come upon him without warning in the dark. Yet when he'd seen who she was, he'd stopped only long enough for her to remove her hand. There'd been no exchange, no feeling or apology for the pain he'd inflicted, only the flat stare of one lost to his own imperative.

Olivia tucked the newspapers in her briefcase and went outside. The sun was just lighting the sky through the corridors of buildings. The air was surprisingly warm. There were fresh mounds of snow along the park and on the steps of the fountain in front of the Plaza. Olivia came to the morning rested and relieved that morning had in fact come. No shots had been fired; no center had yet fallen away. There was still time. Bulagwi was not due to arrive for several hours. She had no way of knowing what events were already conspiring, but for a moment she could almost believe nothing was occurring except the dawning of this first crisp day of February.

She started down Fifth Avenue with the sunrise. She wanted to walk and let the air clear her thoughts. She peered in at store windows: at four-foot-high bears and lions and giraffes in FAO Schwartz, at diamond necklaces and rings in Tiffany's, chocolates at Lady Godiva's, where one thumb-size candy cost the hourly wage of a worker in the hills. The wealth and plenty of her country overwhelmed her. She stopped in front of Fortunoff's where two men were polishing the three foot-high chrome letters. Next door at Gucci's, polishers were scrubbing the brass. When the sun finally made its ascent over the buildings, it would glint off these facades whose metals likely originated in Africa. "Ah, Olivia Turner, your country is in love with the image of itself." The words sounded so clearly in her ear that she turned expecting to see Jamin there whispering to her or perhaps in the taxi at the curb waiting for her. But he was not there. Only his voice, like an alter ego, offering commentary upon her life.

At the corner she brought a cup of fresh orange juice and a hot pretzel from two vendors wheeling up their carts for the day. She then crossed the street and settled on a bench at Rockefeller Center where she opened the *Tribune* and looked for Kay's byline. It was over a short lead-in on the front page which jumped to a full article with pictures on page three. There were two pictures of Bulagwi: one in a leopard skin robe with a staff. He was standing with a lion on one side of him and a Mercedes Benz on the other and the caption read: "The best of past and present drives us into the future." The picture was a standard. The slogan was plastered all over the Capitol like a car advertisement. She'd always wondered which European public relations firm had contrived this image for Bulagwi. The other picture showed Bulagwi in full military dress reviewing his troops also dressed with plumage and epaulets. They stood at attention on a dry field in front of the Capitol building. The building itself resembled the White House except that sprouting off the cupolas were Greek and Roman statues of Prometheus and Venus with the heads of Africans. Olivia skimmed the article:

A Man and His History:
Amundo Bulagwi Arrives
To Quiet Diplomatic Storm

By Katherine Bernstein Walsh
Tribune Staff Writer

NEW YORK — Fifty-five-year-old Army General Amundo Bulagwi arrives at the United Nations today to explain the reported massacres of an estimated 6,000–8,000 of his countrymen. Insisting that he owes explanations to no one, President Bulagwi said in a telephone interview that he was coming to New York simply "to visit with my old friends and allies at the United Nations."

Prime Minister and President-for-Life, Amundo Bulagwi has held the reins of power in his small African nation for the past 15 years in spite of half a dozen coup attempts and the de facto secession of a quarter of his population into the barren hills of the north.

To understand the forces now at play in this country, one can start with a brief history of the man who rose from the son of a peasant farmer and sorceress to the multimillionaire potentate who counts among his friends kings and queens.

Ngwami Amatari Joseph Amundo Bulagwi was born August 31, 1929 in a small village in the south. He was the ninth son of his father, the first son of his mother. When Bulagwi was eight, his father converted to Christianity. Heeding the warnings of the priests about the sins of sorcery, his father took Bulagwi from his mother and sent him to a parish school thirty miles away. He cast Bulagwi's mother, his third wife, from his compound.

His father's conversion opened the way to lucrative business opportunities with the church which purchased his crops. He sent two more sons to the mission school. From the age of eight, Bulagwi spent 11 months of the year at school. The other month he lived in his father's compound with his 20 brothers and sisters.

A competent though not outstanding student, according to reports, Bulagwi went on to the mission secondary school where he finished the equivalent of the tenth grade before he enlisted in the Army. It was the Army where he began to distinguish himself. He rose quickly through the ranks, eventually earning his training in England. He was in an African detachment during the

Suez crisis and returned to his country as a colonel in 1957.

By the time he returned, the political climate had heated up in neighboring countries which were agitating for independence. In his own country Robert Nyral, a secondary school teacher, had founded the Party for National Liberation, predecessor to the current National Liberation Association. Nyral, however, was considered a radical and a threat by colonial authorities, who arrested him on conspiracy charges in 1958.

Bulagwi's more moderate stand and his popularity with the army found him favor with the colonial government. In an effort to appease growing dissent, the colonists appointed Bulagwi adjunct Governor General in 1962. One of Bulagwi's first acts was to release Robert Nyral from prison. Gradually an alliance grew up between Nyral's party and the people of the north and Bulagwi's predominantly southern base; this alliance led to independence in 1969.

A coalition government then ensued and lasted for seven years. However, charges of corruption and brutality by the army increased. Finally Robert Nyral resigned his portfolio in a week which began with the killing of the Finance Minister, a political ally of Nyral's. The bloodshed which followed was the beginning of a storm which has stirred ever since and this week sweeps again into the chambers of the United Nations . . . ."

Kay's story went on to elaborate charges against Bulagwi, to offer opinions from opponents and supporters and then to discuss the possible consequences of the ensuing meetings. Olivia noted that the article was filled with secondhand information—much of it gleaned from her own firsthand accounts years before—organized in a clear, flat chronological structure. She didn't finish the story.

She set the paper down beside her and unwrapped her pretzel. She didn't bother picking up the *Times*. As she ate, she looked up now and watched the jets of water shooting the gigantic gold

Prometheus at Rockefeller Center. As water sprayed into the cold air, she found herself thinking of Nyral's fish flapping between water and sky yesterday, of the view it must have caught of a new world no longer beneath the sea, a world both astounding and terrifying, for in it the fish was not equipped to breathe. She thought again of her purse flying out the window, her own scraps of identity thrown to the wind. And she thought of Jamin who, by the very action he contemplated, was forcing her to her own ascent and action.

As she drank her juice and ate the twisted bread, she rehearsed what she knew. From her briefcase she pulled out the questions she'd asked herself yesterday and checked off those she'd answered. She'd at least found Jamin and Nyral. She was fairly certain now that Western interests had provided the financing for the NLA visit, either privately through businessmen like Benjamin DeVries or covertly through the CIA and other intelligence agencies of its allies. How committed or united the West was in its sponsorship, she wasn't sure, but the U.S., probably France and Britain, and perhaps Belgium and Western-leaning African countries, recognized that Bulagwi might soon topple; they saw, or at least had seen, Jamin and Nyral as replacements. That the United Nations had been willing to hear a bid for separate statehood, she assumed, as Bulagwi must have assumed, was simply the first step towards a shift in power. Yet Olivia also knew, and Jamin and Nyral knew, that no commitment could be counted on unless the power was secured, and so she felt sure the West had not entirely abandoned Bulagwi. She wondered if DeVries too were playing both sides.

She wasn't clear about the source of the uprising in the hills, though she tended to account it to Jamin's explanation: that in the end his people had simply been unable to wait and had plunged into a battle they could not win. She had no doubt that there were forces like DeVries pushing at them and manipulating their fears, but in the final analysis they had staged the raids and had yielded to the manipulation. She didn't know where the Soviets stood in this scenario except as spoilers of whatever would shift the balance of influence from them.

Olivia feared that Jamin, for all his intelligence and worldliness, had also fallen victim. She thought of what Nyral had said on the pier: that it was Jamin who believed in the evil and, fighting it on its own terms, gave it power. She thought of other countries in Africa, those governed by humane and rational men, and it seemed these too eventually fought their version of evil on its terms, thus turning it loose in their land. Nyral had held longer than most to his ideals. Yet she wondered how he could keep his hold after the massacres and in the face of the superpowers' bid for his land. The conspiracies against ideals were too great and the weight of history too compelling, she thought. The necessity of taking a side for one's own survival seemed inevitable.

She drew her coat around her. On the ice rink below, great machines were rolling out to clear away the old crust then spray a new layer of water on the ice. Olivia suddenly stood. Tossing her cup and napkin into the trash, she picked up the newspapers from the bench and checked her watch. It was 7:45. Bulagwi arrived at eleven. A press conference was set for 2 o'clock in the White and Gold suites of the Plaza. She had a few hours. With luck she might have a few days. She tucked the *Tribune* and the *Times* into her briefcase; then she set out, back up Fifth Avenue.

Chapter 26

Jenny awoke with a start. Beside her Mark slept on his belly, his head flat on the mattress, his mouth opened; he was sleeping hard, deeper than she ever slept. She didn't know what had jolted her awake, but suddenly alert, she got out of bed. She picked up the Afco file which had fallen to the floor and set it on the bureau, then dressed quickly. She smelled coffee brewing.

In the living room Kay was sitting on the couch reading her own story in the *Tribune*.

"You're up early," Jenny said, stepping over to open the shutters.

"I never sleep more than a few hours. Didn't Olivia get back last night?"

Jenny glanced around the room. "I guess not. When did you get in?"

"Around two. You were asleep, but Mark was up."

"Oh?"

"He's really worried about that mining deal, isn't he? You know, I may be able to help him. I have some contacts in Washington. He's worked so hard. The business could be such a help to those countries though I swear some of them seem determined to slit their own throats." Kay sipped her coffee holding the saucer and cup in front of her.

"I'm afraid not everyone considers American business their benefactor," Jenny said.

"What do you mean?"

"I simply mean there are other points of view. Mark's hard work isn't the issue."

"You constantly amaze me, Jenny. Mark is about to lose a major investment, and you sit around considering other people's points of view." She laughed lightly then picked up the newspaper. "I suppose I never will understand you. But in any case I can help Mark when I get back to Washington. There are several people in the State Department who are also concerned with stabilizing that area of Africa. Mark can come down and speak to them."

Jenny picked up Cassie, who had jumped onto the footstool. She held the cat firmly with both hands. "That's very thoughtful of you, Kay, but I think Mark can handle his business on his own."

"Oh?" Kay looked up from under one eyebrow. "He seemed to think it was a good idea last night. In fact I was about to make a few calls for him before I go over to his mother's."

"You're going to Helene's?"

"It was generous of her to offer her apartment. You're lucky to have such in-laws. You should have met mine." Kay poured herself another cup of coffee from the pot she'd brought to the table. "Even if I'd had a chance of making my marriage work—and that's doubtful—my mother-in-law did all she could to scuttle the odds. We lived in a tiny apartment in East Boston, and she used to drive in from Newton every week and complain about how messy I kept the place and how I was neglecting Randy. I'm sure when I finally left Randy, she crowed: 'See, I told you what sort of girl she was.'" Kay lit a cigarette and leaned back into the pillows of the couch. "It's odd, Jenny, isn't it, the way things turn out?" Jenny stroked Cassie. She didn't answer. "I always did like Helene though," Kay went on, "the few times I met her. Don't you?"

"I didn't know Mark had asked you about his parents' apartment."

"It really is a help. I've called the hospital; David can be

247

released Wednesday with a nurse, and Mark's offered to pay for the nurse so I can keep working."

"I see." Jenny set the cat down. She began sweeping up seeds in her hand which the new bird had scattered on the table. "When are you going over?"

Kay glanced at her watch. "I'll make those calls, then Mark said he'd stop by with me on his way to work. I can run to the hospital from there before Bulagwi's arrival. You know today is a big day for us." Jenny wondered who 'us' was when Kay added, "I wonder where Olivia is." An anxious look passed over her face as though she feared Olivia might already be on the story.

"I'm sure she'll turn up."

"I wonder if she's found out anything." Kay lit another cigarette; then all at once she smiled as Mark walked into the room. She raised her cup. "Breakfast's in the kitchen," she announced. "Lox and bagels as you requested. I went out early this morning for them."

Mark glanced at Jenny, who stood holding a handful of birdseed. He hadn't had a chance to tell her about his talk with Kay last night. From the look on Jenny's face he realized that in his depression he had confided too much to Kay. "I'll just have cereal," he answered. He glanced back at Jenny. "You want to help me?"

"Don't tell me you can't make your own cereal, Mark," Kay quipped. As Jenny went into the kitchen, Kay reached for the telephone.

"I thought I'd take Kay by mother's after breakfast," Mark said facing the cabinet. "She can move in tomorrow." He turned, holding a bowl. "It'll be nice to have our apartment back to ourselves, won't it? How long is Olivia staying? Did she come in last night?"

"No." Jenny stood watching him from the doorway.

"I worked at my desk after I talked to Reynolds; then Kay came in, but Olivia never did. I wonder where she is." Mark strained for a casual tone, but he felt Jenny's tension, and she heard his strain. She shut the kitchen door and went over and sat down. She reached into the bag on the table for a bagel.

"You want to have dinner together tonight?" he asked. "Just

the two of us. I think mother would love to have Erika over before they go, and we need to talk."

"About what?"

"Just talk and be together." He averted his eyes as he began eating. "I'm sorry about last night. I was upset about Afco; it's out of control."

Jenny stirred her coffee. "Kay said she was going to help you."

Mark glanced at her. "She offered. I don't see that people in Washington can help much, but I'm willing to consider anything." He continued eating.

"Anything?"

He looked up. "What do you mean?"

"I just wonder what you mean by anything."

"I mean anything within legal and moral limits. What are you suggesting?"

"I'm not suggesting anything. I just asked what you meant. I'm not sure the people you speak with will have the same definition of *anything*."

"Oh Christ . . ." Mark reached into the bag for a bagel.

"What would you expect our government to do?" Jenny tried for a neutral tone.

"I don't know if there's anything to be done, but I'm willing to talk. What's wrong with that?"

"Nothing," she said. "Only make certain you're not assuming that your interests and those of the African countries are the same."

"What does that mean?" Mark crushed the bag and tossed it at the trash can.

"You know what it means," Jenny said. She picked up the bag and dropped it in the trash. "Are you helping perpetuate Bulagwi just so Afco can survive?"

"I'm not perpetuating anyone. I don't have that kind of power, Jenny. I'm trying to keep our investors from losing their money."

"Of course you have power; your investment has consequences. You're not value neutral here, Mark."

Mark pushed up from the table. "I don't have time for this," he said; he set his bowl in the sink.

Jenny wondered if he accepted third world politics as the cause of dissent between them, or if he too were relieved to let it rest there. "Are we still having dinner?" she asked.

He took his coat from the chair. "I don't know. I'll call you."

The Washington Tribune lay in a shaft of sunlight on the brass coffee table. Mark and Kay had left with Erika whom they were to drop off at school. Jenny was sitting on the couch holding her cup of coffee. She was reading the end of Kay's story, or rather she was reading where the paper was opened, not paying attention to the words but forcing them into the empty space opening inside her. Her eyes glided down the page with little heed of the meaning until they caught on a sentence: "I cannot allow crocodiles to eat my people." She backed up and started the paragraph again.

"Among stories coming out of the country is one in which Bulagwi is said to have driven a school bus of prisoners onto a bridge above the Izo River. At one end of the bridge his soliders were stationed with machine guns and orders to shoot anyone who tried to cross. At the other end a swarm of deadly vipers were let loose. Below in the river crocodiles waited. Bulagwi then opened the doors of the bus and released the barefoot, manacled prisoners and told them they could chose their path to freedom. Those who jumped from the bridge were quickly pursued by the crocodiles. After the crocodiles' attack was complete, Bulagwi took his rifle and shot the offending reptiles. 'I can't allow crocodiles to eat my people,' he is reported to have said. Those who chose to charge the soldiers were shot down. And those who chose the path of the vipers were bitten and left to fall in the forest nearby. "'So you see, I allow even my enemies the freedom of choice,' Bulagwi is said to have told one of his aides as they re-entered the empty school bus to drive back to the Capitol."

Jenny looked up from the paper. She stood and began pacing the living room. She sat back down on the couch and reread the report. Then she took up the paper and went into her study where she clipped the story. The menace of Bulagwi's choice chilled her even as she found herself plotting her own escape. She was a strong swimmer; she would have jumped from the bridge, tried to dive deep enough into the river to escape the soldiers and the crocodiles. Perhaps the report had come from one who had escaped in this way, disappearing under the waters. Or had it come from one who had gone into the forest and knew enough about magic or medicine or prayer to cure himself of the deadly bite of the viper.

As she considered the options, she sensed she was missing some key in Bulagwi's riddle, but the answer eluded her. She glimpsed it as through a haze which thinned for a moment, then grew dense so that she couldn't see beyond it; and instead she found herself considering again the choices of Bulagwi.

She picked up the phone. She called Mark's office, but he wasn't in yet. She left a message with his secretary that she was counting on dinner with him tonight and would make arrangements for the restaurant and for Erika. Next she called Helene, who said Mark had just left. He hadn't mentioned dinner, but she said she'd be glad to take Erika for the evening.

Jenny then went into the bedroom for the Afco folder. She wanted to study the projections and the balance sheets, study the details of this plan Mark and DeVries had devised in the hope that she could find a way to grow comfortable with it and with her husband. Perhaps if she studied hard enough, she would forget the complacent look on Kay's face as she'd set forth from the apartment that morning with Mark and Erika.

Jenny picked up a brush and pushed it through her hair which hung limp and shapeless on her shoulders. As she looked into the mirror, she sank down at the dressing table with its ornate wood carvings of cherubims eating grapes. Staring back at her was her own square, serious face, without make-up, with lines already forming at her eyes and mouth. Her face seemed to her unbearably plain. She set the brush down. She was holding the Afco folder in one hand; she stared at her hands, chapped and ragged at the nails. She put the folder aside and reached for the phone book by the night table. She opened the Yellow Pages to "Beauty." She went to a beauty parlor only two or three times a year to to have her hair trimmed, but she studied the ads now as if returning to ancestral custom.

She picked up the phone and made an appointment in thirty

minutes at Vidal Sassoon's on Fifth Avenue for a styling, a shampoo and set, and a manicure. She made another appointment next door at Christine Valme's, for a facial. She wasn't even sure what a facial was, but she took the recommendation of the Sassoon receptionist. She watched herself as she made these appointments, wondering what was causing her to move out on this tangent. She seemed to be acting against her own will; and yet she proceeded, impelled suddenly by a need to invent herself.

She left the apartment at 8:30, her work undone, the Afco folder under her arm, her thoughts ruminating on the choices of Bulagwi. Only those who knew her well would have understood how aberrant this path was for her. As she plunged into the center of high-fashioned make-up and hair styling, she sensed that she too was jumping off a bridge.

Chapter 27

Mark left word that he did not want to be disturbed; then he told
his secretary to get DeVries on the phone. Shutting the door to his
office, he dropped his briefcase on his desk and began pacing
before the windows forty-eight floors above the ground. The clear
blue winter sky pressed in upon him.

The intercom buzzed. "Yes?. . . . What do you mean unavail-
able? Where is he? . . . Well, find out where he is and get him."

He sat down at his desk and began flipping through the pink
slips of phone calls he'd already gotten this morning. He set them
aside and buzzed Louise.

"Could you get me a map of Africa? . . . Any map, the one Afco
sent, where is it?"

Mark rifled through his coat closet, and from the top shelf he
pulled out a tube with a map inside. He unrolled it on his desk.
Outlined in red were a cluster of three countries where Afco had
its mines. He stared at the countries and at the surrounding countries as though they were pieces of a puzzle he might, if he were

ingenious enough, rearrange. Why couldn't they ship ore through the western nations, he wondered; then he remembered there were no rail lines or adequate roads. Why was that? He studied the geography. That's right; there were mountain ranges to the west. As he studied the map, he realized he didn't know the area to the west very well. He'd visited the mines with DeVries before the initial investment; he'd sent geologist teams over and talked to area specialists. He had studied maps of the terrain, but he didn't have much firsthand knowledge of these countries—of the land or people or politics. He'd relied on DeVries for this information, and he realized suddenly how helpless he was to effect a change. If it were a recapitalization problem, he could handle that. If it were only a question of financing, he had as much imagination as anyone he knew to find solutions, but here Jenny was right. He had little knowledge of who these people were, what motivated them or governed them. Jenny knew the area from years ago; Olivia had lived there, but he resisted seeking their knowledge, for he didn't want to have to contend with their politics. Instead he was dependent on a man he was beginning to doubt. Had DeVries taken a spread on the debt as Jenny suggested? When she'd asked that question, it had flashed like a light in a corner of his own doubts which he'd been unconsciously accumulating. He had trusted DeVries in his negotiations with the banks. At the time he himself had been swamped with the Greyson closing. When he'd asked DeVries for the records of the transaction, DeVries had put him off as if the records were incidental. He couldn't remember now if he'd even received them. He buzzed Louise and asked her to look. His anger at Jenny was at least in part because she expressed doubts he couldn't afford to express.

Louise buzzed back. "Your father's on the line. You want to speak to him?"

Mark hesistated. "Okay . . . Hi, Dad." He tried to sound cheerful. "What can I do for you?"

"You got your box on? I hate that thing."

"Sorry." He punched off the speaker phone.

"We didn't get to finish our conversation yesterday, and I'm leaving tomorrow. I wanted to know if you'd made a decision about DeVries' partnership."

"Ah . . . No. Right now I'm more concerned about putting out a fire five thousand miles away I have no control over. I don't even know where the fire extinguishers are."

"Anything I can do?"

Mark forced a laugh. "I wish."

"Well, I wanted to tell you, for what it's worth, I think the opportunity DeVries is offering you is unique, a real chance and very generous in my opinion."

"Yes . . ."

"Frankly I don't understand why you haven't snatched it up. He may not wait forever. I hate to go away and have that hanging."

"Jenny and I haven't had a chance to talk," Mark evaded.

"Then talk. I'm sure Jenny won't stand in your way."

"What do you know about DeVries?"

"What do you mean know? I know he's one of the giants of the past several decades. He's moved out of the center of the action a little lately, but that's why he needs you."

"Jenny doesn't trust him."

"Why not?"

"I'm not sure. Woman's intuition I guess."

Irwin laughed. "Well, I'm the last one to argue with that. But a lot's at stake here, Mark. There are other considerations."

"Also, his history, the trail of rumors that have followed him . . ."

"You live on a big screen in the big world, there'll be rumors," Irwin said. "Look at his accomplishments; that's what to look at."

"I'll wire you if I make a decision while you're away," Mark answered.

"Do that."

"Leave the information with Louise." Mark hung up. He stared back at the map, then he buzzed Louise. "Any luck with DeVries?"

"His housekeeper says he left early this morning, didn't leave any messages. Jan, his secretary, swears he's not there. I'll keep trying. Reynolds is on his way in to see you."

Mark turned towards the door as Reynolds knocked and opened it. He was holding *The New York Times*. "Did you read this?" he asked.

"What?"

Reynolds spread the paper on the coffee table. "They attacked one of the mines." He opened to the inside and began to read a paragraph at the bottom of one of the stories.

"Guerrilla forces attacked a platinum mine in the southeastern section, looting and burning barracks where the Army housed its troops . . ." Reynolds looked up as if he were presenting evidence.

Mark nodded. "I know." He picked up his squash racket and began to bang the ball against the window. "DeVries phoned last night. It's a small mine; the damage is limited."

"What do you propose to do?"

Mark laughed. "What do you want me to do? Go over and put out the blaze? I've been trying to get in touch with DeVries all morning."

"We're exposed here, Mark. I've had four calls just this morning from our investors."

Mark caught the ball. He turned in his chair. He lifted his own stack of pink slips and dropped them back on his desk. "I know. As soon as I talk to DeVries, I plan to call them all back.

"Reynolds . . . ," he said emphatically, "I have never let our investors down. I don't intend to start now."

"At least we haven't made the final payment." Reynolds pulled a nail file from his pocket.

"I'll protect our investors," Mark repeated.

"We're not making that payment either. " Reynolds looked up. "I assume you know that."

Mark didn't argue. "Let's get by this, see what can be done. We don't have to make that decision yet."

Reynolds began to clean his nails. "You broke the glass, Mark," he said in a dry voice.

"What?"

He nodded towards the window. "The glass, it's cracked."

"Where?" Mark looked over at the middle window where the small dark smudge of his squash ball was wiped clean each night by the maintenance staff.

"There." Reynolds pointed with the nail file.

Mark stood and went to the window. There he saw the crack the size of two small intersecting rivers on a map and in the center, a hole the size of a pin prick where the wind rushed through.

"I'll have Robert call maintenance." Reynolds pulled a black notebook from his pocket. "We better replace it before the crack spreads." He got up then and started out the door. He left the newspaper on the table and left Mark with his finger over the hole.

Chapter 28

Jenny emerged from the mirrored catacombs of Sassoon's and Valme's polished and fluffed. She was prettier at first glance, yet she was anxious about the time she had wasted and uncertain of the results. She had let the hair stylist talk her into streaking her hair with blonde and lightly perming it; she had let the manicurist persuade her to get a pedicure as well as a manicure; she had allowed the facialist not only to massage but to make up her face. She went through all the rituals without believing in them. As she moved from chair to chair, she took with her the Afco balance sheets and her legal pad. She studied row upon row of figures trying to understand what the cash flow was between Afco, DeVries and Bulagwi and trying as well to give purpose to her time and this pursuit of vanity.

As she studied her image now in the window outside Valme's, she was considering where she could go to set it right. Her hair curled in several layers about her face; it was a brightened brown and blonde with the frontpiece swept to one side. The squareness of her face was mitigated by the curls, but the style looked frivolous and absurd, she thought. Her face was thick with make-up;

three shades of green shadow moving out from her almond-shaped eyes and two shades of toner on her cheeks to accentuate the hollows and again relieve the squareness. Her lips were brushed with a copper color and outlined in a deeper brown. To the average observer she might have appeared glamorous. Her tall figure, clad in a loose purple dress, carried the fullness of face and hair, and the cautious look in her eyes and her obvious pregnancy played against the excess of fashion.

She checked her watch. It was past noon. She had to pick up Erika in less than an hour. She wanted to stop by her old news bureau and check the files. She wanted to review the circumstances surrounding DeVries' resignation from Generale de Metaux. She vaguely remembered a rumor of impropriety, though DeVries had made the company so much money, nothing had ever been confirmed.

In studying the Afco flow of funds statements, she had noticed one discrepancy: an increase of almost two million dollars in the noncash charges this quarter. She had only a limited accounting background, but she thought the increase was unusual though she wasn't sure what it might mean. She wanted to read the business files on DeVries and on Afco at the time the first financing was announced. She also wanted to read files on Bulagwi. However, the bureau was on 42nd Street, and she wouldn't be able to slip in unnoticed. She'd have to greet everyone and explain herself; and so she decided she'd call the editor and see if she could stop by before her dinner with Mark tonight.

Instead she headed across the street to the Plaza which had the closest restroom. There she pulled out her brush and began trying to reconstruct her hair. She brushed hard, but the curls sprang back. The more she brushed, the more recalcitrant the various layers became, until they butted out in odd directions.

Finally she gave up and returned to the lobby. A throng of people crowded around the main entrance. She edged her way towards the door, but a security guard told her she would either have to wait or use another exit. She was so involved in her own thoughts—whether she could pick up Erika on time, how she might yet get work done, whether Mark would call about dinner—that she didn't realize what was happening. She glanced out the window from the corner where she'd been pushed and saw a fleet of limousines drawing up with red, green and black flags flapping on the hoods. Suddenly cameras thrust into the air; flashbulbs blinked at the sun.

A celebrity must be arriving, she thought. The door to the first car opened. There was a break in the crowd, and Jenny saw two tall, elegant women in African gowns emerge, followed by a short black man in a three-piece suit holding a staff in his hand. A goatee sprouted from his chin; a pleased smile spread on his lips; an almost mischievous glint shined in his eyes as he bowed to the awaiting press. Quickly body guards moved in, and she lost sight of him and the women. She realized at once that she had just seen Amundo Bulagwi. The discrepancy between the man and the picture of him she had formed in her mind made her rise to her toes and try to get another look, but the crowd pressed upon him. She had never seen him in person; she had always imagined someone of much more imposing stature. Instead he looked almost humorous with his goatee and glittering eyes. He looked as if he too appreciated the humor of this spectacle. She strained but didn't see him again, for he entered the hotel en masse, moving in a block of dark suits to the elevators.

The gathering began to break apart then. As Jenny moved out from her corner, she caught sight of Olivia standing to the side jotting notes and glancing about as if searching for someone. She looked disheveled; her pants were wrinkled, her short hair uncombed. Jenny pushed over to her. "Olivia . . ." she called.

Olivia glanced up. For a moment she didn't see who had spoken, but when she spotted Jenny, she frowned. "What are you doing here?"

"I just happened to be here. I didn't realize Bulagwi was coming now. I had my hair done . . ." But the state of her hair was not what she wanted to tell Olivia about. She wanted to tell her about the anxiousness she'd felt when she'd read in the paper this morning what Bulagwi had done, to tell her about Mark and Kay. Yet even as she rehearsed the worst of her anxiety, it paled in the light of the story Olivia was pursuing.

"I've been studying the mining financings," she said instead. "You should take a look at Afco's flow of funds statements."

A pained look crossed Olivia's face. In the look Jenny saw what she herself was feeling: that she was irrelevant to the moment at hand.

"Well . . ." Olivia interupted, "I will, but I'm afraid I've got to go to the press conference now."

"Of course."

As Olivia hurried away, Jenny fell silent. She had seen in Olivia's face her seriousness of purpose; and though she didn't know the full extent of that purpose, she compared it to her own that morning and felt chastened.

"Will you be coming back tonight?" she called, but Olivia had already disappeared around the corner of the Palm Court.

Jenny started towards the door. She glanced around. Kay would be here too she realized. She couldn't bear to face Kay right now. She hurried outside, waved down a taxi, and sped across town to get her daughter.

Jenny took Erika to the zoo after school rather than straight home. She wanted to be with her and see the world through her eyes for a while. On the way home Erika fell asleep in the cab. Jenny carried her into the apartment. As she passed through the back hall, she saw Kay sitting at Mark's desk talking on the phone. Kay smiled and waved as Jenny went by. Jenny continued on to Erika's room, where she lay her daughter on the bed. What was Kay doing in her apartment in the middle of the day? How had she gotten in? Mark must have given her a key. The thought of Kay having a key to her home suddenly agitated her so that she made herself sit in the rocking chair in Erika's room until she could gather her composure. She glanced at the snake on Erika's shelf. Partly hidden in the sand, the snake didn't look threatening, and yet the keeper had said if she took away its hiding place, it might strike. She stood and placed a cover over the cage. She wasn't ready to lay bare anyone's hiding place right now. As she finally turned from Erika's room, an expression of enforced calm was on her face.

Kay was still filing her story at Mark's desk, and she raised a finger to indicate she'd be off in a minute. Jenny went on into the living room, where she stood by the window. She wouldn't say anything to Kay. She would maintain control, for she didn't trust her strength in an open contest.

"All done," Kay announced. "What a mad house that was." She stepped down into the living room. "I figured your phone was

261

as easy to file from as any." She stopped when she saw Jenny full face. "Jenny . . . what have you done?" She gestured to her hair. "Well . . ." She walked around to the side of Jenny. "What a difference. You look . . . well . . . older, don't you? Yes. I wonder what Mark will say. Why did you do it? The luxury of a morning at the beauty parlor . . . I can't even remember."

Kay sat over on the couch. "So, tell me, why did you do it? I mean you colored it too, didn't you? I never imagined your dying your hair. Very bold, Jennifer. You do constantly surprise me." Jenny heard the ease in Kay's voice and wondered why she was feeling so confident. Kay went on, "You should have been with us. Everyone was there . . . even *The Auckland Star*. It was madness."

"You've written your story already?" Jenny sought to keep the conversation away from herself.

"I knew most of it in advance. It was only a matter of plugging in Bulagwi's quotes. The story could get interesting though. I can't say exactly how, but I have a feeling. Olivia was there. I think she knows something though she wouldn't say. You haven't talked to her, have you?" Kay tossed the question off casually, but Jenny saw the friendly chatter had in fact been aiming at this question.

"No."

"Well, she was there and acting very secretive. I don't know why she's gotten that way; she didn't used to be. I suppose it's because she's insecure, don't you think? I was rather hoping she might have come back here."

Jenny stared out the window. She understood now, at least in part, why Kay was here. "Anyway, I wanted to gather my things. Helene said I could bring them over early if I wanted. She's so thoughtful. Did you know she'd already set up Mark's room for David. She even brought out Mark's old train set for him. She said David and I could stay there as long as we needed." Jenny felt Kay watching her. She strained to show no emotion, yet she was sure Kay knew the wound she had hold of and was now spreading it open.

Kay continued: "David is much better. Do you think Erika could visit him when we move to Helene's? You should see the two of them together; it's very sweet. I think it would do him a lot of good. If you wanted to work some afternoon, you could drop her off.

I'd take care of them, and then Mark could pick her up on his way home from work."

Still Jenny didn't answer. She stared at the cockatoo chipping at the cuttlebone in its cage. Yet she saw it only as one looks at a two-dimensional picture for she was deep inside herself now as the coil tightened. She was afraid at any moment it might spring and send her shooting out the window. She turned and walked slowly towards the door.

"Where are you going?" Kay asked.

"I have to call Mark."

"Oh . . . I almost forgot. When I got in, the phone was ringing. It was Mark's secretary. Let's see, I wrote down the message . . ." She fumbled through some papers on the coffee table. "He has a dinner meeting with DeVries at 7:30 so he can't make dinner, but he said you can come for dessert if you want. He'll call you from the restaurant . . . you could meet him around 9:30."

Kay looked up smiling. "I asked his secretary which restaurant—I thought you might want to know. She said she'd have to call DeVries' office to find out, but I said I'd do that for you. It's the Jockey Club on Central Park South. DeVries thought I was you so he picked up to say hello. That was nice of him, don't you think? When I explained I was a friend staying with you and reminded him we had met the other day, he invited me to come too. Mark had mentioned that I'd offered to help with some contacts in Washington, and he wanted to talk. I'm sure his contacts are as good as mine, but I'd enjoy meeting him again. I told him I wasn't sure if I could though. I wanted to check with you and Mark first to make sure you wouldn't mind. I don't want to butt in if you'd rather I didn't. But I am rather curious to talk with Benjamin DeVries. He is something of a legend, isn't he? Tell me, what's he like?"

By the time Kay asked the question, the spring had burst, and Jenny had fled, though she was still standing in the middle of the living room. Kay's involvement in her life was too complex for her to cut through any more. Mark was either too naive or too indifferent to help extricate them. It was only a matter of logistics now for her to pack her own and Erika's bags and bring their bodies along in her flight.

Chapter 29

Bulagwi had managed the press conference that afternoon like a master. He had stood poised before the microphones and lights in the White and Gold room wearing a navy pinstripe suit with a navy tie, diamond tie stud and a leopard skin fez on his head. He joked with reporters, frowned at questions about the massacres, protested ignorance of the worst reports, agreed that some grievous incidents had taken place, insisted that responsible parties were already being brought to justice.

"You must understand," he had explained in a halting, accented voice, "we have been an independent nation only fifteen years. Our people are still learning the responsibilities of citizenship. Fifteen years is but the blinking of an eye compared to two centuries of freedom here in the United States and many more centuries in Europe. Yet in that short time we have educated one hundred percent more students every year; we have increased our college graduates twenty times." From three to sixty, Olivia noted. "We are developing our own manufactured goods . . ."

As Bulagwi had listed his accomplishments, a reporter had interrupted with a question about the secession of the North. At this point Bulagwi slammed his fist onto the podium. "The call for separate statehood is a plot of greedy foreign powers who would divide our country to achieve their own ends," he declared. His voice accelerated, "The plot is as old as Africa's history. Reports of massacres are from these same powers. I am surprised if five hundred people have lost their lives. I invite the Red Cross, the American Congress and anyone to come and see for themselves, then report back to the world how we have been slandered. I invite every person in this room to come and see." He'd held out his hands as if inviting them on board a ship.

While he talked, his security men circulated in the room dressed in black suits and sunglasses. They seemed to have a definite purpose as they moved among the reporters. Olivia guessed they were looking for Jamin and Nyral. Bulagwi knew they were alive. He must have concluded what she had: that they might try to kill him. She too had been searching the faces for Jamin as she took notes. She checked the waiters manning the bar and the table of food; she studied the other reporters, but no one was of his stature. Even Jamin could not hide a 6'4" frame.

When the press conference ended, Bulagwi had been quickly ushered away by his body guards, and the reporters were left to talk among themselves. Olivia moved to the table set with crackers and vegetables and dip. Bulagwi had been smooth; she'd never seen him so adroit at handling the press. She wondered who had rehearsed him. His charges of foreign interference in efforts to divide his country were sure to find sympathy among African leaders who feared the same spectre. He had turned the stories coming out of his country into regrettable, but hardly savage, acts of over-zealous soldiers.

As Olivia stood at the table, she could hear the disquiet among her colleagues whose obligation it was to present the facts. Reporters who covered the story only from the sites of New York and Washington were at a loss to know which reports were true. Their natural skepticism made many believe the sketchy accounts of atrocities, yet they had not been there themselves to see. Bulagwi knew this, and he had played to their limitation. Olivia was sure his invitation for anyone to visit would be rescinded as soon as the U.N. meetings were over. She didn't doubt the leaks herself, including the report of the incident on the bridge which she'd read while she waited for the press conference to begin. Bulagwi could be charming as he'd shown today, but only until he was contradicted; then he would turn as he had on the reporter asking about secession. His face had drawn tight; his eyes flattened. In that look which he'd once turned against her, Olivia saw a man capable of disposing of anyone who challenged his will. In an interview with him years before, Olivia had pointed out a contradiction in information he was giving her. Suddenly he had grown silent; his face had transformed. For a moment she had feared for her own safety. He announced the interview was over. She had never been allowed to interview him again. Twice she had sought an appointment but was denied and the third time she was warned not to ask again.

As Olivia stood eating from the hors d'ouevre table, making the crackers and cheese and raw vegetables her lunch, she backtracked. Where was Jamin? She feared for his safety, yet she also feared that he might suddenly appear threatening everyone's safety. She kept glancing towards the door. She pulled out her pad and jotted a note to herself to check the Afco filing. She didn't know what Jenny meant, but the memory of Jenny's words rose now to Olivia's attention. She folded the note in her pad. She'd been disturbed at seeing Jenny looking as she had, talking about her hair, but Olivia didn't have the time nor the understanding of how to attend to Jenny.

"So . . . what do you think?" A voice spoke from behind. Olivia turned. "Is he telling the truth?" Kay reached over and dipped a tree of broccoli into the yogurt dressing.

"I don't know," Olivia evaded. "What do you think?"

"He is hardly what I expected. But you know him . . . was that an act?" Olivia shrugged. She feared anything she might say would tip Kay off to the real story of Jamin and Nyral. She saw Kay was watching her closely.

A cluster of waiters entered the room carrying trays. Olivia scanned their faces. "So where were you last night?" Kay asked. But noting Olivia's expression, she turned. "What's wrong?"

"Nothing." Olivia turned back around quickly. "I'm sorry. I

have to go." She picked her briefcase and coat off the chair beside her.

Kay put out a hand to restrain Olivia. "What's happening?"

"Nothing."

"I don't believe you."

"Fine, don't. I still have to go." She pulled away from Kay's hand and left the room.

Kay went over and got her own coat and followed through the door, but Olivia had disappeared. Kay hurried down the stairs, but she saw no trace of Olivia. It had been then that she'd decided to go back to Jenny's. It had been a long shot, but it was possible Olivia might go there. She had not found Olivia. Instead she'd found Jenny, who was at least as agitated as Olivia though not nearly as adept at hiding the cause.

Among the waiters who had stepped into the room that afternoon was Willie Williams. Olivia had been so taken back when she saw him that she'd been unable to contain her surprise. She'd left as soon as he set down his tray of food and made his exit. She knew Kay would follow so she'd stepped into an empty conference room until Kay went by; then she traced the path of the waiters to the service elevator. The appearance of Williams suddenly made real for her the threat she had been chasing all day. With the uneventful passing of each hour that threat had begun to seem more and more her own invention. Yet Willie Williams was not her invention. And he was not a waiter either.

Inside the elevator a maintenance man watched her as she faced the two banks of buttons, her briefcase in hand. She wasn't sure where she was going, but she chose a button and pressed it, only the button didn't light. Quickly she pushed another button on the other panel; the light blinked on, and the door closed. She wondered if she'd given herself away. She wondered too where she was headed. The Plaza had four levels of basements, numerous service elevators, each with two panels of buttons. The life underground here was intricate and bustling in order to serve the decorum above.

In the corner a security camera aimed downwards. Edging her way under it so it couldn't track her, she imagined some anonymous eye recording her path these last few days as she'd wandered about the Plaza. There were security cameras everywhere. Had someone watched her sleeping in the hallway last night? Would this eye eventually recognize her and alert a higher authority?

As the maintenance man got out at K, Olivia realized that was where she wanted to be, but she rode the elevator down to her button, SB, where she got off lest the eye find her behavior suspicious. She found herself in a gigantic room with brown and orange walls, a red metal floor and enormous, bulbous yellow generators humming. Off to the side of the elevator huge baskets of sheets and towels were piled up. She moved cautiously down the aisle between the generators and wire screens, behind which blue lockers rose to the ceiling. A sign suddenly caught her attention: "Absolutely No Strangers In This Area." She looked over her shoulder to see if the eye was watching. What were they hiding here? She kept walking, disobeying the order which appeared again on the next wall. Not until she passed the third sign did she realize she had read it through her own paranoia, for the signs did not say "Strangers," but "Storage": "Absolutely No *Storage* In This Area." Yet discarded randomly about the area were old French provincial chairs and sofas with velvet cushions and golden backs, forgotten among the boilers.

As she turned the corner into a hallway, she arrived at another set of elevators. In her mind she was devising the story she would tell if anyone questioned her. She would say that her grandfather used to wash dishes at the Plaza and that she simply wanted to see where he'd worked. His name, his name . . . Chester Dunbar; she chose the first and last name of authors. Did you know him? He worked here over twenty years. In her mind she elaborated her story and felt a vague nostalgia for her own invention.

She pressed K. She wasn't sure in which kitchen area she might find Willie Williams. She didn't really want to find him. She was afraid of him, but he was her only clue to what was happening and to where Jamin might be. She decided to search the large basement kitchen first. This room too was enormous, with stark white walls and whirring machines and fans. As she got off the elevator she noticed in a corner the boxes she and Jamin had left. All at once she exhaled, realizing only then that she had been holding in her breath. Suddenly she felt rooted, as though she'd at last come across a landmark she recognized.

Stowing her briefcase behind the pipe, she picked up the boxes and changed her strategy. She would use Jamin's invention and pretend to be delivering the boxes. If she was asked what was inside, she would say it wasn't her job to know, only her job to deliver. If possible she would say nothing and simply fade into the bustle of the waiters and the chefs, who were hurrying down the aisles in tall white paper caps.

Negotiating her way around several dozen room service trays, their dishes tied up in blue table cloths, she began to explore the corridors of the kitchen, carrying the boxes of veneer like a shield, past the pastry room, down a cold white hallway lined with giant freezers. As she went, she searched for Willie Williams. She didn't know what she would do if she spotted him or what he might do if he saw her. She walked with her back towards the wall so that no one could come upon her unaware. She looked for a place where she could stand unobserved and watch who passed by. She reached the end of the hall and turned back.

So far no one had stopped her. She set her boxes in a corner and moved now to the center of the room, where dishwashers in aprons stood at a giant stainless steel counter. She took an apron from a hook. Offering a smile to a girl who was watching her, she stepped up to an empty space. Over the years of reporting she'd learned that if she acted as though she knew what she were doing, most people assumed that she did: the first rule of improvisation, one which she and Jamin both understood. There were no dishes in front of her so she waited as she searched among the faces for Willie Williams.

She'd been in place only a few minutes when someone dropped a tray of plates in front of her. She glanced at the man beside her to see what she should do. She began scraping the plates into a trash can then slipped them onto a conveyer belt. She processed several trays in this fashion, prying loose stubborn bits of food with her hands, all the while searching the room.

"I see you have many skills," a man said from the other side of the counter. A partition divided the counter so that she could see only the hands and the top of the head of the person across the way; yet immediately she knew the voice of Nyral. She looked under the partition. He smiled. His sleeves were pushed up.

"I saw you come in." He answered her unspoken question. "I've been waiting to see what you would do."

"What are you doing here?"

"The same as you: cleaning dishes."

She stepped around to his side. Nyral stood in old trousers, a faded yellow shirt and an apron. He slipped plates and cups onto the conveyer belt with the ease of an experienced washer. His gentle eyes mocked her own agitated expression. "I've got to talk with you," she said.

"I don't know where Jamin is either. I've been looking for him. He didn't show up for work today."

"You mean he works here too?"

"It is a place to hide and observe. Étienne is one of our country-men." He nodded to a stout, dark man scraping plates beside him. The man smiled showing pink gums. "Étienne has been in your country seven years."

"So where do you think he is?" Olivia asked.

Nyral wiped his hands on his apron. "This is not a safe place to talk." He glanced at a clock on the wall. "In a quarter of an hour I will take a break; we can talk then." He nodded for Olivia to return to the other side of the counter where plates had already stacked up for her.

The constant flow of dishes made the fifteen minutes pass quickly. Yet as her hands cleaned the plates, Olivia's mind raced. What was Nyral doing here? Did he know Willie Williams? Did he know what had been planned? In all her searching for Jamin this morning she had been wishing she could find Nyral. Of all people, Nyral knew Jamin the best. He might stop him. Yet now she was doubting Nyral. Perhaps he too had agreed with the plan. Maybe they planned to poison Bulagwi's food and that's why Nyral and Willie Williams were in the kitchen. The CIA, she knew, had used such tactics before. She suspected both Willie Williams and Moreau were CIA, though she had trouble believ-ing Nyral would comply. She was considering the possibility when Nyral tapped her on the shoulder. "Follow me."

She rinsed her hands and without speaking followed him out

270

the door to the basement where he led her down several flights of stairs into the bowels of the hotel. Finally, at the bottom of a narrow stairwell in front of a bolted door, he stopped. He sat down on a step. "We can talk here," he said. She sat on the step below him. He leaned his head against the wall and shut his eyes. After a moment he opened them. "So . . . you have seen him now."

"Seen who?"

"Amundo."

"Oh . . . yes, though he didn't see me."

"And what did you think?"

"About what?"

"Our friend. Do you think people believe him?"

"Bulagwi? I hardly thought he was your friend. But yes, I'm sorry to say, there will be many who do. It's convenient to believe him. To break with him causes too much trouble. But you know that."

Nyral nodded. "Yes. Perhaps I have been a fool to expect otherwise." He was subdued, almost as if he had resigned to his new lot, not as a head of state, but as a dishwasher inquiring about the lives of those in power. Olivia saw why Jamin would rebel against him.

She leaned forward. "You really haven't seen Jamin?"

He shook his head. "Not since yesterday. I returned last night, and he was not there. I thought perhaps he was sleeping with you."

The allusion to her relationship or lack of relationship with Jamin made Olivia uncomfortable, but she realized Nyral's reference was only one of logistics. "Don't you know what he's planning?" she asked. Nyral squinted; he didn't answer. "When we came back here last night, there were three men waiting for him . . ."

She recounted what had happened. As she talked, she kept glancing up to the top of the stairwell. She half expected to see a dark face peering down at them. They were trapped where they were sitting, with no way out except back up the stairs or through the door in front of them, which was sealed shut. She wondered why Nyral had brought them to this place. Didn't he know the perils right now?

As she was telling him about the incident of her crushed

fingers, she heard footsteps at the top of the stairs. She looked up, but in the dark she couldn't see clearly. She could discern only a man in a uniform with his hand on his side as if he were about to draw a gun. She felt her heart quicken. The walls and the stairs funneled down to her, circumscribed and without an exit. She didn't think she was being paranoid or dramatic. If Jamin were plotting an assassination, then there must be counter forces equally as violent and dangerous on the other side. Yet Nyral sat at the bottom of this thirty-foot staircase with no apparent concern. Perhaps Jamin was right, that the peace she felt in Nyral was only his ignorance of the evil around him.

Nyral raised his hand. "Hello, Asa."

"Oh, it's you. Hello," the man said. "I was just coming on."

"Well, have a good night."

The security guard waved and walked away. "Am I paranoid?" she asked. "Or do you think I'm right about what's being planned?"

Nyral frowned and rubbed his head as though it suddenly ached. His hands were cracked and ashen. He stared at the black door in front of them. "I do not think you are wrong," he answered. "I have been afraid of this, and yet I turned from it, refused to consider it; and now it is my fault."

"It's not your fault," she declared. "Jamin is a grown man."

"He does not know what I know," Nyral answered quietly. "He believes too much in Bulagwi's power. Have you have looked for him well today?"

She told Nyral of her early morning searches up to the Bronx, then to the veneer factory warehouse in Brooklyn. "I tried to think as he would, but I realized how little I know him."

Nyral didn't answer. Instead he stretched out his hand. "How are your fingers?" He took them in his own. She had not thought of the fingers much today except that she used them stiffly. The two middle fingers were bruised and swollen. Nyral placed them in his palm and stroked them gently from top to bottom then on the sides.

"I do not think they are broken," he offered. "They will mend in a few days." Olivia didn't answer. His touch was so soft and his face so attuned to her pain that the emotion she'd been holding back suddenly rose. She wanted to cry. "We will find him," Nyral responded.

"Where?"

He was silent for a moment. "You are a reporter," he answered finally. "Later I will tell you what I know, and together we will find that answer." He stood then. He started back up the stairs. He climbed with effort, holding onto the rail to pull himself up. His collar was soiled; his shoes were worn and too small for his feet so that he appeared to hobble. Olivia followed behind. As she watched him, she remembered that he was seventy-two years old, that he had overseen his country from within and without the corridors of power for longer than she had been alive.

At the top of the stairs he turned. "But first I must finish washing dishes," he said. He gave her a room number and told her he would meet her there in an hour. "Meanwhile," he added, "you must call and try to talk with his sister again."

Chapter 30

Nyral sat in an arm chair with his shoes off and his size eleven feet stretched out in brown socks. He was eating from a plate on his lap: fish and potatoes and carrots which he had prepared himself when he got off work. He had brought a plate up for Olivia too. She ate at the desk in the small, dim room similar to the one she had sat in the night before with Jamin.

"You see, we used to chase the lizards and cut off their tails," Nyral was telling her. "We'd see who could collect the most tails. The tail would jump around for a long time as if it were alive, but the lizard would run off into the bush and eventually grow a new tail." Nyral took a bite from his plate.

"So which are you seeing as Bulagwi . . . the tail or the lizard?" she asked.

"I don't know that I see him as either. Of course if he is killed, that is the end of him, and the lizard *will* grow a new tail."

"Then you're saying someone just as bad may step into his place?"

Nyral smiled and laughed gently. "I didn't know I was saying anything so profound. I've just been thinking about all those stump-ended lizards lately. Did you know Amundo twenty years later used to play the same game as a boy? We talked of it years ago after he'd released me from prison, and we were first planning an alliance. I've been thinking of him as a boy running through the bush after lizards."

"That was a long time ago."

"Yes. I've been thinking of how he tracked the lizards. He told me he used to sneak off with his father's machete. When he saw one, he would chase it and slash down upon its tail with the blade. It's a wonder he didn't cut off his own toes or those of his friends. Many lizards got away of course. He also killed a good many. Sometimes, he told me, he would spend all day hunting just one lizard that had gotten away. On his very best day he collected twelve tails. Like myself he could still remember his highest count." Nyral smiled. The lines around his eyes spread on his copper-colored skin, and his grey-flecked moustache drew into a straight line across his top lip.

"What was your best day?" Olivia asked.

"Thirty-three."

"So were you a better marksman or were you older."

"Neither," Nyral answered. "We were both seven. Would you like to know how I collected the tails?"

Olivia nodded. Nyral took another bite of his fish. She watched him quietly eating from the plate on his knees, reminiscing with her as if there were nothing more pressing upon them. She wondered if he understood what was at stake here. And yet she wanted to hear how he caught lizards, for as long as he told his story, it seemed to her the disorder outside this room was held at bay.

"I had several methods. First I set traps. I would dig holes in the ground and put whatever kind of container I could get from my mother into the holes. If a lizard came along, he would fall in. It was not a perfect method, but I could usually catch four or five this way. Every afternoon I would check my traps and dig more. I'd also go out when the sun was high with my lizard noose." He smiled at the memory. "It was a long stick with a little hoop of string at the end. I'd sneak up behind the lizards and hook it over their heads. I also went about turning over rocks and logs and catching them with my hands. I kept my own kraal of lizards. I didn't like cutting their tails though, but I'd seen lizards break off their own tails. When threatened, they'd just snap off. They'd leave the tail behind wriggling. A predator would go after the tail while the lizard ran away. So I tried to get them to break off their own tails."

Olivia smiled. "You were clever at an early age, I see."

Nyral sipped a glass of water. "At an early age I understood there were many ways to get a lizard's tail."

"Why have you been thinking about how Bulagwi caught lizards?" Olivia asked. "These are not random thoughts."

Nyral's full lips drew together: he rubbed them with the back of his palm. "Because Bulagwi is still as that child: of small imagination but dogged will. That is a dangerous combination. But to kill him would be to kill the mindless tail of the lizard."

"But a lizard's tail can't harm others," Olivia suggested.

Nyral didn't answer. He set his plate on the floor as if he had suddenly lost his appetite. "Jamin is tracking down the worst of Africa to slay it. But I fear it is he who will lose even more. He believes too much in the evil; he believes it has power and that he can use its power for good. But if he kills Amundo, I fear he may destroy himself."

"Are you afraid he'll be killed instead?" This was Olivia's foremost fear.

Nyral sipped a glass of water. He was silent for a moment. "Jamin has not yet killed a man face to face. To do this he must lose himself, and I fear the mask he hides behind will not so easily release him." This was Olivia's second fear.

"What would you do?" she asked.

Nyral closed his eyes. "I have been considering how to get the lizard to let go of its own tail. You see, in my heart, I believe evil destroys itself." He opened his eyes. "Men like Amundo would have us think we have only his ways to choose from—either we must prove ourselves more powerful or submit. I do not accept this choice. That is where I start. I do not accept the choices of evil."

Olivia frowned. She didn't understand what he meant or what other choices might be available. She felt suddenly anxious over what she didn't understand and over the powerlessness of her own and Nyral's position.

"I will tell you what I know," Nyral went on. Olivia reached for her notepad and picked up the Plaza pen from the desk. "Amundo is superstitious. His power depends upon deception, and that deception begins with himself. He has come to believe his will is omnipotent, even divinely protected. He tells of having dreams in which he is given answers about national policies. A few years ago, soon after you left, he sent out an order that all children under ten must be taken out of school. It was revealed to him, he said, in a dream that the schools were poisoning the minds of the children. Until ten they were to attend indoctrination classes which taught them, among other things, the history of Bulagwi himself. When they finally went to school, they could then decide for themselves whether a teacher was deceiving them or not, he said. If a teacher was reported by a student to be teaching falsely, the teacher could lose his or her job and on occasion even his life."

"I'd heard of that," Olivia said, "though the press hasn't had access for some time."

Nyral nodded. "Bulagwi has no overseeing principle governing his policies. In truth he is neither capitalist nor Marxist, Christian nor Moslem. He looks only to himself and to spirits he doesn't understand; and since there is nothing larger to turn to, he is often afraid, for there is much he cannot control."

Nyral leaned forward with his elbows on his knees, and he waited for Olivia to catch up with her notes. "As you know, he has accumulated vast wealth—some report as much as $500 million. And yet the country is almost bankrupt. The treasury shifts money from one account to the other to cover itself, but it is a dwindling amount."

"What about the new mining revenues?"

"At least a third of the revenues go to Bulagwi and his friends and family and a part more, I would guess, to Afco officials."

Olivia sat forward. "What officials? You mean above and beyond their royalties?"

Nyral smiled. "Above and beyond and through the back door. I don't know for certain, but sources have told me there is a sizable stream flowing out of our country, and it is not all to the numbered accounts of our president and his family."

"Do you have proof?" Olivia wondered what information Jenny had uncovered, and she felt suddenly the pain of her friend if Jenny were on a trail that looped, however inadvertently, near her husband's door.

"Not as yet, but we do have agents locating the tributaries to that stream and getting closer to its final deposits. When the time comes, we will know where at least several large reserves of our nation's wealth have been hoarded. So you see Amundo is scared right now. Though I would not have forseen it, I would say Benjamin DeVries may be scared too. Otherwise he would not be turning against his partner. Perhaps he is scared of what Bulagwi will reveal if pressed. Or, it is possible that Bulagwi has tried to extort from him further 'contributions.' I do not know what deal DeVries has struck with Jamin, but DeVries is smart enough to know that deal will not necessarily hold. I fear for Jamin. Unlike Amundo, Benjamin DeVries is a man of sizable imagination."

For a moment Nyral stared off over Olivia's head as if considering his next words. He took another sip of water. "Both men use their wealth as power, confuse it with power. Bulagwi spreads his money among those he needs as friends. His lapses of rationality are overlooked by these people, within and without our country, because they no longer know how to separate themselves from him. However, I have seen a weakness in him which I think I can use."

"What?" Olivia looked up.

"In my presence I have seen him become outraged, almost to a point of madness. This has happened twice. On both occasions the rage came upon him suddenly as though he had no control over it. On reflection I realized that I was the cause of this rage. As you saw today, his image in the international community is important to his ability to keep power. Because he is greedy, our country is in debt to many nations. It is within their power to change our leadership. That is a sad confession, but I fear it is true. From your meeting last night you have learned of one side who would seek a change for their own reasons. I do not trust these men. To my view they are no better than Bulagwi—in fact I think they are worse, for with all that they have in the world, they want more. They think nothing of using a man like Jamin to get their ends."

"But Moreau . . . if he's from the CIA as you say, then he must represent U.S. interests?" Olivia asked.

"Your government is very complicated. One part does not always know what the other is doing. I am not sure who Moreau represents though I have come across him before, if he is the man you describe. He had been in the Congo during the unrest and the assassination there. He knew DeVries then. When he was in my country, I knew he was from the CIA. He was there to spy on our neighbors though today he is perhaps more interested in us. But I am told that the right arm of the CIA does not always know what the left is doing. Your government, like most, represents itself with many faces."

"So what is your plan?"

Nyral reached to the tray on the floor and set down the glass of water. "I will take from Amundo his mask."

"And what is that?"

"His power to deceive. He is to speak before the Security Council tomorrow. I will be there. I shall confront him and let him reveal himself."

"But how can you do that?"

"I have thought long on this. I believe I shall know what to say. I believe the mask will of its own fall away."

Olivia frowned. "That sounds dangerous and speculative."

Nyral stared across the room, his gaze remote, as if he were rehearsing some memory of his own. "You be there," he said finally. "You will see. You will then have, as they say, a scoop."

"But what's to keep Jamin from showing up before then?"

Nyral set the glass of water back on the floor. "I have thought of that. Have you spoken to his sister?"

"She said she hadn't seen him or talked to him. I believe her. I told her to leave a message for me at my friend's if she heard anything. I think she understood how important it was. Do you know her?"

"Only when she was a child, but from Jamin I know there is something strong between the two of them."

Olivia nodded, for she also saw but could not name what they shared: it was perhaps the knowledge Rhekka had of Jamin and Jamin's need for someone other than himself to have this knowledge.

"I will watch for him," Nyral said. "And Étienne and the few friends we have here, they will watch. But of course if Jamin does not want us to see him, he will find a way to hide."

"Will you be in this room if I need you?" Olivia asked.

Nyral began stuffing his feet into the hard brown shoes he had borrowed. Olivia wondered what he had done with his own soft leather ones and the silk suits. "I don't know. It is necessary I keep changing my place so I won't be found."

"Will you at least be in the kitchen?"

"I have been told Bulagwi's men will be coming down to supervise his food. They may recognize me. I think I shall have to find another place." He stood. "The security has grown very tight."

"But if I need you, how will I find you?"

"I won't be far away. I shall find you." He moved to the door with the tray of his and Olivia's dishes. "Now you had better go find out what our friend in the presidential suite is doing." He opened the door. He cast a glance up and down the hall. He set the plates of half-eaten food on the floor. As Olivia started towards the elevator, she looked back, and she saw him slip out the door in his worn clothes and disappear down the stairs.

Chapter 31

In a corner booth with his back to the wall and a phone at his elbow, Benjamin DeVries was picking the anchovies out of a Caesar salad and emphasizing to Mark why a decision on their partnership had to be made soon. He was trying not to press too hard. From years of negotiating, he'd learned how to hook a deal and how to reel it in. He knew that too insistent a tone could cause a wary prospect to turn away, while too relaxed an attitude could as easily lose what he wanted.

Earlier on the phone this afternoon he'd again assuaged Mark's concerns over the burning and looting at one of the mines, explaining that the mine was among the smallest and was in a territory known for such outbursts; the incident did not represent a larger threat, he insisted. He also told Mark that he'd arranged an alternate route for shipping the ore and that Afco could expect the first shipment by the end of the month. He then insisted he and Mark have dinner to discuss their partnership.

He'd spent months now courting Mark and studying the way he

operated. Mark's firm was about half the size of DeVries Holdings but had much more liquidity, a strong base of U.S. investors, and Mark had a reputation for integrity, a reputation DeVries valued. Mark was a genuine talent. In ways he reminded him of himself at that age. Yet he'd also spotted Mark's weaknesses, and he thought he knew how to play these to his advantage. Mark's first weakness was that he was too idealistic. For all his natural skills and instincts at making money, he still needed to feel he was acting to benefit some larger cause. DeVries accounted part of this idealism to his wife, whom he was beginning to tally as Mark's second weakness; she held too much sway over him. She was strong- minded, yet naive and suspicious of DeVries; therefore DeVries did not trust her either. Yet years had taught him the necessity of getting along with a colleague's wife or, on occasion, helping him part from a wife who was an impediment. He had not yet determined that Jenny would stand in Mark's way; however, he was interested in this other woman who had appeared more than once. She seemed friendlier, and unless he had lost his skill in reading a woman's eyes and voice, she was interested in Mark. If possible he preferred not to interfere directly. Rather, he assessed the forces already at work and aligned himself with those which would play out to his advantage. Had he known Robert Nyral, he would have agreed, at least in theory, with the strategy of inducing the lizard to release its own tail.

In a remote chamber of his thoughts now, he was considering the women in Mark's life even as he was saying, "Because the situation has altered over the weekend, I need a decision soon." While he spoke, he set tiny pieces of fish on the side of his plate. He concentrated on this task as a way of defusing the urgency in his voice.

"I don't understand how the two relate," Mark said.

DeVries continued his attention to his salad. "After twenty years of serving me, you'd think they could remember to hold the anchovies." He looked up; then he answered Mark's question without transition. "The destruction of certain rail lines is a setback. I've located a temporary route, but we must quickly establish a permanent solution."

"But how does that relate to our partnership?"

"Everything relates, Mark," DeVries answered with a slightly patronizing tone. "Surely you understand that by now." He leaned forward. "There are costs. It has occurred to me that one way to extend the life and the cash flow of Afco is to incorporate it into a larger money stream. The losses derived from these past setbacks could be written off by the other company, and the cash flow to Afco could continue until the political obstacles are hurdled."

"You want our partnership to absorb Afco?"

"What do you think?"

Mark didn't answer. He ate a bite of his salad. "I'd want to run through the figures," he said cautiously. "Offhand it seems to me we'd be tying ourselves to a very unpredictable asset . . . the fish swallowing the whale, possibly a dying whale, even with the tax benefits." DeVries didn't answer. He waited for Mark to go on. "I'd assumed Afco would remain an independent arm of DeVries Holdings," Mark said. This new idea seemed to Mark to have sprung up out of the blue though from the intense way DeVries was watching him, Mark saw the suggestion was not random but carefully come to. He wondered how long DeVries had been considering it.

DeVries turned back to the salad, having revealed more than he intended. He could not let his will overbear here nor his pride show through, for it was in fact a point of pride with him that Afco should not fail, a pride among colleagues far senior to Mark in the financial worlds, legends like himself. When he'd started DeVries Holdings half a dozen years ago, he'd bought interest in existing companies. Afco, however, was his own creation, his first company formed out from under the umbrellas of his Belgian bank and Generale de Metaux. He had invested too much money and too much of his prestige to let it fail.

DeVries flicked one last speck of anchovy from his plate then took a bite. Still aware of Mark's attention, he thrust his fork into the air. "Waiter!" he called. The waiter hurried to the table. "How am I expected to eat this?" he asked. "Next time you prepare me a Caesar salad, I suggest you consult your superiors." He handed the bowl and the plate of dead anchovies to the man. He then turned back to Mark noting that he'd succeeded for the moment at least in distracting Mark's attention.

"As you know," he resumed, "whatever I do calls attention to itself. That has its advantages, but if one wants to be discrete . . .

and here I think discretion is to everybody's advantage . . . then we need someone else as a figurehead." Mark frowned at the word. DeVries amended, "Of course that is not all you are to be, but your name on the company will not attract the same attention as mine. The transfer of funds to Afco and the assumption of its liabilities should take place discretely and as quickly as possible both for tax reasons and because there is an immediate need for cash."

"You mean in Afco?"

"Yes . . . among other projects."

Mark leaned forward in the leather booth. "What other projects?" He picked up a spoon and began tapping it back and forth between his fingers. He'd felt agitated all day, starting with his argument with Jenny. Yet he'd been running at such a pace that he hadn't had time to sort through his feelings. Now, as he faced DeVries across the table instead of his wife as he'd originally planned, his uneasiness heightened. He'd tried to call Jenny, but no one had answered. Finally he'd had to leave it to his secretary to pass on the message about dinner. He knew Jenny would take the breaking of the date personally after their argument this morning. "I'm afraid my wife and I haven't had a chance to talk," he said.

"Mark . . . " DeVries' voice rose. "This is an important decision. I must say I'm not used to being put off like this."

"We were supposed to have dinner tonight to discuss the proposal," he countered.

"Then why aren't you?"

"Because you said it was urgent that we meet." Mark answered, suddenly annoyed that he'd let DeVries once again come between him and his wife.

A new waiter and busboy arrived at the table, along with the maitre d' who was full of apologies for the mistake over the salad. "I have spoken to Claude severely," he assured. "And he will not serve you again, Mr. DeVries. Gustov, our finest, will serve you from now on, and I will make you a new salad myself."

DeVries waved his hand with indifference. "*Cela n'a pas d'importance,*" he dismissed. "I've lost my appetite for salad. You may bring dinner." Gustov gave a stern order to his busboy, who quickly cleared the plates.

Suddenly uncomfortable, Mark stood. "I need to call Jenny," he said.

"Here, use this phone," DeVries passed a white telephone to him."

"I'll use the pay phone." And he left the table.

When Mark returned to the dining room, Kay was sitting in his place talking quietly with Benjamin DeVries. Mark stood for a moment in the entry staring at them, trying to figure out what she was doing there.

As he approached the table, Kay read the question on his face. "I know I'm a little early," she greeted, "but I finished my interviews much sooner than I expected. Mr. DeVries said you've finished your business for the moment."

"What are you doing here?" Mark asked. DeVries watched his face and noted that Mark did not seem pleased.

"Didn't Jenny tell you?"

"Tell me what? I haven't talked to Jenny. Where is she?"

"Oh, she should be here soon. Your secretary said to meet you at 9:30."

Mark saw DeVries watching him; he tried to hide his annoyance. "I still don't understand . . . did Jenny invite you?"

"I'm sorry, Mark," DeVries interupted. "I had no idea you were planning such an important meeting with your wife." Kay's attention focused on the words. "When Miss Walsh called my office this afternoon for your wife to find out where we were dining, I invited her along as a courtesy. I also thought it would be an opportunity for us to discuss what, if any, strategy is possible in Washington with this mess that has occurred."

"I've been telling Mr. DeVries . . . "

"Benjamin, please." He smiled.

"I've just been explaining that I know at least two assistant secretaries sympathetic to your problem," Kay said. "They also feel the only hope for keeping that part of Africa in line with the West is strong economic ties. They are very concerned that the Soviets are behind the latest unrest."

"What do you think your friends in Washington might be willing to do to aid us," DeVries asked as Gustov arrived with the dinner.

"They would have to answer for themselves, but I know they are not sitting on their hands."

"Well, that is good to hear. Neither are we."

"Oh? What are you doing?" Kay asked.

DeVries smiled. "I see you are a reporter who lets nothing get by you. I'm afraid I must answer with no comment."

Kay glanced at Mark to see if he shared the intelligence, but he was hardly listening. He checked his watch then cut into a two-inch lamb chop.

"Are you sure you won't have something?" DeVries asked Kay.

"I've been eating all day at receptions. Kay touched the gold belt on her black wool sheath. "I'm afraid this may pop open at any minute."

"So tell me," DeVries asked, "what did you think of Bulagwi? What do you think will come of this visit?"

"Do you know him?"

DeVries applied his knife and fork to the small wing of the pheasant on his plate. "I have met him a few times, but I don't know him well." He took a bite.

"I thought you might."

"Why is that?"

"You were quite involved in African affairs at one time." Kay phrased her words carefully. Like DeVries, she kept her attention on something else—in this case pouring milk into a cup of coffee—so that her real intent might appear casual. "I was hoping you might tell me about him." She stirred the coffee, then lifted the cup and met DeVries' eyes over the top.

"That was a long time ago and in a different country." He sipped a glass of white wine. The waiter quickly stepped over to refill it.

"Of course. But even now, with Afco, your interest remains. I've never been to Africa myself, but I've noticed it has a hold that persists for those who've lived there. Do you find that's true?" Kay was beginning to circle. She had her target in sight, and she was quietly, indirectly aiming towards it. She wanted to ask DeVries about his role in the Congo and how he might apply that situation to the current one and to his own plans for "not sitting on his hands."

DeVries, however, was as sophisticated with the press as Kay was at interviewing the sophisticated though at the moment he was enjoying this non-interview. "Yes, you might say that. You should go sometime."

"What is it for you that is so attractive?" she asked.

DeVries looked at Mark; then he laughed. "Shall we tell her the truth? We're among friends, right? Now, off the record: there is a hell of a lot of money to be made there." DeVries drank more wine. He patted his small mouth with his napkin. "Unfortunately the countries can be as volatile as a whore with a bee up her arse. That's why there's not too much competition among investors these days. But if you can hang onto the lady, you can get a hell of a ride."

Mark frowned. He hadn't heard this language nor this rationale from DeVries before. He imagined Jenny's response; he was answering her as much as Kay when he said, "The investment also offers jobs and income for the countries we're in."

DeVries passed Kay a glass of wine and smiled as if he gauged now was the time and the company in which to crack through some of Mark's idealism. "Of course at least half of the benefit will go into the pockets of whoever is in power as it has to our friend Bulagwi. We in the West have made him a very rich man . . . much richer than any of us. It could be argued that we have even spurred on civil wars in several countries by sweetening the pot for whomever comes out on top. Whatever rebels may say about capitalism and imperialism, you can be sure when the revenues come in and the pot is divided up, their pockets are as deep as anyone else's. If you could dye the money red, I could tell you who would have red hands at the end of the day."

"I'm sure you're right," Kay said. "Was it the same in the Congo?"

At the mention of the Congo, DeVries' face altered. He had been smiling, enjoying the wine and the company, but now his pale skin flushed and his eyes blinked quickly. The change was subtle, but Kay had a fine eye for such changes. She added quickly. "It seems to me someone had to do *something* there, whatever the general opinion may be."

DeVries didn't answer. He turned his attention to the bird on his plate, cutting into the breast. Aware that she had lost the moment, Kay released it and directed her attention to Mark. "By the way, I stopped by your mother's before I went over to the U.N. this afternoon," she said. "She told me to tell you to be sure and call to say goodbye." Kay looked over at DeVries. "Do you know Mark's parents? They are very special."

DeVries glanced up, interested in her assessment. "I know Irwin," he answered.

"Oh, of course. You were with Irwin when I met you. I'd forgotten." Kay held her glass out to him, for the moment retreating into a comfortable social zone in order to reconsider her approach.

DeVries poured her wine and approached on his own. "So tell me, what do *you* see coming from Bulagwi's visit?"

"I'm told there's a chance he'll get the Security Council to pass a resolution barring foreign troops and military aid to the rebels. He has the support of several major African leaders. A who's who in Africa has been parading in to see him all day."

"But the man is a barbarian!" DeVries declared. He set his knife and fork beside his plate. His face again flushed. This time even Mark noticed. "He will not listen to reason. He blackmails his allies, demands more and more to line his pockets. He's murdered thousands of his own people. How can they support him?" DeVries' voice rose, and the people at the adjoining table looked over. Kay exchanged a quick glance with Mark. The reaction was so abrupt that she didn't know what to make of it. "Surely, you must agree," he demanded.

Kay treaded carefully. "I don't know why they support him. It is still only a rumor."

Steadying himself, DeVries picked back up his knife and fork. He returned to his bird, dismembering the second wing. His mouth pursed as he concentrated on picking off the small bits of flesh from the bone with an intricate flicking of the fork. "I do not usually show such fervor," he said, smiling at his own outburst. "But I find men such as that incomprehensible . . . like Africa itself I suppose. I find it even more incomprehensible that they are tolerated in a civilized world."

Mark pushed his plate aside. He felt suddenly uneasy. He stood.

"Where are you going?" DeVries asked.

"I want to try Jenny again."

Kay glanced at the thin gold watch on her wrist. "It's just now 9:30," she said. Mark hesitated. "You know Mark's wife used to be quite a good journalist," Kay offered. "In fact I helped her with her first story, if I recall, when she came to the paper."

DeVries lifted his fork to Mark. "A man who doesn't know where his wife is . . . that's a bad sign," he chided.

But Mark didn't answer. He turned and went towards the phones. As he left the table, DeVries turned to Kay, "Tell me, does she hold him by the short hairs?"

Part Four

Chapter 32

The light rose up to meet Jenny from the inlets and peninsula around Logan International Airport as the Eastern shuttle circled to land. Beside her, Erika lay sleeping with her head on the arm rest. Jenny peered out through the mist streaking in drops across the window pane. It was 9:30, the time she had been told to meet Mark. She had set 9:30 as the deadline to be bound in her own direction. She leaned her head against the back of the seat. She felt drained. She longed for rest but could not sleep.

Even after she had decided she must go away and let events take their course without her, Kay had lingered about the apartment, prodding her with small talk as if Kay knew where she had arrived in her mind and wanted to secure her there. Finally Jenny had excused herself, saying she needed to work. Only then had Kay gathered her briefcase and headed to the United Nations.

Jenny stared out at the water of the bay, dark and shimmering with fragments of light. In its mirror the plane looked like a giant torpedo speeding across the flat black surface of night.

The seat belt sign flashed on. Jenny tucked the blanket around the small stocking foot of her sleeping child, then stroked her daughter's hair. The wind outside roared as the plane made its final descent, closing the distance with its image on the water. The "No Smoking" sign blinked red in the dimly lit cabin. Jenny looked over at Erika and caught both their faces in the window. For a moment she saw Mark in Erika's face—the softly lidded eyes, the straight nose, the olive-toned skin. She could not escape him, though she was trying.

After Kay had finally left the apartment this afternoon, she had gone into Mark's office. With a sweep of her hand, she had knocked his lucite cubes and triangles and rectangles off his shelves, left them scattered upon the ground like so many broken toys. Only they didn't break; they only lay there, some with their edges nicked, but with the little slips of paper listing the hundreds of millions of dollars intact inside, behind walls of lucite. So Mark and DeVries could have dinner together; Kay and Mark and DeVries could eat lucite cubes together.

Outside, the plane and its reflection almost merged: a great silver shaft on the water. The double image shimmered a moment longer, then disappeared as the plane flew over the land.

The stewardess walked by and pulled Erika's seatback forward. As her daughter awakened, Jenny drew her close and pointed to the lights outside the window. Together they watched the ground and the sky meet on the runway of Boston.

In the taxi Erika leaned into Jenny. As they gazed out at the streets rushing by, Jenny concentrated on the motion; the blur of lights along Storrow Drive and the Charles River she saw only as confirmation that she was moving. She wasn't sure why she had come here, to this city of her independence, but she had not come casually. And though she couldn't have said why, she was heading to Olivia's apartment rather than to a hotel, the destination and the lodging had presented itself as one, a place where she could both remember and reinvent herself.

She had tried to reach Mark later in the afternoon, to tell him calmly that she was leaving for a while. But he wasn't in his office. She left a message for him to call her. She phoned her mother and told her that when Mark called to let him know she and Erika were all right.

"What's wrong?" her mother asked.

"I can't talk now. I'm going to Olivia's." Her mother knew Olivia's, had stayed there herself. "I'll call you."

"Do you need help?"

For a moment Jenny fell silent. The question touched so closely her vulnerability that she was afraid if she spoke, she might break down and not be able to put herself together again in time to act. Finally she said, "Yes."

"You want me to come?"

"It's not necessary."

"You know, R.B. Lipscott's headquartered in Boston. I just interviewed half the Houston office."

"It's not necessary," Jenny repeated.

Jenny paid the taxi driver and asked him to wait in front of the brownstone on Commonwealth Avenue. With her suitcase in one hand and Erika in the other, she mounted the steps. She felt in the crack behind the mailboxes where Olivia kept her spare key. Drawing it forth, she waved the taxi on.

Inside, the hallway was lighted from the top by a wooden chandelier which cast a dim glow on the stairs. Olivia's apartment was on the fifth floor. Jenny began mounting the steps, dragging the suitcase and Erika from landing to landing where she rested; the weight of the unborn child pressed upon her. Finally at the top were two doors without numbers. On one, a sheet of yellow paper was taped: DO NOT DISTURB in Olivia's thick block letters. From inside Jenny heard a barrage of typing. She hesitated. She was sure Olivia was still in New York. She knew Olivia wouldn't mind if she stayed, but she hadn't counted on someone else being there. She knocked. The typing continued. She knocked again. There was a pause. Then she heard fumbling on the other side and a chair push back. She picked up Erika to be prepared for whomever she met. The door opened.

"What are you doing here?" Jenny exclaimed.

"The landlady let me in," a greying, blond-haired woman answered. A pencil jutted out from behind her ear; she held another pencil in her hand. She was Jenny's height and build with a broad face, full lips and gentle grey eyes. She wore slacks, a navy cardigan and slippers. "Come in." She reached out to Erika, who went eagerly to her. "You've grown just since Christmas. I have something for you . . . over there on the couch." Erika wiggled down. "Not much . . . " she turned to Jenny, "just a few things I picked up at the airport."

"But how did you know to come here?"

"You said you were going to Olivia's. The landlady—did you know she used to live in Lubbock?—she let me in. I tried to call you back, but your line was busy, and I was on deadline. When I finally got through, the babysitter said you'd gone out. I decided just to come. R.B. Lipscott is based here anyway. They just completed two huge shopping malls that came in way over budget and are half empty . . . "

Erika was rummaging through her grandmother's overnight case, pulling out a stuffed frog, a car, a pad of paper with colored pens. Jenny took off her coat. She couldn't believe her mother had come. She hadn't intended for her to come. She wanted to be alone, and now here was her mother talking about the landlady and toys and Texas real estate developers. Yet as she watched this lean, sunburned woman digging through a Samsonite suitcase, she couldn't help but be touched. Her mother was not easily moved from her routines nor was she easily alarmed. "Thanks for coming," Jenny said.

Dorothy Reeder nodded. She was sitting on the unmade couch looking at instructions for the car she'd brought which was supposed to roll over and change directions whenever it hit an object. "I won't stay here," she began explaining. "I've already got a room over at the Copley Plaza. I thought Erika could stay with me to give you some time to yourself."

Jenny started to answer, but her eyes filled with tears. After her outburst in Mark's office, she'd drawn her emotions in and had been keeping them in a tight hold all afternoon while she called her mother, made airline reservations, went to the bank, waited in the bank line, packed, waited till the last minute for Mark to call, then finally caught a taxi and went to the airport. But now her mother's clear, unstated knowledge of what she needed touched her; her composure broke. The tears started to roll down her face. Erika looked up at her confused. Jenny turned away, yet Olivia's apartment had only one room, and there was nowhere to go.

"Erika, honey, wait till you see what I saw in the bathroom," her mother interceded.

"What?"

"A bathtub with feet." She led Erika away to the old-fashioned bathroom. A moment later Jenny heard water running. In a few more minutes her mother reappeared. "Erika's taking a bubble bath."

Jenny was sitting at Olivia's desk now, staring at the story in the typewriter. "Is this yours?" she asked, reaching outside herself for her composure.

"I hope Olivia doesn't mind if I used her typewriter. I'm right in the middle of a series investigating developers. That one's on Hutchinson Construction . . . you remember Nina Hutchinson? You were in sixth grade together. That's her father, a shady character . . ." Even in the middle of a crisis her mother had a way of turning to the most recent gossip for conversation, whether to distract her or allow her privacy, she didn't know.

Her mother went to the kitchen and began making coffee. She'd stayed here when Jenny was a reporter in Boston and Olivia was out of town on assignments; she'd even stayed after Jenny had moved. Olivia and her mother had gotten along right away.

"I'm afraid I have to be back Wednesday morning, honey." She set a cup by Jenny and one on the coffee table for herself. "Now," she said, "tell me, what is this all about?"

Jenny stared at Olivia's old Royal typewriter, fixing her eyes on the space bar so she wouldn't cry. "I feel as if I'm losing Mark. There are forces larger than us pulling us apart." She told her about Afco and DeVries, about the partnership DeVries was offering, about the pull of his world of money and power. "I don't trust the man. And I don't trust his world."

"What does Mark say when you tell him how you feel?"

"He thinks I'm paranoid." For a moment her mother grew quiet. Jenny hadn't mentioned Kay. She didn't know how to tell her mother the story she herself had lived through a decade before, had only come out of in the past few years, trailing her father's rejection as though it were a judgment she must carry with her.

But her mother asked on her own. "Tell me, is there another woman?" Jenny stared, surprised by her intuition; then she nodded. Dottie frowned. "You're sure?"

"No. I mean not exactly, but . . . " She began explaining how Kay had come back into their lives, how she was attracted to Mark and Mark didn't seem able or willing to step away or to understand how it was hurting her. "I keep thinking of you and Dad . . . " She glanced up to see if she were touching her mother's pain, but her mother appeared calm, as though the wound were no longer personal.

Instead she was watching Jenny, whose hair flared in its high-fashion waves, whose eye make-up had washed down her lids and radiated in tiny black lines from the edges of her eyes. "There's a difference between you and me and Mark and your father. Don't you know what that is?" Jenny shook her head. "Your husband loves you. Your father, for whatever reason of his or mine, quit loving me a long time ago." Her mother said this matter-of-factly as if her father's love had finally ceased to be her measure. Then she added: "You don't have to live my life."

Jenny pressed the space bar on the typewriter. The statement, so simple and direct, struck at the root of her fear that in the end history and life had a force outside her control. That in spite of her payments to the gods, the gods might still grow angry or act according to whim or to patterns already set. In needing, in fact willing a faithful husband, she was willing the existence of God, for she did not see how she could survive in a world where there was no governing, faithful Principle.

"But how do I know?" she asked, though already she suspected that her fear blocked the very faith she sought and also blocked the perception of her own husband.

Her mother shook her head. Her greying hair was pulled behind her ears in the pageboy she'd worn ever since Jenny could remember. "You make your own life, sweetheart, whatever Mark does. He can't make your choices. And you can't make his."

From the bathroom Erika called, "I'm ready." Dottie squeezed her daughter's hands, then rose to get Erika.

Jenny stood and went over to the bay window where she stared out at the Charles River and the lights of Cambridge in the distance. She had lived on her own where those lights now shined. Her mother's words had been so certain: "Your husband loves you. You don't have to live my life." Her mother, who was no sentimentalist, no giver of false assurances, inserted a wedge under her fear which had grown incarnate in the past weeks. She still felt its constriction, and yet she also felt a shifting of the weight.

"Erika and I are going to walk the Freedom Trail tomorrow," her mother said as she led Erika into the room wrapped in a pink bath towel. She stood her by the wall furnace and opened Jenny's suitcase. "And then we're going to have lunch at Hay market and go look at the boats. We'll call you in the afternoon to see if you want to have dinner with us. Right, Erika?"

Erika smiled. Her cheeks had grown rosy in the warm bath, and beads of sweat glistened around the roots of her black hair. She looked content and sleepy in her grandmother's arms. Dottie pulled out a clean pair of underpants and a pink flannel nightgown and dressed her, then changed from her own slippers back into short brown heels. "Now why don't you call a cab so Erika and I can get to the hotel?"

Jenny phoned the taxi and packed Erika's clothes into her mother's suitcase. Her mother went over to the typewriter and removed her story, then picked up the rest of her pages from on top of Olivia's manuscript. "Olivia's got a hell of a book here," Dottie Reeder said. "Have you read it?"

"Not yet."

"It's good, very good." She went to the kitchen and began ferreting about the shelves, taking a jar of coffee, a box of crackers and putting them in her shopping bag. "Olivia won't mind, do you think? I need to work late tonight, and Erika's hungry. You restock her for me in the morning."

Jenny nodded. She helped her mother downstairs with her suitcase and typewriter and shopping bag full of provisions. "You call me if you need me," her mother said, sliding into the taxi.

"Thank you," Jenny answered.

Her mother reached out and again squeezed her hand. "Now go in and do some looking for yourself. We're going to leave you alone till you do."

Chapter 33

In the taxi home from the restaurant, Kay positioned herself so
that the rim of her coat and the edge of her knee touched Mark. It
was eleven o'clock. Jenny had never shown. As the cab sped up
Madison, Kay could feel Mark's distance, and she felt slightly in-
timidated by his silence. She reviewed to herself what she'd said
to Jenny this afternoon to make sure she was guiltless. She had
been friendly and forthcoming. She had even offered not to come
tonight if Jenny didn't want her. It was not her fault that Jenny
had stood up her husband; yet she couldn't help but feel that
Mark was blaming her. Perhaps DeVries was right; even he had
noticed that Jenny held an unusual sway over Mark. At the appropriate time she would mention this. He should know what his
business colleagues thought. She had liked Benjamin DeVries,
and it was clear that he had liked her. But now was not the time
to mention Jenny. Instead she said, "I saw David today." She
opened her hand in her lap and reached over and touched his
hand. "He asked about you."

Mark turned. "Oh? How is he?"

"A little bored but happy about leaving the hospital, I think. I
asked your mother if I could bring a bird into your room, and she

said that was all right so I told David I'd get him a cockatoo like Erika's."

"Fine." Mark stared out the window.

"You know, you were right," she went on. "I never have given him any pets. I think he was pleased when I told him, though with David it's hard to tell." She pulled a cigarette from her purse. Up front the radio crooned a Spanish love song. She leaned forward to the driver and asked for a light.

When she sat back, she positioned herself a few inches away from Mark. "I wouldn't worry about Jenny," she said in a slightly arched tone. "She's a big girl." She drew on the cigarette. "You know, if you don't mind some constructive criticism, you let her push you around too much."

Mark looked over at her. "What do you mean?"

"She manipulates you. You don't see it. She has you so well in control, you don't even know it. Actually it surprises me that she's so good. I never will figure her out. But even Benjamin has noticed."

"Noticed what?"

"When you went off to call her, he asked me if she held you by the short hairs. I didn't answer of course, but I will tell you to your face that I think she does."

Mark was silent for a moment. Then in a quiet voice he asked, "What did you say to her this afternoon?"

Kay looked at him; her voice exploded in exasperation. "Oh Christ!" she declared. "Nothing. I said nothing to her. I don't know why she didn't come. She was probably out buying Erika another snake. Honestly, Mark, I even told her I'd put off Benjamin's invitation if she'd prefer, but she raised no objection."

Mark didn't answer. Kay felt his stillness deepening. Suddenly she worried that she'd said too much. She reached out and took his hand. "Mark, I just want us to be friends. I want to help you if I can, but I swear Jenny is like a lioness protecting her cubs with you and Erika."

Still Mark didn't answer. The fact that DeVries would discuss him and his wife in those terms with Kay disturbed him. That Jenny had been overly possessive lately he would agree. He might have argued the point with Jenny except he was beginning to wonder if she had cause after all. He considered her discomfort over DeVries. She had said she didn't trust his motives in the partnership. It was clear from the discussion tonight that DeVries' motives were more complex than he'd allowed. Right now he was confused and wanted to talk with his wife, and yet he was wary of coming in so late with Kay, though according to Kay, Jenny knew it was DeVries who had invited her. Then the fact that he even had to worry about Jenny misinterpreting his actions angered him.

"Now that I remember, Mark," Kay said in a more sympathetic voice, "there was something odd about Jenny this afternoon. Did you know she's dyed her hair and has it . . . well . . . " Kay spread her hands about her head. " . . . all curled up and out. She doesn't look very much like Jenny."

"What are you talking about?"

"Apparently she went to the beauty parlor this morning and got the works. Maybe you'll like it. I don't know. She had her face made up too, very sophisticated . . . I've never thought of Jenny as sophisticated, but . . . " Kay stopped. She saw that Mark looked concerned. "I don't know what brought it on," she offered, stamping out her cigarette in the ash tray and drawing another from her purse. "It may be nothing, but frankly I'm not so sure." She folded one hand around her waist, cocked her elbow, and smoked the cigarette perched between two fingers.

"What do you mean you're not so sure?"

Kay hesitated then turned towards him. "Well, I've been there, Mark," she said. "Before my nervous breakdown, when my marriage was falling apart, I did something similar. I went out on a shopping spree. We had very little money, and I spent all of it and to the limit of the two credit cards we had. I suppose in some irrational way I wanted to bring on the end. I knew Randy would blow up when he found out what I'd done." She smiled. "David was about six months old. I spent all day shopping. I went to the best stores in town, and I bought everything on sale so I couldn't take any of it back."

Mark listened with a puzzled look on his face. "I don't see how that applies. Jenny can spend whatever she wants, however she wants. It's her money too."

"You're missing the point. You can't see her with her hair and her face all made up without knowing she's saying something to you. She isn't happy, Mark. That's been clear to me. I don't know what's wrong, but believe me, I recognize the signs."

The taxi stopped at the apartment. Mark paid the driver and hurried up the steps with Kay following behind. At least she had spoken the truth, she thought. Mark had winced at what she'd said, but he had to know. She felt oddly tranquil as Mark opened the door and plunged into the apartment calling: "Jenny!"

Kay saw the note first. It was propped against the music stand on the piano, not the most logical place for a note, she thought; but then Jenny knew what Kay did not, that Mark would eventually end up there when he realized she was gone. It was there that she wanted him to read what she had to say as if by its placement she might assure him that she had gone in search of order, not dissolution. But Mark hurried to Erika's room first. The sight of the empty bed sent a sudden pain through him. The pain was followed quickly by anger as the possibility arose that Jenny had left and taken Erika with her. He went to the bedroom and saw the closets open, but he couldn't tell if anything was missing. He hurried to Jenny's office. Her writing of the morning still sat on her desk as though she intended to return any moment; his panic lessened. Maybe she'd simply gone to a friend's or perhaps to his mother or father's to say goodbye before their trip. He returned to the living room.

He didn't see the note. He moved past Kay and back into his study where he picked up the phone and dialed his parents. As he waited for an answer, he flipped on the light and turned to lean against the desk. It was then he saw his trophies strewn across the floor, dozens of them under the chair, the desk, as if some force had swept through the room. Had someone broken into the apartment? Had Cassie leapt up on the shelf and knocked them down? Only as his father was answering on the other end did it occur to him that Jenny had done this. He took in air.

From the thickness of his father's voice, he knew he had awakened him. "I'm sorry, Dad. I just thought Jenny might be there."

"What time is it?"

"What's wrong?" Mark heard his mother ask. "Who is it?"

"It's 11:30," Mark answered. "I'm sorry. Listen, have a nice trip."

Kay stepped into the study and handed Mark the note. "I think it's from Jenny," she said.

"Who's that?" Irwin asked. "Where's Jenny?"

"Everything's all right. Have a good trip."

"Who's voice was that?" Irwin persisted.

"Just Kay."

"Where's Jenny?" he asked.

"I think she must be out to a movie or at a friend's." Mark strained to sound casual, but his father didn't yield.

"What is that woman doing there with you?" The tone of his father's voice chafed at Mark, but Mark was anxious to read the letter, and he didn't want to start in with his father.

"We're going to bed now," he said. "Good night." And he hung up.

He stood for a moment staring at the trophies lying at his feet: he tried to understand what had happened. What would cause his wife such anger? He tried to check his own anger until he had read her letter. He took the envelope into the living room and sat on the couch.

Kay stood in the doorway; her eyes fixed on Mark. She felt her own heart beating. Her hands, at a loss to occupy themselves, reached into her purse for a cigarette. She began to pace behind the couch while Mark read.

When he finished the letter, he sat staring at the page. His dark eyes were fixed on the words though he wasn't reading them or even seeing them. His mouth opened then shut. Again Kay felt the stillness taking him deep inside himself. She felt at a loss to know how to approach him. She quit pacing and moved over by the window. She felt suddenly breathless. She wanted to ask Mark what Jenny had said, but she didn't dare break into his thoughts. She was unaccustomed to feeling timid.

The moment was broken by the ringing of the phone. Mark gave a start then went quickly into his study and shut the door. He left Jenny's letter on the coffee table.

Kay didn't hesitate. She went over and sat on the couch. She didn't pick up the letter for fear Mark would return and find her prying, but she leaned over the table as though to get a magazine and in that fashion read the contents.

Dear Mark,
> *I've gone away for a while. I've taken Erika*
> *with me. I need her more than you just now, I think.*
> *I tried to call but was told you weren't available.*
> *I'll phone in a few days.*
> > > *I love you,*
> > > *Jenny*

Kay turned the letter over to see if there were more on the back when suddenly Mark stepped into the room. She started and set the paper down.

It had been Irwin on the phone asking about Jenny, and Mark had done what he rarely did with his father; he had lied. He told him Jenny had just come in from a friend's, and he had missed seeing her note. Had he heard any sympathy in his father's voice, any opening for his own failings and misjudgments, he might have told him what had happened, but he heard only judgment and censure in Irwin's questions.

In fact Irwin had heard the panic in his son's voice and had called hoping Mark would talk to him, but his tone with Mark was a habit, and the habit carried too much history.

Mark hung up twice as angry. His father's call had brought forth the fear he had been trying to dismiss. Jenny was gone; she'd taken Erika; and he didn't know where nor understand why she had left. She had no right to take Erika. The tempered, pleading tone of her note eluded him right now. In the past when they'd argued, she'd always gone out alone, with her work, and eventually had come back. It was unstated, but understood, between them that however angry they got at each other, they would never stay away over night. And they would never take their child into the battle. That Jenny had violated this stricture agitated him most of all for it struck at the root of his fear: that when a final accounting came, in the courts or in the heart or wherever such accounts were tallied, the child, if divided, would fall to her mother. He, the father, would stand helpless, dismembered of the one person in the world he loved the most.

He also loved his wife. He needed her right now and had counted on her to be there for him. He felt betrayed, almost as though she had gone off with another man. It might have been easier if there were another man, he thought, for at least then he would have someone to fight, but she left him only himself as the battleground.

When he opened the door to the study and saw Kay reading Jenny's letter, the full rush of his anger broke. "What do you think you're doing?" he demanded.

Kay dropped the letter. Her eyes darted up to him.

"I ... I ... I just thought maybe I could help."

Mark's face was pale. "That letter is personal," he declared, sweeping it out of her hands. "You have no business . . . Goddamn you, Kay, you have no business reading it." His voice faltered he was so angry. "Goddamn it, why did you come back?" He threw the letter across the room.

Kay sat stunned. She had never seen Mark this angry, and his words struck her like a whip, lashing at her hopes. Her hands began to shake. She stamped out her cigarette. "You're not the only one," she declared. "You're not the only one, Mark."

"One what?"

"You're not the only one who hurts. Goddamn *you*! Can't you see? What have *I* done? Nothing. Not one blessed thing except try to be your friend. To help you with your work. To be here when your wife skips out. To love you without saying a word. Yes, without a word. To suffer Jenny's and Olivia's abuse . . . and . . . " Her voice pitched so high here that she had to break off and start again in a lower tone. "And to allow Jenny to nearly disable my son for life and have him blame me. Yes! You didn't know that. I didn't tell you. He blames me. And what have I done? Nothing! Goddamn it, Mark, why don't you open your eyes." Kay was sobbing now, and she turned her face from him.

Mark stared at her, taken for the moment out of his own anger as he watched her. "What do you mean David blames you?"

Kay sucked in air; she couldn't stop crying. "Today . . . when I saw him . . . I wasn't going to tell you . . ." she spoke in broken sobs. "When I told him he could leave with me, he said he didn't want . . . he didn't even want to live with me. That I'd tried to kill him!" She looked up at Mark, her eyes wide. "That I wanted him dead . . ."

"No . . ."

"I didn't know what to say. I don't know what to do with him." Kay wiped the tears with the back of her hand. "Oh shit . . ." she said, reaching for a Kleenex on the table and blowing her nose. "He blames me for everything. I see it in his eyes. I can't bear looking into his eyes."

Mark sat down. He put his hand on her back to steady her. "I'll talk to him," he offered.

Kay leaned towards him. "Oh Mark, I'm sorry about Jenny. I am. But honestly I didn't do anything."

Mark stared off over her head, which she leaned on his shoulder. "Oh, Mark . . . " her voice pleaded. She reached up and touched his cheek. "The biggest mistake I ever made was stalking out on you that night at the banquet and leaving you to Jenny." She reached up with her other hand, and she kissed him. He didn't resist. She kissed him again and then again; and because he felt the injustice of the way he had treated her and felt profoundly the injustice of the way Jenny was treating him, he returned the kiss. She touched his lips with her tongue, then inserted it into his mouth. She drew him down beside her. Still he did not resist. He tried to lose himself in the caring and the need of this woman, in his own need for caring, relinquishing for the moment his will. Kay accepted the lead, kissing him, stroking him, drawing him on into his need. She unloosened her dress and slipped it off her shoulders, guiding his hands to her breasts, concealed in silk and lace. She began unbuckling his belt with quick fingers, reaching down towards the hardness she felt rising in him. Her fingers slipped into his slacks, but her touch, which stirred suddenly his passion, also drew him up, even as the hand on a brow can both start and awaken one from a dream. Part of him longed for the dream to complete itself, yet the awakening begun, pushed the dream away so that its pursuit became an act of will. He opened his eyes.

There he saw not his passion, but a woman almost ugly in her desire; her eyes streaked with mascara, her lips swollen and dry and reaching, her hands maneuvering, pushing for a destination, her body arching up and down beside him. Yet he also understood that he had brought her to this point. He knew with even greater clarity, however, that to continue would be to throw over what he cared for. Wherever the world had come to in the easy coupling of men and women, he could not account himself so easily.

Kay was straining at him now, pulling him to her. His own body longed to burst even as his mind issued its protest. He tried to hold Kay still beside him, removed her hand, tried to pull them both back into the world where order could reign. Yet she was insisting and moaning. "Oh Mark . . . please . . . please . . ." She pushed his arm aside and began to climb on top of him.

He sat up. "No," he said.

At first Kay didn't understand what was happening and reached down to him at the same time he was pulling himself up, and his elbow knocked her in the face. She opened her eyes. He tried to put his arm around her to help the transition. "What's wrong?" she asked.

"Kay. I'm sorry. I'm very, very sorry."

"What?"

"This is a mistake."

"Mistake?" She stared at him as if needing a translation. Slowly she asked, "I'm a mistake?"

"I'm so angry at Jenny . . . but it isn't fair . . . it's not you."

Kay's hair fell in a tangle over her face, and she pushed it aside with the back of her hand. The slackness of her mouth, lost only a moment before in passion, tightened and her gaze grew cool. She looked about the room as if orienting herself. Mark stood and quickly zipped his slacks. Kay lay there for a moment then slowly sat up. "I can't believe this," she said. She pulled her dress back on her shoulders, then reached around and tried to zip it. Finally she turned her back to Mark. "Please . . ." Her voice was brittle. Mark leaned over and zipped the rest of the dress, then stepped back.

She too stood. "What's happened to you?" she accused. But Mark didn't answer. "You don't mind if I sleep on the couch tonight, do you? I'll be moving out tomorrow, but it *is* midnight."

"Of course. Take my bed, and I'll sleep on the couch."

"Ha!" she laughed. "And what do you tell Jenny if she comes back and finds me in your bed? You'll be explaining yourself for weeks. No, Mark, I prefer the couch."

In silence they stretched a sheet across the sofa and tucked in the blanket. As Mark turned towards the back of the apartment, Kay added, "You needn't lock your door."

Chapter 34

Mark couldn't sleep. When the phone rang at six the next morning, he was already dressed. He grabbed the receiver before it finished the first ring for fear the noise would wake Kay. He wanted to leave before she got up. He'd written her a note promising to go see David today. It was a cowardly exit, he knew, but he had too much on his mind—Jenny, DeVries, Afco—to face her.

When he'd gone back to his study last night to pick up his lucite cubes from the floor, he'd seen the Afco folder returned to his desk. On it was a brief note from Jenny suggesting that he check the noncash charges this quarter. He wondered which had come first: her financial analysis or the tantrum in his office, and this swing of her emotions disturbed him. Yet when he analyzed the sheets, he saw what she had: an increase of almost two million dollars. Since noncash charges represented depreciation allowances for plant and equipment, they should be uniform quarter to quarter. That his accounting department hadn't flagged this increase concerned him. That the discrepancy could represent a larger problem agitated him even more. Were there costs DeVries hadn't told him about? Were there other problems? Or might DeVries or someone have been understating noncash charges and overstating cash charges for his own use? As soon as this doubt rose, he dismissed it until he could investigate further. Yet it wedged under his peace of mind. Jenny had signed her note "J." No closing, nothing, just "J."

Only as he spoke into the phone now did he consider that Jenny could be on the other end. But Olivia answered instead. "I'm sorry . . . I thought my watch said seven. Did I wake you?"

"No. I was about to leave."

"Oh? Well, is Jenny up?"

"She's not here."

Olivia hesitated. "Where is she?"

Mark heard another receiver pick up. "Olivia, I need to talk to you," he said.

"What is it?"

"Could you meet me for breakfast?"

"Now? What's wrong? Where's Jenny?"

"In half an hour. Where are you?"

"I'm heading to midtown; I have half a dozen leads to follow up by noon. I called to see if I'd gotten any messages."

"Not that I know of. Do you know Wolf's Delicatessen on Sixth?"

She said she did, and though she hesitated, she agreed to meet him. "I'm leaving now," she said.

"So am I." As they hung up, Mark heard the other receiver quietly disconnect. He put on his jacket then took the note and his briefcase and stepped into the front hallway. Kay was back on the couch feigning sleep; he was glad for the pretence. He set his note on the hall table, lifted his coat from the hook. As he opened the front door, Kay said in an ironic voice, "Good morning, Mark." For an instant he hesitated, wondering if he should turn but decided to keep up the pretext and pretended not to hear as he shut the door behind him.

Olivia was sitting by the window staring out at the street when Mark arrived. Seeing her, he felt strangely shy. He had been so insistent that they meet, and yet now he didn't know what he expected her to do. He was afraid she would lay the blame for Jenny's leaving on him. He had been up all night going over the events of the past days, trying to understand what had caused his wife to leave him, straining to see her point of view. Yet even allowing the worst interpretation of all that had happened, he came up with one conclusion: Jenny didn't trust him. As soon as he arrived there, he began defending himself, though he knew a defense was not what was called for right now. He had come to Olivia hoping she could offer a view he could use.

Olivia watched him approaching. Spread before her was a yellow pad with names of those she had yet to contact in her search for Jamin. At the bottom of the pad, Jenny's question: Afco flow of funds? She had so many questions, it was hard to know which to focus on. It seemed clear that Benjamin DeVries—and thus the company Mark was part of—was playing a role she didn't yet understand. As Mark drew nearer, making his way through the red vinyl booths, she considered what questions she should ask him.

She took off her glasses and rubbed the bridge of her nose. She felt tired and irritable. She'd stopped late last night at Peg's apartment in the Village on her way back from Brooklyn. Peg was up writing on deadline for *Newsweek*. Olivia had taken a bath then slept on Peg's couch for a few hours. When she'd awakened at 5:30 this morning, she felt immediately behind schedule. She'd paused long enough to press her beige pants suit and have coffee. She'd borrowed a fresh blue blouse from Peg, who was larger than she, and now the soft bow at her neck made her look uncharacteristically feminine even as her broad hands cleared the table of papers.

Mark sat down. He glanced out the window rather than at her. Olivia saw in his face the same pain she'd seen a few nights ago. She still didn't know how to relieve it. She hadn't wanted to come here. She couldn't afford anyone else's troubles right now. She had to stop Jamin. Yet looking into Mark's face, she saw he was thrown off balance. "What's happened?" she asked.

Mark turned to her. "Jenny's gone. I don't know why, and I don't know where, and frankly I'm mad as hell; but I'm also worried."

Olivia sipped her coffee. "Is Kay still there?" Her tone was cool. Mark nodded. "Christ," she said.

"She's leaving today. Jenny knew that. I arranged for her to stay at my parents, but I couldn't throw her out."

"Why not?"

Mark frowned. "Don't start in on me. I need your help, Olivia, not your judgment."

Olivia drank her coffee. She didn't know how to help this man. Why was he coming to her? She gazed out the window then turned back to him. "You can't ignore how Jenny feels, you know, just because you don't agree. You're hoping she'll change, when you're the one who's got to act and make some choices."

"There are no choices," Mark argued. "That's what you and Jenny don't understand. I made my choice eight years ago. It was Jenny. Kay is not an option."

Olivia didn't answer. She signaled the waitress for coffee. "You want to be the nice guy, do the right thing by everyone, is that it?" She put back on her glasses and tried to moderate her tone. "There are worse faults, God knows, but in the long run, Mark, you may hurt more people than the ordinary bastard who's only out for himself." She hesitated. "It's not enough. You've got to take on the demon."

"What demon?"

The waitress set down coffee then returned with cereal and toast. Olivia doused the cereal with sugar and milk and began to eat. After a moment she looked up. "Nyral described Bulagwi as a man of small imagination and dogged will. Maybe that's one side of the demon. A sort of giant smallness that creates havoc to make itself grand or strikes at others out of some panic of its own. To get rid of the panic we fight wars, murder, rape, anything to fill up the hole."

Mark frowned. He glanced at the pictures on the wall: eggs, pancakes, fish. "I don't understand what you're saying. I don't see how it applies."

"When you were a child, did you ever play chicken on the tracks?" Mark raised his eyebrows as he sipped his coffee. "Where I lived, there were railroad tracks a few blocks away, and the boys in the neighborhood used to go there and play after school. When they heard a train coming, they'd dare each other to stand on the tracks until it roared around the curve on Bay Street. That gave them about thirty seconds to jump off before the train would smash into them. It was a terrible game; all the adults forbade it, but they played it anyway. The girls used to hide in the bushes watching, superior in our wisdom, yet thrilled at the boys' affront.

"Well, one day Johnny Talmadge, a blonde, blue-eyed boy from over on the white part of town, came down and took the dare. Only he didn't jump off when the train turned the corner. I don't know what he was doing. I don't know if he was trying to prove he was braver or what, but I still remember staring through the bushes as though the world stopped in that second when Johnny

Talmadge's face slammed against the front of the train. I remember the wail of the whistle and the metal wheels screeching on the track as the train tried to stop. Everyone froze in place, then just as fast, we found our feet and flew through the brush back home. None of us knew why, but we ran like the devil himself was after us, which of course he was for within hours the police were all over the place. Finally they arrested three boys.

"No one had touched Johnny Talmadge; he'd stepped on that track for reasons of his own and stayed there for who knew what reason, even when the other boys were screaming at him to get off. But some force froze him. Three black boys were brought to trial on charges that they had pushed him in front of the train. "The violence of Johnny Talmadge's death set off a reaction that had to fulfill itself. The demon flew around our town playing havoc for months. What was that demon? I can't tell you exactly, only I knew it even then. Sometimes it screams like Johnny Talmadge as he hit the train. Sometimes it's quiet and insinuates itself. But it's a force. Or maybe a fear. But to get rid of that fear, we do irrational, sometimes terrible, things. I know you've got to take it on or it takes you on; and you can't ignore someone it's gotten hold of."

Mark shifted uncomfortably on the seat. He took off his jacket then stretched his neck above his collar as though his collar suddenly constricted him. "So how do you take it on?" he asked, his voice skeptical and slightly defensive.

Olivia ate her toast. She thought of Jenny decked out like a society wife. "I'm not sure I can tell you," she said. She stared for a moment at the bottom of her cereal bowl as though the configuration of cornflakes might yield an answer. She glanced up and saw Mark watching her, trying to understand what she was saying but not yet putting the pieces together for himself.

"I've never been married," she went on, "but I've always thought if the marriage worked, it could extend who you were, or rather what you could see and understand about the world. I mean if it works, it's a leap of imagination, isn't it, being so close to another human being?"

"Olivia," Mark declared, trying to restrain his impatience. "At another time, I'd enjoy talking philosophy with you; but right now, my wife has left, and I don't know what to do."

Olivia paused. She set both arms on the table, her large brown palms face down. "Get rid of Kay."

"Done."

"Go after Jenny."

"Where?"

"Call her mother."

"I did. She's not home."

"Call her office."

"I will. No one's there yet."

"Make sure if Jenny calls you, she can get to you no matter where you are."

He nodded.

"And when she comes back, listen to her. See what she's seeing, not what you think she should be seeing." Olivia pushed her bowl and plate aside. She looked out the window now; her own face filled suddenly with emotion.

"What's the matter?" Mark asked. She shook her head. "Where've you been the past few days?" he persisted.

"On this goddamn story," she said. Her eyes were shadowed with dark circles; small beads of sweat sprouted at the roots of her hair though the restaurant itself was chilled. She didn't look well, Mark thought.

"You've been lecturing me on seeing," he said quietly. "I see something's wrong. You want to talk?"

She began gathering up her notes and papers. "Jamin's alive," she answered.

"Where?"

She glanced around the restaurant. The crowd had increased in the last half hour, but the booths near them were empty. "I don't know. I've spent the last day and a half looking for him."

"He's in New York? What's he doing?"

Olivia didn't answer. She wanted to share with someone the burden she felt for Jamin, to have someone help her catch the demon she knew was loose but could not contain. She wanted to lean for a moment on Mark's connection with the world which she felt so disconnected from, to tell him about the plan to assassinate Bulagwi. She wanted to ask what he would do. Yet the consequences were enormous, and she and Mark were not bound by the same loyalties. She sipped her coffee. "What do you know about Benjamin DeVries?" she asked instead.

Mark picked up the salt shaker and held it between his fingers. "Why do you ask?"

"I've come across him." She hesitated. "Do you trust him?"

"We're partners with him," Mark answered. "At least our investors are. What do you mean you've come across him?" His eyes

315

bore down on her and her question in the same way Jenny's did, she thought.

"Would you tell me about Afco? Jenny suggested I check flow of funds statements."

"She did?"

Olivia nodded. "Do you know why or what she meant? Is Afco supporting any of this political activity? Are you supporting Bulagwi or the NLA? Or are you playing both sides?"

"We're not playing sides," Mark declared. "We're trying to run a company."

"Then do you know what Jenny meant?"

Mark took a sip of Olivia's water. "She found a discrepancy. I'm checking it out today. I'd appreciate it if you'd let me find out the problem before you write anything."

"I'm not going to write anything," she said. "I'm writing a book, Mark, not the daily news. Jenny knows that. She wouldn't expose you."

"There's nothing to expose," Mark defended. He sat the water down. Then he asked, "In what context did you come across Benjamin DeVries?"

Olivia considered again telling him what she knew. But what if Mark told DeVries or called the police? What would happen to Jamin and Nyral? No, she didn't know Mark well enough. She didn't know the loyalties that held him; she couldn't take the risk. Instead she said slowly, "I don't know exactly what you're doing in Africa. I don't know if you're there just to make a lot of money, or if you think you're doing some good. But don't assume that because your intentions are good and you're good at what you do, that the consequences will be."

Mark leaned back in the booth and shut his eyes. He wouldn't argue with Olivia. Instead he asked again, "Where did you come across DeVries?"

Olivia began putting her papers away. She closed her briefcase and set it on the table between them. "It's possible," she said in a low voice, "that Benjamin DeVries has been skimming from you and your investors, possibly taking an extra cut from Bulagwi or not reporting all the revenues.

"I don't know. Maybe that's what Jenny found. This is only a guess. I would also guess that Bulagwi knows and is part of the scheme. In a colossal misjudgment he may have tried to squeeze DeVries or even blackmail him. In any case I do know DeVries is now taking events into his own hands."

Mark sat forward. Hadn't DeVries used a similar phrase the night before? "Do you have proof?"

"On the finances, not yet. But someone I trust has access to evidence and to the bank accounts. I may be wrong. But I do know firsthand that DeVries is involved in ways I assume you know nothing about. I'd advise you to be very careful."

"Involved in what ways?"

"I can't tell you. And you can't tell anyone I've told you this much. There's too much at stake."

"But you don't have evidence?"

A sadness returned to Olivia's face. "No, and I have very little time." She took her briefcase onto the seat beside her. She looked up. She hesitated, but finally she offered, "If this is ever over and Robert Nyral survives, maybe I can introduce you. Perhaps you could help each other."

She opened her briefcase and pulled out a five dollar bill for her breakfast, but Mark took the check. She nodded, then she slid out of the booth.

On the street she gave Mark her hand. "You picked the wrong partners, Mark," she said. And she turned down the block and trudged into the wind, shoulders rounded, head thrust forward, up 57th Street.

The phone rang again in Jenny and Mark's apartment at 6:30. Kay was sitting up on the couch in her slip, a blanket wrapped about her shoulders. Her bare feet were propped up on the coffee table. As she sipped a cup of black coffee, she wondered if Mark had really failed to hear her this morning or if he had ignored her on purpose. She was certain the latter was the case. Her hand trembled as a slow rage spread inside her. She had laid herself open to him last night, and he had not only turned her away, but he did not have the balls, yes, the bloody balls, to say good morning. He had instead made a breakfast date with Olivia. For what purpose, she could not even imagine, most likely to lament his skittish wife who also lacked, biology aside, balls.

She'd always liked Jenny well enough in the past. Jenny posed no real threat to her, she thought, except that she'd had the insight to marry Mark. But then she'd also settled for a husband and family and let her career slip away. She'd always felt superior to Jenny. Since Jenny didn't challenge this order, she considered they were friends of a sort. Lately, however, Jenny had challenged her, quietly challenged her access to Mark. She'd never made a secret of her feelings for Mark. She'd always acted openly, never tried to meet Mark behind Jenny's back. She prided herself on being direct. As to what might come of the friendship, well, she made herself available; that was all. If Jenny or any wife didn't have what it took to hold her husband, that was her problem. Sooner or later most men she was interested in, married or not, made an advance. Mark was an exception. She wasn't convinced that his action was final, however. They had almost made love. She knew he had wanted to, even if his conscience had won the battle. If he was really not tempted, then why hadn't he spoken to her this morning? They were adults after all. That Mark didn't know how to deal with this ambiguity interested her, but at the moment, the phone was ringing.

She got up and went into Mark's study. "Hello . . . oh, Jenny. No, I'm afraid he's not here. Let's see . . . " she said, "we got up around six I guess. He had an early meeting. Where are you?"

Jenny hesitated. Finally she answered in a voice that almost betrayed her but held steady. "I'm at Olivia's. I'll try Mark at the office. Goodbye." She hung up before Kay could insert any more between them.

Kay smiled as she set the receiver back in the cradle. So everyone fled to Olivia's. If Olivia was the best solace they could find, then there was hope for her. Yet as she rose to dress, the rage again stirred. Jenny, in her quiet, matter-of-fact voice, denied her, rejected the significance of her presence. Suddenly she wanted to strike out at this house and at this woman she didn't understand. She stood in the middle of Mark's study trying to find an object. She saw a note in Jenny's handwriting on Mark's desk: "Check Afco flow of funds noncash charges v.v. past quarters. J." She paused. She didn't know what the note meant, but she jotted it down for herself on a separate sheet of paper. Afco was DeVries' company, a fact she hadn't explored yet on this story. She'd call *The Tribune* and get someone to check the figures for her.

She headed into Jenny's office. Here was where Jenny was most vulnerable: in her work which had not seen the light of print for four years except for one children's book. How could she work for four years without being published, with no assurance that her book ever would be published? Yet Jenny had been writing on her own, for some reason of her own, and like Olivia, remained obscure and in her own world.

Kay picked up the pages on Jenny's desk. Her first instinct was not to read them but to destroy them, destroy the whole goddamn pretense of this woman. She went back to the living room to her purse and took out her cigarette lighter. She returned to the study and flicked on the flame. She stood with the lighter over the pages, waiting for some force outside herself to push her arm and make her drop the fire, but no force moved her.

Finally she closed the lighter. She looked about for another outlet. She went into Erika's room. Cassie was curled on the red gingham pillow in the rocking chair. In the corner the king snake was making a hissing sound from its cage as if it sensed Cassie's presence, but so far Cassie didn't appear to notice the snake. Why Jenny had bought such a creature for her child was beyond her. She watched the snake coiled up flicking its tongue. She wondered if it would strike the cat or if the cat would instead kill the snake. An interesting question. She lifted the lid of the cage and dropped it to the floor, leaving the two creatures to enact their fates; then she returned to the hall and shut the door behind her.

Kay had dressed and was making herself toast when the intercom buzzed. She couldn't understand the name of the person who was seeking entry, but it was a young woman's voice, so she rang her in. Through the peep hole, she saw a brown-skinned girl with dark hair halfway down her back.

"I am sorry to come so early," the girl apologized as Kay opened the door. "But Olivia said I should come at any time. She said you were a friend."

Kay tilted her head. She couldn't imagine Olivia calling her a friend. The girl glanced behind her as if someone were with her or following her. Kay invited her in, but she stepped only so far as the foyer. "Olivia said I must tell her as soon as I heard anything, that it was very important. She said she would be in touch with you."

Kay realized the girl thought she was Jenny. "Yes, what is it?"

"Jamin. I think I know how he will appear."

"Jamin?" Kay asked. "Jamin Nyo?"

Her surprise made the girl cautious. "You are Olivia's friend?"

"Yes, yes . . . how will he appear?"

The girl hesitated. Kay smiled encouragingly. "Tell Olivia that I do not know for certain, but that she should look for a woman."

"What woman?"

"Jamin. Tell her I think he will come as a woman."

Kay frowned. This didn't make any sense to her. "Where is he? Is he alive?" she asked, but her tone was too eager.

The girl stepped back. "That is all I know." She was already moving towards the door.

"But he's alive?"

Rhekka stared at Kay and felt instinctively she had made a mistake, that this woman was not who she represented herself to be. She opened the door.

"Please . . . " Kay followed her into the hallway, "just a few questions . . . who *are* you?"

Suddenly panicked, Rhekka hurried down the stairs and disappeared into the street.

Jenny had fallen asleep on Olivia's bed in her clothes. She slept fitfully. When the sun finally streaked through the window, she awakened with a start. The heat had gone off during the night, and she'd drawn tighter into herself for warmth, vaguely conscious of the cold, yet too far into sleep to act. When she woke, she felt unrested. Quickly she climbed under the covers, rubbing her legs back and forth on the sheets as she'd phoned Mark. She had rehearsed the past days and events to see what had gone wrong. The only conclusion that had risen clear was that she could not run from what she feared. She must talk to him, only Kay had answered instead.

She hung up the phone now. She lay motionless on the couch. She started to shiver. She curled her body tighter into itself; she could not get warm. She heard Kay's voice insinuating in her ear: "We woke up around six . . . *we, we, we* . . . " What was Kay doing in her home at 6:30 in the morning? The sun shown brightly through the window. She turned her face to the wall, curled her body in a fist and fell asleep.

At eleven she awoke. Finding herself still in Olivia's apartment with papers crumpled over the bed, she got up. Her head ached. She felt drugged from sleep, yet exhausted, as though she had not slept at all. Her white turtleneck and jeans were twisted around her body. She put on her boots and coat. She must get up, go outside, do something. She went to the desk to get her purse. She stared out the window at the river, a triangle of blue between the soot-backed buildings. She knew from the past that this break in the view was the river, though from where she stood, it shimmered only as an intensified patch of color. She looked down into the alley below, into the grey light caught in the shadows of the buildings. She stared for a long time into this emptiness and felt herself lost in it, flying towards it, the darkness folding over her and separating her from the pain. She longed to be alone, without pain from another. In her mind she took the leap.

She didn't remember what happened next, but she found herself in her coat, holding her papers, standing outside on Commonwealth Avenue. On either side of the wide street, brown snow banked against the curb and the trees. The trees were exposed and naked. The cold penetrated her own layers of clothes. The sun, a bright ball in the clear sky, gave off no heat. She stared up at it, suddenly impatient at its deception. Crossing the street, she turned towards the river.

A catamaran with red and white sails pitched on the white caps, its hull diving into the waves then heaving towards the sky. She thrust her hands into her coat pockets and sat on a bench under a chestnut tree. She used to come to the river and sit watching its unhurried flow through the city, to the harbor, to the ocean beyond. It moved at its own imperative, without effort or will. But today the river was roused. Jenny sat very still watching it. By her stillness she tried to contain her own panic within. She tried to resist the urge to plunge into the water herself or down a dark alley as her friend Elise had done, towards some absolution of feeling. She recognized this urge, a helpless nihilism that would throw all away in the very hope of redemption.

She remembered her mother years ago bolting out of the house one night in the rain, in her nightgown, when her father had

322

finally come home after two unexplained days away, and she knew he had been with another woman. Her mother left him to take care of her while she drove pell mell down the highway without destination or caring, speeding into her own void to avoid what she could not face and did not know how to bear, until finally she had run out of gas and had to be towed, nightgown and all, to a gas station somewhere outside Texarkana. As she sat in her car sipping a warm Dr. Pepper at four in the morning, watching the truckers speed by on the highway, she knew she had survived this plunge over the edge and must now go back and take up her child and her sundered life. With the breaking of the day and the lifting of the clouds, she had slowly pulled into the driveway of their house, picked up the morning paper as she did each day in her nightgown and gone inside to set about a new order.

She remembered her father that morning waiting by the window where he had not slept all night, in blue cotton pajamas, defeated in his unhappiness. She had heard only the beginning of the confrontation which had eventually, years later, brought the end. She remembered her father's words: "I am not happy here." And her mother, letting go that morning, had started again.

But she *was* happy or had been happy with Mark, and Mark with her, so why was she bolting? What force was driving her from her own home? As in dreams she sometimes barreled down mountainsides without brakes or wings or any means of controlling speed, she plunged in her thought, leaving Mark, starting again, independent, contained, invulnerable, yet out of control because of the love she had left behind and thrown away. What had Kay been doing in her home at 6:30 in the morning? *"We got up around six. We . . . we . . . we . . ."* Kay's voice shot into her like venom, freezing her heart and negating her feelings.

She stood and walked to the edge of the river. The water slapped at the stones on the bank. She reached down and touched the cold water. She was a strong swimmer. Could she swim fast enough to get warm if she took the plunge, swim towards that catamaran, past the catamaran? In her mind she saw bodies flying from a bridge in Africa.

323

On the surface of the waves a duck bobbed. She remembered the duck on the Izo River, the grey-brown, plain-suited duck she'd watched that day near the dam as he paddled against the current drawing him to the edge of the giant spillway. Whenever he stopped paddling, the current carried him closer to the edge. Finally he took to diving beneath the water, disappearing for a long moment, then surfacing slightly upstream; but with the slightest pause, the current propelled him towards the precipice. She had worried how he would save himself from crashing over the forty-foot drop, under the weight of tons of water. Then, nearby, another duck, also paddling against the current, suddenly lifted its wings and flew off the water. She'd laughed out loud. Of course. She had been so caught up watching the struggle that she had forgotten ducks could fly. She wondered why her duck didn't do the same. And then just as the current drove him to the edge where the water must have rushed hard under his soft belly, he too lifted his wings and flew above the falls.

She pleaded now for an answer within herself, pleaded for the wings to lift her from this edge. The answer rose so naturally that at first she dismissed it. She found herself thinking about Erika, wondering what she was doing right then, probably exploring the docks with her grandmother. Erika was a false mirror in which she tried to see herself. But no, Erika was more than that, infinitely more. She was an opening to love which demanded not that it be returned, only that it be given. And she heard in herself the reply: you have a loving heart.

The answer drew her up. She snapped a branch from a tree beside her and dropped it in the water. It lapped back and forth until the current caught it, pulling it out into the river where it began churning over and over in the waves. With the branch she also lay her answer on the water to see if it would hold. The river took them both and carried them beyond her view. Before Mark, before Erika, through no power or will of her own, she had a loving heart. This was her power. When she looked deepest into her feelings about Kay, what troubled her was that in confronting Kay, she confronted a part of herself which did not love. Because Kay triggered this smallness of heart in her, she felt bound to Kay as if Kay had secured around her neck an albatross which only a larger power could set free.

She began to walk along the bank. She followed the river to the band shell where she'd attended concerts so many summers ago. She had sat under the stars listening to the music. The band shell was deserted now. The ground was covered with patches of ice. A light snow was beginning to trace a path through the trees. Snowflakes landed in a thin crown on her head. As she listened to the quiet, an idea opened within her.

Chapter 36

Jenny hadn't been back to *The Boston Record* for years. As she made her way across the marble floor of the lobby, into the wood-paneled elevators, down the beige corridors, she saw no one she recognized. She had called ahead, and the personnel director's assistant was expecting her. "I used to work here as a reporter . . ." Jenny explained as she sat down. "I need to find the former husband of a colleague. I don't remember his name. Her name is Katherine Bernstein Walsh."

The woman took down Kay's name, then went over to a filing cabinet. After a few minutes she returned with a manila folder which she opened on the desk. "It says here she's divorced."

"I know," Jenny said. "But does it mention her husband's name?"

The woman scanned the sheet. "Randall . . . Randall Walsh."

Jenny asked if she might use a phone. At a desk in the corner she checked information and found there were two Randall Walshes listed. Her first call located the Walsh she was looking for in Arlington. His wife said he wouldn't be home till 5:30. When Jenny asked if she might stop by around six, the woman hesitated, but finally agreed.

Jenny headed next towards the newspaper's library. She would use the time to track down information on Bulagwi and DeVries. Outside the editorial pages she paused to look into the glass trophy cases. There, among dozens of other plaques and loving cups and trophies was the award with her name on it that she and two other reporters had won as a team: "For Excellence in Local Reporting. Joseph F. Pulitzer, 1974."

"Jennifer Reeder?" a voice spoke from behind. "Is that you?"

For a minute she didn't recognize the bald, beak-nosed man peering at her. "Vince?"

"I'm the copy editor now," he announced without being asked. He had been her city editor when she'd started. "And I see what you're up to." He gestured towards her belly.

"Actually, I was hoping to use the library files," she said. "I need to check some information."

"Well . . . " he hesitated, "they're pretty strict about access, you know. It's against the rules really, Jennifer. You understand. If everyone who'd worked here came back and wanted to use the files, the real reporters wouldn't be able to get what they needed."

Jenny smiled. Vince hadn't changed, a bureaucrat till the end. With her smile, he relented. "But I tell you what, I won't say anything if Stella lets you."

"Thanks."

He nodded, then strode down the corridor.

Jenny turned into the library, a high-ceilinged room, flanked on all sides by grey metal filing cabinets where recent news clippings were kept according to subjects. A bank of microfilm viewing machines had been installed under the windows on the south wall. The room itself, a dull green when she'd worked here, was now a dull beige. In the center of the room, surrounded by stacks of newspapers, sat a bespectacled lady with dyed brown hair. She was ripping out a story from a newspaper with a ruler.

"I don't know if you remember me . . ." Jenny began.

The woman looked up, over her wire glasses. Her face opened into a fan of tiny wrinkles. "Why Jenny . . . Jenny . . ."

"Reeder."

"Jenny Reeder. Of course." She thrust out her small hand. "Excuse me, let me just finish . . ." She ripped off the fourth side and set the clipping in a stack. "Nice to see you. Yes, I remember. I forget some of them, but I remember you . . . and Elise Ward . . . and who was that other girl, big black girl . . ."

"Olivia Turner."

"That's right. Olivia. I remember all three of you used to run me ragged. Did more research, the three of you, than half the newsroom. You a reporter somewhere else these days?"

"I've been writing books . . . or actually, a book. I'm just in town for a day. Do you suppose I could use the files? I won't bother you."

"Bother me if you want." She looked over her shoulder at half a dozen assistants clipping at tables behind her. "I've got more help these days. It's after first deadline anyway so it'll be slow for a while."

The woman stood. She showed Jenny where the clipping index and the microfilm desk had been moved. She gave Jenny a yellow request pad and a xeroxing card and told her to tally any copies she made, then pay the petty cash box. Jenny withdrew to a table where she spread out her papers, and for the next three hours she read and took notes on articles in magazines and newspapers over the past quarter of a century.

Finally, before she left, Jenny went to visit the newsroom. She stopped briefly at the city desk, where a new editor and staff were installed. At the national desk she asked if she could see the latest copy on Bulagwi's visit. The editor handed her the wires.

"When are you going to write for us again?" he complained as she scanned the copy. "We miss you."

She glanced up and smiled. "I've got a few other projects to attend to first."

"So I see. Well, just as long as you don't forget us." Jenny nodded.

On her way out, she stopped at the business page. She'd rarely visited this area as a reporter, but since she'd married Mark, she'd gotten to know the business editor. On occasion he'd call Mark for comment or background on issues. As she entered his cubicle, Taunton Embers rose. "Why, Jenny! I've just been on the phone trying to reach Mark."

"You have? Why?"

He handed her a sheet of wire copy. "You know anything about this? It'll be in tomorrow's *Trib*. The story claims discrepancies have shown up in Afco's books, and *The Tribune* is suggesting funds may have been diverted to Bulagwi, though the story seems soft to me."

"Who wrote the story?"

"Kay Walsh. You didn't talk to her and not us, did you?"

Jenny sat down in the chair opposite him. "I didn't talk to anyone, Taunton." She skimmed the story.

"Well, can you tell me if there's any truth to it?"

Jenny looked up. "I can't tell you anything. But I'd get the facts straight before I chased Kay's lead."

"That's what I've been trying to do, only Mark's not picking up."

Jenny stood. She started towards the door; then she turned. "Keep trying . . . please."

Hurrying out of the white-columned *Record* building into the five o'clock traffic, Jenny searched for a taxi. The street lights were flickering on; the snow had stopped. How had Kay gotten that story? Surely Mark hadn't talked to her. There was only one way: Kay had gone through their desks and had found the papers she'd left for Mark. All at once she wanted to get home. But she had to make a stop first. A taxi pulled to the curb; she got in and asked the driver to take her over the bridge to Arlington.

The Walsh's double-decker clapboard house was set away from the street at the rear of a narrow lot. By the time Jenny arrived, the sun had set. The clouded sky concealed the moon. Jenny asked the taxi to wait; then she walked up the dark driveway.

Mounting the steps to the front porch, she considered what she wanted to ask Randall Walsh. Do you know your son is in the hospital? Do you know your son? Do you have a son? She wasn't sure what she hoped to accomplish here. All at once she wondered if she were here on a goodwill mission or if she were simply trying to get Randall Walsh to take Kay and his son out of her life. She wouldn't know the answer until she walked through the door which was now opening to her.

A short, thick-set woman about her age and about as far along in pregnancy greeted her. Holding onto the woman's skirt, a child in training pants and a Boston Patriot's sweatshirt peered out.

Another child scooted a tank across the floor behind his mother. "Bam—Bam—Bam!" he thundered as he rammed the tank into his little brother, who let out a howl.

"Stop that, Randy. Go play in your room," the mother declared. "Go on now. And Joshua, you go with him." She scooted the toddler along with her hand, then turned back to Jenny. She offered an uncertain smile. She was dressed up in a tailored red wool maternity dress; her brown hair was piled on her head; her small face was freshly made up. She didn't look like a mother at the end of a day, rather like a woman who had dressed up for this visit from a friend of her husband's first wife.

"I'm sorry to intrude," Jenny offered. "I won't be long." She saw the wariness in the woman's eyes.

"I'll get Randy."

As she disappeared, Jenny stepped into the entry hall which opened onto the living room. On a sofa a girl of about nine sat doing homework in front of "The Jetsons" on a large screen TV. The living room was furnished in early American pine and maple, big block furniture set on a braided rug. Spread out on a knobkneed coffee table were *McCall's*, *Readers' Digest*, *TV Guide* and a Book-of-the-Month-Club selection brochure. Jenny tried to imagine Kay in this house with three children, sitting on the braided rug. She saw her instead running out the door screaming. She tried to imagine herself and knew she could accommodate at least to a point, though at the arrival of the fourth child or the fifth *Readers' Digest* she feared she too might run from the house, down the driveway into the quiet, unbearably quiet streets outside. She wondered if the woman at the door were also treading an edge or if she had created a refuge here for herself and her family.

"Yes?" The voice from behind was stiff.

Jenny turned. A tall, balding man with a thickening waistline watched her from behind horn-rimmed glasses. He was dressed in a brown suit and orange tie. For a moment Jenny just stared trying to picture this man with Kay.

"Can I help you?" he asked. His wife stood beside him, the toddler in her arms now.

"I'd like to speak with you for a minute . . . " Jenny glanced at the woman. She was prepared to explain the situation in front of the second Mrs. Walsh, but Randall Walsh nodded. "We can go into my study."

As Jenny passed through the doorway, the woman stepped aside. Jenny tried to assure her with a smile that she wasn't going to disrupt her home, that nothing was going to happen, though Jenny sensed already how much might be put on the line.

Randall Walsh positioned himself behind a large pine desk before he motioned for Jenny to sit down. The room was dark and drafty with little furniture and no rug on the hardwood floor. On the walls were Randall Walsh's trophies: an elk's head on one wall and a smaller deer on the other. Jenny wondered if his wife had a study.

As Randall Walsh lit up a pipe and took a puff, Jenny began without introductions. "I don't know if you've heard," she said. "Your son is in the hospital in New York."

Randall Walsh looked up. A bewildered look passed across his face as if he had been expecting other news, though Jenny couldn't guess what.

"At New York Hospital," she continued. "He was in an accident. I don't know if Kay's called you."

"I haven't spoken to Kay in a year."

"David is your son?"

He nodded, but he didn't speak. His full cheeks had turned florid. Finally he said, "Kay takes care of him."

"Do you see him?"

"In the summer for a few weeks," he answered. Then he added, as if wanting to make sure he didn't misrepresent himself, "He didn't come the last two summers because of the baby."

"I see."

"Was he hurt?" Randall Walsh asked the question in a voice that could have been inquiring about a stranger.

Jenny wondered suddenly if she had made a mistake coming here, inserting herself into this family she knew nothing about. She'd expected this man to step in and claim his child, to *be* his father. For a moment she found herself thinking of Benjamin De Vries inserting himself between Mark and his father. "He was in intensive care," she offered. "But he's out now."

Randall Walsh watched her, seeking from her his own response. "I never saw him very much," he said finally. "We have four children. The baby's due in the spring." Then he added, "It's been hard."

Jenny nodded. "Yes. I see." She realized she couldn't judge this man. "Well . . . " She stood, suddenly awkward and uncertain of why she had come here. "I just wanted to let you know."

Randall Walsh stood too. "What hospital did you say that was?"

"New York Hospital in Manhattan."

He looked down at his desk. He tapped his pipe on the corner. "Do you think I should call him?"

Jenny rested her hand on her own unborn child. She felt sad that this man didn't know what to do. "Yes," she said quietly. "I think that would be a good idea. He needs a father right now." And when she said this, she knew that she had not come only to carve out territory for herself; she had come, at least in part, to attempt some restitution.

Randall Walsh didn't answer. For a minute he didn't move to show her out. Instead he stood puffing his pipe behind his desk, in this study with no carpet, no pictures on the walls, only an elk and a deer staring at each other at opposite ends of the dark room.

Jenny took the taxi back to Olivia's where she waited for her mother's call. She tried to phone Mark, but he wasn't at home or at the office. She wondered if he'd heard about the *Tribune* story; she wondered if Kay had tried to interview him. There was no evidence in the wire report that she had.

As Jenny sat waiting at Olivia's desk, she began to read the first chapters of Olivia's book. Her mother was right. Olivia had at last gotten hold of her story: the story of an African boy in search of a father and a land to claim him and for him to claim. It was the story of his disenfranchisement through powers greater than he, of his struggle not to betray the father he found. It was the story of Jamin and Nyral. While its lyric pace had not suited *The New Centurion*'s analytic style, as a book Olivia's story triumphed. Olivia had ended chapter seven with ellipsis for the story was not yet complete.

At 7:30 Dottie Reeder phoned. Jenny arranged to meet her at the airport. At nine o'clock Jenny and Erika boarded the last shuttle back to New York.

Chapter 37

Olivia was waiting across the street from the United Nations, scanning the pedestrians and peering into each cab as it landed at the curb. Against the sky flags beat at the wind in a geometry of colors. Above her, inscribed in grey granite, was the United Nations motto: *They shall beat their swords into plowshares, and their spears into pruning hooks; nation shall not lift up sword against nation, neither shall they learn war any more. Is. 2:4*

Peg was to have met her here with press credentials twenty minutes ago. She had to make sure she got into the meeting today. Bulagwi was speaking before the Security Council, and Nyral planned to confront him. She'd almost given up looking for Jamin. She'd called the Patels four times since yesterday, annoying Mr. Patel to the point that she was reluctant to phone again. She'd gone back to the Flatbush Veneer Company twice but had found no sign of life. She'd patrolled the back halls and basements of the Plaza, even the subbasement, wandering among the boilers and lockers, but the more she moved about trying to track Jamin by her own logic, the more elusive he became for her.

She paced now in front of the steps leading up to the inscription, more concerned at the moment about whether Peg could get her a pass than about where Jamin was. In the corner of her eye she glimpsed an off-duty taxi make a circle to the curb then suddenly veer away to the honking of horns. She didn't think much about the car until she saw the same cab pull to a stop across the street as Bulagwi's limousines started up First Avenue. Though she couldn't see inside the taxi, her instincts suddenly awakened.

She darted across the street. The cab was about twenty yards up the block, but she recognized the license plates. She was afraid at any moment the cab would pull out, but she couldn't rush upon it. Approaching from the rear, she walked quickly along the wall of the United Nations, out of range of the rearview mirror. She controlled her step to keep from running and attracting attention. She heard her shoes clattering down the sidewalk. It seemed to her she couldn't move fast enough or quietly enough to catch this man whose destiny she no longer pretended to understand, yet whose life it seemed imperative to her be saved. She was within feet of the taxi now. Her eyes scanned the doors. The back door on the street side was unlocked. She made a dash for it.

"Jamin . . . Jamin . . ." she intoned as she dove inside. She uttered his name as an incantation to protect her. This time she understood the danger of coming upon him without warning. She landed on the floor for safety, her ungainly body spread out the length of the cab. "I-have-to-talk-with-you. Nyral-sent-me. And Rhekka," she added quickly. Rising slowly, she saw she had not over-dramatized her incursion, for Jamin pointed a gun at her. His expression was so rigid, it was almost unrecognizable. His eyes, bloodshot and piercing, allowed no bond between them, only the cold fact of the gun.

"Jamin . . ." she gasped. Yet she didn't believe he would hurt her. She saw the telescopic sight and knew its object. "Please. If you kill Bulagwi, you can't come back. You'll destroy yourself, or they'll destroy you."

The limousines turned into the United Nations grounds now. She had at least aborted this chance, she thought, though she sensed that he had only been staking out contingencies.

All at once he pulled away from the curb. He pressed the lock on his door, locking her in. "Jamin?" She leaned towards the plexiglass barrier between them. All she could see was the upper part of his face in the rearview mirror. His eyes peered back at her coldly, almost with hatred. She had seen this look in others in his country, this deep suspicion, this ultimate distancing, but she would not believe Jamin hated her. He had never hated her.

As he turned onto the East River Drive, she tried again, "Where are you going?"

"You should not have come," he said finally in a toneless voice.

"I can't sit by . . . " she began.

"Goddamn fool of a woman!" he exploded. Then he fell silent.

Olivia shifted in the back seat. She tried to see his face more clearly, see something she recognized, but his cheeks, roughened with the growth of beard, and his eyes, flattened by withdrawn emotions, looked alien to her.

Half an hour later Jamin pulled up to the rear of the Flatbush Veneer Company. The sun was low in the sky. The shadows from the trees across the street cast skeletal patterns over the scrubby backyard. As Jamin unlocked the doors, Olivia's first impulse was to bolt, though she knew Jamin could catch her in three paces if he wanted. She would have to run almost two blocks before she found people, for there were only boarded-up stores here. She made this calculation even as she determined she would not run; she had known Jamin too long to be afraid of him.

Jamin took her by the elbow and led her up the back walk. "Where are we going?" She pulled her arm free. He looked at her, his eyes momentarily questioning what she would do. In the question was a flicker of recognition. "You broke my fingers the other night, did you know that?" she asked. She held out her hand to show him the swollen, bruised fingers twice their normal size. He didn't reply. "Who did you think I was?" But still he didn't answer. He turned up his coat collar and continued up the path. Under his arm he carried a bundle wrapped in brown paper. "Jamin!" she demanded. He opened the back door then stopped and waited for her. "Answer me or I'm not coming." She was standing near the door, and in the same moment she turned to leave, he grabbed her arm, forced her inside, then locked the door behind her.

"You're frightening me, Jamin. What's happened? Please talk to me." She looked quickly about. The only light was from the sunset diffused through the smudged windows where she'd wiped streaks of dirt two days before. The room was bare, no furniture, no pictures, no sign of activity. She glanced into the other empty rooms and wondered if anything had ever been made or stored here or if the building had always, only been a pretence.

"What do you want with me?" She pulled away. They were in a room now with no windows. It was cold, and the darkness was settling upon them, obscuring their faces so that try as she did to penetrate Jamin's expression, she could barely distinguish his features.

"You have taken too much," he said in a quiet voice. "I will not allow you to take more."

"Taken what?"

He stepped over and shut one of three doors opening into the room. He locked it with a key. He went over to the second door and locked it. Olivia tried to stay calm, but each door shut out light so that only a dim slash of grey remained. She bolted for the last door. Jamin stepped in front of her and slammed it.

"Jamin, please, don't close me in." She heard the key clatter to the floor. She sank to her knees and tried to retrieve it, but Jamin took hold of her. She sucked in air. "Why are you doing this?" There was no light in the room now. She couldn't see him even though he was beside her. She could only feel his hold on her wrist and his thick warm breath near her. She felt him bend and pick up the key and lock the door. He let go of her then.

She moved away, feeling her path with her hands. She held her breath lest the panic of breathing give away her position. She heard Jamin's breathing, slow and regular. Did he want to hurt her? Why?

"You think I can't see you?" he asked. "Crouched in the corner like an animal. Get up for god sakes!"

Olivia stood. She didn't know how he could see her when she couldn't even make out his outline.

She tried to find her voice. "Jamin, please, just open a door. I won't run," she said.

"I am always accommodating you, Olivia Turner, turning on lights for you. Remember when I arranged for the one powerline in our village to bring light to your hut so that you might work at night? How many had lights? But you had a light. I prefer now the dark."

336

"Jamin . . ."

"Was it not from the dark on the same day that you and I were born? Or have you forgotten?" She had not forgotten that they shared the same birthday. "Only you are frightened that I too came forth."

"I'm not frightened."

"You do well to be. I am frightened that you came forth."

"Jamin, just open a door."

There was a rustling on the other side of the room, then the sound of water from a faucet and a buzzing noise Olivia half recognized but couldn't place. "What are you doing?" she asked.

Jamin didn't answer. For several minutes he remained occupied. "Of course," he said finally, "we are in a factory, not a womb now, a factory which doesn't exist except to produce illusions which we believed. I believed most of all. I believed in a postmark: New York City. I wrote letters to that postmark, outlining our plans for the future, letters dropped through the slot of this empty address. I do not know how long this address has been empty. But for the past years my letters, along with the trash, have been picked up once a week.

"The letters were a source of much amusement I am sure. They were answered by third-rate clerks hired to monitor dreams and subdue dreamers with promises . . . and with markets. Markets for our veneer. MORE VENEER, they cried from New York City. Keep sending your exotic African veneer for us to cover our televisions and tables. Your future will be as broad and wide as the sheets of veneer you send. So we worked and stripped our trees and sent our veneer while they used our factory to monitor radio transmissions between our neighbors and to keep a finger on our area of Africa. We were given compensation of course for our veneer, and we thanked them for this allowance."

"So the factory is only a sham?" Olivia asked.

Jamin laughed. "You never change, do you? To your blackest end you will be asking questions, Olivia Turner. May this reporter who asked too many questions rest in peace."

Olivia grew silent. "What do you want from me, Jamin?"

He laughed again. "The truth? I want to fuck the soul out of you. The soul out of you and the dreams out of myself until there is nothing left but two carcasses in the middle of the floor without illusions or souls."

He moved to her. His body rose so close that she could almost see it because of the density of the space it occupied. She raised her hands, and she felt the chilled skin of his bare chest, naked before her. She gasped, not at the threat of his flesh, which she would have allowed without violence, but at this man she did not comprehend, for he was not touching her but laughing.

"Jamin, please . . . I don't understand."

"You never have."

"You don't have to take from me. Surely you know that," she said.

"So instead I allow you to take from me."

"What have I taken?"

"You would take my manhood if I would let you. But I will not allow you or any woman to do this." He drew off her jacket now, not roughly, but as he might undress a child.

"I won't fight you, Jamin. I am not your enemy."

He unbuttoned her blouse and pulled it off then asked her to give him her brassiere. In the darkness of the room she knew her own nakedness only by the cold air which pierced her skin for she could not see herself, and Jamin did not touch her. Instead he withdrew to the other side of the room. She stood for a moment trying to see. Finally she said, "Jamin . . . I'm cold."

He threw her his shirt and jacket. She heard him moving about, heard the rustling of paper and clothes, a final buzzing, and then he was still. He stood or sat in silence for a while. She felt calm suddenly, for she understood now that he would not hurt her. She didn't understand what he felt towards her or what he wanted from her, but their bond held.

Finally she heard a key in the door. "What are you doing?" she asked.

"You will stay here for twenty-four hours. I cannot take the chance that you will try to stop me. There is food on the floor and a blanket and a bathroom in the corner. You are right; you are not my enemy. I will send someone to let you out. You do not understand me, Olivia Turner, but I wish you no harm."

He unlocked the door and opened it. In the thin shading of light, she saw him towering in the elegant headdress of his tribeswomen and in her soft blue blouse and a long patterned skirt. He turned for a moment and smiled with irony. "You see, I have decided to approach Bulagwi from his weakness. He is vain and blind in his lust, and he will, I believe, allow me near him." Jamin's voice had subtly changed, still in his resonant tones, yet feminine. His face was shaved close now, and he held a long shawl around his shoulders. Yet the transformation was not complete.

"You don't look enough like a woman, Jamin. You'll be shot for impudence."

He smiled. "I have only changed my clothes, it is true; but before the night is over I will have changed my soul."

A clock ticked somewhere in the room. Olivia had not heard the sound before Jamin left, but now it was all she could hear. She could see nothing, not even a shading beneath the door offering the promise of light. Outside the night had come without mitigation.

She listened to the clock, taking odd comfort from the sound for it fixed her in time and space. The relief she'd felt over Jamin not wanting to hurt her suddenly seemed meager compensation for the prison he had left her to. She moved along the wall, feeling her way to the door. She tried the knob, but it was locked. She moved along the next wall to the second door then to the third. Each was firmly locked. As she went, she counted the corners of the room so she wouldn't lose track of where she had begun.

She stopped in the corner where she'd started. Listening, she moved now towards the clock. She wondered why Jamin had left her a clock. Why hadn't he left her a light too? At least then she could work. But he'd locked her in the dark, and she hadn't known how to fight him. This passiveness stagnating within her suddenly enraged her so that when her foot knocked against the clock and the store of food, she kicked them across the floor. "JAMIN!" she shouted. But only the ticking of the clock answered back.

Feeling along the floor with her foot, she found the clock. She pulled off its cover to feel the time with her fingers. She counted the spaces. It was 7:30. She rested her fingers on the face and tried to feel time moving. Jamin had said someone would let her out in twenty-four hours. She couldn't wait twenty-four hours. "Help!" she shouted. "Help!" But there was no one anywhere to hear her.

On the clock she felt a third metal rod: the alarm. Again she counted the spaces. The alarm was set for five and the alarm button was pulled out. Why did Jamin want to alert her at five in the morning? She could think of no reason and pushed the button in. She felt suddenly frightened for herself and more frightened than ever for Jamin. He was lost in his own world, diving dangerously into himself, trying to find the woman in him who might conspire to accomplish his will. The forces he was up against were far too subtle and complex, she thought, to be outwitted by his masquerade. And yet she understood his sidestepping better than he realized. She understood too his violence. In an odd way she even understood the wrath of Bulagwi—the self-consuming anger which struck out at all he feared and could not control. This ultimate powerlessness stirred one to rage. She understood this response better than Nyral's ideals, though it was Nyral's ideals that she aspired towards. She had pleaded with Jamin in the taxi to talk to Nyral and listen to his plan, and yet she too believed the gun had more power.

A door slammed somewhere in the building. Olivia had dozed off, but the sound jolted her awake. She reached for the clock and felt the dials: 10:30. Only 10:30. Or was it 10:30 in the morning? Had the clock stopped? She listened. She heard the ticking, and then she heard footsteps. She grew still. The footsteps were moving from room to room towards the center of the building. She couldn't imagine who was here. Had Jamin returned, or had some transient wandered in out of the cold? If it were a transient, at least she was safe; the room was locked with a key. Yet she didn't feel safe. She stood up, ready to meet whomever might come through the door.

Quietly she gathered her case. She listened. The footsteps were approaching the door on her left. She moved to the door and pressed herself against the wall. Whoever entered would come upon the room in the dark. Even if he carried a flashlight, there would be a few seconds in which she could slip out then bolt for her life into the streets of Brooklyn.

She heard a key slip into the lock. Her body tightened. She quickly checked to make sure she was ready: her case was shut and held to her chest; Jamin's jacket and her coat were buttoned around her. The knob turned. She prepared. But instead of the person entering the darkness or scanning it with a beam, a hand reached in and flipped on a light switch. All at once light filled the room. She gasped. She hadn't even considered a light switch, so convinced had she been by Jamin's terms of imprisonment. The light blinded her. She couldn't see who stood before her. She thought she might still disappear into the dark factory, but every room was illumined.

A voice spoke: "Jamin told me he had locked you here. I insisted he give me the key." Olivia squinted. Nyral stood before her in his patched jacket and cap with the ear flaps. "I've come to ask your help."

"What? My help?" What was Nyral doing here?

He stepped into the room. An ordinary, uninteresting room she saw now, with grey-green walls, a cracked linoleum floor, no furniture, a small bathroom off to the side where Jamin had left a wad of clothes on the floor. "Jamin came to me to see if I would recognize him," Nyral said. "I knew him instantly. He told me of his plan and said that he had seen you. I couldn't stop him, though I know, as you must, that he will not survive."

Olivia nodded. Her fingers suddenly ached. The chilled air made her start to shiver. She drew Jamin's jacket and her coat around her. "But what can I do?"

Nyral was silent for a moment; then he said, "Remember I told you Jamin would not be able to kill unless he lost himself behind a mask?"

Olivia nodded.

"Now we know the mask."

"You mean as a woman?"

"I should have thought of it myself. Many of our men are afraid of women for the powers of life they control. Bulagwi of all is afraid, though he lusts after women—tall, beautiful women—whom he hates and fears and would control. Lately stories have spread out of the palace over what he has done to his women.

So Jamin, you see, has taken on the mask of Bulagwi's fear so that he might control *him* and then kill him."

Olivia glanced about this cold lighted room, afraid suddenly that the light would alert others. "I don't understand what I can do."

"As a tall, beautiful woman you can reach Bulagwi."

"Beautiful?" The concept surprised her even then. She frowned. "I don't understand. And frankly I'm not willing to risk my life."

"I wouldn't ask you to."

She looked at him skeptically. He had said the same to the hundreds he'd sent armed only with food into a town filled with Bulagwi's soldiers.

"First, however, we must leave here. There are others who may come tonight. Jamin stole his key to this building. In the basement he has found weapons under a false floor. It is from here I believe they are shipped to our country and others. This is not a safe place." As he started from the room, Olivia reached up to turn out the light, but he stopped her. "Leave them on." He smiled then with mischief. "Let whoever comes wonder who has been here before them."

Chapter 38

Benjamin DeVries leaned forward over the Louis XIV desk and presented Mark with a small box lined in rose velvet; then leaning back into a green leather desk chair too large for him, he waited while Mark opened the lid.

Mark stared for a moment before looking up. "What is it?"

"A coin," DeVries answered.

"I see it's a coin," Mark said with slight impatience. He'd been trying to reach DeVries all day. When DeVries had finally phoned him this evening, he'd insisted Mark come right over as though he were irritated Mark wasn't there already. But when Mark arrived, DeVries greeted him leisurely, strolled in his lounging jacket and slippers back to his study, where he was now handing Mark this old coin.

"The coin of the realm," DeVries elaborated, stretching back over the desk and lifting out the heavy greenish blue coin and holding it up on its chain. "Do you know how old this is?" Before Mark could answer, DeVries answered his own question, "Almost twenty-two hundred years old. Older than Christ, Mark. Older than Julius Caesar himself. And it's still solid. Here, hold it." He extended the coin to Mark, who accepted the small weight in his palm.

"It's dated around 147-135 B.C., found near Tunis, or ancient Carthage, from the days when Rome destroyed Carthage and created a new province called . . ." he paused, ". . . Africa. The coin has lasted all these years. On its face is Minerva herself."

Mark set the coin on the edge of the desk. At the moment he didn't care about Carthage or Minerva or coins, and he suspected neither did DeVries. But he allowed DeVries this diversion while he decided on his own tack. During the past eight hours, he'd taken no phone calls, including two from Kay. Instead he'd been studying all the Afco files, personally checking the flow of funds statements, balance sheets, projections. He cross-examined his assistant about where and why an increase of almost two million dollars in noncash charges could slip by without notice.

He called the banks where DeVries had bought the sovereign debt of Bulagwi's country and asked that confirmation of these purchases be sent to him directly. DeVries had provided the confirmations which were currently in the Afco file. Over the phone he'd asked the lending officer if he recalled the purchase price. The man had hesitated, but finally said he thought it had been around 18 1/2 cents on the dollar but he couldn't be certain. Then he'd backtracked and said he really wasn't at liberty to discuss the matter over the phone.

Mark calculated the spread: if the debt had been purchased at 18 1/2 cents and sold at 20 cents, then DeVries had pocketed almost eleven million dollars. If this quarter's noncash charges betrayed a regular siphoning of similar funds each quarter, then he could add over ten million to that total. He didn't even know how to approach the allegations Olivia had made this morning or to calculate their worth. At the moment he had no proof of anything. He had enough just to consider the evidence of his own that Afco and the mines would soon be out of money unless cash and a route for the ore were found. His foremost concern right now was to protect his investors. He'd come ready tonight with a plan which he knew DeVries was not going to like.

But before he could set out his own agenda, DeVries declared, "You see, Mark, if you expect to have influence beyond the deal of the moment, if you are going to have an influence on the world at large, you have to make commitments which will ride through temporary political storms. Every great man has understood this. I am counting on you to come through."

DeVries took the coin from the edge of the desk and replaced it in its silver box. "We have the opportunity here to create both wealth and history if you make that commitment. We can reshape these countries." Mark stood; he felt suddenly uncomfortable. DeVries went on, "Surely you've seen the implications. If we are successful, we could shape a whole area of the world." He paused. "And make a lot of money."

"Benjamin," Mark stopped him. "If you want a coin with your face on it, go to Coney Island." DeVries laughed. "I'm serious. I persuaded a group of investors to put up their money on the basis of your figures and projections and, frankly, on the basis of my reputation as well as yours. They are expecting a return. They are not expecting to influence history or to be heralded by archeologists two thousand years hence. And they are not expecting to lose their shirts."

DeVries smiled now. "We seemed to have switched places, haven't we?"

"How's that?" Mark paced across the green and red Persian rug.

"I recall your telling your lady friend the other evening that our presence in Africa was expanding roads and schools, and what else?"

"Tell my what?" Mark asked.

DeVries rose from the desk and went to the bar in the corner where he poured himself a drink. "You want anything?" Mark shook his head. "Your lady . . . Katherine . . . was that her name? You were telling her how our presence would benefit the economy at large."

Mark stopped pacing between a shelf of Roman artifacts and a three-foot high statue of a Nubian woman. He stared at DeVries, smiling indulgently in his bedroom slippers and lounging jacket. Why was DeVries bringing up Kay? Was he probing for a weak spot? "Kay is a friend of Jenny's and mine; that is all," Mark said quietly.

DeVries raised his hands as if to say "as you please." Then moving to the desk, he handed Mark the box with the coin. "Then this is for your wife, as it should be. I had it set in gold to remind us all how we endured this trying time. I assume you and your wife have had an opportunity to discuss our partnership by now. My lawyer has assured me he could rush the partnership papers through, and we could be up and running in a few weeks at most."

From the desk Mark picked up what looked like a letter opener and began hitting it on his palm as he resumed pacing though it was hard to move in this room so filled with art and artifacts. He and Jenny had not talked; he resented the pressure DeVries was putting on him; yet he didn't want to tell DeVries they hadn't spoken.

"Mark," DeVries said in a patient, almost patronizing voice, "that dagger you're holding is over twelve hundred years old. I don't think it will withstand your vigor."

"Oh . . . sorry." Mark set the dagger back on the desk. "Benjamin . . ." he began to speak with his back still turned. "Why do we have a two million dollar increase in the noncash charges this quarter?"

He tried to ask the question off-handedly, but DeVries grew suddenly still. For a moment he didn't answer. Finally he said, "We had to replace some equipment at higher depreciation rates."

"Then why didn't it flow through the income statement as an additional expense? You never said anything to me."

"I'm not aware I must report every expenditure to you," DeVries countered.

"To neglect telling your banker of a substantial capital improvement..."

"What are you suggesting?"

Mark turned, his feet planted slightly apart. "I'm not suggesting anything. I'm stating a fact. Both Reynolds and I ran through all the papers and the figures. There's no mention of new purchases. Is your accounting department slipping up?"

DeVries moved towards the bookcase. "Well, I'll certainly check with them," he said. "You'll have to show me precisely what you mean." He began pulling out books.

"I've also asked the bank for the confirmations of the debt purchase. To be honest," Mark sat back in the chair, "I'm not prepared at this point to put my business into a partnership to buffer a loss in Afco. I don't believe in the long run it will help. And I'm not willing or able to raise any more money for Afco given the present circumstances. We are not in control. Neither are you. So I've spent the past two days working on a plan which I believe can get our investors out and leave the governments their assets for when the political situation stabilizes." Mark reached down to his briefcase and opened it. "Here's what I've come up with . . ."

But as he sat up, DeVries was rotating a panel of the bookshelves to reveal a small room behind the case. "I'd like you to see something, Mark," he said. "Very few people have seen this."

Mark stared, his hand on his new projections and plans. DeVries was stepping into a chamber approximately five feet square whose walls were padded with wine-colored velvet and lined with glass-enclosed shelves. On the shelves stood gold and bronze and iron figurines and implements. DeVries sat down at a small table in the middle of the room. "Come," he said.

Slowly Mark rose. Ducking under the low doorway, he stood at the edge of the room as if at any moment he might turn and leave.

"Sit down, Mark. Sit down. I want to show you something." He pulled out his ring of keys from his pocket. Without moving from the chair, he opened each of the cabinets in the room. Reaching up to the cabinet on his right, he took down a six-inch iron figure of a woman. "Have you ever heard of the Kingdom of Kush?" he asked. Mark shook his head. "Neither have most people walking the streets today. But Kush remains one of the great unsolved mysteries of the ancient world, a kingdom in its time—around a thousand B.C. until the fourth century A.D., a kingdom which rivaled Egypt, situated on the third and fourth cataracts of the Nile River, known for its sophisticated iron manufacturing and iron work. Just look at this . . ." He held the figurine up to the light, showing off the delicate lines and complex tool work on the body.

"The people of Kush very likely fashioned weapons and trained the elephants the Romans used in their conquests. But much of their culture is a mystery to this day, for no one has yet deciphered the language of Kush. An entire civilization and period in history. The record exists, but we can't read it. It may hold links between East and West Africa. This civilization may hold keys to other civilizations, but there is a knowledge gap of well over a thousand years because *we*, twentieth century man, cannot decipher *their* language. What do you think of that?" DeVries set the small woman or goddess back on the shelf and brought down several implements.

"I'm afraid I'm wondering why you're showing me these right now?"

"Ah!" DeVries reached to his left and took out a small tablet with markings upon it. "You see, Mark, if you haven't guessed, civilization is my hobby. Over the years I have become a scholar of sorts on various ancient civilizations. Now some may accuse me of being a dilettante. I would have to agree that a true scholar spends years in concentrated study and focus, so perhaps I should say I am a dilettante scholar. In studying the past, I have come to see that civilization moves forward because of the vision of a few great men and a strong aristocratic class with the power to implement that vision. We see this in Egypt, in Rome . . ."

347

He looked up from the tablet which he had been examining with a magnifying glass. "For the past few years, I have employed a team of scholars to study the language of Kush, and they are hopeful they will soon come to a breakthrough. We will then be able to understand how civilization was passed westward. But that is, as you have pointed out, not clearly relevant to this present moment. It is the present in Africa that is ripe for shaping. There are few areas in the world still so malleable, so undeveloped both in political and economic structures. There are few areas where one's impact can be so profound and where the resources exist to make an impact.

"You see, Mark, when you suggest that I would purloin two million dollars from Afco, it is . . . well, it is a bad joke as well as an insult in the face of what we are talking about here." DeVries replaced the tablet.

Mark leaned his head back, but hitting the glass case, he pitched forward. "I didn't say you *purloined* anything, Benjamin." He tried to stretch out his legs, but he couldn't move. "I'll admit that sum may be inconsequential to you," he began, "but there *is* a discrepancy."

DeVries' face flushed suddenly. "Do you have any idea the value of the objects here?" He swept his hand across the tomblike room. "In this room alone is art from antiquity which might draw six or seven million dollars if it were to be put up for sale. In this apartment, perhaps seventy-five million dollars worth. I'm employing scholars around the world to research great questions of civilization and history, and you are accusing me of filching a million dollars." His voice had risen until now he was shouting. "Even if I were, look at what use it is going towards." His face was a deep pink; he was breathing hard. Mark sat quietly watching him, trying to remember exactly what Olivia had told him.

"Benny . . ." a voice suddenly interrupted. Rosa DeVries stepped into the room in a red sweater and long denim skirt. "Some reporter's on the phone. You want to talk?"

"What . . . ?" DeVries' hand was in the air clutching his keys. He blinked as if trying to focus on where he was. "No . . . no. We're busy!"

Before she retreated, Rosa DeVries leaned over and kissed her husband on top of the head. DeVries' hand and the keys lowered to the table. He adjusted a figurine on a shelf; he began locking the cases around him one by one from where he sat. Finally he stood. His voice was calm now. "I'd appreciate it if you kept this collection between us," he said.

"Why?" Mark followed him to the door.

"It's personal to me. I'll make it known when the time is appropriate."

Mark didn't answer. He found himself wondering if the seven million dollars of Kush artifacts represented clues to an undeciphered civilization or loot from embezzled funds. He sat down in the chair by the desk. He felt suddenly disoriented, balanced on the edge of a precipice. His wife had left him; his family was gone; his business and reputation were about to fall over the edge. He didn't understand how he had arrived here. He was struggling to see how to step back. He picked up his briefcase from the floor. "Benjamin . . ." he said, "I'm going to call for an independent audit of Afco."

"A what?"

"A special audit of the accounts. I think we should jointly engage the auditors so there'll be no misinterpretations."

"No one has ever . . ." DeVries protested. "Who do you think you're talking to? You don't have the authority."

"I hope you'll understand," Mark said, trying to keep his own calm, trying to pull them both back from the edge he only hazily glimpsed before him. "To protect ourselves we need an independent accounting right now. It's to your benefit too if questions should be asked."

"Rosa! Rosa!" DeVries called. He looked about frantically. "Rosa!"

"Benny . . . I'm right here." Rosa got up from the couch in the corner as though emerging from the Renoir painting behind her, as though the sofa and the dark-haired, pale-faced woman were one with the art. Mark wondered if she had been sitting there the whole time.

"Show Mark out."

She smiled at Mark. Mark closed his briefcase. "I'll just leave this here for you to look at," Mark said, setting his plan on the desk. On the edge of the desk he left behind the Roman coin.

Chapter 39

In a brown bag by the door the king snake lay lifeless on top of the garbage. Mark had left it there to take out in the morning. When he'd come home from DeVries', he'd gone first to Erika's room. He'd stood in the doorway staring at the stuffed bears and rabbits and dogs waiting for Erika to return. He'd sat in the rocking chair and tried to draw close to his child in his thoughts. Jenny had had no right to take her from him. He was agitating the rocking chair back and forth when he saw the snake under the curtain, its black and red body twisted in a parenthesis. As he bent forward to retrieve it and return it to its home, he saw on its stiff body the slashes of the cat's claw.

Cassie lay sleeping on Erika's pillow. Mark wondered how the snake came to be out of its cage and Cassie shut up in the room. He picked up the lifeless body by the tail and carried it into the kitchen where he dropped it on the trash bag; then he set the bag in the hall so he wouldn't forget to take it to the incinerator. He never had understood why Jenny bought the snake; he would leave it to her to replace.

He returned to the kitchen where he opened the freezer and took out a frozen pizza and stuck it in the microwave for dinner.

He made himself a salad, poured a bottle of seltzer water into a glass, and ate dinner at the kitchen counter, watching a basketball game. After dinner he dumped the empty pizza box into the trash with the snake and remembered to wash the dishes.

Returning to the living room, he sat down at the piano. The apartment was quiet, so quiet he could hear the mumble of a television downstairs. He began playing a composition of his own from years before. He tried to remember what had led him to write this music, but it was from another place in his life. He could no longer remember its origins. As he played these jazz renditions, he realized he couldn't lose himself to the music anymore. He got up from the piano and went in to bed where he fell asleep with the light on, reviewing his plan for Afco.

During the cab ride home from the airport Jenny held Erika close, telling her a story in a quiet voice about Nugundi Heath, the street orphan in her children's books. "Out of pity a noliad showed him a magic tunnel lined with mirrors . . ." she intoned. But in her thoughts she was with Mark. She wondered if he'd seen Kay's story. She had looked for the *Tribune* at the airport, but the paper wasn't on the stands yet. As she held the warm body of her child beside her, she sought within herself the stillness she had felt earlier in the day.

She hesitated at the door of the apartment, then opened it firmly. A single lamp was turned down low in the living room. She glanced quickly about for some sign of Mark and saw his coat on the hook. Beside his coat hung Kay's white fox. Under the coats she saw the trash bag and the dead snake draped over a yogurt carton and a pizza box. She picked up Erika so she wouldn't see the snake and stepped into the living room. She stood for a moment taking in air. The piano was opened; nearby Kay's briefcase leaned against the stool.

"I'm tired," Erika complained.

Jenny drew her child's head to her shoulder. "I know. We're going straight to bed." She moved into the back hallway where she heard voices from the darkened bedroom. She took Erika quickly to her room and turned down her bed. "You run to the bathroom," she whispered, "then climb in bed, and I'll be in in a minute to kiss you goodnight." She shut the door as Erika hurried off.

Jenny knocked once loudly on the bedroom door then opened it. She shut the door behind her before she could even focus so that Erika might not come in. The light from the closet was on, and she saw Mark in bed in his blue pajamas. Sitting on the side of the bed, barefooted, with one stocking leg raised up under her chin sat Kay, fully dressed.

"Jenny!" Kay's voice leapt out of her. "My god, you scared us!"

Mark was sitting up, leaning against the pillows. He turned when Jenny entered, but he didn't speak. His face was stern.

"Now don't get the wrong impression," Kay began lightly. "Mark has been a saint; I hate to confess that, but it's true . . . well, almost a saint. I just came in to thank him for going to see David today."

Jenny watched her husband. His eyes were steady upon her, offering no apology and no explanation. She knew they would not be able to explain their way back to each other. She had been formulating, then discarding explanations all the way home. "I thought you were at Helene's," she said to Kay in an even voice. "It was so lonely there," Kay protested, "at least till David gets out tomorrow. I thought since you weren't here, I might stay one more night. I didn't know you were coming back so soon." Kay's tone was bright and casual, but there was a tremor in it, a pleading not to be found out or perhaps simply not to be made to sleep alone. "I won't take up much room. I'll just sleep on the couch." She started putting on her boots.

"No," Jenny said. Kay looked up as if she hadn't heard correctly. "You can go to a hotel if Helene's is too lonely."

"It's almost midnight, Jenny. I'll go first thing in the morning."

"Hotels are open at midnight," Jenny answered. "I'd like you to go now."

"Mark . . ." Kay turned to Mark then back to Jenny. "Are you throwing me out?" she asked.

Jenny didn't look at her husband though she could feel him watching her. "I'm asking you to leave." She picked up the phone and asked for the number of the New York Sheraton.

"You don't have to get dramatic, Jennifer. If I'd known you'd be running back from Olivia's so soon, I never would have imposed."

Mark glanced at Kay. "You didn't tell me you knew where she was."

"She called this morning. You weren't here. I see now who runs this family." She laughed lightly, but again Jenny heard the tremor and in it the insecurity of Kay.

"Have you shown Mark your story for tomorrow?" Jenny asked.

Kay's eyes darted up. Slowly she finished zipping her boot.

"What story?" Mark asked.

"I tried to phone you," Kay answered without looking at him, "but you never returned my calls." This last she added with a slight triumph. "What story?" Mark repeated.

"It seems there's a discrepancy in Afco's finances," Kay answered matter-of-factly. *"The Tribune's* been investigating the figures. It's been suggested that Afco funds may have been used to finance the recent political upheavals."

"Who suggested?" Mark asked.

"I can't say."

"What does your story say?"

Kay zipped her other boot. "You can read it in the morning," she declared. "I'm sure it's nothing you don't already know." She stood from the bed. "By the way, David's counting on that trip you promised him," she added without transition.

"What trip?"

"You said you were coming down to Washington and would come see him."

Jenny glanced at Mark; she turned to leave the room. She wouldn't fight Kay's hydra-headed assaults.

"Where are you going?" Mark demanded.

"To put Erika to bed."

Erika lay cater-cornered on her bed, her head nestled into Cassie's fur. The cat slept with her back curled against the child, a favorite sleeping position of both. Beside the bed Erika had turned on the clown night-light. She'd changed into a blue gown which she'd put on backwards, and she'd taken a book to bed. She had put herself to sleep in the same manner Jenny and Mark did every night, and this imitation touched Jenny. Mark had followed her into the room and now stood next to her. Jenny bent over and kissed her daughter then turned her around and tucked the covers about her. Cassie opened one eye and nuzzled back against the body.

Mark stared at his sleeping child. He wanted to be conciliatory to his wife, but suddenly the fear he had been suppressing all day roused. "Never take Erika away again," he declared.

"I wasn't taking her from you," Jenny answered.

"Oh?" Mark looked at her. The hurt he'd felt, rose up insisting now on compensation.

"You're missing the point, Mark," she said.

"What is the point?" He stood holding one post of the canopy bed. He felt so far from Jenny right now that the distance frightened him and held him to his anger.

Jenny sat on the edge of the bed. "The answers I'm looking for are independent of you," she said.

"What does that mean?" He tightened his grip on the bed post. He didn't know how to bridge the space between himself and his wife. Suddenly he felt desperate that she would leave him to it. He looked down at Erika; for a moment neither spoke. Finally when Jenny didn't answer, he glanced at the cage on the toy shelf and grasped at an object apart from them. "Cassie killed the snake," he declared.

"I saw."

"Did you leave the cage open?" he asked.

"No."

"How did he get to the snake?"

Jenny met Mark's gaze, her eyes steady. "Perhaps someone else opened the cage."

Mark grew silent, considering this possibility. "Who?"

"You tell me."

Mark didn't answer. He asked instead, "You think Erika will be upset?"

Jenny shrugged. She stroked Erika's cheek with the back of her hand. Mark watched her, then reached down and did the same. Erika stirred and rolled away from them both.

"What did you and Erika do at Olivia's?" he asked. His tone was more accusatory than he intended, but he seemed unable to find the tone and the ground on which to approach his wife.

"Mother took her so I could be alone."

"Dottie was there? I tried to call her." That his mother-in-law, whom he liked, might judge him harshly disturbed him.

"What did she say?"

"That I don't know you as well as I think."

Mark watched her. For the first time he noticed her hair—curled and frosted with long bangs swept to the side. She looked . . . what? Freer, he thought. Her blue-grey eyes met his. "You think that's true?"

"I didn't leave to hurt you, Mark." She touched his hand on the bedpost with one finger, lightly. He raised a finger to meet hers. Outside the door Kay stirred in the hallway.

Mark lifted his hand and stretched it over his head, grabbing the top of the canopy. "Reynolds told me today he wants to retire by summer," he said. "DeVries may in fact be siphoning funds off Afco. I'm calling for a special audit. Needless to say that ends the possibilities of a partnership. If DeVries has skimmed money, I may be in trouble too." He listed the problems; they were his defense. He began pacing beside the bed. His pajamas hung loosely from his burly shoulders; black hair curled in fists on his chest. "Goddamn it, Jenny, I wouldn't have left you."

Jenny watched him. She moved over to him. He turned and shook his head as though he didn't know how to make his own way back.

There was a knock at the door. "If I'm leaving tonight, at least help me catch a cab," Kay insisted.

Mark hesitated. Then he started for the door.

"Where are you going?" Jenny asked.

"To get Kay a cab."

"Mark . . . ?"

He looked at her. But she didn't know what to say. Her pain was still near the surface, and it silenced her. When she didn't speak, he opened the door. He went into the bedroom to dress. Kay remained in the hall glancing occasionally at Jenny, who was sitting now on Erika's bed as though the breath had been knocked out of her.

Jenny waited for Mark in the living room at the dining table. She stared out the window, watching the light on the sidewalk below. The night was cold and clear; the light looked brittle, shattered into a thousand shadows on the concrete. Mark had been gone almost half an hour. She had brought out her manuscript so

355

she wouldn't watch the clock. She felt panic again beginning to spread inside her. She focused on the light. If she concentrated hard enough, she thought she might check the panic. Whatever Mark was doing or not doing, whatever he felt about Kay was not the point, she repeated to herself. How she acted, that was the point. She stood and began to pace in front of the window. She wouldn't allow herself to look out for Mark now. She could not let her peace of mind balance on her husband, always outside herself.

In the blue velvet chair Cassie watched her with one eye opened. In front of the window the cockatoo clucked: "Whee . . . hey, sweetie . . . hey, sweetie, give him the business." She went over to the bird, picked up a cracker he'd dropped on the floor and considered stuffing it into his face; but instead she held it between the bars, and the bird chipped at its edges.

The key turned in the lock. She looked towards the door. She waited, her expression expectant, vulnerable when Olivia came in. At first Olivia didn't notice her in the dimly lit living room. She tiptoed to the closet where she dragged out her suitcase.

"Olivia. What are you doing?" Jenny asked.

Olivia dropped the suitcase as if she'd been caught stealing. "Jenny." She let out breath. "I didn't know you were here. I didn't want to wake anyone so I used the key." She stepped into the room. She'd hoped to sneak in, change clothes, take her belongings and leave. It was past midnight. She thought Mark would be asleep. Her only fear had been that Kay might still be here, but Mark had said Kay was leaving today. She stared at Jenny. She couldn't stop right now.

For her part Jenny felt suddenly trapped and at the same time relieved to see Olivia. She wanted to be alone with Mark, yet Olivia gave her a context, drew her out of herself and away from the inward pull of her emotions. "Are you staying?" she asked.

Olivia opened her suitcase and began digging through the small nest of clothes. Nyral was waiting for her at the Plaza; she was already late. She glanced up. She saw Jenny's eyes filled with emotions she didn't understand. "I can't. I only came to change. I've got to go back."

"Where?"

Olivia pulled out a long cotton dress with a black and red and yellow pattern in an African weave. She looked at Jenny and paused for a moment. After all the years they had known each other, surely she could trust Jenny. Yes, she could trust her, but in Jenny's face was another imperative, that same need she hadn't known how to address before and didn't have the time to consider now; and yet could not ignore. "Where have *you* been?" Olivia asked.

"I went to your apartment."

"My apartment? Why?"

Jenny sat on the hall step into the living room. "I'm not sure I can give you a rational answer."

"Mark was quite upset, you know."

"You were here?" For the first time it occurred to Jenny that Olivia might have been here last night with Mark and Kay.

"No, but I had breakfast with him this morning." Olivia pulled out a pair of low black heels from the suitcase. "Look, Jenny, I don't have any time right now, and I'm the last one to know how to give you advice about marriage, but the man loves you for whatever that's worth to you." She closed the suitcase. "Where is Mark anyway?"

"Helping Kay catch a cab."

Olivia frowned. "I didn't see him on the street."

"He should have been back a while ago." Olivia watched her. Jenny shrugged. "I can't keep fighting this battle," she said.

"So what are you going to do?"

"I'm alternating between trusting Mark and asking him where the hell he's been for the last half hour."

Olivia smiled appreciatively. Taking up her dress and shoes, she moved to the bathroom. Jenny followed. "So which will you do?"

Jenny stood by the door as Olivia changed. "I don't know. You want to stay and find out?"

Olivia laughed. "I pass."

"When I was at your apartment," Jenny said, "I read your first chapters. I hope you don't mind."

Olivia looked over, her eyebrows raised.

"You've done it," Jenny said. "Goddamn, the book is powerful." Her eyes suddenly misted. She reached over and hugged Olivia.

"I'm really proud of you." Then she stepped back into the doorway. "You're writing much more than politics and history, aren't you?"

"Sometimes I'm not sure what the hell I'm writing." Olivia pulled her long gown over her head. "You know, when I was in Boston," Jenny went on, "I also stopped at the *Record's* library. I spent three hours reading about DeVries and Bulagwi. Did you know they knew each other from the start?"

Olivia zipped her dress. "The start of what?"

"Before the country even got its independence, DeVries had *hired* Bulagwi as a 'consultant' at Generale de Metaux. He hired a number of politicians in various nations, not only in Africa, but wherever Generale de Metaux did business. There was a brief scandal about the diversion of funds, but the story seems to have been hushed up, at least I could only find a couple of small articles in the U.S. press. You could probably find more in the European papers. I would guess he helped get Bulagwi into power."

Olivia nodded. "DeVries among others. Bulagwi owes so many people that no one constituency can lay claim on him."

"I haven't found the funding link yet for the NLA though Kay has a story tomorrow suggesting Afco may have helped Bulagwi topple the NLA." Olivia turned towards Jenny. "Unattributed speculation," Jenny added. "No sources. I read the story on the wires."

"What does Mark say?"

"We haven't talked. I can't believe Mark knew anything about it, though that doesn't speak too well of him either."

"For what it's worth, Kay's got the story wrong," Olivia said.

"What do you mean?"

"I can't tell you more right now."

"I came across one other story that may have meaning to you. Just a minute . . ." Jenny went into the hallway where she dug through her briefcase and extracted a xerox of an article and a photograph. "This is the best copy I could get." She handed the photograph to Olivia. I don't know if you can recognize the man. The article didn't note any significance, but it seemed to me it might have some."

Olivia stared at a picture of Benjamin DeVries dated two months ago in Paris with a short African man dressed in a military uniform. The picture was simply illustrating a feature story on European business connections in Africa.

"That's the NLA's Minister of Transport," Olivia declared. "Remember I told you about him, the one with the amoeba necklaces. DeVries is playing both sides, Jenny. I know that firsthand. Now here's evidence. Can I have this?" Jenny nodded. "I'd like to give it to Nyral. He'll know how to use it. DeVries has been paying off Bulagwi for years, but Bulagwi is out of control. He's looted his country; he owes everyone. DeVries is in deeper than Mark knows, Jenny."

"In what way?"

Olivia set the article on the sink. She wanted to trust Jenny; she did trust her as well as anyone she knew. She also needed to lean on someone right now. "You have to keep this in the strictest confidence."

"What?"

"Jamin is alive. DeVries and a man named Anton Moreau, a CIA operative DeVries knew from his days in the Congo, have hired Jamin to assassinate Bulagwi."

"Olivia." Jenny stepped towards her.

"Nyral wants me to visit Bulagwi and warn him not to allow anyone into his room tonight. He's afraid Jamin will show up."

"Why would Bulagwi listen to you?"

"I don't know, but Nyral thinks he will. I'm headed over to meet Nyral now."

"Olivia . . ." Jenny started to caution.

But Olivia nodded. "I know. I'm appropriately scared."

Jenny was quiet for a moment. "You know," she said, "you're the one friend I've always aspired towards." Olivia turned towards her with a questioning look. "You have talent in the largest sense of the word."

Olivia laughed. "I don't know how much talent will be worth tonight."

"Don't underestimate yourself. Your talent's from the heart. Nyral sees that."

"I hope you're right." Olivia turned back to the mirror. "While you're wrestling with your own demons tonight, will you include a prayer for me and mine?"

Jenny nodded.

"Now," Olivia added, offering a quick, ironic smile. "I need to borrow a purse. Something appropriate . . ." She held out her arms in the full sleeves and full length gown.

Jenny went to her closet where she dug around on the top shelf and brought down a black evening bag with a gold clasp. When she returned, Olivia was combing her hair. She'd applied a deep rose blush and red lipstick, mascara and gold eye shadow. She turned and smiled uncertainly.

Jenny smiled. Oliva looked striking: a tall, gentle-faced woman dressed in the robes of a country she loved. Jenny handed her the evening purse into which Olivia tucked her remaining money.

"Someday we'll sit in your kitchen and sort out these past weeks," Olivia said. "But for now I've got to go."

"When will I see you again?"

Olivia stepped back into the hallway. "God only knows." She reached out and took Jenny's hand, her broad brown fingers unadorned fitted around Jenny's own thin white fingers. "This plan is Nyral's," she said. "*He* would probably tell you to trust yourself. Or more likely he'd say something like: the egret rides without fear on the hippo's back; and then he'd ask you to figure out why. Anyway I know you two would like each other." She embraced Jenny and then hurried back into the night.

Mark came through the door at a little after one. He'd been gone almost an hour. He felt suddenly wary of having stayed away so long. After he'd sent Kay off in a cab, he'd intended to go home, but he found himself walking instead.

Kay had been cold and sarcastic as he'd taken her to the corner. When he'd asked again what she'd written, she retorted, "Buy the paper, Mark." But then as they reached the corner, she'd suddenly taken his hand. "I *promised* David you'd come visit us. You have to come. I told him you'd stay with us a few days. Bring Jenny and Erika if you must. But I don't know how else I'll get him to go home with me."

"Kay!" Mark protested. "You lied to him. Don't you see that? I told him I couldn't come." Kay brushed her hair out of her face and quickly scanned Mark's. "I am not his father," Mark insisted. "You're leading him to believe I am."

Kay stared for a moment; then her eyes went flat and hard. In this look Mark saw her will which tried to create for herself what life denied her. For the first time he glimpsed the devastation of such a will. "Good-bye, Kay," he said as he shut the door of the cab.

He'd started down Broadway towards a late-night bookstore to buy the *Tribune*, only the bookstore didn't have the paper and suggested he try the newsstand on 72nd Street. He needed to go home, and yet almost against his will, he started walking towards 72nd. Part of him rebelled at the hold his wife had upon him. He needed time to think. He loved Jenny more than she understood. He depended upon her as the one person to know him. He sensed, though he did not articulate, that he had made her custodian of his ideals, and this power, unwittingly held by her, now oppressed him. That she could split off from him and leave him to himself startled and then angered him.

He walked the sixteen blocks to 72nd Street where he bought the *Tribune* and stood reading the story under a street lamp. Kay had two stories in the paper. The one on Afco was on an inside page at the bottom. It was a loose, speculative article, quoting unnamed sources. The story presented figures which had already been made public, but it used them out of context so that the article left the impression that the losses in Afco were due to misappropriation of funds for political purposes. The article was below Kay's standard, and Mark wondered if she had written it out of spite.

Rereading the story in the taxi home, he tried to appraise the damage it might do, but the damage was impossible to assess. Finally he glanced at Kay's front page article:

NLA Leader Clashes With Bulagwi At UN;
Jamin Nyo Reported Alive, In Disguise

The damage from this story he didn't even think to calculate.

When Mark came through the door, the light was on in the living room, but the rest of the apartment was dark and silent. Jenny's suitcase still sat in the hall, along with the garbage. He picked up the brown paper bag with the dead snake on top and walked to the incinerator. A note requested that the incinerator only be used during certain hours, but he carefully released the latch and opened it. The wind whistled up the tunnel. The flames reached through the wind to draw down the snake and coffee grounds and cereal boxes into its craw. Mark pitched the bag then shut the door. Returning to the apartment, he took off his coat dropped it on a hook, then went back to the bedroom.

Jenny was sitting up with a single light on, working. A clipboard was propped on her knees and papers were spread on the bed. She didn't speak when he came in; neither did he. As he began to undress, she finally asked, "Did you find a cab?"

He listened for the accusation in her voice. He nodded. He sat on the side of the bed untying his sneakers.

"I was worried." She listened to her own tone and was relieved to hear its calm, relieved to feel the poise inside herself. After Olivia had left, she'd felt this calm returning within her, recognized it as one does a familiar face coming slowly into the focus of memory. Because the egret can fly, she'd answered Olivia's question. The egret is not afraid to ride the hippo's back because it can fly. And Olivia knew she could fly, knew her independent, creative self, as she knew Olivia's. She'd gone into the bedroom and changed into her nightgown, spread the last chapter of her book over the bed and begun to work.

"I went for a walk," Mark said. He looked over at her. "I needed to think." He bent back down and untied his other sneaker. He was wearing the grey and blue sweat suit Jenny had given him for Christmas, his legs long and strong in the sweatpants, his jacket zipped halfway over a navy tee shirt.

Jenny closed her folder and set it on the night table. "Think about what?"

"Us." He looked back at her, watching her face which he'd assumed he knew so well. Had it changed? Years ago he'd been drawn to the openness of her face as to a resting place where there was no need for pretence or defense or guile, where he could be who he was. Only lately he'd been in a hurry and had only paused with her, not rested; and now he saw the strain in her face, the lines settling in, beginning to break up the openness. He feared suddenly that he could lose what he'd searched long to find.

As if sensing his thought, Jenny reached out and covered his hand on the bed with her own. They stared at their hands; then Mark raised them clasped to his lips and kissed hers.

"I've missed you, Jenny," he said finally. "I've needed to talk with you, as a friend as well as a wife, but . . ." He hesitated lest what he say back them into an argument. "I guess I haven't seen what you needed very well."

Jenny reached up to him. "I am your friend, Mark," she said.

He touched her newly curled, golden-brown hair and smiled.

"Were you also trying to be the other woman in my life?"

She smiled too. "I hope you have better taste."

He touched her cheek then kissed her. He put both hands on her face, held her firmly between his hands and kissed her again and again. He reached over to turn out the bedside light, but Jenny stopped his hand.

"I want to see you," she said. "I need to see you."

At 3:15 the phone rang. Jenny grabbed for it as out of a dream. Kay's voice on the other end merged with her dream.

"Give me Mark," Kay demanded.

"Kay?" Jenny asked.

"Give me Mark!" Her voice cracked in its demand.

Jenny handed the phone to her husband, who sat up on one elbow, his bare chest emerging from the blankets. "Hello . . . What? . . . Slow down." He glanced at Jenny. "Kay . . . I can't understand you." He listened. "My God. I'll be right over . . . or better I'll meet you at the hospital . . . Okay, I'll come get you. Wait in the lobby."

Jenny watched him as he spoke, his sleepy face and body which moments before had been merged with her own, warm under the blankets, at last at peace with one another, was suddenly alert, drawn away from her again and held by someone else's world.

"What is it?" she asked as he hung up the phone.

"David tried to kill himself. He got hold of a razor. They found him unconscious."

"Oh no."

Mark got up and began to dress. "Kay's hysterical." He hesitated. "I have to go."

Jenny offered no argument though inside she started to rebel. "Does anyone know why?" she asked rising from the bed and going to the dresser.

"Kay didn't say . . . I didn't ask. She was screaming that I'd abandoned him."

"What?" Jenny turned. "Mark . . ." she warned.

"She's not rational." Mark's face pleaded with his wife. Jenny pulled out a pair of white sweatpants from her drawer and put them on. "What are you doing?" he asked.

"I'm coming."

"You can't."

"Why not?"

"What about Erika? We can't take her out at this hour."

"I'll call Mrs. Rousseau."

"Jenny . . ." Mark put his hand on her shoulder, but for a moment she wasn't sure if it was to comfort her or to hold her at a distance. "It's not a good idea."

"Why not?"

"Kay's pretty upset. I think . . . frankly I don't think you'd be very comfortable. I won't stay longer than I have to."

"I'm not coming to be comfortable," Jenny answered.

Mark hesitated. "Kay blames you," he said finally.

"What?"

"She said you tried to kill her child, and if he died . . ." Mark stopped. "Look, she's irrational. I'm afraid you'll make things worse."

Jenny paused for a moment considering this point, then she drew out a sweatshirt from her drawer and pulled it over her head. "I'm coming," she answered. She spoke with such determination that Mark didn't try to argue further. She went to the phone and called the Rousseaus, apologizing for the hour but explaining that it was an emergency.

She considered calling Randall Walsh, but she thought of his wife, of the children she would wake, of the bewildered look on his florid face; she set down the phone. Later she would suggest to Mark that the hospital call the boy's father. For now she didn't want to be carving out territory. She simply wanted to be with her husband.

Five minutes later Madeline Rousseau padded up in carpet slippers and a terry cloth robe with curlers in her hair. "I hope it's nothing serious," she offered.

Jenny just nodded and told her she could sleep in their bed where Erika would come in the morning. "We'll be home as soon as possible."

Mark and Jenny didn't speak the whole cab ride to his parents' apartment. Mark was uneasy over the scene he anticipated between Kay and Jenny, and he felt sick at heart about David. There had been something so pitiful in the boy's face when he'd told him he couldn't come stay with them in Washington. David had taken the news with resignation, one more disappointment in a life full of broken promises from his mother and non-existent father. He was still too young to understand his life in a context much beyond the one given him; yet already he knew he should have been able to expect more. His face had a wariness and a resignation far beyond his eleven years, Mark thought. He wished he could speak to Jenny about him, but he found himself wondering if she had come tonight out of the large-mindedness he counted on her to have or out of a need to possess him.

As Jenny stared at the empty streets, she couldn't have answered that question; she wasn't entirely sure herself. She had simply known she had to come. What her presence would mean or how it might change what was to happen, she couldn't anticipate. She too felt uncomfortable at the prospect of facing Kay and even more uneasy at facing her own responsibility, no matter how accidental, in what had occurred both to Kay and her son. She didn't know if she could find within herself the generosity to reach out to Kay. As she stared at the street lights, she felt this constriction in herself, threatening her, this quiet hostility which she'd accounted as her only defense, her sole means of keeping Kay at a distance from her family. She also knew what a poor defense she was offering them all.

The cab pulled up to the curb on Fifth Avenue. Kay ran out. Unlike the night Mark had brought her wild and ragged to the apartment after the accident, she looked meticulously arranged as if she'd stood before a mirror and hair by hair, eyelash by eyelash achieved order. Yet as Kay ducked into the taxi, Jenny saw in her eyes the same frenzied look she remembered from that night.

When Kay saw Jenny, she let out a little cry as if someone had slapped her; then recovering, she sat back, wedged between Jenny and Mark. She looked over at Jenny and stared without dissembling then turned to Mark. "I can't believe you brought her."

"Kay," Mark protested.

She laughed in an unnatural pitch. "This is too much. Really. My God!"

Jenny sought words to assert herself, for Kay was speaking as though she weren't there; but then Kay turned to her. "If David dies, if I lose him, I won't forgive you, Jennifer. I want you to know that. I can't believe you had the temerity to come. Why did you come?"

Jenny felt herself wavering, wondering if she should have come, but she met Kay's glare. Kay's eyes were all frantic motion, insistent need. Jenny saw how vulnerable she was. She saw too that Kay didn't really see her, and so she couldn't threaten her. "I came to help," Jenny said.

Kay laughed, dismissing the possibility. She turned back to Mark. "I want you to see David with me." Her voice was high-pitched and strained. "But I will not allow Jennifer into his room."

Jenny leaned her head back onto the seat. Hadn't she said the same thing only a few days ago when Mark suggested Kay sleep with Erika. These small concentric circles of the heart suddenly stifled her. She longed to plunge outside herself, to shed the skins of other people she had been wrapping so carefully around her. My God, let Mark go, she cried to herself, let him care for Kay and her son if he must, but let him go, let herself go.

"Kay," Mark answered sternly, "Jenny had nothing to do with David trying to kill himself, and you know it. For God's sakes face the problem . . ." But he stopped short of stating the problem, reluctant to strike at the heart.

"Me?" Kay asked in a voice so remote that it wasn't clear whether she were asking if she were the problem or the one being addressed.

"Jenny came to help. I want her with me."

The cab pulled up to the hospital; Mark paid the driver as

they got out. The three of them entered the reception room where they were told to wait. They sat on hard white plastic chairs. This time Mark sat between them. Kay leaned her head against the wall turning away from Jenny and Mark. In the harsh florescent light she looked brittle as if she might snap at any moment. Her slender arms and legs were pale; blue veins showed through in the cold. Her make-up offered only a transparent cover to her face, and two or three small pimples showed on her chin. The light in her large eyes had flattened, and her face was tight with the effort at control.

A doctor came in. "Mr. and Mrs. Walsh?" she asked. Kay rose. Mark rose with her. Jenny remained in the chair.

"We caught him in time, I believe. I don't know how it could have happened though, of course, we took no special precautions. We were given no reason to . . . I mean for a child so young. Did you have any indications?"

Kay stared at the doctor as though she weren't sure what the woman was asking. "No," Mark answered for Kay.

"Well, Mr. Walsh . . ."

"Mr. Rosen," Mark corrected, "I'm a friend of the family's."

"I see. Well, Mr. Rosen, he's sleeping now. I'd like someone to be there when he wakes up, but I'm afraid I can't let all of you in . . ."

Jenny rose. "Mark, you go with Kay. I'm all right."

Kay glanced at Jenny without expression. Mark nodded, and taking Kay's arm, he supported her down the beige corridor towards the child's room.

Jenny returned to her chair. She sat for a moment staring at the wall. She picked up a magazine then set it down. She opened her purse for a book but had forgotten to bring one. She stared at the clock above the reception desk. It was 3:45. No one else was in the room. At the desk a nurse appeared every fifteen minutes. When he entered the second time, Jenny went up and asked him if there were any news of David Walsh. He said he'd find out and let her know. She asked if she might borrow some paper; then she went back to her chair. She stared again at the clock and listened to the quiet of the room. She listened to the quiet in herself. The stirring and agitation of the last weeks had stilled. As she'd watched Mark move down the hallway with Kay, she had felt a momentary panic that she was letting her husband go, for she saw that he was not able to turn from the need of this woman and her child right now. Yet for the first time she felt herself rising through her own pain to another place, independent of Mark or Kay or anyone. If she was not yet able to extend herself to Kay, her heart opened to Kay's child, to the child in them all. As she waited for Mark's return, she began to sketch a cover for her new book; she began to sketch birds.

Chapter 40

The flame from the gas jet glowed yellow and red in the fireplace of the White and Gold suite where Nyral and Olivia sat talking quietly in the corner. At the other end of the room two men in custodial uniforms—expatriates of Nyral's—were vacuuming the rug and cleaning up after the reception which had been held there earlier in the evening. Another man, also in a grey uniform, kept watch at the door. Nyral himself was dressed as a custodian. He had arranged to meet Olivia here because he said it was an unlikely place for Bulagwi's men to look yet a logical place for Olivia to be should anyone observe her. Olivia had given Nyral the news photograph of DeVries and the NLA Transport Minister.

Nyral simply nodded. "I know. I allowed our expenses for the United Nations visit be paid by this man, Benjamin DeVries. I was against complicity with the patrons of Bulagwi, but finally I was persuaded that our cause was more important than my objections. I allowed myself to believe that this man asked nothing in return, that he sought alliance with us because he was convinced that Bulagwi had grown too corrupt to govern. I did not count that it was Jamin's soul which would be demanded in exchange."

Nyral put out his hand. "Could I have the photograph?" he asked. "It will be of interest to Bulagwi's men who think Benjamin DeVries is their patron."

Olivia handed the clipping to him. She'd made a note of the date and newspaper. Nyral sat forward on the edge of the white Louis XIV chair, his hands clasped in front of him now. "I'd like to tell you another story which may interest you," he said.

Olivia nodded.

"More than ten years ago, before I left the government, before our country divided, when Bulagwi was a man of too much ambition and too much will but not yet an evil man, he took a young girl for a mistress. He had a wife and two daughters at the time. He employed the girl as his secretary. She was very pretty and very bright, especially for a village girl. He put her in charge of his appointments and his personal business; then after a few months he took her to his bed. I don't know how she felt to be his mistress. I have never asked her. She was young, from my part of the country. The city and Bulagwi must have been a glamorous, new world for her. It was a time when we believed all things were possible. Bulagwi kept her as his secretary and moved her into rooms at the palace. I do not know how his wife felt about this girl, but then our women are not allowed to say much about such matters.

"The time arrived when this girl got pregnant and bore Bulagwi a son. From an early age this son was a most unusual boy. He too was bright like his mother and curious and handsome; and he was a kind child. His father by then was growing in greed and power; he had little time for this son. He had taken himself two more mistresses, and soon he converted to Islam so that he might make his mistresses his wives. He wanted to marry this girl, but she refused.

"I had come to know her by then, rather like a father. I felt sorry for her. This was also the time Untoro was making his plan which would have exposed Bulagwi, the time when Untoro was killed. As the terror began, this girl knew I would have to flee. She came to me and asked if she and her son could come with me, for she feared rightly that she would be killed if she continued to refuse Bulagwi. I agreed to help her escape. She and her son came with us into the hills. There she started our first school."

Olivia's mouth opened in surprise. "You have guessed by now?" Nyral asked. "Yes, I am speaking of Mushambe and Albert."

"I had no idea."

"Few people know. Their lives would be in danger both from our people and from Bulagwi. Albert is Bulagwi's first son. I am not certain if Jamin even knows. I do not know what he would say should he discover, for in Mushambe, he found a woman who understands his heart and in Albert, a child who has touched his soul."

"Mushambe and Jamin?" Olivia asked. "Mushambe never told me."

"She has learned to be cautious. She knew you too cared for Jamin. She knew that you could talk with him as she could not, for you are educated as she is not and have seen the world." Olivia fell silent for a moment as she took in this information and tried to understand what it meant to her. Suddenly she laughed.

"What is it?" Nyral asked.

"It's just . . . Of course. Of course. Why didn't I see? Jamin and Mushambe." Nyral nodded for he understood what she meant. "But what's happened to Mushambe and Albert?"

Nyral shook his head. "I have heard that the whole village was destroyed. They too may be dead, but Mushambe is a woman of resource. I cannot believe that she stayed to be destroyed. Jamin, however, feels this loss above all, I think, though he will not see what he feels, and instead he is driven by feelings he does not govern."

"Does Bulagwi know he may have killed his own son?"

"That is what I am moving towards." Nyral leaned forward in the chair. "For many years I have believed that Bulagwi left us alone because he knew his son lived among us. More than once he has sent spies into our hills to find his son. However, I always found out about the spies first for they were neither smart nor loyal; they could be bribed. Bulagwi did not try too hard to find Albert or I think he would have. He has other sons now and other children and many wives.

"I thought perhaps in time he would forget about the boy, though in my heart I knew he would not. The best I hoped was that Albert might live among us and grow in knowledge until the day he would return to his father. I have always seen Albert as the one who could unite our people. But you see now I have been told by our spies that Bulagwi had a dream three weeks ago that his first son rose up against him. In the dream the boy appeared as a python which coiled itself around his body then ate his father whole until from the snake's mouth the boy appeared and took his father's staff. It was this dream, at least in part, which sent Bulagwi into his rage through our hills. When our men were captured outside the capitol, he took this as a sign that his dream was coming upon him. He came into the hills, I believe, to kill his own son."

Olivia sat back in the chair. Her eyes fixed on Nyral, who was staring into the fire as he talked. She had sorted out all the political possibilities, the alliances of power that might have precipitated the attack, but she had not allowed sufficiently for the personality of Bulagwi. She wondered whether Nyral was right, whether the historical and political forces poised were finally set in motion by this most personal fear.

"Our informer has told us that since Bulagwi has come here, he has had another dream. He has slept poorly and was up most of last night. He called his wives to him to soothe him, to make love to him and put him to sleep, but at last when he did fall asleep, he dreamed that a woman came to him and slipped into his bed. As he was opening his arms to her, she drew forth a viper, and it struck him. He awakened with a scream which brought our spy, his aide, to him. Bulagwi told of this dream. He then rose and called his other guards and ordered them to bring his wives that he might strike them down and punish them. He was persuaded, however, that should such an act be found out here in America before the United Nations meeting, it would ruin him, so instead he has sent his wives back. They will be imprisoned until he returns."

"Oh God . . ." Olivia muttered. She had also not counted on the dark tunnel of this man's will.

Nyral went on in a flat, matter-of-fact voice. "Bulagwi is near a breakdown, I believe. At the meeting today at the United Nations, I stood up in the audience as I told you I would. I said nothing. I merely stood while Bulagwi was speaking until his eyes slowly rose and met mine. When he recognized me, he started shouting. I said nothing. He called for the guards to take me away. At first no one understood what was happening. Bulagwi kept shouting, "Son of a dog! Bastard! Bastard! Son of a dog!" Finally Bulagwi's aides came to the podium; they persuaded Bulagwi to sit down. They apologized, explaining that Bulagwi had been ill and was suffering from exhaustion after the trip.

"During the reception this evening, I am told that Bulagwi kept losing himself in thought. He would be in the middle of a sentence then drift somewhere else. When he returned to finish the sentence, he would not recall what he was saying and grew angry at his listeners. His aides cancelled most of his appointments and cut his appearance at the reception short tonight, insisting that he must rest for his meetings tomorrow. Before the reception, Bulagwi asked his closest aide, our informer, to find him a sorceress who would meet with him tonight in his room."

"Why does he want a sorceress?"

"To tell him the future so that he can act to change it if he wishes. The future is what frightens him for he has no control over it. Jamin, as well as myself, was told of this request; and Jamin, I am certain, is planning to go to Bulagwi's room tonight as that sorceress. After the fortelling, it is Bulagwi's practice to commune with the sorceress as a way of sealing his powers over his fate."

"Commune?" Olivia asked.

"Take her to his bed," Nyral clarified.

Olivia rubbed the bridge of her nose and shut her eyes trying to comprehend what she was hearing.

"Yes," Nyral agreed. "It is a dark world into which Amundo has sunk. You remember that his mother was a sorceress."

"Is he committing incest in his own thoughts?"

"I wouldn't attempt to suggest what is in his thoughts. I know only the facts I am given."

"But he'll recognize Jamin." Olivia leaned forward in her chair. She pulled from her evening bag a small pad and a pen.

"It is possible he may not. The room will be dark. It is possible he will see only what he wants to see. He has sent for the sorceress at five o'clock. I want you to arrive at the room at 4:30 as that sorceress. I have arranged with Bulagwi's aide to take you in."

"What?" Olivia's voice sprang out. The guard at the door looked over at her. "You said you wanted me to *interview* him, to tell him I'd heard rumors and that he shouldn't admit anyone to see him."

"Yes," Nyral answered thoughtfully. His small, intent eyes met Olivia's. "That is the best I could think of at the time. I didn't know the depths to which he had descended. I doubt he would listen to such rational advice right now. You must instead find him where he is. At the moment he is living in his deepest fears. It is a dangerous place for him and for the world. And yet . . ." Nyral hesitated. He touched his forehead lightly with his fingers as if literally drawing forth an idea. ". . . because they are so dark, they may be all the easier to illumine."

"I don't understand."

Nyral watched Olivia taking notes. He reached out his hand and gently set it on hers to stop her. "My plan is simple," he answered. "You go to his room and enter in silence. Indicate to him that you do not want him to speak. Ask that he lie down and shut his eyes and think of nothing but his mother holding him as a child. Do not allow him to touch you and speak as little as possible. Hum perhaps some soothing song, even a lullaby. He is exhausted. I think he will sleep. If you need to prove yourself a seer, use the information I have given you of his own child and his dreams. Your only task is to have him sleep. When you are sure he is asleep, leave the room and tell the guard he is to admit no one, that this is Bulagwi's order. I will take precautions to keep Jamin from getting to the room."

"Why would he possibly let me do that?" Olivia exclaimed. "First of all he'll recognize me."

"I don't think so. He isn't expecting you. Tell him you must work in the dark and in silence. He is looking for what he wants to see: a person who can deliver him from his own will which is dangerously near collapse."

"I don't know . . ." Olivia protested. "What if you're wrong? What if he wants to commune with me?"

"You must only do what you think you can, Olivia. I can't argue with you. It is the best plan I have come to. If I could go, I would. I fear if Jamin gets to the room, they will kill each other. Or if he kills Bulagwi, he will lose himself at the very moment his country and I need him most."

Olivia looked up at the ceiling then out the window. "Do I look like a sorceress?"

Nyral smiled. "You look like a woman whose gentleness could put a crazed man to sleep."

Olivia leaned her head against the back of the chair and shut her eyes. "You want my opinion?" she asked. Without waiting for an answer, she went on, "You are the one to lead your country, Robert." She opened her eyes. "You are crazy enough."

He smiled. "But I am growing old."

Outside a clock sounded a single chime on the half hour; it was 3:30. Olivia glanced at the other men in the room and saw that they were sitting now on chairs waiting for Nyral to finish his conference. Once again Olivia felt time receding in the company of Nyral. They were at a point of crisis, yet Nyral was ruminating as though the hour did not press upon him; she too felt its weight momentarily lift. "Am I wrong," she asked, "or do you feel some sympathy for Bulagwi?"

Nyral stared into the fire. "I wouldn't call it sympathy, but I do feel some link to him. We've been adversaries for so long, I know part of myself through him. And of course I know where he came from and where he wanted to go. Had he stayed a sergeant or even a general in someone else's army, he may have lived with only the vices of the average man. But he thrust himself into a place in history for which he was ill-equipped." Nyral looked over at her. His thin grey moustache was rimmed with small beads of sweat although the fire before them gave off little heat, and the room was cold. "You know, sometimes good and evil appear to exist side by side, so close that you can't see how to separate them or distinguish them. The one says it is the other, justifies itself in the name of the other. But I have come to believe, Olivia, that good and evil are not two faces of a whole. And they are not personal. I believe evil is denied its power when confronted by good.

"Jamin of course argues correctly that history does not support me, but I do not look to history for this conviction. In any case, it is how I must conduct my life. When I speak of Bulagwi, I see a man in whom evil has grown such tendrils that it will, by its own nature, choke itself."

Olivia leaned towards Nyral. "I can't do it," she said. "I don't have your courage or faith. Bulagwi will see in a moment I'm a fraud."

Nyral took her hand, the one with the bruised fingers. "I think you have both," he said. "And you are not a fraud."

Her pad slipped from her lap to the floor. As she started to reach down to pick it up, Nyral let go of her hand. She hesitated, then left the pad on the floor. "I wish I could see what you see," she said. "I wish I had even a small part of your faith. I don't even know what you have faith in, but I wish I had it."

Nyral was silent for a moment as if listening for an answer. "You must do what your heart tells you," he said.

"I don't want to see Bulagwi kill Jamin or the other way around, but I don't see how I can convince Bulagwi."

"You don't have to convince him of anything," Nyral answered.

Olivia laughed. "You just want me to sing him to sleep? If I had my guitar . . ."

"Yes, I remember your guitar."

Olivia gazed into the simulated coals which glowed red and orange. She thought of all the times she had stepped aside when challenged by power that seemed larger than herself, of how her own history had set her on the outside of power, how she'd felt for the past years that others had control of her fate. She looked back at Nyral. "But I have to do it, don't I?"

"No, you don't."

Olivia picked up the red spiral pad from the floor and stuffed it in Jenny's purse. "Yes," she said, "I do." She stood up.

Nyral stood with her. At the end of the room the other men rose. They checked the hallway, then joining Nyral, they escorted Olivia to the elevator.

In a black silk robe on the couch of the presidential suite Bulagwi lay listening to music. The room was dark except for the glow of street lights at the edge of the curtains. On the coffee table beside the couch incense burned. Next to the incense a Sony walkman sat upright with the earphones stretched over and wrapped about Bulagwi's head. The mellow voice of Diana Ross filled his ears.

There was a knock on the door, but he didn't respond. His eyes were shut. The knock grew louder. Still he didn't answer. Finally an aide stepped in and crossed over to him. He nodded. The aide opened the door for three armed guards dressed in khaki pants, brass-buttoned shirts and black berets. Between the guards stood Olivia.

Bulagwi turned his head slightly. He made a low, guttural "eh-h-h," and waved his hand. The guards retreated. Olivia glanced at them as they left, wondering which might be her ally should she need one, but their expressions were masks behind which she saw only suspicion. As the last aide stepped out backwards, he met her eyes and nodded. This recognition gave her courage. She glanced quickly around at the elaborate furnishings.

Sitting up on one elbow, Bulagwi gestured for her to come nearer. He still wore earphones over his thick hair. His slightly bucked teeth showed as he smiled at her approach. On the table she noted his gold-rimmed glasses and took comfort that he wasn't wearing them. She also saw a stack of newspapers with the *Tribune* on top, and catching sight of the headline: *Jamin Nyo Alive, in Disguise,* she almost gasped.

But Bulagwi was speaking, "I didn't ask for no brown-skinned woman," he said. "Who sent you to me, brown-skinned woman? Brown woman got white father, tell white fortune I think." His manner was teasing and flirtatious, yet menacing.

Olivia remembered Nyral's advice to speak as little as possible so she merely bowed to him. "What numbah fortune tellah are you?"

"Number?" she asked, and hearing her own voice, educated and American, she understood why Nyral told her to remain silent. Bulagwi didn't seem to notice. "I think you are numbah 13 for bad luck." He reached out and grasped her hand. "Humm? Numbah 13. That your numbah?" He raised himself to a sitting position and took off his headphones. He peered intently into her face so that she felt sure he would recognize her. "You are pretty fortune tellah I see. Who sent me pretty brown fortune tellah numbah 13?" When she didn't answer, he began to grow agitated. "I don't let *white* man's daughter tell my fortune." He spat out the word "white"; his eyes glittered. A narrow smile curled at his lips. "I don't trust white man's daughter. White man's daughters whores, eh? Hmmm . . . you a whore, brown-skinned woman? Make a man dirty, eh? My enemies send you to make me dirty, brown-skinned woman fortune tellah numbah 13?"

He rose from the couch. He stood before Olivia several inches shorter than she, his legs astride, his robe half-opened showing silk tiger pajamas underneath. When he saw Olivia looking at him, he said, "Eh, you like me? You want to have me? You have heard of me, I think. I make you rich, give you strong black babies you think. I am very rich man, very, very good with women, you have heard? You must tell me my fortune; then we shall see what comes. You tell me good fortune, maybe I let you have me, eh?"

He laughed a mocking laugh she had heard before. The careless violence within this man frightened her. She couldn't help but feel he was playing with her, feigning simplicity so that he might trap her. He was brutal, yet also cunning. Like Jamin, he would play the role an audience expected as a way of controlling them, for then he possessed the power of surprise.

He took her hand and drew her onto the couch. She realized she would have to act quickly or lose what little initiative she might have in this room. Bulagwi felt her resistance and peered into her face. "You are afraid of me? How you tell my fortune, you be afraid? You not tell me true fortune I think. You sent here to trick me I think."

He reached up, and with the palm of his hand, he suddenly rubbed Olivia's cheek so hard that she let out a cry. "Eh . . . I make sure you not white woman underneath, not my enemy dressed up to fool Bulagwi." He nodded to the newspapers on the table. "They say my enemies will come dressed in disguise. You know my enemies?" He took his glasses from the table and put them on. He stared at her. "Do I know you, brown-skinned woman?"

"No," Olivia answered quickly, standing.

"No? Eh, you lie. I do not like a woman who lie to me." His voice was harsh now. "Woman corrupt a man, lie to him all the time. Lie and lie and lie. I *eat* woman lie to me." He laughed then at his own fierceness. "You lying, spying fortune tellah, I must eat you up!" He spread his hands and laughed.

Olivia stepped back. She wondered what she had been thinking to come here. She couldn't have sung a song right now if her
life depended upon it, which she assessed it might.

"Now what I do with you, eh? You tell me what my enemies
plan, maybe I let you go. Maybe not." His face had a feverish expression. He stood before Olivia, within inches of her, his legs
pressed against her so that she could feel his tight muscles and
smell his sour perfumed body. "Ah!" he exclaimed. "You must
think Bulagwi is a stupid man. Mistake of my enemies if you
think Bulagwi a stupid man. I see you. I know you . . ."

All at once Olivia began to hum. As if following instructions
from within, she started softly; then in a low quiet voice she began to chant a children's refrain: *"La din-din-din. La din-din-din.*
La la din-din." She wished dearly for her guitar to hold to steady
her and accompany her. *"La din-din-din. La din-din-din. La la*
din-din."

Bulagwi grew silent. He stared at her with suspicion, yet also
with curiosity.

I have come to tell you what I saw.
I have gone and seen for you,
And this is what I saw.

She gestured for him to lie upon the couch as she began to sway.
To her surprise, he did.

A mother had a child
A beautiful, smart boy child
A beautiful, smart boy child.
The mother loved her child.
La din-din-din.
La din-din-din.
La la din-din.

But the child he lost his way,
One day he lost his way
In the bush he lost his way
And the mother lost her son.
La din-din-din.
La din-din-din.
La la din-din.

Olivia made up the words, miming the simplest rhythms of songs she had heard in the hills, songs and stories invented by Mushambe and others around a fire at night or as dinner cooked on the hearth. Bulagwi sat back on the couch, but his eyes remained alert regarding Olivia, who quickened the chant, improvising from somewhere within herself and her knowledge of the man and his land. She took themes Nyral had given her and sang to this potentate she feared as she had to the children at Mushambe's school.

The mother went to find her son.
Into the bush I come.
Into the bush I come.
I will come for you, my son.
La din-din-din.
La din-din-din.
La la din-din.

But you must sleep, my son.
Don't speak, my son.
Go to sleep, my son.
Or the Leopard will find your way.
La din-din-din.
La din-din-din.
La la din-din.

The son he goes to sleep.
The Leopard searches the bush.
The Leopard searches the bush.
But he cannot find the way.
La din-din-din.
La din-din-din.
La la din-din.

So Mother finds her son.
You see, my sleeping son.
You see, my sleeping son.
Mother always finds her son.
La din-din-din.
La din-din-din.
La la din-din.

Olivia swayed before Bulagwi humming the refrain as she sought more verses. His eyes had closed. *"La din-din-din. La din-din-din. La la din-din."* She kept humming, not daring to stop for fear he would awaken. She was in awe that the song was working. She didn't know where it had come from. She couldn't possibly have repeated it or planned it, and she could not, had she the objectivity to see herself, have believed her own courage or her naturalness swaying in African dress in the gilt-edged room of the Plaza. Yet Nyral had known what she must do, and trusting him and then herself, she had begun to sing. Nyral, however, had not told her how to stop.

"La din-din-din. La din-din-din. Hummm-hummm-hummm." She moved slowly towards the door as from the bed of a child, fading out the music, waiting to see if the child would awaken when the music stopped. Bulagwi did not stir. His face was turned upward, his mouth parted; his breathing was heavy and regular. He had been exhausted, as Nyral had said, and now he was asleep. She had been in the room she thought about half an hour and was about to turn the knob to leave when a clatter arose in the bedroom of the suite, and a light flashed on.

Bulagwi's body twitched. Olivia looked towards the opened door where suddenly she saw towering with a mane of straightened black hair and thick red lips, the absurdly voluptuous figure of Jamin. "Sweetness, sweetness," he crooned in a low mellow voice from the American South. "Sweetness of the humming bird, sweetness of the nightingale. Sing an evil man to sleep."

He swayed into the room dressed as he had been earlier in a long skirt and her, or rather Peg's, sheer blue blouse. The top three buttons flapped open. Jamin had rounded out his form so that the effect was both lewd and enticing. Olivia stared at him as if at the incarnation of lust and desire. "I shall take that evil man from sleep," he said. On the mantle above the fireplace a gold Louis XIV clock chimed five times.

"No!" Olivia whispered. "Jamin!" She uttered his name as if this recognition of who he was might bring him back. Yet even as she spoke, she couldn't take her eyes off this form who seemed neither man nor woman, African nor American, but some Nemesis dressed up like a whore.

Bulagwi roused at the voices and opened his eyes. Seeing the wanton body of Jamin coming towards him, lips wet and opened, he licked his own lips. As if from sleep, he reached out to embrace this woman-man. Jamin leaned down towards him, but at the point of embrace he pulled a pistol from his bosom. "No!" Olivia cried. "Jamin, no!" Without thinking or planning, she hurled the small black evening bag at the gun. It missed the gun but hit Jamin on the side of the head. He turned, startled, his expression opened, exposed for a moment behind his mask of make-up. In that moment Bulagwi reached for the alarm button on the table. A guard rushed in, over to Bulagwi. A shot fired. Olivia turned. Jamin ran into the bedroom. The guard stood with his gun drawn. Bulagwi's eyes opened wide as if seeing for the first time, then he fell. Olivia grabbed Jenny's purse from the floor as half a dozen guards hurried towards the collapsed figure of Bulagwi, his head on the table in what seemed to Olivia an absurdly red pool of blood. Olivia hesitated, then fled into the hall which was momentarily cleared. She darted towards the stairs. Was it Jamin or the guard who had shot Bulagwi? It had to have been the guard, she realized. As she opened the door to the emergency exit, she glanced back to see if Jamin had gotten away; he was nowhere to be seen. Then suddenly two men took her arms and propelled her down the back stairs.

Chapter 41

"But I'm his father!" Randall Walsh declared to the nurse at the admitting desk. He leaned across the curved wooden counter, a garment bag draped over one arm, his bulk bearing down on the pale man on the other side. "The hospital phoned me in the middle of the night."

Rousing from where she'd dozed, her head against the wall, Jenny rubbed a crick in her neck and peered at the expanse of overcoat across the room before she recognized the voice.

She stood. Randall Walsh turned. "They won't let me in," he complained as if he'd expected to see Jenny here and now expected her to arrange things for him. "They say he has his quota of visitors."

Jenny approached the nurse who'd given her coffee and paper and progress reports all night. She explained that this man was in fact the boy's father and she was sure the man with him now would trade places. The nurse said he would check.

As he left the room, Jenny asked, "How did you hear?"

"I phoned the hospital after you left. I gave them my number. Someone called me in the middle of the night and told me David had tried to kill himself."

"When you called, did you talk with David?" Jenny asked.

"Yes. But he didn't have much to say. He never has much to say to me. Why did he do it?" Randall Walsh peered at Jenny through his horn-rimmed glasses, waiting for her explanation.

But Jenny was wondering suddenly if Randall Walsh's phone call had sent his son over the edge, this final voice of a stranger, his father. Rather than speculate, she answered, "I don't know." Then she added, "You did the right thing in coming."

He stood awkwardly before her, holding his garment bag over his shoulder. "I wasn't sure." He set the bag on a chair; he reached into the zipper pocket. He held out a box for Jenny to examine. "I bought him a present." She opened the lid. Inside was a watch with the time illumined under the nose guard of an NFL football helmet stenciled on its face. "I got it at the airport. I don't know if he'll like it."

Jenny stared at the watch. She didn't even know this man's son. Why didn't anyone know him? "I don't know what he likes," she said. Then she offered, "But you bought it for him; that's a beginning." She handed him the box.

The nurse came back. He motioned for Randall Walsh to follow. Further down the hall Jenny saw Mark turn the corner, walking slowly, his grey-flecked hair uncombed, his hands deep in his pockets, returning to her.

When he approached, she reached up to draw him beside her, but he said, "Can we walk instead?" She folded her paper and stuffed it in her pocket, then stood.

The streets were just beginning to grow light. The street lamps still glowed against the grey sky. They walked for a moment in silence. Finally Jenny asked, "How is he?"

"He woke up for a few minutes; then he fell back asleep. He's lost a lot of blood, but he'll live. That was his father who came in. Kay told me she didn't know where his father was."

"I know. I went to see him yesterday." Mark looked over at her. "He was living in Boston," she explained, "in Arlington. Kay hadn't told him anything. I'm so sorry for the boy, Mark." Her voice sank. She reached across the distance between them and took his hand.

"You had nothing to do with what happened," he said.

"I'm not so sure . . ."

Mark stopped walking. He placed both hands on her shoulders. "You didn't. A lot of people did, but you didn't." He put his arm around her. They turned west.

"How's Kay?"

"They gave her a sedative and a bed in David's room. I don't know what she'll do when she wakes and sees David's father. But for now she's asleep."

"You'll need to go back," Jenny offered.

"Perhaps not, now that his father's here."

Jenny and Mark emerged from the dark street into the wide expanse of Fifth Avenue. The early morning sky was clear; the air was crisp. "Can we keep walking for a while?" Mark asked, turning south rather than north. Jenny nodded. "I told David I'd come see him in Washington when he got back. Will you come with me?"

"You want me to?"

"Jenny . . . why don't you know I do?"

"Then I'll come. We'll come as a family with Erika." Mark dropped his arm from her shoulders and took her hand as they walked along the stone wall by the Central Park zoo. "I was thinking about you as I was waiting for David to wake up," he said, "about how much I need you and believe in you. I'm sorry if I haven't let you know that. Olivia told me I was looking at everything with the wrong end of my anatomy."

Jenny smiled. "She said that?"

"She tried hard not to say I had my head up my ass, but I think that was the point."

"I hope she's all right."

"She seemed worried though she wouldn't really talk to me. I hope she'll trust me someday. But she's tough, Jenny. A survivor."

"I know."

"I understand why you two are friends."

Jenny looked over at Mark. "You need to talk with her, Mark. You need to know what she knows." Jenny wanted to tell him what Olivia had told her about DeVries and the plot to assassinate Bulagwi, but she had promised Olivia she wouldn't. She would persuade Olivia to tell him. "It's time the two of you became friends. You could help her too."

"Will she be at the apartment?" he asked.

"I'm not sure."

"I'll call her," he said, "and see if I can help."

They walked for a while without speaking. The city was slowly coming awake. A bus pulled up to the curb and a lone passenger stepped on. "You know," Mark said, "when I was trying to find you yesterday, I also started thinking about Dad. When he comes home, I'd like to ask him if he'd work with me. You think he'd do that?"

"If you asked him."

"I don't know why it's been so hard between us. I could use his help right now." Mark glanced over at Jenny. The wind scattered his hair; his mouth turned up at the corners in a self-mocking smile. "I'm thirty-five years old, and I still want a father." He grew serious then. "I don't know what's going to happen with Afco," he said. "I'm vulnerable, Jenny. I'm really vulnerable here. Kay's story puts me immediately on the spot. I've got to figure out what to do about DeVries. If Olivia's right, he's been diverting funds all along. I can't understand that. The man is a legend."

"Mark . . ." Jenny said quietly, "a legend is a stack of news clippings. I read DeVries' 'legend' when I was in Boston. I went back to the *Record*, to the library. What Olivia's suggesting isn't a new accusation."

Mark glanced across the street at a fountain shooting jets of water into the cold air. "But why? When he has so much? It doesn't make sense."

Jenny didn't answer for a moment. "Maybe he set out his path a long time ago, before he could see the end. Even when it didn't make sense anymore, he stayed on it because it was who he'd become."

Mark didn't answer. He stared straight ahead. His expression turned inwards; his dark eyes tracked another place. "What is it?" Jenny asked.

He glanced at her. "What do you mean?"

"Something else crossed your face."

Mark peered at a small crowd in the next block by the Plaza. He stopped walking. "Jenny, when I came home and found you'd gone, I was so angry. I was confused and hurt and angry . . ."

Jenny nodded. "And Kay was there. I lashed out at her. I tried to blame her for what had happened, and I hurt her; then I felt even worse." Jenny felt the coil inside . . . was it tightening? Mark hesitated.

"What?" she pressed.

He stared at her. "I . . . we . . ." But in his wife's eyes he saw the hurt still close to the surface. Nothing had happened between Kay and him, nothing that had any meaning. He sought for a way to tell Jenny this truth so that she could see as he did.

"Nothing that mattered happened between us, Jenny, nothing, but I haven't been fair to you. I'm sorry. That's all I can offer. I don't want this ever to happen again."

Jenny sensed she wasn't being told everything. She grew still. She heard the distant calls of the birds in the zoo, the honking of a car. Inside herself she heard old voices stirring, but above them she heard an even older voice, a voice so old that it had achieved the clarity of finely fired glass, of sound pitched in the highest register, of wisdom born: You have a loving heart. She trusted this voice; she trusted herself; she could trust Mark. She had come that far. Though she hadn't yet won the peace, she would no longer fight this war.

Opening a side door beneath a security camera scanning to the east, a large man in a grey uniform checked the street, then motioned for Olivia to hurry out towards the west. Olivia asked again to see Nyral. Her escorts had led her into the basement where she was instructed to wait in the laundry room among hampers of dirty sheets and towels. She waited on a three-cornered stool for over half an hour. Finally one of the men returned and led her to the exit.

"Please, where can I find Nyral?" she insisted as she stepped outside.

The man glanced across the street. She followed his gaze. There, in the back of a taxi, Nyral sat watching her. He nodded to the man. Olivia darted over to the cab.

"Bulagwi was shot," she announced as she slipped into the back seat. "I think a guard fired the shot."

"I know. Bulagwi is dead. His own people have killed him." Olivia sat forward.

"Jamin was there," Olivia said. "Did he get away?"

Nyral kept his eyes on the side entrance of the hotel. He'd changed clothes and was dressed in the tan slacks and buttoned-up jacket that was the style of his country. "I am not sure. But I must believe he did."

"What are you going to do?" Olivia asked. Her eyes scanned the cab, picking up details: the valise on the floor, the suitcase in the front, the dark glasses in Nyral's lap.

"I am returning," he answered. "Our fate will not be decided here."

"And Jamin?"

Nyral was silent for a minute. "If he escapes, he will find his way." In his voice Olivia heard a resignation she hadn't heard before, as if he had also faced the possibility that Jamin might not return.

Nyral shut his eyes then. He didn't speak for a moment. Finally he said, "Rhekka came to see me today. She was very frightened. Jamin had come to her to say goodbye, and he told her what he was going to do. I don't know why he would tell her unless he was desperate himself. She pleaded with him, but he left. She said she tried to find you. I assured her I would intervene. I have been waiting here hoping I might see her or Jamin. She told me that she planned to help him whatever he did. It is my hope that she can; she knows his heart. If he did not fire the shot, if he did not kill Bulagwi, it will be easier for him to come back. But now I must go before I am seen."

Police sirens wailed down Fifth Avenue and turned into the Plaza. Their red lights flared against the lightening sky. Olivia leaned her head onto the back of the seat. Nyral put on his sunglasses. Unlike Jamin, who looked menacing behind the dark lenses, Nyral looked like an old man shielding his eyes from a sight too harsh.

"What will you do?" she asked.

"When I return, I will be led to what I must do."

"But how will you know?"

"I will listen."

Olivia wondered at the simplicity of faith in a man who had spent his life in and out of conflict, in and out of the corridors of power both in his own land and abroad. She wondered if his struggles had reduced him to a sort of blind mysticism or if they had instead beaten the world out of him and left him with a hard kernel of truth.

"I also have an idea or two," he added with a smile. "The workers in several of Bulagwi's mines have gone on strike, I am told, and the soldiers there have refused to intervene. The nonviolent revolution may already be underway. But now you must go home and finish your book. Your book will help us, Olivia Turner."

"How will I contact you?"

"Leave me your address. I will contact you."

Olivia opened Jenny's purse and quickly wrote down her address and phone number on the small red pad inside, though as she handed it to Nyral, she wondered if he would remember to write her.

He folded the paper and slipped it into his pocket. "Now I know where you are," he said.

All at once she wanted to lean over and kiss him. But she refrained, for he sat here as the senior statesman about to return to his nation which he had fought for his whole life: as a young man in the schools with his early ideas of nonviolent struggle, as a middle-aged man spending years in jail for his resistance to colonial rule, and now as an older man, returning to try to wrest his nation from the failure of ideals. She offered him her hand instead. Outside the street lights switched themselves off. Olivia slipped out of the cab.

As Étienne turned the taxi into the empty street and across Fifth Avenue, Olivia turned in the opposite direction, walking west. Behind her an ambulance whined to a stop at the entrance of the Plaza. Olivia hurried on. She too believed that Jamin had gotten away. Like some grand illusionist he had disappeared in a puff of smoke. But if she couldn't find him before, she knew she wouldn't be able to find him now. She no longer knew who he would be if she did find him. She should perhaps hunt the back corridors of the Plaza or return to the veneer factory; yet she felt an overwhelming need to go home. She could pursue the news and pursue it without end, for it never ended. Next must come the succession to Bulagwi, the opposition, the search for Jamin, his flight, his possible capture, and the struggle, always the struggle for power. The news shifted patterns like pieces of glass trapped in a kaleidoscope, turned by time, never falling in quite the same pattern, yet never transcending themselves. Jamin had once told her that she had accumulated more words and information than his people were worth but that she didn't write because she didn't trust herself enough to say what she knew.

Yet a few weeks ago she had begun to write. She longed now to get back to her desk and attend to what was awakening within her. She had not saved Bulagwi's life tonight, but she had acted, and her act had had consequence. It had, she believed, prevented Jamin from killing Bulagwi and that fact had consequences she couldn't measure. In the room something of herself had been saved or perhaps born, some courage. It was not much in the face of the violence that ensued, but it was what she had. She wanted to take it to herself and to her work and let it lead her.

Jenny and Mark walked by the entrance of the zoo, around a vendor selling fresh orange juice off a wagon. Across the street reporters and limousines and police cars were gathered at the main steps of the Plaza Hotel. Jenny and Mark crossed instead to Central Park. The snow was piled up on the sides of the benches. Two carriages drew up to the curb; the drivers pulled out their feed bags. Jenny and Mark walked hand in hand over the cobblestones, down the steps, into the park to the footpath where solitary joggers and bikers had already arrived. At the Central Park Pond they stopped. An early morning flutist was setting up his stand. They paused for a moment to watch as he opened his case, assembled his instrument, then raising his flute towards the water, announced the day.